BEYOND THE
SAND CREEK BRIDGE

*For Neil —
Best wishes —
Scott Wyatt*

SCOTT WYATT

ISBN: 0988238802
ISBN-13: 9780988238800
Library of Congress Control Number: 2012915678

Also available in electronic form for most e-readers

This is a work of fiction. Names, characters, businesses, places, events,
and incidents are either the products of the author's imagination
or used in a fictitious manner. Any resemblance to actual persons,
living or dead, is purely coincidental.

HIGHLAND HOUSE PRESS
P.O. Box 350
Issaquah, WA 98027

ACKNOWLEDGEMENTS

I am grateful for the opportunity to acknowledge those who elevated this book with their generosity and vision. I wish to thank in particular Brenda Wilbee, Molly Strange, Cheryl Hauser, Frank Winningham, Amy Dahl, Linda Deiner, John Gamache, the late Zola Helen Ross, Miathili Gandhe Telang, Barbara Carole, Sandy Nygaard, Martha Hobson, Kim Pearson, Andy Carmada, Nellie Williamson, Ann McRill, Jason Frazier, Meina Cheng, Laura Sealey, Linette Wyatt, and Sandra Judd.

Special thanks go to Aaron Denke, Janet Powell and Linda Allardice for their wonderful cover photographs, and to model Amy Frazier and makeup artist Arianna Scott.

I owe an enormous debt of gratitude to my mother, Betty Wyatt, my sister, Christine Wyatt, my sons Aaron Wyatt, Todd Wyatt and Aaron Denke, and my daughter Teija Bielas. My mother's editorial contributions were especially useful.

I thank my life-long friend Mike Dreisbach for showing me the Chinese gráves at Hope, Idaho when we were boys.

Whether he knows it or not, that was the spark that started it all.

Finally, I could not have completed this work without the encouragement, love, editorial and constructive criticism, financial support, and unending patience of my wife, Rochelle Wyatt, to whom this book is dedicated.

For Rochelle

1

Kwangchow, China
1882

Mei-Yin stood shivering beneath an umbrella of bamboo and oiled paper. She clasped a rain-soaked blanket about her neck that overwhelmed her narrow shoulders and threw its excess to the ground in deep muddy folds. Her aunt, Lai-Ping, stepped out of the cover of the umbrella holding a candle that burned feebly in the bottom of a tin cup. She knocked on the door of the dark house, then stepped back. Neither woman moved, except Lai-Ping to place her hand over the flame after a rain drop hissed in the bottom of the cup. The stench of night soil—human waste left in buckets on doorsteps up and down the crowded alley, to be collected before dawn and taken to the fields outside Kwangchow to be used as fertilizer—was unusually strong. There was no wind to attenuate it.

Her aunt did not turn, did not utter a word. Despite the near silence in the deserted alley—only a chorus of drips from the eaves all around them could be heard—and the more perfect silence of the house, she seemed certain of the adequacy of her three reserved and evenly spaced knocks upon the brightly painted door. Mei-Yin wasn't so sure. Two minutes passed. The rain began to fall more heavily again, albeit unevenly, but a great downpour could be heard approaching, dancing raucously over the tiled rooftops. Lai-Ping's robe grew black with rain, and by the time the door opened, spears of her wet hair clung to her throat and her broad forehead like streaks of gray paint.

A plump, gray-haired woman with one eye closed sidled into the half-opened doorway. Her face was puffy, marked by sleep. She wore a white mourning robe, loosely tied over a heavily embroidered sleeping gown, and carried in her right hand a white candle whose flame flickered furiously when she pushed it forward. "Who goes there?" she croaked. Mei-Yin, who had been awake for hours, was startled by her harsh tone. "Lai-Ping, is that you?" The woman's teeth were as black as the shadows in the room behind her.

"It is I, Jong Suk-Wah."

"What are you doing here?" Suk-Wah thrust the candle in Mei-Yin's direction. "And who is this?"

Mei-Yin felt her heart sink. She willed it to rise up and beat again, her breath to return. "I am Mei-Yin," she tried to say, but Lai-Ping stopped her with a sidelong glance and a tilt of her head, as if to say, "Remember what I said."

"This is Mei-Yin," her aunt said. "She is the firstborn of my youngest sister. I have told you about her. She is the beautiful one."

The householder made a halfhearted attempt to examine the girl. Mei-Yin shrank back then caught herself and inched forward into the circle of light, her eyes lowered respectfully. "The firstborn of your youngest sister," the householder mumbled. "I do not know this girl." She seemed about to ask Lai-Ping for more information when she remembered herself. "It's raining. Forgive me, Lai-Ping. Come in, come in. Both of you. You're soaking!"

She led them into a small room ringed by faint, quivering shadows. In the corner, near an arched passageway, a brazier burned low. Mei-Yin removed the blanket from her shoulders. The householder took it and pointed them toward two large plaited mats covering the floor of pressed earth. She placed her white candle on a table beside the doorway. Three low wooden stools were brought out from a back room. "I am a poor hostess," Suk-Wah moaned, shaking her head. She set another white candle on the table and lit it with the flame of the first. She took the tin cup from Lai-Ping and blew out its candle. "I will make tea."

Mei-Yin sat quickly on the stool placed to the left of the two remaining, as etiquette required, and began to look around. So this is Suk-Wah's home, she thought. How odd that I haven't been here before.

Suk-Wah and Lai-Ping had been friends for more than forty years. Mei-Yin had heard her aunt speak of the widow Jong Suk-Wah countless times. Seeing the old woman now, and sitting in her home, it was all just as she'd imagined. She felt as though she, too, had known Suk-Wah for years.

In the undulating candlelight, Mei-Yin spotted a painting of the God of Wealth hanging near the doorway. It was identical to the one that hung in her father's house—last year's standard. In the opposite corner of the room, on a low, round rattan table, were the stunted remnants of four white candles, a wilted chrysanthemum, a bowl of fruit, and two incense trays, meticulously arranged around a framed portrait of a young man. Suk-Wah's son, Gok-Wing, was quite handsome, thought Mei-Yin. This is as Lai-Ping has told me. I'm sure this shrine does not go unnoticed in heaven. She looked away the moment Suk-Wah entered the room.

"Your grief and kindness are well met," whispered Lai-Ping, receiving with both hands a porcelain bowl of steaming tea from her friend. Lai-Ping set the bowl on the grass mat in front of her, placed her hands in her sleeves, and did not speak again until Suk-Wah had served Mei-Yin and was settled on her stool. Then Lai-Ping bowed her head and after taking up her tea and sipping it, said, "This is the rose bud and orange spice tea I brought to you last week."

"Yes," replied Suk-Wah slowly. "There is none more delicious."

A soft hissing arose as embers in the brazier shifted. Mei-Yin felt the weight of each passing second. She was sure these two older women were prone to sit in long, companionable silences, sipping tea. Can there be any doubt that my father has discovered me gone by now? she wondered. Hurry, Lai-Ping! Please! Ask her!

Lai-Ping eventually glanced at her niece and turned to face Suk-Wah. She drew a long breath. "I seem to remember that your son Gok-Wing was under contract with the House of Huang before he died, to return to America, the land we call Gold Mountain. Do I remember correctly?"

Mei-Yin shuddered. She stared through the ornamental grate of the brazier at the languid glowing flame. The House of Huang was among the leading trading houses in Kwangchow, but it had acquired most of its reputation and wealth serving as middleman for foreign shippers in the coolie trade, or as agent for British companies importing Indian opium through the southern treaty ports after China's defeat in the Opium Wars. Following gold discoveries in California, the House of Huang turned its attention to the demand for cheap foreign labor to work the placer mines, and, years later, to build the great American railroads. It contracted with American companies and labor purveyors, promising to fill their quotas—and the holds of their ships—with Chinese men, men who thought of themselves not as "Chinese" but as "sons of Han," or "Tang people."

Once under contract, a son of Han was no longer his own man, but the "stock in trade" of the House of Huang. Mei-Yin had heard stories of cruelty and mistreatment visited on men who failed to honor their agreements with the House of Huang.

Suk-Wah's shock at the mention of her son's name within a week of his death was not lost in the dim, uneven light. The shape of her eyes made it plain she was no longer half-asleep. "Yes." She glanced at Mei-Yin, then back. "Why do you ask this, Lai-Ping?"

"And the ship that was to transport him? Was it the *China Sea*, the American vessel that lies at the quay as we speak?"

"Why, uh, yes, I think so. The *China Sea*. How did you . . . ? He was to depart tomor—No, it's after midnight, isn't it? He was to leave today! Today was the—"

"Today then," snapped Lai-Ping. Suk-Wah froze. Mei-Yin was sure she was preparing to cry over such talk of her son when Lai-Ping changed her tone and spoke quickly and preemptively. "What time today, Suk-Wah?"

"I don't know these things. Why do you ask me such things?" She turned to face Mei-Yin again, this time with a look of pleading in her eyes. "My son is only just dead."

Mei-Yin bowed her head and nodded. She imagined Gok-Wing's limp body being pulled from the Pearl River. He had been fishing with a friend. Their boat overturned. He couldn't make it to shore.

Mei-Yin pushed the dreadful image out of her mind. Stop it! You weren't there. You don't know anything about it. Mei-Yin pressed her lips together.

A silence descended upon the room. Then the ship will be leaving any minute, Mei-Yin realized, looking up quickly. Oh, Lai-Ping. Perhaps it's left already. Perhaps it's too late for this plan of yours. She moved her hand toward her aunt but did not touch her. Lai-Ping seemed determined to ignore her. The gray-haired woman had fixed her gaze on Suk-Wah. Lai-Ping seemed to be bearing down on her, so unmercifully, in fact, that Mei-Yin found herself glancing across at the old woman to see what affect this was having. She watched Suk-Wah raise a trembling cup of tea to her lips. Mei-Yin bowed her head again, swallowing back some of her impatience. On the other hand, it's still dark. Perhaps, if Suk-Wah will agree, there is time.

"There is a favor I must ask of you," said Lai-Ping. Her voice was firm and unfriendly, or at any rate not modulated in the manner of friendship. Mei-Yin could not help thinking how terrible it was to be making so little room for the other's grief. But then she considered the fact of their long friendship, all they had been through, the grief they had known together in these difficult times, and realized that Lai-Ping's way was direct, not inconsistent with compassion. "It concerns the girl. She is a virgin and is promised to a sojourner. What is his name, child?"

Mei-Yin started. "Hok-L—"

"*Promised?*" interrupted Suk-Wah. "I assume you mean their fathers have arranged a marriage?"

"No," answered Lai-Ping flatly. "Not in the traditional sense. It's what, dear?"

"Hok-Ling."

"Yes. Hok-Ling. His father was the fish vendor who for many years sold live eel and carp near the Flowery Pagoda. Do you remember him, Suk-Wah? He was dark and wiry, with a dirty pigtail, but his barrels were always clean and freshly painted, yellow, black, and red." Suk-Wah shook her head vacantly.

Lai-Ping waved her hand in the air. "Well, never mind about him. He's old now, and wealthy in his years. But his third-born son, Hok-Ling, is away to the Gold Mountain, just as your son might have been had Heaven not unexpectedly thrown open its doors to him. It's been more than the three years, and the man-child has not returned to Kwangchow. Mei-Yin's father has received no word concerning him."

"*Her* father?" asked Suk-Wah, trying to catch up. "Do you mean *his* father?"

"No. Let me explain, although we have little time. Hok-Ling and Mei-Yin have known each other since childhood. He

6

attended school near her father's house in the years before the famine, and in their adolescence there were not hairs enough on a pig to count the half-truths they told—including to me—or the artifices they employed to ensure meeting at one place or another. After his eighth year of education he was chosen for the civil service examinations, but the famine hit that spring, and his mother was taken ill. He was forced by circumstance to forgo the examinations.

"When Mei-Yin was old enough to bear sons, Yeung Men-Hoi, the husband of my sister, who, as I've told you before, is a man of evil destiny, threatened to sell his daughter on the street. Many, many times he threatened, for he recognized a price in gold for one so beautiful. Twice he brought home drunken men from the teahouses, men who reached through their robes to pull up their girdles and put on important faces, calling out, "We are here to see this treasure your husband brags about," but each time my sister refused to let them see her, and she railed openly against her husband, and for this, while the men watched dumbly, she received his hand. Twice she has picked up teeth in the door yard, but, as you see, Mei-Yin is here. She has not been sold into concubinage.

"Four autumns ago, the man-child Hok-Ling brought baskets of oranges and eggs, and two handsome carp, and he presented them with a sincere blessing to Mei-Yin's father. After he made the proper apologies for the absence of his own father, who was ill, he begged permission to step into the street and speak frankly to Men-Hoi on a matter of great importance." Lai-Ping leaned forward a little. "It may be supposed," she added confidentially, "that Mei-Yin's father did not see Hok-Ling make eye contact with the blushing girl as they passed out of the house. But my sister? Do you think she is capable of missing such a thing?"

Mei-Yin remembered a kiss stolen in the twilight of a summer's eve near the home of Hok-Ling's father. Hok-Ling was sixteen then. He kissed her, then held her shoulders, and staring intently into her eyes, said, "I wish to be with you always, Mei-Yin. I will never be satisfied with anyone else." And it was exactly so for her then, although she did not say it. Would she feel the same now? And what about him?

"Well, it was then that Hok-Ling persuaded Men-Hoi to enter into a solemn agreement. In exchange for the promise of his daughter, Hok-Ling would contract with the House of Huang to sojourn three years on the Gold Mountain, there to work on the American railroads. He would receive the customary daily wage of one silver dollar, and, as the men lived in camps along the route and could live cheaply, he would be able to return a large portion, perhaps as much as two-thirds of this amount, to Kwangchow. It was agreed that one-half would be paid directly to Men-Hoi."

Lai-Ping stopped. She picked up her tea and sipped it, while her eyes, still and dark, held the balance of her story above the steaming liquid. She swallowed, licked her lips, and her brows shot up, involuntarily signaling once again her approval of the drink.

It was all Mei-Yin could do to hold her tongue. Was it not in her nature to speak freely on matters of importance to her? And here, after all, was the picture of her life being drawn in words. Slow words. Unnecessary words. Wasn't *she* the one to be doing this? But Mei-Yin bit her lip, remembering her aunt's stern warning: "When we arrive, you will remain still. Do not interrupt. Leave everything in my hands."

"You see," Lai-Ping finally continued, scrutinizing the dark specks at the bottom of her bowl, "half the money was to be Men-Hoi's, to do with as he pleased. This was his requital. The other half, however, he was to hold in safekeeping until Hok-Ling returned. This would be held as a dowry, for it was agreed that when Hok-Ling returned to take the girl from Men-Hoi, not a penny more would change hands between them. Such was their agreement.

"But," Lai-Ping added, looking into Suk-Wah's eyes, "Yeung Men-Hoi is not an honorable man. You know this,

Suk-Wah. His words are—how should I say?—empty and vile."
She lowered the bowl to the ground. "And now, dear, I must
speak very quickly.

"The man-child has not returned from the Gold Mountain,
although the three years of his contract ended many months
ago. There is still some money paid out on his account at the
House of Huang, but it is a fraction of what it was before. It
can be assumed he is alive. Perhaps he is ill or injured, or in
some extremity. We don't know. No one has heard from him or
about him. Since this is all in the hands of the gods, it is not
something to worry about. But, unfortunately, there is more.
You see, my sister's husband, Men-Hoi, arrived home only a few
hours ago this very night and announced to my sister that he
had just lost Mei-Yin at the mahjong table."

Suk-Wah gasped. She covered her mouth and looked at Mei-
Yin across the new distance created by her pity. Mei-Yin felt the
sting of tears. Suk-Wah turned back to her friend, disbelieving.

Lai-Ping nodded. "He has instructed my sister to collect
Mei-Yin's things and make ready to deliver her over to a water
carrier at the hour of sunrise. When Men-Hoi went into the
street to relieve himself, Mei-Yin fled the house at once and
came straightaway to my door. My sister could not come, you
see, for her feet were poorly bound all those years ago, and she
suffers greatly. It is for this reason that she refused to have any
of her daughters' feet bound. But never mind . . . we have come
here, for the gods have instructed me to ask a favor of you."

Mei-Yin's frightened eyes swung to Suk-Wah.

"I don't understand. What favor could I do?"

"It is this, gracious lady. Give my luckless niece the papers
that Gok-Wing received from the House of Huang, those that
authorize him to board the *China Sea* and return to America.
Also, bring out a suit of his clothing and his hat. Mei-Yin must
go in his place. We must leave at once—do you see? For the
ship will sail with the first tide." Lai-Ping paused. "Why do you
look at me this way, Suk-Wah? There is no other way."

Suk-Wah's mouth had fallen open. Then her lips began to move around words that she had no breath to utter. Her eyes bulged.

Mei-Yin shifted forward and went to her knees. She extended her arm, preparing to appeal to Suk-Wah, but Lai-Ping once again checked her, lifting a finger and shaking her head sternly. She cleared her throat again as if to remind Mei-Yin of her earlier warning.

"What you ask is impossible!" cried Suk-Wah. "It's out of the question!"

"We will bind her bosom, of course." Lai-Ping said, giving no sign of having heard Suk-Wah. "I have given her a small amount of money, one and a half *tael*. It will not be easy for her. How could it be? But I believe she will manage. When she arrives in San Francisco, she will go to the home of Cheng Tien, the son of Cheng Xio Ping, the barber. He is a friend of mine. He will help her find Hok-Ling."

Suk-Wah wailed softly, "What in the world are you talking about? Do you even know what you're asking?"

"She is my niece. I told you that."

"I know she is your niece! But what about . . . !"

Suddenly, Lai-Ping lunged forward and took hold of Suk-Wah's shoulders. *"Shhh! What's that?"* With her finger pressed to her lips, she turned toward the door. Mei-Yin had heard it, too, and her heart sank momentarily, then rose up again, flailing in her chest. It's *him!* she thought. He's found us!

The noise grew louder. They could make out the pounding of horses—two or three—galloping over the muddy road, splashing through puddles. The sounds grew louder still, and the sharp jangling and squeaking of bridles and saddles rose up in a sharp crescendo. There was no subsidence, no change until at the point of its most jarring effect inside the small room, the noise began to modulate as quickly as it had arisen. A few moments later, it was a distant, fading rumble and thrum in the night. Lai-Ping sat back. "It's nothing," she sighed. "Forgive me, Suk-Wah, but, you see, Mei-Yin is in great danger. We must go quickly."

Suk-Wah looked at both women, frightened. "But if the House of Huang were to find out . . . ?"

"If you are asked, Gok-Wing's papers were stolen. Mei-Yin is prepared to confess that she acquired them from a thief. It is she who will be punished, not you."

Yes, thought Mei-Yin, her heart racing. I will. But I can't stay here. I must get to the Gold Mountain. I must try to find him. I don't care what happens. I have at least to try. When Suk-Wah saw the determination and courage in Mei-Yin's eyes she turned away at once.

"What about the man, Lai-Ping? The husband of your sister? What you ask me to do, I cannot, for it would bring shame to him. I cannot cause a man, even such a one as Yeung Men-Hoi, to lose face."

"You won't," replied Lai-Ping. "Surely you can see that he has brought dishonor upon his own name, and that of his family and ancestors. He has suffered the loss of face already, and those who dwell in the house of his ancestors will no doubt suffer by the same token. He is beset by *gui*, evil spirits." It went without saying that Men-Hoi was in danger of never gaining complete redemption, for the solemn agreement that he had made with the man-child Hok-Ling, and his failure to keep it, were facts widely known. The sojourner's money had been squandered. "He has spent the money on prostitutes and opium," Lai-Ping went on. "We have talked about this before, Suk-Wah. There are so many good and reasonable, hard-working men. But he is not one of them."

Lai-Ping turned and stared blankly at Mei-Yin, as though some new thought were just forming in her mind. "She *must* go in Gok-Wing's place. You have heard of the Chinese Exclusion Act, the law passed by the American government? For the next ten years, all Tang people are forbidden from immigrating to the Gold Mountain to work. A single exception has been made

11

for laborers like Gok-Wing, who have already been there, and who were there before the eleventh month of their year 1880. His documents are proof of this. Were this not the case, I would not have come."

Suk-Wah frowned. "Still, Lai-Ping, I could never . . . I must consult a fortune-teller before considering this."

"Forgive me, gracious lady," interrupted Mei-Yin, "but there is also the matter of the advance."

"Mei-Yin!" snapped Lai-Ping.

"The *what?*" cried Suk-Wah. "What are you talking about? What advance?" The old woman turned to her friend. "What is she talking about, Lai-Ping?"

But Mei-Yin didn't wait. She leaned toward Suk-Wah and fixed her eyes on the collar of the white mourning robe. "Surely, my lady, you are aware that your son received fifteen silver dollars when he contracted with the House of Huang? It is called 'the advance.' It is the same amount paid by all of the great houses of the Crown Colony, when men are hired for the demon companies in America."

"Oh, *that*," croaked Suk-Wah, letting a little relieved smile bend her eyes. "Yes, yes. We received that. But that was—"

"Why, don't you know? You must repay—"

Mei-Yin stopped. Has it really come to this? Look at her. The poor, dear woman. What must she think of me? How selfish I am! How unwomanly, and in the hour of her grieving.

Washing over these thoughts, however, she began to hear the echo of her mother's voice, the choked words that had come to her through the darkness of shattered sleep only hours before. "Daughter, listen to me! I have tried to protect you, but there is no more I can do. Do you understand? You are old enough to bear sons, and your father has spoken. He is a man . . . my husband . . . and I must obey him. If you are to find safety, you must act for yourself."

And she remembered Lai-Ping's words, spoken to her two hours later as she sat, exhausted and wet, at Lai-Ping's table.

"Your mother and I have lived all these years in fear of only one thing, Mei-Yin, that one day you would be harmed by a man. That a man . . . I presumed it would be your father . . . would dominate you and control you and break your unusual spirit. I cannot stand the thought of this. I cannot stand the power that men have when it is used in disregard of a woman's life, of her well-being. A mahjong game. I hate this man! Go to the Gold Mountain, child. There, at least, a woman is not a man's property. There, you can find safety and comfort. Be free, child, and you will find your own happiness. This is your destiny. I'm sure of it."

Mei-Yin turned partway toward this powerful, independent woman who had been her favorite aunt for as long as she could remember. Lai-Ping sat with eyes closed. And to think I have questioned the source of my spirit and independence. *Who* is here with me? *Who* is trying to save me now, when my father has spoken?

It would be months before Mei-Yin, reliving this anguished night, would realize that neither her mother nor Lai-Ping had mentioned Hok-Ling. "Be free. Find your happiness," is what they said, the two women who loved her most.

Mei-Yin turned and began to search the dimly lit face of Suk-Wah. "Kind lady, you must refund this money if Jong Gok-Wing does not board the ship this morning. If his name is not crossed off. It is an advance against wages, you see? It is paid initially by the House of Huang, in addition to the cost of passage to Gold Mountain. The House of Huang is reimbursed by the American labor agents for each man who reports to the ship, as promised. Later, the money is deducted from each man's wages on Gold Mountain. In this way, both the House of Huang and the demon company are reimbursed in full. Only the man's wages are advanced. Hok-Ling called it a 'credit-ticket system' or something like that. In any event, if Gok-Wing does not board the ship, the House of Huang will demand repayment."

"But . . . ! How can this be?" cried Suk-Wah. "Are you absolutely sure of this, child?"

Mei-Yin nodded. Not only did Hok-Ling explain this arrangement to her but she had heard the same thing from girlfriends whose fathers and brothers had gone off to work on Gold Mountain. Suk-Wah lowered her eyes, and when she looked up again, turning first to Mei-Yin and then to Lai-Ping, her mouth formed a terrible smile. "I cannot replay this." She pressed her right hand to her forehead and began to rock gently back and forth. "I cannot repay this," she sobbed. "I cannot. I cannot."

Mei-Yin and Lai-Ping sat with Suk-Wah without speaking for several minutes. Eventually, Mei-Yin saw that her aunt's hands were extending to take up her tea again.

Suk-Wah cried into the night, "I have spent this money for a monument . . . a beautiful monument to be placed near the wall of the city in honor of my son. Don't you see? It's gone!"

Suddenly, Mei-Yin reached for the woman's hand. "Let me go then, gracious lady! Let me go! I will board the ship and see that your son's name is crossed off the list!"

2

New London, Connecticut
June 27, 1879

"**W**eigh enough!"

Eight broad-shouldered oarsmen stopped rowing on the coxswain's command. The blades of their oars skimmed the surface as they sat back and let the sixty-five-foot racing shell *Lexington* slide effortlessly beneath them.

Several of the rowers reached back to grip the gunwales. Weary of the long warm-up, they lifted themselves free of the wooden sliding seats. Others stretched their necks and backs elaborately in anticipation of the race to come. Twenty-three year old Jason McQuade, resting the grip of his oar against his torso, winded and breathing heavily, leaned slightly forward. Scanning the faces along the shoreline, he raised his head to acknowledge the waves of a handful of strangers. *"Go Ha-vard!"* came a shout from an older child, a boy of ten or eleven. Jason and three teammates raised appreciative, answering fists.

If the race doesn't kill you, the warm-up will, Jason thought. He looked down at the crimson blade of his oar bouncing along the rippled, gray-blue surface of Connecticut's Thames River. A reflection of the June sky, towering clouds framing wide patches of brilliant blue, passed in splendor beneath the oar's shaft. He took hold of his oar and lifted the blade above the surface, turning it one way and another, as though inspecting it, but his thoughts were elsewhere.

He'd sought out only one face in the crowd, he realized, but it was all in vain. A fool's errand. If he's anywhere, he's at the finish line, Jason told himself. Yet in the next instant he banished that thought. Good God! How many times will you do this? he asked himself, letting the blade fall back to skim along on the surface. And when will it end?

At that moment, Bernie Page, the number three oarsman, turned in his seat and extended a hand to Jason. "Let's do this, McQuade!" Jason gripped the hand firmly. "You got it, ol' man! One more for the Commonwealth, huh?" At the same time, he felt the strong hand of John Sullivan, the number five rower, squeezing his left shoulder. "This one's ours!" In similar fashion all nine men, eight and cox, knitted their spirits together before the eyes of the crowd. A small contingent of Harvard students, having traveled over one hundred miles from Cambridge to New London by train to see the race, waved crimson banners and cheered their varsity team on with boisterous enthusiasm.

The ten-minute gun sounded. The cox pulled a pocket watch from under the neck of his sweater, opened it, then stuffed it back underneath. "All right, Ha-vard! Port forward, starboard back! On two, one . . . " Jason mechanically followed the commands of the cox and the movements of his teammates as they slowly turned the *Lexington* on her heels and inched (mostly by dint of current, although the stroke and number seven were put to use occasionally) toward the starting line. "Weigh enough! Let her run!" Jason turned to look down the course toward the New London Bridge in the distance. As he did so, the Yale boat, having just completed its warm-ups, slid alongside. The Yale coxswain, dressed in a white-and-blue-striped sweater, turned to face his counterpart in the stern of the Harvard boat. The gold rims of his glasses were just visible above the edge of a white megaphone with the familiar blue "Y" painted on each side. "A wager of shirts, gentlemen?"

The Harvard cox, Austin Camby, seeking the advantage of standoffishness, didn't reply in words, but raised his hands above his head and applauded as the Yale boat slid past.

John Sullivan chuckled quietly. "You tell them, Austin."

Jason idly examined the crimson material on the back of Bernie Page's jersey. *He's not here, okay?* Forget about it! He spit over the gunwale, then reached down and splashed cold water onto his legs. *Why do I make excuses for him? God, I've done this forever! Why do I pretend that "I'll try to make it, son" means "I will make it"? How important is a damn crew race anyway?*

It wasn't the race itself, of course, but the effort to get here. The endless hours of training. The dedication. Didn't that count for anything in his father's mind? Did Jason matter to him at all? That's what he really wanted to know. No, Robert McQuade wouldn't be at the finish line. Of course not!

The question of "mattering" had given shape to inexpressible recurring sentiments that barred Jason from the scales by which people measure self-worth. He had struggled to overcome this, as most children will, instinctively. He performed feats and excelled at everything to which the laurels of virtue (according to his father's lights) were attracted. On that score, he'd conformed himself to the black-and-white outline of his father's likes and dislikes, and in the process paid scant attention to his own. In fact, he could not have spoken authentically to his own likes and dislikes, and would have found a probing question in that direction distressing.

Why had he gone to Harvard? It was his father's alma mater. Why did he row at Harvard? His father had rowed for the crimson in the first Harvard-Yale Regatta in 1852, to be followed by his older brother Andrew in 1873. Why did he excel at the piano? His father didn't play, but had taken Jason, without his older brother, to a performance of Chopin's F minor concerto for two pianos at age six. In the carriage ride home his father had lavished unceasing, heady praises on "men like this." Jason knew he meant Chopin and heard mention of Liszt and Beethoven in the bargain. Men of genius who "actually made something of themselves." Was it a surprise that Jason asked to take piano lessons three weeks later?

But where was his father now? Where had he been during all those piano recitals? Not the first one at ten, which he'd fumbled so terribly, but later, when what the *Boston Daily Advertiser* described as "an unusual, seemingly effortless talent" was displayed? What use was it to work so hard at something if . . . ?

"Your father wanted to be here, Jason," his mother would say, "but his Theosophy Club meets on Thursday nights." Or, "he's only just returned from Philadelphia and he's simply too tired." Or, "your father will be so happy when I tell him how splendidly you played, darling. Wait till he hears what Mayor Cobb said about your duet with Josephine this afternoon—how moved he was. Did you hear? It nearly brought him to tears!"

"Ready to row!" shouted the two coxswains one after the other as each maneuvered his vessel to a point just upstream of the starting line. A cheer went up from the crowd of onlookers lining the Thames and occupying the spectator boats that were anchored in patches of eel grass at the edge of Bartlett's Cove. Jason and fifteen other oarsmen slid forward as though animated by a single mechanical arm. Their sliding seats struck the front stops with a thud. Fully extended now, the brightly painted blades—Harvard's crimson, Yale's blue and white—hovered above the surface of the water at the end of twelve-foot oars, and thirty-two powerful arms angled over coiled knees. Each man waited for the cannon shot.

The starter, a pudgy, bearded man dressed in a black frock coat with a black vest and a string tie, stood in the bow of a launch anchored midway between the two shells. As the *Belle* and the *Lexington* drifted slowly, ever so slowly, toward the starting buoys, he stood erect, looking through binoculars toward the first referee boat—a twenty-eight-foot gaff-rigged sloop with its mainsail unfurled—anchored a mile and a half downstream. He raised a large red-and-white signal flag over his head and waved it vigorously. The crowd, too, set binoculars and telescopes on the distant sloop. The sloop returned the signal, and a few moments later a second signal went up signifying that the "All ready" had been relayed successfully to the other referee boats and to the referees stationed at the finish line four miles away. The starter lowered his binoculars and picked up a large green megaphone, which he held to his lips. Swinging it side-to-side with two hands, addressing first the white-clad Yale crew with great blue Y's stitched over the front of their jerseys, then the Harvard crew in crimson tops and shorts, with a small white H visible over the heart of each man, he bellowed, "Best of luck to you, boys! Ready now . . . "

The cannon's thunderous report came from the eastern shore two miles away. It reverberated over the streets of New London and Groton. By the time the first of three distinct echoes reached the starting line, Yale's *Belle* and Harvard's *Lexington* were charging away with already 150 yards gained. Each surging vessel was overhung with spray from the catch of blades in furious motion. Fully at racing speed within five or six strokes, the oarlocks of the two boats knock-knocked, knock-knocked like metronomes. Jason pulled with every ounce of his strength. The oars, port and starboard, feathered in snapping unison to clear the roiling, eddying surface of the water. Both coxswains leaned forward now, at extreme, unnatural angles, shouting, exhorting their crews in full voice. The slides on the seats sang on their tracks, and sixteen young men—ages nineteen to twenty-three, all white, all from well-to-do eastern families, their eyes dull, downturned, unfocused—sixteen young men in the peak of physical condition, mindless of the screaming crowds, grimacing in the extremity of effort, rocked forward and back, forward and back with an uncanny grace and symmetry. From the starter's launch the blades of the two boats bound for the New London Bridge flashed crimson and blue, crimson and blue, rising and plunging beneath the surface again and again in what became—especially as the mechanical sounds of the race receded and the boats grew smaller—a spectacle of sublime and sympathetic rhythm, the beating of wings, as though the cannon shot had frightened two great sea birds from a respite on the Thames to take up again the uncertainties of their home on the Atlantic.

* * *

Boston, Massachusetts
June 28, 1879

Jason took one last deep breath within the sanctuary of her neck and hair. He kissed Josephine lightly on the cheek and lifted himself, preparing to roll onto his back as he had done so many times—lifting his muscular frame over hip and knee without applying pressure, without hurting her. Landing on his back, on the pillow, being no longer inside her, was a kind of freedom to him.

Thirty-one-year-old Josephine Carter turned onto her side and shifted toward him—also in a familiar, practiced way—and Jason slid his arm under her pillow to bring her closer. She pulled the white sheet up over her shoulder, but otherwise lay silent. With her head on his chest, she stared into the swivel mirror on top of the mahogany dresser opposite the bed. His entire 6' 1" length was visible to her, his brown disheveled hair, his strong right forearm and hand hanging limply over the edge of the bed, the angle and set of his jaw, the irregular movement of his blue eyes staring up at the ceiling. "Did your father attend the race?" she asked at length.

"No." He'd never really understood how she did it, how she knew what he was thinking almost before he did. When he was younger, much younger, twelve or thirteen, he had thought it came from their focusing on the same pieces of music, the same notes and progressions, for hours on end, virtual days spent sharing the same piano bench. Then, he realized, no, it must have something to do with the intertwining of their bodies, with his penetration of her, which she'd taught him, which she instigated and controlled with gentle and clever urgings. Or perhaps it grew out of the rhythms that began and ended in storms of breathing and sighs on the basement stairs and later, when his brother Andrew was at Harvard, in Andrew's room. She was an adult, after all, twenty-one when it started, and he was but a boy of thirteen. But now that he was twenty-three? It had to be something else. In any case, it was not new to him, this strange ability of hers to read his thoughts. Not a few conversations had begun as this one had.

"I'll never understand that man," she said. Josephine slid her hand down his chest and let it come to rest on the flat of his abdomen. She raised her head and looked into his eyes. A swath of her long auburn hair clung to a cheek still moist with perspiration. "He's a *figlio di puttana!*"

"He is, huh?" Jason had no idea what this meant. Josephine had studied Italian for four years along with piano theory, composition, and symphonic performance at the Boston Academy of Music. Music was her escape, her lifeblood—she trusted it and made sure that all that truly mattered to her maintained a recognizable orbit around music. She'd gone from a simple piano teacher at age nineteen to playing concert halls up and down the East Coast by age thirty-one, as far west as Chicago, and as far north as Montreal. Her Italian, on the other hand, was but a favorite toy, and she seldom used it without feigning a growl, a triumphant shout, or a look of sudden, tragic urgency, her brows steeply knit above sparkling brown, mischievous eyes. Jason, as he usually did, went along. "Who can deny it?" he added. "I mean it's right there for everyone to see. He's a fig-eelio . . . "

"A *figlio di puttana*, exactly." She set her head back down, satisfied that only one of them knew that *figlio di puttana* meant "son of a bitch."

Sunlit white lace curtains billowed at the partially opened window. Jason felt the relief of ribbons of cool air traversing his outstretched leg. He stared at the coved ceiling of the hotel room—a familiar sight. How many times had they met here? Six? Eight? Even the carefully rendered patchwork in the corner of the ceiling near the door with a thumbprint visible in the plaster held a kind of significance for him. Josephine had discovered the room originally. "Oh! This is fine!" she'd smiled the first time she saw it, throwing her hat on the bed and stepping to the window. She'd wiped a circle in the condensation on the window to reveal large snowflakes drifting down beyond the glass. Two hours later, with Jason in tow, she'd repeated these same steps. "Look, Jason! We can see the harbor from here! Isn't this . . . ? Well, this is very fine!" She'd spun back to him, and with a playful grin, spreading her arms wide, cried out, "Darling! Home at last!"

Jason closed his eyes to the memory, raised his arm, and rested his wrist against his forehead. A sigh escaped his lips as he sensed the winds of melancholy returning, its leading edge, self-rejection, rattling the sashes and threatening the foundation of what lovemaking had so hastily constructed: a temporary sense of wholeness. Oh, for those minutes of peace! A sense that *he* was—and therefore *all* was—as it should be, and could be.

He bit down on his lower lip. Despite the warmth of Josephine's soft skin . . . It was there, still there. Her tantalizing scent, still there. The gentle pressure of what he considered in the throes of sexual hunger dizzyingly beautiful, large, exhilarating breasts. Still there. Despite the room's resplendence, its sunlit window, the cool fingers of moving air, the bright, clean walls that had given them both privacy in perfect measure . . . . Despite his recent successes . . . Hadn't he just graduated with honors? Wasn't he offered a position in his father's firm that would guarantee his financial future for years to come? Despite all of it, his thoughts began to sink in a familiar way toward self-negation, or to come to the point, the belief in "self-not-mattering."

Josephine propped her head on her fist and watched this change come over Jason. She said nothing as he swung his legs over the edge of the bed and sat up, reaching for his shirt. She let him dress in silence. Only with minutes to go before he would turn to her, as in the past, and offer an awkward apology before leaving, she said, "You remember about tomorrow tonight, right? The Villard reception?"

"Yes."

"They've asked us to play our duet at seven. Is that going to work for you?"

"Yes." Jason tilted the swivel mirror up so that he could watch himself tie his four-in-hand necktie.

"The Mayor wants us to play my *Two Roads to Appomattox* again."

"Sure."

"They'll have a second piano there."

"Mmm. Good. I'll be there."

"It'll just be the one piece. We're to follow the dinner speaker, an attorney or something from the Idaho Territory."

"All right."

"The way my friend Sally describes it, Villard's trying to get more Americans, especially German Americans, interested in investing in his railroad. Apparently this guy is going to talk about the possibilities for expansion, or his experiences out west, or something. I don't know. Anyway, it might be interes—"

"Look, Josephine," Jason interrupted, turning to face her. "I feel bad about today."

"What do you mean?"

"I . . . I shouldn't have contacted you last night. I was frustrated. I should have just left you alone." He turned back to the mirror to recheck his tie. He was drawn back to the previous day, recalling first the weight of the shell, and the weariness of his arms, as he and his teammates, knee-deep in water, in a single practiced motion lifted the dripping *Lexington* out of the water and held it upside-down over their heads. Then, on the cox's command, how they lowered it gingerly to their shoulders and marched slowly up the bank to the grassy shore and the boathouse beyond. He remembered the shifting weight as they walked over the uneven ground, the gunwale digging into the saddle of his left shoulder. He'd stuffed his newly won Yale jersey beneath the gunwale, but it had slipped out. He remembered, too, the cool blades of grass beneath his bare feet as they climbed toward the boathouse. He was over-conscious of these details, for he had bound himself to them in the certain knowledge that he was alone now. That none of the smiling, cheering faces lining the path to the boathouse were there for him. Not one—and certainly not *the* one.

Ten minutes later, as he'd stood with teammates, coaches, and well-wishers toasting victory, singing *Fair Harvard,* a desire had begun to creep in behind Jason's obliging smile and friendly banter. A desire to board the train and get back to Boston as quickly as possible, to get a message to Josephine Carter that he wanted her, needed her, needed to see her soon—the next day, if possible. He didn't know if she was in town. Their last contact had been a short letter she'd sent from Philadelphia in May, congratulating him on his upcoming graduation. Still, he knew what her answer would be if she *were* there. She would find a way. They would be undressing each other at the first opportunity. Holding each other, falling into bed together. She would give of herself freely, holding nothing back. Her body would be his, and all else would disappear.

"I feel I've used you. I . . . I shouldn't have."

Josephine sat up on the edge of the bed, turning her back to him. She drew the sheet up to her chest. After a long pause, she turned to face Jason. Her face was flushed, her brown eyes fixed on his intently. "You didn't *use* me, Jason. You . . . you've never done that. In fact, I'm not someone or some*thing* that *can* be used." She leaned over the bed to pick up her camisole. "Please be more careful with your words. Besides, I don't want to have this conversation again. Things are what they are. I know I've told you I love you, but I don't expect anything from you. I've made that clear."

Jason slipped on his waistcoat. "Yes, I suppose you have." But against that thought he pictured a time when it was not clear at all to a twelve-year-old boy why his piano teacher's hand would suddenly be resting on his right knee as he played, or why this would happen again—by what bizarre coincidence?— the following week near the end of his two-hour lesson. And in the third week, and the fourth, why the position of the hand changed—he suspected he might have caused this himself, perhaps because of the way his leg moved when using the sustain pedal. In all events, the hand's placement became routine, its movements a caress, sometimes in time to the music, at times randomly along his outer thigh or with a lighter touch, in small expanding circles on the inside of his leg just above his knee. It seemed to a twelve-year-old boy that his twenty-one-year-old piano teacher had asserted a claim of partial ownership of his right leg! Over time he began to expect and then want these explorations, which she punctuated in new and exciting ways. In an unspoken conspiracy, they both began to listen intently while he played—or while she played for him, demonstrating some fingering or phrase—for the sounds of his mother leaving the house or the domestic busying herself upstairs.

Jason picked up his frock coat and walking cane and moved to the door. Without turning to face Josephine, he set his hand on the doorknob. "You're okay, then?"

"Yes."

"And you can get yourself home?"

Josephine did not answer. Jason hesitated, then opened the door and left.

* * *

"There you are, old man!" said Bernie Page, rising from the table and shaking Jason's hand. "I've saved a seat for you."

"Excellent."

"Gentlemen," Page began, turning toward the four other men seated at the table. "The late Mr. Jason McQuade, may he eat in peace."

Jason took his place to a chorus of laughter. Introductions and pleasantries crisscrossed the white linen tablecloth topped with silver flatware, Wedgewood bone china, and crystal goblets, until (with evident relief) conversations veered and narrowed and were managed at close quarters again. Jason winked at his teammate and friend as he unfolded his napkin.

Page leaned over the man sitting between them. He raised his voice to match the noise that swelled around them. "Emory is a school chum of my father's. They grew up together in Genesee County, New York. Fought in the 151st Infantry Regiment, C Company. Emory's staying over at the house this week."

"Oh, I see." Jason smiled and nodded at a man in his mid to late fifties, of medium height and build. He had a thick salt-and-pepper mustache and a full head of graying brown hair that he wore rather long in a nonconforming style fashionable during the war's waning years. He dressed in a brown ditto suit, which, while only gesturing at the formality of the evening, seemed to have the advantage of being expertly tailored. The addition of a string tie gave one the impression that his calling card would be unfamiliar to the people in attendance.

"Yeah, he's like an uncle to Sally and me. Anyway, Emory's speaking tonight. Villard's people brought him out to talk about his experiences in Idaho, where he's living now." Page put his hand on Emory's arm. "Jason, in addition to a variety of other, very meager talents, is quite the piano player. You're going to get to hear him play tonight with his former piano teacher."

"Wonderful," said Emory.

"What do you do out there in Idaho, Mr. Morse?"

"Me? Oh, I'm an attorney. I've set up a practice in a little town up north called Sandpoint."

"Is that right?"

"Of course I'm here to talk about Henry Villard's interests. I started out working in acquisitions and easements for the Oregon Railway and Navigation Company—the legal side of things, you know. It's no secret that Villard has had his eye on the Northern Pacific route for years. And once the N.P. cleared bankruptcy and got operations going again, they sent me and a couple of other fellows up into the Pend d'Oreille country to work on right-of-way issues."

"The Pend d'Oreille country?"

"Yeah. Lake Pend d'Oreille. Idaho Territory. It was named by French Canadian fur traders. It's a beautiful big lake. In fact, the whole area is some of the most scenic country you'll see anywhere. High, snow-capped mountains, native forests, miles of untouched lakeshore, deer, elk, beaver, eagles, fish as thick as fleas. It didn't take me long to realize that this is exactly where I wanted to live. After a few months, I resigned officially (although I still do work for Villard's people occasionally) and I opened up a little office. I've sunk my roots there in Sandpoint."

"Huh. Sounds nice." Jason was struck by the calm certainty in Emory's voice, his self-possessed manner. "Sounds very nice."

"This is the fellow I was telling you about," Page said to Emory, apropos of nothing.

Emory explained, "I was telling Bernard the other day, I'm looking for someone to come out and apprentice with me—someone who'd be interested in joining my practice within two or three years. I've got more work than I can handle."

"Oh."

"It involves a lot of reading, of course, but, uh—"

"I thought of you, old man," interrupted Page, pointing at Jason. "You've got the right temperament for it, and you used to talk about all those people migrating out west, remember?"

"*Me?*" Jason blurted. "Are you kidding?"

"No, not at all. In fact, I told Emory you're the perfect candidate. First off, you've graduated. That leaves me out. But you're also a hell of an arguer, right?" He feigned a confidence with Emory. "Don't ever try to win an argument with this one. He's a regular Protagoras." Bernie lifted his white linen napkin, unfolded it, and placed it carefully on his lap. "I think it's a great opportunity, and I kind of hate to see you go to work in your father's firm, if you know what I mean."

"No, I'm afraid I don't," Jason lied.

"Well, that's really none of my business, but if I were you I'd grab a little adventure—that's all. Go to Europe or Africa or something. Or hell, go out to the Pacific Northwest. See the world. You've always had a hankering for something out there, Jason. You just haven't known *what*. When Uncle Emory mentioned this the other day, I thought of you immediately. Who better to go out and wrestle bears and dodge arrows than Jason McQuade!"

"Oh, thanks," Jason chuckled.

Page continued talking over the outstretched arm of a waiter who was leaning over, pouring water into his goblet. "Beats Atlanta anyway. You'll admit that, won't you?" Page looked at Emory. "That's where his father wants to send him, to manage a textile mill."

Jason wasn't sure he wanted to argue. But what a difference! On the one hand, the potential for adventure and excitement on the frontier—living independently in an untamed land, reading for the law, living by his wits; on the other, working in a hot, stuffy office in the heart of the old Confederacy, relying as much on his father's whims as his own wits.

Father hates lawyers, he reminded himself. Although on more than one occasion Robert McQuade had declined dinner table entreaties from his sons to explain his reasoning, he'd at least been consistent and thoroughly negative. "Can't trust them," he'd say. Or, "the law, at bottom, is an unseemly affair." No doubt because of this, Jason hadn't so much as entertained the slightest idea of becoming an attorney. Yet now he looked over and was caught by the seriousness in Bernie's expression.

"A lawyer?" he queried incredulously.

"Yes!" Bernie shot back. "Why, you'd be top-notch."

The idea of going to law school held no appeal whatsoever for Jason. He was tired of school. But "reading the law," as it was called, apprenticing oneself to a practicing lawyer, was different. He knew it was how most attorneys became attorneys— Abraham Lincoln was a case in point—and he calculated that it carried one particular advantage: exposing the professional candidate to a host of practical realities. *I don't know that I'm totally opposed to it,* Jason thought, surprising himself.

Page turned to Emory. "His father is Robert McQuade, of McQuade Textiles. You and father probably huddled under a McQuade blanket or two in your day."

It was as if Jason had been hit with a jolt of electricity. His spine stiffened and he leaned back in his chair. He was seized by a sudden, overwhelming realization, one that he'd managed to ignore—or smother—his whole life. It had always been there, he knew, but he had not dared to hold it up to the light. And now, as though a great façade were crashing down around him, he could not escape the truth. On top of everything else, he was ashamed of his father, the same man whose approval he had sought all this time! His father, who had paid to have someone else serve in his place, who had profited almost beyond measure during the war years. Jason looked closely at Emory's blue eyes and could not help but see (or was he hearing?) the horrors of battle, the heartbreak of loss, the stone-coldness of personal sacrifice. While others of his father's generation had gone off to fight, to risk their lives, their hopes, their aspirations, to preserve the Union, what had Robert McQuade—*his* father—done? Nothing, except hire hundreds (or was it thousands?) of women and girls—mostly Irish girls—at low wages to sew uniforms and weave blankets for the fighting men. Oh, he'd wrapped his "war effort" in patriotic boasts, all right, but what had he really done for the cause, other than criticize Lincoln's management of the war from the comfort of his mansion on Beacon Street, while other men bled and died? He'd sold merchandise to a government too distracted, too mired in lethality, to look closely at the profit margins built into each bill of lading.

Jason pushed this out of his mind.

"You ought to think about it," Page concluded, taking up his water glass.

The table conversation mercifully pointed in new directions. Fifteen minutes later, in the midst of enjoying a witticism shared by one of his tablemates, Jason felt a familiar hand on his shoulder.

"Hello there."

He couldn't help taking in all of Josephine, from the gown of striped green silk damask, to the short apron overskirt trimmed with white Duchesse lace, to the basque bodice with its low-cut square neck. She held a fan of lace and sage green silk. She wore her hair up in a chignon under the management of a diamond and silver comb, and had about her neck and left wrist the work of the same jeweler. Josephine stepped back and took a position next to a man with exceedingly short, sandy-colored hair and rather hard brown eyes. He wore a dark blue single-breasted officer's uniform with gold shoulder knots, an aiguillette of gold cord beneath his right shoulder, and the red facing and piping indicative of artillery service. His trousers were of dark blue with a black stripe. Beneath his tunic appeared a starched white shirt and black cravat. His thin lips supported an even thinner mustache. "Jason, do you know Captain Stephen Osgood?" asked Josephine, blushing slightly.

Jason rose from the table and took the man's hand. "I don't think I've had the pleasure. Captain. Jason McQuade."

"How are you, sir?"

Josephine looked from one man to the next. "Captain Osgood is a regimental adjutant recently returned from Plattsburgh Barracks."

"Oh. All right."

Josephine took the captain's arm. "Jason is a former student of mine. My prize student, I'd guess you say."

"You're too kind," Jason said, bowing slightly.

"I look forward to hearing your piano duo," the captain said stiffly. As he spoke his attention wandered to a different table, and then to a third. He let his gaze return slowly and condescendingly to Jason. He could not have exhibited greater indifference had he produced a stalk of beach grass and stuck it between his teeth.

"We'll do our best, won't we, Miss Carter?"

"Of course," Josephine replied, her color deepening. "I just wanted you to know that I'd arrived, Jason. We'll be sitting over there somewhere," she added, pointing toward tables beginning to fill up in the back of the hall. Jason nodded. Josephine looked around the room. "Oh, and I see the pianos are here."

Jason glanced up toward the dais, below which could be seen the raised lids of two grand pianos. He looked back at Captain Osgood and slapped his arm good-naturedly. "I get the one that's in tune," he winked.

The captain took a long, slow breath. "We better find our places."

"Before you go, Josephine, I want to introduce you to Emory Morse. Mr. Morse, Miss Josephine Carter. Miss Carter here was my piano teacher for many years, and now we perform together on occasion. She's the real pianist, as you might imagine."

"Miss Carter, it's a pleasure."

"The pleasure's mine, Mr. Morse. Are you from Boston?"

"Mr. Morse is an attorney from the Idaho Territory. He's just asked me to apprentice with him out in a little town called— what was it, Mr. Morse?"

"Sandpoint."

"Really? You would *do* that? What does that mean? That you'd become a lawyer yourself?"

"Yes, I think that's the idea. Whether I'd do it or not . . . well, probably not. But it's very flattering, and gives one some-thing quite unexpected to think about."

"What would you think of your piano student becoming a lawyer, Miss Carter?" Emory asked.

Josephine closed her fan and folded her hands in front of her. She tilted her head to look at Jason as though a fresh angle might provide a clue in one direction or the other. The look in her eyes was strictly for Jason and he knew it. "I'm afraid I've never imagined such a thing. I don't think I've ever heard you mention it."

"Perhaps he was playing too loudly at the time," offered Captain Osgood. "Shall we go, Josephine?"

"Oh yes, of course. Will you excuse us, gentlemen?"

Josephine took one step, then stopped and turned back to Jason. "Your father would certainly be disappoi—" She cut her-self off as though suddenly realizing her mistake. "Well, let us hope that tonight is not our last performance together, Jason. I would count that a great loss."

3

Mei-Yin was stunned then relieved to see the dim outline of three masts and a tangle of shrouds, stays, yardarms, and sailcloth looming ghostlike above the rooftops. She thought for a moment she heard men calling and answering in a strange language from invisible perches in the dark heights, but Lai-Ping gave no sign of having heard, or of having seen the ship, so Mei-Yin said nothing. Squeezing her aunt's arm, and carrying Gok-Wing's heavy drawstring bag over her shoulder, she and Lai-Ping continued along the dark street half-walking, half-running, sidestepping only a fraction of the puddles in their way. Mei-Yin worried about her aunt's ability to maintain such a pace—hadn't her feet been bound in childhood as well?—but Lai-Ping neither complained nor slowed. A few minutes later a buzz of activity, orders being barked, pulleys straining and squealing, could be heard. Only one more corner, thought Mei-Yin. Ahead, shadows flickered across the wall and high, arched

33

entrance of the Customs House. When not blocked by the black silhouettes of men passing and crisscrossing in front of them, the flames from the barrel fires lighting the quay were reflected in its large windows.

"Almost there," Lai-Ping wheezed.

They edged closer to the foreign factory buildings and offices that lined the south side of the street. There they could move virtually unseen in the cover of night shadows. Yet they soon found themselves surrounded by the encroaching noises and penumbral movements of scores of men, wagons, and draft animals, all converging on, or departing from, the circle of firelight ahead. They leaned out behind the corner of the last building and saw for the first time the great hulking figure of a ship, its black, shiny planking dimly reflecting tongues of flame dancing above the barrel rims. It was the *China Sea*.

Mei-Yin rolled back against the wall of the building. Her conical hat—Gok-Wing's bamboo hat—was pressed up against the bricks and rose up awkwardly, framing her face. Her freshly shaved forehead and temples gave her a more masculine appearance. "I can't do this!" she gasped. "I . . . "

"Yes, you can," answered Lai-Ping calmly, still surveying the situation. She turned back to Mei-Yin. After ascertaining that no one was within earshot, she said, "There are many stories of women disguising themselves in this way, traveling the seas on ships and junks—some even as pirates! My grandfather once told me of a Persian woman who was married to a spice merchant. He'd lost two ships at sea, and the captain of his only remaining ship attempted to extort extravagant wages. He was sacked. His wife took over in the guise of a sea captain. For the next eight years, she made deliveries between Kwangchow, Ceylon, and Zanzibar. Her true identity was never discovered."

But that is not me! Mei-Yin protested inwardly. I could never do such a thing!

Lai-Ping leaned out past the corner of the building again. "Look over there, Mei-Yin. The men are lined up at that table—

see—over there under the tarpaulin. There are two white devils seated there, and a son of Han. They are checking each man's papers by lantern light, no doubt against names written in those two large books. From there the men are hurrying toward the front of the ship—over by that red wagon, do you see? Each man shows his papers again, then walks up the ramp to the deck. At the top, there's a devil directing them where to go." Lai-Ping turned back to Mei-Yin.

Tears glistened on Mei-Yin's cheeks. Her hair, tightly queued by Suk-Wah, hung over her shoulder. "I can't defy my father, Lai-Ping. It will destroy the harmony of the family! It will bring them dishonor and awaken the wrath of our ancestors!"

"You are frightened, child," answered Lai-Ping. "This is to be expected. There is room for your fear. I, too, am afraid." There is room for your fear. How many times had she heard her aunt use this expression? The memory of Lai-Ping squatting next to her when she was just eight years old, saying these words as the two faced the prospect of crossing a narrow footbridge over a swollen river, flashed through her mind. Over the din of the raging river, Lai-Ping had added, "Remember, fear—what we feel together—is not everything. It does not consume all that is happening here. Perhaps it nibbles at the edges of our toes. Yes? Let it then! But it's what's in your heart that matters. That's what must be done!" Mei-Yin felt her aunt's fingers touching her forearm. "It is your father who has destroyed the harmony of the family, not you. It is *he,* Yeung Men-Hoi, who has torn the nest. He will know this when he is sober, although he may never admit it to himself or to your mother. But that doesn't matter. The ancestors surely know it. His brothers and uncles know it. They know of his broken promise to Hok-Ling, of his dissipation, of his mistreatment of your mother these many years.

"Has your mother ever told you what happened when your father's oldest brother, Siu-Kai, was stricken with fever several years back, and for three months could not work to support his family?"

"No," Mei-Yin said, wiping the tears from her cheeks with the wide sleeves of Gok-Wing's blue coat.

"Men-Hoi offered to go to Siu-Kai to work in the fields with his three other brothers, but then he put one excuse after another, and he never went! He provided neither money nor rice to his stricken brother's family. Had it not been for his other brothers, surely they would have perished.

"And now he would throw away his youngest daughter on the mahjong table!"

Mei-Yin straightened, drew a ragged breath, then exhaled deliberately through pursed lips as though trying to impose calm upon herself. She forced a partial smile and embraced her aunt with a newly found strength. "I will never forget you, Lai-Ping," she whispered. Then she bent down to open Gok-Wing's bag. She took out the papers that Jong Suk-Wah had given them. They fluttered in a cool, freshening predawn breeze. She touched her aunt's face and nodded. "I'm ready."

"Good, good! Then it is as it should be!" Lai-Ping looked left and right to see that no one encroached too closely, then squatted, and with a well-placed hand encouraged Mei-Yin to squat beside her. "Listen to me now. You are Jong Gok-Wing. You are twenty-two years old." Lai-Ping reached around to examine the tightly bound queue tied into Mei-Yin's hair. "Your father, Bo-Tai, is dead. He was a fortune-teller for many years, and before that a courier. You live with your mother, and she and her two elderly sisters are dependent upon you." Lai-Ping interrupted herself only long enough to rub some dirt over the side of Mei-Yin's chin. "You have contracted with the House of Huang for three years to work on the American railroads. You are a sojourner. This is your second trip to the Gold Mountain. You have promised to return to the Middle Kingdom when your contract is up—do you understand?"

"Yes, Aunt."

"All right. Now, you must go get in the line by the table. Answer questions asked of you, but say nothing unless spoken to. Bow and say as little as possible. Speak in low tones—always. When you get on board, go where you are told but look everywhere for hiding places, places of privacy. You must find these at once. Do not drink or eat until you have determined how and when it will be possible for you to relieve yourself. Do you understand? And this must be done silently. If you are given a bucket, put rags or straw at the bottom before you use it.

"Suk-Wah and I put several rags in your bundle for bleeding. All of these articles must be washed without anyone seeing, hopefully at night. Remember Mei—Jong Gok-Wing—you are a man! You must think and act like a man! You will be exposed to crudeness and vile language. You must be indifferent to it, and mind your affairs solemnly."

Mei-Yin's sudden composure widened the eyes of Lai-Ping and anguished tears fell to her cheeks, as well. The old woman tried to wipe them away with her dirty hand, leaving marks that made Mei-Yin laugh softly. "Oh, now look what you've done," Mei-Yin said, trying to erase them with her own hand.

Lai-Ping sniffed and turned the conversation again. "When you arrive in San Francisco, get away from the ship at once. Go to the home of Cheng Tien. *Cheng Tien*, can you remember that?"

Mei-Yin nodded.

"He and his wife will help you. Now listen carefully, Mei-Yin. Your mother has heard from the parents of a man who knows Hok-Ling, has worked with him. They believe Hok-Ling and their son are part of a Tang work crew working in the north. They are building the railroad eastward into what is called the Idaho Territory, near a place called Sandpoint. Can you remember that word—'Sandpoint'? You must learn to pronounce it correctly in English, for somewhere near this place there is a labor camp along the shore of a great lake. This is where you'll find Hok-Ling." Lai-Ping hesitated, then took hold of Mei-Yin's wrist. "Your fate now is in the hands of the gods. If you arrive safely on Gold Mountain, you will know that the gods smile down on you. But still, be careful. Do not trust the white devils. Do not be led astray. Do you hear me? Trust your own judgment before anyone else's." She released Mei-Yin's wrist. Her face hardened. "Go now, Jong Gok-Wing."

* * *

Her bunk mate's arm slid smoothly over Mei-Yin's hip. He mumbled something incoherent as she pushed it away for the third time in the last two hours. The ship pitched and rolled beneath them. His limp body sagged against her buttocks and the small of her back, waking him up temporarily. He turned over and went back to sleep.

Mei-Yin lay with eyes open, her face mere inches from the weeping black interior wall of the ship. A low-burning lantern swinging from a chain near the companionway sent the stark shadow of her cheek and temple rising and falling over the silvery, malodorous sheen. When she was sure he was asleep, she rerolled her blanket into a thick tube and stuffed it carefully between them. She pulled her blue coat up to her chin, closed her eyes, and tried to sleep.

They had been nine days and eight nights at sea. She had slept little, mostly during daylight hours. She had avoided the other coolies for the most part, spoken little, given wide berth to knots of men playing cards or mahjong on deck, or sitting around sea lanterns telling stories while they ate. She was careful not to make eye contact or draw attention to herself. She skipped meals of rice, fish, and cabbage, or waited until the others had finished. She feigned seasickness and stayed in her shared bunk most days. But the greatest danger of discovery came from the accidental groping, the wandering legs and hands, of her bunkmate, a plump, round-faced, taciturn man of thirty-five from Macao named Lei Zheng-Ping. He slept unusually heavily, but with expansive tendencies that kept Mei-Yin in constant fear of invasion. If his hand found her hip or her breast again, or the small of her waist, she resolved to take drastic action.

She did not have long to wait. Pushing him away for the fourth time, she waited, listening to his breathing settle again. Slowly, she rose up and slid off the bunk. She put on her coat and carefully lifted the rolled blanket. She made her away around the prone, snoring bodies crowding the floor, to the companionway ladder. Beneath the ladder, blankets had been hung to hide buckets for the men to relieve themselves in during the night. She listened. Hearing nothing, she peaked in between two of the blankets to make sure no one was there who would see her climbing the ladder. The ladder groaned and squeaked with each upward step, so she went slowly, trying to synchronize her movements with the sounds of the ship's moaning and creaking. Finally, she was through the companionway door and onto the deck, where she crouched down, taking account of the number and placement of lanterns, and insofar as possible the location of the ship's crew.

She shuddered as she looked up into the enormous assemblage of white, billowing sails towering overhead, sweeping the star-studded sky in silent arcs of unimaginable breadth. Underfoot, the ship's movements seemed to triple in intensity all of a sudden. She quickly grabbed the casing of the companionway door to steady herself. Just past the mainmast she saw her target, the canvas-covered longboat resting on blocks at the center of the ship's well. She had noticed it several times while walking on deck. It sat atop a pile of extra spars. If I can get inside, under that canvas, that will give me some privacy, she thought. A neatly constructed pyramid of water barrels secured to each other and to the deck stood near the longboat's stern. Perhaps it would give her cover—enough time to untie the canvas and slip into the longboat to sleep!

As she started for the longboat, two voices sounded behind her at the starboard rail. A few words of English followed by subdued laughter. Mei-Yin ducked behind the mainmast, pressing her back hard against thick, rough halyards and belaying pins, seeking every inch of available shadow. The voices grew louder, and despite the howling of the wind in the shrouds she could make the words out clearly, although she did not understand them. The men were coming toward her. They had turned and were about to walk directly past her. She pushed her head back, turned away, and closed her eyes. The two men stopped within inches of her. Their tobacco smoke blew over Mei-Yin's face, entering her nostrils. After a few moments of silence, they began to speak again, and she heard their steps slowly moving away. She turned and opened her eyes to see the two crewmen round the companionway door and continue on their way astern. They hadn't seen her! She put her hand to her heart as she watched them disappear behind the cookhouse wall.

Mei-Yin struggled to keep her balance as the ship conspired through a chaotic series of violent rolls and yaws to prevent her gaining the pyramid of barrels, but at last she made it. By mere good fortune, the lacing on the canvas cover of the longboat was tied off within arm's reach and she was able to untie the knot and struggle aboard the twenty-four-foot boat. She tightened and retied the lacing from the inside and very quietly felt her way to the middle of the vessel, where she wrapped herself in her blanket, lay down, and fell into a sleep far deeper than any she had ever known or imagined.

She awoke once. A narrow seam of gray light surrounded her but was insufficient to illuminate the gloom where she lay at the bottom of the boat. She heard voices and the bustle of the crew on both sides of the ship, the shouting of orders, the squeal of pulleys and blocks, and the occasional knock of wood spars hitting the masts. In the distance, she heard Cantonese being spoken. The ship was rising and falling to a much greater degree than before, and the howling that descended from the rigging had a new, higher, more sustained pitch. Mei-Yin was comforted by the knowledge that she was well hidden, and then, too, by the fact that she was warm, and had wedged herself snugly between two of the longboat's benches. One bench lay smooth and firm against her back, while the other provided a brace for her knees. She was secure. As she drifted back to sleep, she noticed the meager brightness that marked the sun's position traversing several inches along the thin line of gray light above her head. The ship was changing course. The bow lifted and crashed heavily, but rhythmically, in a following sea.

Sixteen hours after Mei-Yin had slipped into her hiding place, the *China Sea* was hove to—at a stop with her bow pointed into the wind—entertaining a full storm. Mei-Yin, however, was sound asleep. All hands save a skeleton crew were below decks, drying out. The few sails still unfurled, straining at their reef points one minute, slack the next, pounded like furious celestial drummers each time the bow edged to windward or walked itself back again. A sea anchor had been eased out by order of the master, and the bowsprit, the foremost part of the ship, leapt heavenward like the head of a stallion and crashed down again and again against the unceasing onslaught.

Suddenly, Mei-Yin was jarred awake by a sense of weightlessness followed by a sharp pain in her right leg. She let out an involuntary scream as her body was tossed like a toy, first against the longboat's starboard gunwale, then against one of its benches. She reached out desperately for something to hold on to as her body was pitched violently in the black, confined space over another bench. She struck her head and shoulder against a floorboard rising up in the darkness, unseen. She tried to swallow back another scream, but it was no use. At last her frantically searching fingers found a cross-brace small enough to accommodate her hands. She gripped it tightly, while her legs continued to bounce and swing uncontrollably. This must be the end, she realized. Why didn't I hear this terrible noise before? The ship is sinking! I'll be swallowed up by the waves! I'm going to die!

Then she saw a flash of golden light beyond the canvas, then another. The lacing holding the canvas cover was being undone. One edge was open now, blowing back, beating hard against the rest. Then more and more of the cover was coming loose. She closed her eyes and turned away as slanting rain and sea spray poured in on top of her. When she turned back a man was standing over her, his face obscured behind the glare of a storm lantern. Thick fingers emerging from a dark green oil-skin sleeve gripped the gunwale as the man struggled to keep his balance. What's happening? she thought. The question was framed in remnants of the dreamlike state that still held her, but then the cries she had let out began to echo in her mind like the wailing of the wind in the shrouds.

Half a face appeared beside the lantern. A gruff voice. *"What the hell . . . ?"*

* * *

Her small hands clung to the ship's rail and to the shrouds as the man who'd pulled her from the longboat was now escorting her toward the back of the ship. Twice she began to fall on the pitching, sea-soaked deck, but each time he caught her under the left arm and placed her back where she could take hold of the rail-ing. Her clothes, Gok-Wing's loose-fitting pants and long shirt, his blue coat, were all soaked through. It was difficult to move in them. He pushed her up the ladder, hurting her, but she didn't struggle. What's the use? she thought. I will soon be dead anyway.

The man took her by the arm. They approached what Mei-Yin assumed was an officer, a tall, bearded man wearing a greatcoat and a small, round cap. The brass buttons on his coat blinked in the glow of the binnacle lamp, which he was using to steady himself. Behind him, two men were bracing themselves at the helm. There were other men struggling in the gloom on the port side of the ship, shouting to each other, trying des-perately to splice a mizzen topsail sheet that was fraying and in danger of snapping. Mei-Yin's escort steadied himself, then confided to the lot in a loud, crowing voice, competing with the roar of the wind and sea. He mimicked her two cries. He held the lantern up to her face, and the others paused in their battle with the storm long enough to look. Their mouths fell open.

On orders from the man in the greatcoat, Mei-Yin was taken below and locked in a cordage locker, a dank hole filled with enormous coils of spare rope, pulleys, blocks, and other fittings. The same man who'd found her in the longboat pointed her toward a hole in one of the coils that would accommodate her in relative comfort until the storm passed. She sat down in it at once. As he started to leave, the man spied a canvas tarpaulin tucked between two barrels of tallow. He pulled it out and, taking it up by a corner, let gravity unfold it. Despite the ship's continual pitching and yawing, he managed (while still holding the lantern) to spread the tarp over her legs. He looked around. In another corner there were two piles of rags, one clean, the others smeared with grease and dirt. He picked up three or four clean rags and tossed them onto Mei-Yin's lap. A moment later, the door to the locker was slammed shut. The lock clicked into place and all was darkness, the unfathomable cacophony of sea and storm, and the strange comfort of a coil of rope.

* * *

She stood before the master, staring down at her hands. He was seated at a wooden table in the middle of a large, well-appointed cabin, head in hand, poring over the ship's manifest. He was dressed in a capacious gray nightshirt, open at the collar. The skin of his ankles and shins, visible beneath the hem of his white breeches, was goose flesh. His thick brown hair, an angry confusion of curls such as she'd never seen before, lapped up around sausage-like fingers. He muttered to himself as his leonine shadow, cast by the bright morning sun pouring through the portholes, slid back and forth across the cabin walls.

The crewman who'd discovered Mei-Yin and secured her in the cordage locker was there. The mate in his greatcoat as well. They were all waiting for Wu Tai-Hing, the ship's bilingual cook, who'd been summoned by the steward. The rolling ship creaked and groaned around them. Listing to port, the *China Sea* was making way. The master turned the pages forward and back, shaking his head.

Mei-Yin's demeanor belied the frenzied racing of her thoughts, the weakness she felt in her knees and back, as though at any moment she might collapse utterly. She willed herself to breathe, to take in everything around her: the tones of the men's voices, their gestures, their movements. It didn't matter that she couldn't understand them. She had to focus her mind on what she could comprehend, on what was possible.

Wu Tai-Hing, hugging a red blanket about his shoulders, sidled through the open cabin door. Mei-Yin glanced up at him. He was a tall, clean-shaven, round-faced man with narrow, deep-set eyes, and short-cropped salt and pepper hair. His forearms—what could be seen of them—were covered in tattoos. She detected in him at once a kind, gentle disposition. But was this just her mind playing tricks on her? She thought of her grandfather, who constantly lectured her on the conclusions we draw about other people, those that arise from awareness of their differences, and those that spring into place when we see parts of ourselves in them. Here was a Tang person like herself. She was giving him the benefit of the doubt. Wu Tai-Hing's eyes were puffy with sleep. "What's this, Master John?"

"You tell me," the master groaned, still flipping pages.

"It's a woman, that's what," declared the first to discover Mei-Yin. He wiped his mouth with the back of his hand. "I found her in the longboat last night. I was checking on the spars when I heard a scream—like a girl what's got her hair pulled. There was one scream and another. Thought my time was up, I did. Thought, okay, this must be how the Good Lord does it—starts things out with a scream or two. Take a good look, Cookie."

The cook stepped closer, examining Mei-Yin. He glanced up at the mate for confirmation, then looked back at Mei-Yin and spoke in Cantonese. "Who are you, child?"

She averted her eyes. What do I tell him? The truth? "Mei-Yin," she whispered softly. "Yeung Mei-Yin."

"And what are you doing here?"

Now she was silent. Her heart's pounding was a drumbeat for embattled thoughts. "They will rape me and kill me" spread like thunder across the landscape of possibilities. But the landscape held other features that she spied, at first, peripherally. She shifted her attention away from the imminent threat of death to the possibility that what filled her now—life, breath, and will—might go on. Perhaps there was a way. But how? Now that this Tang person is here, I can communicate with them, she thought. But what do I say? How do I account for myself?

"Well," said Tai-Hing.

"Seamstress." The word tumbled out of her mouth, surprising her. Her eyes darted side to side as she sought to collect the bits and pieces of a story.

Wu Tai-Hing turned to the shipmaster. "Her name is Mei-Yin, sir. She is very frightened . . . "

"Mei-Yin, huh?" the master snarled. "I don't see any goddamn 'Mei-Yin' here, Cookie. Ask her what the hell's she's doing on my ship?"

"The master wants to know . . . "

The cook had bought her time. Her brow arched as she regarded the story that was taking shape in her mind. "Please tell him that I . . . I came aboard as Jong Gok-Wing, a dead man. I purchased documents stolen from the home of Jong Suk-Wah, Gok-Wing's mother."

The master slammed the manifest book shut and fell back in his chair. His bleary, red-ringed eyes glinted up unevenly. "Oh, isn't that nice!" He turned to the mate. "Jesus, Stevens, who was responsible for taking on these coolies? Wasn't it Johnson?"

The mate cleared his throat. "Yes, sir. Johnson and myself. But you'll recall the wind backed, so we had to ship a bunch of them in a hurry. No doubt she came aboard with the last group."

"Oh, she did, huh? So you're saying we just opened her up—let anybody who wanted come on board?" bellowed the master. He slammed his fist down, then stood up and marched away from the table. Mei-Yin jumped at the outburst.

"No, sir."

"*No?*" the master countered, spinning around. His face was red as a cranberry. "Then how do you explain—?"

"By the document, sir," interjected the mate. "She had this other man's authorization. Nobody got on board without written authorization."

The mate's reply seemed on the verge of satisfying the master. He looked away, shaking his head. A moment later, angry questions were crowding his eyes again. He stared at the mate, then sat down, and began chewing his lower lip as though the resolution to his problem somehow required this. It would not have been a propitious time to interrupt him. No one did. "Ask her what the hell she's doing, cookie. Is she a prostitute, someone's daughter—what?"

She looked anxiously at the cook as he translated. She nodded.

"My father is a businessman," she began slowly. "He lives on Gold Mountain. In a letter to my mother he gave instructions. 'Tell Mei-Yin to come to Gold Mountain at once to work.'" Mei-Yin looked directly at Tai-Hing. "He said I should make arrangements with the House of Huang. He gave me twenty silver dollars and said he will pay another twenty silver dollars to the master of the ship upon my arrival. 'Don't worry,' he said. But the House of Huang made this impossible. 'The ship is full,' they said. I was desperate to see my father, to honor his wishes. A few days later—no, it was the same day—I heard from a friend of a friend that someone had stolen the authorization papers of a coolie who had drowned. This man stole the papers for himself, intending to go to Gold Mountain, but then he got—how do the demons say it?—hot feet? His wife said to him, 'No, do not leave me here with four children. We will all starve.' So this man set out to sell the papers, and as no one would buy them he grew desperate. I purchased them for twenty dollars."

Tai-Hing's eyes arched with growing concern as the story unfolded. "I see," he said in Cantonese. He covered his mouth with one hand to give himself time to think. Then he turned to the master. In English he began, "This woman . . . " But then he turned back to Mei-Yin and said in Cantonese, "This is an interesting story. Do you think they will believe it?"

Mei-Yin's heart stopped. He doesn't believe me, she thought, looking down at the table. Then she raised her head and stared directly into Tai-Hing's eyes. "Yes. Of course. It's true."

Tai-Hing hesitated. "Well, perhaps you're right. Tell me, though, where are you going on Gold Mountain? Once you get off the ship, I mean."

She glanced quickly at the master then back at Tai-Hing. Why does he ask this question? What difference does it make where my father lives? Then a thought occurred to her. She followed a thin line of hope. Perhaps he wants to get me as close as possible. "I am going to a place called Sandpoint, in the Idaho Territory."

Tai-Hing pursed his lips and nodded. He turned back to the master. "This woman is seamstress." Tai-Hing looked at Mei-Yin again and assumed a detached, businesslike demeanor. In Cantonese, he said, "I'm telling him you are a seamstress, as you said. This he will believe. All Tang girls know how to sew."

"Thank you," whispered Mei-Yin. Her heart was in her throat, for she sensed that Tai-Hing had set himself the task of saving her life.

He nodded matter-of-factly and resumed in English. He told Mei-Yin's story but amended it to say that her father waited for her in Tacoma, not San Francisco. Tacoma was the second port of call for the *China Sea* before returning to Kwangchow, known in the West as Canton. Tacoma was much closer to Idaho than

San Francisco was. "And, as I said, this man, her father, waits with twenty silver dollars in pocket for master."

"I need coffee," the master groaned.

Tai-Hing hesitated, pointed toward the cabin door. "Shall I . . . ?"

"No, no. Later. Go on."

"Well, this woman is very daring and foolish, but now has become afraid. She pay a heavy price to do as father wishes. Is afraid to stay any longer on sleeping deck with men. This is why she snuck onto longboat. Is very sorry to have frightened Mr. Corrigan."

The master stared blankly at the far edge of the table, shaking his head in disbelief.

"May Cookie suggest something?"

The master looked up. "Go on."

"If this woman stay in cookhouse under my protection, it will be possible to protect her. That way, we—you—can deliver her to her father in one piece and collect money. If no girl, no money. No money, no girl. Very easy. She will work with me, also do sewing for crew. No charge."

The master looked at the first mate. The mate showed his palms and shrugged. Mei-Yin struggled in vain to understand what they were talking about. The only thing she dared believe was that their tone suggested she would not be killed. She would live another day.

The master sat back and folded his arms over his chest. He let out a long breath and took one or two more bites of his lower lip. "All right, here's what we'll do. She'll stay with you alright, Cookie, until we get to Tacoma. But I'm not dragging her back to China under any circumstances. If her father isn't there with the money, you'll pay the twenty dollars yourself, out of your wages. You got that?"

The cook's face darkened. He resumed the same posture as before, with his hand to his mouth.

4

Washington Territory
1882

When he had been lowered approximately forty feet, the basket slipped suddenly, then caught. Hok-Ling's heart leapt into his throat. After a long pause, the basket began to trip down again, under control.

He held on, fixing his eyes on the minutia of the granite wall, commanding his mind to appreciate the color and pattern of the lichen—pale to bright green, yellow, golden-brown— growing on the sheer face, to marvel at insects at home on the tiny ledges, to wonder at the dry, brown pine needles wedged in the crevices (so far from any trees)—in short, to think of anything but the three-hundred-foot drop to the Spokane River below, or the incessant screeching and squealing of the rusted pulley overhead.

How much farther? he wondered. He couldn't bring himself to look down. Nor did he find solace in the breathtaking view of the valley over his shoulder.

The square basket, just big enough for a grown man, fell free again, this time a shorter distance. Hok-Ling crouched down in its center, gripping its edge with dirty, calloused, white-knuckled hands. He squinted up into the bright glare at the top of the cliff. Two brown faces shaded by conical Asian hats appeared briefly at the rim, then disappeared. It wasn't like this when he was lowered this morning by the others, he reminded himself. They were much more careful. Changing places with Tai-Hu might not have been such a great idea.

With the basket descending again, Hok-Ling ventured a peek over the edge. This time he saw his friend Soo-Kwan squinting up at him from another basket thirty feet below. Soo-Kwan's drill was sunk deep into a bore. His hammer rested heavily on his shoulder. In the next basket over, pounding with one hand, turning the shaft of his drill with the other, concentrating mightily, was Dak-Wah.

"There you are," Soo-Kwan called up. "We were wondering if you'd make it. Your bore is down here." Soo-Kwan's almond-colored shirt slid away from his wrist as he pointed to a spot on the precipice a few yards to his left. Hok-Ling leaned over, holding himself with the rope. He could see the hole started by Yee Tai-Hu.

Good! he thought. Enough of this dropping. He blew a relieved breath. Now we'll see how well they've marked the line.

The basket continued down and jerked to a stop with the bore directly opposite Hok-Ling's shoulders. He smiled at Soo-Kwan to hide his nervousness. "Right on the money, as the demons like to say."

Soo-Kwan laughed, and Dak-Wah, in the basket behind him, nodded at Hok-Ling between ringing hammer blows. Dak-Wah, who was perpetually cold, had on his blue coat, and both men were covered with peppery granite dust. The fronts of their black pants looked as though they'd been faded to gray. Hok-Ling, who'd brushed himself off during lunch, was clean by comparison. He wore black trousers and a blue, heavily soiled work shirt, the sleeves of which he'd removed. All three wore rounded dome coolie hats.

Dak-Wah stopped. "So," he sniffed, "Yee Tai-Hu agreed to trade places with you, huh? I think your request surprised him." He reached up to wipe debris away from the opening of his bore. "Anyway, welcome to our little piece of paradise."

Hok-Ling looked back up the length of his line. "I think I know why he agreed. Did you see the way they were lowering me? Twice I thought the rope had broken! If I'd have known what I was getting into, I would never have suggested this. I can talk to you two anytime."

He ignored his friends' sniggering and gazed out across the palisades. Dozens of Chinese workers hung from baskets and rope ladders in the shadows of the cliffs, preparing blast holes. Like him, each man was staking his life on a wicker basket and a length of dark, weathered rope stretching below the scaffoldings. He made out the light green coat of Yee Tai-Hu 250 yards away. This brought a smile, for Tai-Hu looked like yet another insect at home on the cliffs. It struck Hok-Ling that the basket he observed was the very one he had been in just an hour before, and he marveled at its smallness there on the black cliff, so high above the glistening river. He could see Tai-Hu tamping clay into the very bore he had drilled a few hours earlier. He could easily imagine himself in Tai-Hu's place, and he wondered what he might look like now, from there. He inhaled deeply. Along the line of men he could imagine the silver track that would soon be laid, and the long, sinuous, smoke-belching trains that would one day ply this route, hugging the cliffs.

Several men on either side of Yee Tai-Hu were charging their bores with black powder and tamping them as well. What Hok-Ling did not see was Bo King, the man on Tai-Hu's immediate right, tamping his charge with an iron rod—the handle of his drill. Ten minutes earlier, Bo King had dropped his wooden rammer into the river while trying to swat a bee. It was not that, but the use of the iron rod to tamp black powder that set a timer off in heaven.

"I see you're drilling right next to my friends Soo-Kwan and Dak-Wah. I'll tell you what. I'll switch places with you this afternoon. Tamping wet clay is easy, much easier than drilling." That's what Hok-Ling had said to Tai-Hu between bites of his noon meal of salt fish and rice. He was hoping to have the chance to lighten his day by working next to his best friends. Tai-Hu had shrugged. "Sure, why not?"

Dak-Wah spat into the void. His spittle would disappear between two rocks on the south bank of the Spokane River twelve seconds later. By that time, both he and Soo-Kwan would have raised their hammers and struck three ringing blows to the ends of their drills.

Hok-Ling lifted his drill and drove it into the orifice. He let out a groan. Do you mean Tai-Hu managed only three feet since seven o'clock this morning? He looked over at Soo-Kwan, but the other was preoccupied. Shaking his head, he reached for his hammer. The basket tilted suddenly. He straightened and grabbed the end of the drill, balancing himself again.

The hammer strokes reverberated through his arms and upper body. It was not mind work, and for a time his thoughts wandered aimlessly over questions as diverse as "Why do some men snore?" and "How fast would a ship have to travel to keep the colors of the sunset constantly overhead?" Yet one subject dominated his waking thoughts. It lacked the speculative quality of the others. He had neither the strength nor the will to fight it. This was the immovable belief that he had violated his filial duty to his family, especially to his father, by entering into this contract with Mei-Yin's father. Coming to the Gold Mountain under *these* circumstances—not for his family's benefit but for his own. Sending money back not to his aging parents and grandparents but to the unscrupulous Yeung Men-Hoi. What had he been thinking? Yes, he had fallen in love with Men-Hoi's daughter. That couldn't be helped. But it was not normal, not in a society where marriages were arranged. His feelings were as nothing compared to the wishes of his father.

Hok-Ling gritted his teeth and pounded harder. She was a beautiful flower—but she had no business going along with this. She knew this was wrong. She is no less guilty than I! Oh, that I had never met her!

Three years and nearly eight months had come and gone since Hok-Ling had seen Mei-Yin, since he'd pushed her gently away and held her at arms' length in the busy Kwangchow street so that he might see her and never forget her as she looked then. But now he strained to see her in his mind. He argued with himself about the size of her eyes or the turn of her lips. He found it unbelievable, yet he knew at times he confused her with other young women he knew or had met working at his father's live fish stall near the Flowery Pagoda. When he heard her voice within, it changed in pitch or timbre, or faded to a whisper, and it all seemed right and wrong at once.

How could one forget such things? It must be an omen, he thought. He hadn't forgotten his father's face, or his mother's. He could hear their voices clearly. But they had not changed! Mei-Yin was only sixteen when Hok-Ling had seen her last. Surely, she would look different now. Perhaps her voice would be different as well.

He remembered the last words he'd spoken to her. "Three years' work, Mei-Yin—that is all. The House of Huang is honorable. They assure me that my employer will pay my passage back to the Middle Kingdom when my contract is satisfied. I will return to you then. And the money I send to your father—our half will make us rich. We will marry and have many sons—and perhaps a daughter, too, who will never be as beautiful as you. Three years—do you hear? This I promise."

He remembered the words but found it inconceivable that he'd spoken them. A pang of deep shame accompanied the memory, for how precipitate he'd been to place his interests ahead of his father's. Did his father ever really approve of

Mei-Yin? Had he consulted him in good faith before hatching this plan? He'd told himself he had, but his father was sick and delirious with fever when Hok-Ling approached him in his chamber to seek his blessing. Was it given? In a sense, yes. But did Hok Xu Guan even comprehend what his son was telling him in such haste? How quickly Hok-Ling ran from his father's side, clinging to the vague nodding that he took as assent. Was this filial piety? Hardly.

For the first year or two, Hok-Ling's conscience had been clear. After all, he'd told his father that he couldn't stand the idea of not being married to Mei-Yin someday, or of her being married to someone else. Yes, she would be an asset to his family, for her intelligence and industriousness. But more than that, she would bear him beautiful grandsons. He remembered his father's vacant eyes. The vague nod. All went well, he thought. But then, with time, his conviction began to erode. My father was sick. He would not have agreed to this arrangement, to tie his family to Yeung Men-Hoi's tainted family, not in a million years. I acted selfishly. Rather than protect him, I took advantage of my father.

He recalled with shame the stories of the Twenty-Four Filial Exemplars that he'd read and, in some cases, memorized as a child—stories that his parents, grandparents, and teachers told times beyond number. The one that returned again and again to him now was *Yáng Xiāng: He Strangled a Tiger to Save His Father.* He knew it by heart.

> When Yáng Xiāng of the Jìn dynasty was four-teen, he often followed his father Fēng into the fields to reap grain. His father on one occasion was dragged away by a tiger. Although at the time Yáng Xiāng had no weapon at hand, he thought only of his father and not of himself as he leapt quickly forward and grabbed tightly at the tiger's neck. The tiger left in defeat, and his father was able to escape injury.

A verse praises him, saying:

In the deep mountains a white forehead reared,
And when it moved the wind was filled with
the smell of its dead prey;
The father and child have suffered no injury,
For he has rescued his father's body from the
greedy mouth.

How far he was from a Yáng Xiāng! Only with difficulty
was he able to push this verse out of his thoughts. Sometimes
he replaced it with visions of returning to the Middle Kingdom
and visiting the homes of his older brothers, of the pleasure that
awaited him as his nephews and nieces clamored for his attention, begged for stories of Gold Mountain or of the sea, sang
songs, or read poetry to him.

I wonder, he asked himself, his thoughts increasingly punctuated by hammer blows—his own and those of the scores
of other coolies up and down the palisades—will *this* be the
day? Will the paymaster come tonight? Will I finally have my
voucher?

Like thousands of others, Hok-Ling had been assured by a
coolie crimp—a middleman working for the House of Huang—
that his return passage would be paid by the railroad once he'd
completed his three-year contract on Gold Mountain. But when
he arrived on Gold Mountain, he was promptly disabused of
this idea. The promise of return passage, he was told, had been
a ruse. There were exceptions, or rumors of exceptions, but the
prudent sojourner put money aside to pay his way home again.

The voucher? That was another matter. By agreement
among West Coast shippers and local municipal governments,
no Chinese was permitted to board any ship bound for the
Orient without producing a signed, stamped voucher proving
that he had repaid in full his initial advance, with interest—
usually on the order of $200. In other words, proof that he was

not leaving debts in his wake. Hok-Ling had done this, had paid the advance in full. He had had no choice in the matter. The moneys had been deducted from his pay by the Northern Pacific Railway and its payroll agent, J.B. Harris and Company. Now he was entitled to his voucher. But where was it?

Hok-Ling visualized over and over how he would explain the credit-ticket system and the unjustified withholding of his voucher to his father and grandfather. Part of his filial duty was to disgorge everything to them. He could see their impassive expressions, the two or three dubious glances exchanged between them. "I asked again and again for the voucher, but the white devils kept putting me off. There was always 'perhaps tomorrow,' or 'you must be patient,' or 'after fifteen or twenty more miles of track are laid.' The paymaster would say, 'It's out of my hands. I've asked Mr. Keating about it. You'll get it in due time.' It was only after arriving on Gold Mountain that I learned that the three years of my contract were exclusive of shipboard time, and time awaiting assignment in San Francisco. There were many unpaid days, as well. Days spent in transit to the north, or days waiting for supplies of rails and ties to reach us. And when my clothes and provisions ran out, these were not replenished by the railroad, but I had to purchase them from the railroad stores, or from the shops of camp followers, and sometimes from treacherous and unsavory Tang people whose enterprising was like a flu unshakable among the sojourning men."

Hok-Ling noticed from the corner of his eye that Soo-Kwan and Dak-Wah had stopped working. He stopped as well. "Slow down," chuckled Dak-Wah. "It's going to be a long afternoon." But none of the three spoke further, for they were too exhausted to speak. They each drank deeply from their water bags, then let the cleansing wind and sunlight on their shoulders restore them. One by one they took up their hammers and returned to work.

When I am finally able to get back to Kwangchow, Hok Ling thought, I'll see where it stands with Mei-Yin. I owe her that, at least. Perhaps the fire will burn in our hearts then as it did before. In any event, I must explain to her what I have come to realize. And I must see about getting my money from Yeung Men-Hoi—no matter what happens!

Father, I promise you this: no effort will be spared. On "spared" he struck a mighty blow with his hammer. He imagined himself bowing deeply before his aged parents, making sincere, lengthy apologies for his long absence, begging for forgiveness. He would do anything to make it up to them now, to ensure their comfort and good health, to honor them in death. This would be his first priority.

* * *

"Why Spokane Falls?" Dak-Wah growled as he removed his drill and squinted into the bore hole. "Of all the places on earth, why here?" He turned and looked out at the expanse of windswept grassland beyond the river. "I, for one, will be glad to leave this place!" he shouted in a voice loud enough to be heard up and down the line of baskets. "I have not been warm here since I arrived! Not once!" He raised his hammer and drill in the air. "Even *this* does not keep me warm!"

Two indistinct replies were shouted back from some distance, accompanied by peals of laughter. Hok-Ling regarded his companion with a smile. "My friend," he said calmly, taking off his hat to let the sweat dry inside, "you have been here only a short time. Winters are cold, it is true, but it is already April. Soon it will be summer and very hot. There is not much here in the way of spring or fall. Is that not true, Soo-Kwan?"

Soo-Kwan had two twists in his long queue, one for each year he'd lived and worked in America. Hok-Ling had three, tied at each end with a piece of black silk. Although required in the Middle Kingdom to symbolize every man's perpetual servitude to the Manchurian government, the queue had a different meaning among the sojourning men on Gold Mountain. Here, in the land of the foreign devils, so far from civilization, the sojourners wore the queue proudly. Here, it was a symbol of their venerable race and culture! The added twists—one for each year spent sojourning for the benefit of their families back home—were not unlike insignia of rank among the Tang people. Accordingly, Soo-Kwan's answer to Hok-Ling was direct and respectful.

"It is true, Hok-Ling. The hot weather leapfrogs over spring here."

"Five twists don't lie, then," said Dak-Wah. "I will anxiously await the summer." He stopped to watch half-smiles develop on the faces of his friends, then added expansively, "But I hope your predictions apply as well to this place they call the Idaho Territory."

"I just heard the head-of-section camp is moving into Idaho in less than three weeks," said Soo-Kwan, clearing gray dust from the bit of his drill. "Master Peters informed me of this last night."

"What's this?" cried Hok-Ling. *"They're moving us to the Idaho Territory? Are you sure?"*

"Why was Master Peters talking to you, Soo-Kwan?" asked Dak-Wah. "Where was the boss, Ho Ying-Chiao?"

"I don't know. Perhaps he was in town. Master Peters ordered me to curry and feed his horse. This is why I didn't return from the river until very late."

"Are you certain he said three weeks?" demanded Hok-Ling. A rising panic swept over him, blurring his vision. "This wasn't to take place until the middle of June!"

"Less than three weeks. Yes, I'm sure. You know how he likes to practice Cantonese. In this case, it was remarkable. He even held up three fingers as he spoke. 'Less than three weeks move camp to Idaho Territory,' he said. Why he told me, this I don't know. Perhaps only to practice."

Hok-Ling took hold of the rope to steady himself. "How could this be?"

"Then I will be glad for it," said Dak-Wah. "Besides, I'm running out of money. What's the life of a sojourner without work and pay?" Dak-Wah hesitated and a frown tugged at his fleshy cheeks. "For the last two months I've been unable to send more than a few dollars home to my family. A few dollars! We were not told that the railroad would cut off our pay when rail shipments were delayed by labor strikes. Look at us, Hok-Ling! We're not black powder men. We're graders. What are we doing up here on these cliffs? Was it our fault the Columbia River fell and they couldn't bring the barges up to Ainsworth? Yesterday, we were replacing ballast on the plain. Before that, we hadn't had a day's work for three and a half weeks!"

When Hok-Ling didn't answer, Soo-Kwan spoke for him. "No. But what does it matter, Dak-Wah? It will also take a week or more to move the camp to this place they called Sandpoint—although I have heard from Ho Ying-Chiao that the camp itself will be on the opposite side of the lake from Sandpoint, at a place called Hope. The railroad has built steamboats to take us across. At any rate, do you think we will be paid our dollar a day for loading the grading equipment and black powder onto the wagons again? Will we be paid for carrying our bedding and belongings on our backs for seventy miles?" When Dak-Wah stared at him, still frowning, and did not answer, Soo-Kwan checked himself. "Ah! You are learning, my friend. It is the way here. Be glad at least that the railroad is building again, that we have work. Soon we will be sending money home again."

"Perhaps tomorrow they will charge us a dollar a day for our rice and tea," Dak-Wah said.

It wasn't the money that Hok-Ling was thinking about. He stood at the end of another winter's work, longing for his home-land, for his family, to be standing in the door of his father's home. "The camp is moving?" he asked incredulously.

"What's wrong with *you*?" grunted Dak-Wah.

Soo-Kwan turned. "What is it, Hok-Ling?"

Hok-Ling didn't answer. His thoughts of returning to the Middle Kingdom were suddenly met by the premonition that he would never return, that circumstances beyond his comprehension would arise to prevent his ever leaving. He turned and looked out over the plain. The images of him kowtowing before his father and receiving his forgiveness tumbled inward like the smoke of a raging fire. The grim prospect of having to move east with the railroad in less than three weeks, into the wilderness beyond the railhead, stirred the imaginary smoke in circles.

"Hok-Ling, what is it?"

But if the movement into the Idaho Territory is to begin in three weeks, he thought, surely they will not ask *me* to go. Will they? His entire purpose in coming to America seemed to fall back into memory. He was displaced, and like one who is awakened from sleepwalking, he reeled and saw nothingness through his eyes. *Would they?*

"Hok-Ling! What is it?" shouted Soo-Kwan. "What's the matter? Are you sick?"

The blast was so sudden, so overwhelming and thunderous, that Hok-Ling had the strange sensation of having heard it before it reached his ears. His thoughts of his father and going home were swept away in an instant. He spun, half-tripped, then fell awkwardly into the bottom of his basket. *What's happening? What is it?* Scrambling to his feet again, he looked out. His jaw dropped. His eyes opened wide with fear and disbelief. An enormous flower of dust and rock had burst from the side of the promontory some two hundred yards to the east. Its terrible petals streamed in all directions, dripping stones like raindrops into the river, shooting others like cannonballs hundreds of feet into the valley beyond. The first echo of the explosion came a moment later. The earth shook for miles. The river below shimmered between blue arcs of fleeing water. Stones began to rain down all along the palisades, dropping among the men, crashing and splintering on the riverbank below. Each man could do no more than hold on, while the ropes above their heads pulsed like guitar strings.

The great cloud hung in the air, as if to defy wind and gravity, until an enormous, crumbling wedge of dark granite slid out beneath it. Then more stone followed, pieces dropping away from widening crevices. In an indiscernible moment, the whole rocky mass had collected and was crashing down at once, dragging the bottom of the plume with it.

When the air began to clear, Hok-Ling saw the severed ends of three ropes dangling forty feet above the blast hole. There were no baskets attached to them. Immediately to the left of the gaping hole, the shredded remains of three baskets were tangled together, with no sign of their human occupants. And to the right, two more, each separate and apparently intact, but empty, as well.

Horrified, Hok-Ling studied the ridgeline to make sure. He traced the familiar features in the face of the cliff. Oh! Great spirits! He looked back at Soo-Kwan and Dak-Wah, but the faces of his friends were frozen with shock and disbelief. "Soo-Kwan! Dak-Wah!"

Slowly, the others' fearful eyes turned, came to rest on his own. "It's Yee Tai-Hu!" He felt his noon meal begin to rise, and with an effort he was just able to hold it back. He looked up again—Soo-Kwan's expression hadn't changed, as though he hadn't heard. Hok-Ling saw Dak-Wah's face over Soo-Kwan's shoulder. His narrow, worried eyes flinched, but gave no sign of comprehension. "It's Yee Tai-Hu!" Hok-Ling repeated. "The man I traded places with!"

5

Hok-Ling followed the cursing Ho Ying-Chiao over a rough stubble field toward a dripping, rain-darkened barn and a muddy corral holding three horses. The ten dollars that had pried the crew boss out of his tent had not purchased enthusiasm. "Are you mad?" the crew boss shrieked as he brought out a gray gelding and backed it between the shafts of a wagon. "The crews are moving to Idaho in three days!"

"I know."

"And there are hundreds of miles of track to be laid this summer. There will be dozens of trestles and tunnels to be built in the mountains to the east of the Pend d'Oreille. Why would the railroad release you now?"

"*Release* me?" cried Hok-Ling. "You talk as if I were a slave. I am a sojourner, *gum san hock*, remember? I came here to work, to earn a fortune for my—for the honor of my ancestors. My contract is over. Still, the Harris Company refuses to give me my passage. I have no voucher. *Why?*" Hok-Ling spit angrily. "The work is much harder here, *much* more dangerous, and far less glorious than I was promised. And the pay? Well, it is meager by these standards, isn't it?" Hok-Ling waved his hand toward the distant silhouette of buildings, telegraph poles, and chimneys marking the outskirts of Spokane Falls, Washington Territory. "But it doesn't matter now. I've worked three years, exactly as I promised the lying agent of the House of Huang. I've been here nearly four years. Do you hear me? Now I wish to return to the Middle Kingdom. It is my right. I demand it. I cannot wait any longer. I will pay my own passage if Mr. Keating refuses to pay it. But surely the Northern Pacific will provide me with a voucher so that I may board the ship. They must!"

"Hmm," answered Ho Ying-Chiao, his narrow face angling over the rump of the nickering horse as he adjusted the crupper. "It must be a woman then. Is that it?" He smiled but did not wait for Hok-Ling's reply. "No one would leave this land, or forsake his employment, unless he were lovesick, pitifully love*sick!* What do you suppose you will do when you return to Kwangchow?" Again, Ho Ying-Chiao paused but did not wait for an answer. "You will love this woman a few times and then you will go out looking for employment. Perhaps you will find a jinrikisha to pull. Or perhaps you will be impressed into a provincial army, so that you may march through the countryside in search of a battle in which to be killed. Have you forgotten?"

"I have not forgotten. But the Middle Kingdom is my home. I did not come here to live forever. I would never choose to live here. I am hated here, just as you are. And the others. This is not our place. What do you think these devils will do with you when the railroad is completed, Ying-Chiao? Will you wash their clothes? Cook for them? Live in a tent until you die?"

Ho Ying-Chiao studied the other behind a crooked smile. "This *is* my place, Hok-Ling. And it may be yours, after all. But if you insist on making trouble for yourself, get in."

They rode into town at midmorning as the wind began to pick up and dark, slanting streaks of rain dipped here and there beneath the scud. A patch of white sky far to the west lit the landscape. Hok-Ling sat next to Ho Ying-Chiao on the wagon seat with his hands folded on his lap. He did not speak. He watched the first random drops land on the gelding's back. The thin, shining circles vanished into its gray hide, but by their number they eventually stained the hide. The ground beneath the wheels began to soften, and the animal, stirred to life by a gentle slapping of reins and Ho Ying-Chiao's clucking, kicked tiny bits of mud against the dashboard and the caked, spinning axle.

"Tell me about this woman," demanded Ho Ying-Chiao at length. "She must be very beautiful."

Ho Ying-Chiao had to listen to the silence that followed his words. The two men were tossed by the pitching of the wagon as it rolled over long, jagged potholes. The sounds of cattle lowing could be heard in the distance. When it became clear that Hok-Ling would not answer, the crew boss slapped the reins harder against the horse's back and the wagon jerked ahead with a sharp and sudden acceleration.

They turned onto Division Street and joined a confused traffic of wagons, pedestrians, and horses. Both men took care not to look directly at the townspeople as the wagon inched along. Ho Ying-Chiao drew back the reins, yielding again and again to any white people in their path. He began to speak loudly to his horse, in English, and Hok-Ling bowed his head and put his hands in his sleeves.

At last Hok-Ling was following Ho Ying-Chiao down a long, dark hallway toward a rectangle of colorless light.

"Mas-ter Keating, sir," stammered the crew boss as he leaned over the threshold. Hok-Ling did not bow, for he was still in the hallway, out of view. He wondered at the markings "William T. Keating, Superintendent, Lake Pend d'Oreille Division" stenciled on the glass panel of the door.

"Yes," came a low voice inside. "What is it, Ying-Chiao?" The crew boss straightened, waved Hok-Ling in, then repeated his obeisance when Hok-Ling entered the room. The man Ho Ying-Chiao had called "Master Keating" was a red-faced Caucasian in his fifties, with reddish-blond hair, watery blue-gray eyes and a prominent nose. His hair was excessively oiled and lay in distinct rows under the lingering influence of a comb. His hands were large and, like his face, prone to color. Hok-Ling bowed, following Ho Ying-Chiao's lead, and when he straightened there was an unmistakable ruthlessness visible in Keating's inquiring expression, in respect of which Hok-Ling quickly averted his eyes. Keating sat behind an immense, square, glass-covered desk. In spots, where the glass was not buried beneath a jumble of maps, papers and books, and Keating's worn, ink-stained writing blotter, it reflected the gray light which seeped through a multi-light bay window behind him. The stub of a cigar burned in Keating's fingers.

As Ho Ying-Chiao began to speak, Hok-Ling swallowed nervously, realizing once again the extent to which a coolie on Gold Mountain must, at critical points, place his trust in the English-speaking crew boss. "Most hon-or-able sir. This Hok-Ling." Hok-Ling bowed again, a second time, at the sound of his name. "From Canton. Work three year rair-road." Ho Ying-Chiao seized the twisted queue at the back of Hok-Ling's head and jerked it around for Keating to see. When Ho Ying-Chiao released his hair, Hok-Ling turned back to Keating and bowed slightly—a third time. "Con-track fo three year. First, with House of Huang . . . then Harris Company. Want go home now. Want voucher."

"Home? You mean back to *China*?" asked Keating.

"Yes." Ho Ying-Chiao smiled. "Yes, yes. Back to China."

Hok-Ling watched a scowl develop on the American's face. Keating raised his cigar to the corner of his mouth and wedged it between his teeth. He squinted as threads of blue smoke climbed up his face.

"Why are you talking to me about this? He works for Harris, doesn't he? Go over and talk to them about it."

"Ah, yes," answered Ho Ying-Chiao. "This has been done. But Master Barlow has not said anything, and Hok-Ling has not received his passage or his voucher."

"Ha!" laughed Keating. "I hope you're not expecting the railroad to pay his passage! We contract our labor through Harris. Whatever arrangements they've made with their coolies is their business." Keating made a point of looking down at the paperwork on his desk.

Ho Ying-Chiao translated quickly for Hok-Ling, then turned back to the superintendent as soon as Hok-Ling started speaking to him in whispers. "No, no. Does not ask passage," exclaimed Ho Ying-Chiao excitedly. "Ask voucher. Must have voucher to board ship in San Fra . . . cisco. Only voucher."

Keating glanced up, momentarily. "I'm afraid that's quite impossible, Ying-Chiao. Besides, we're in need of every man. We're moving the head-of-section camp up to Hope. I've got orders to complete the roadbed as far east as Heron before the snows fall this winter. You know that."

"Yes, yes," answered Ho Ying-Chiao. He turned to Hok-Ling as if preparing to explain, then back again to Keating. "Hok-Ling work *three* year here, almost four, yes, and with O.R.N. See? Promise hon-or-able agent work three year. Keep word. Now want go home. Back to China."

Keating sat back. He examined Hok-Ling as he chewed the slimy butt of his cigar. Hok-Ling returned the gaze uneasily, for he had learned that this was the way of the demons, to look upon one another, no matter the circumstances, without averting one's eyes. He saw that each one of the American's teeth was outlined with a bead of gold. Such a thing astonished Hok-Ling, and he made a mental note to remember so that he might tell his father and his nephews and nieces what he had seen.

"This man is going to run no matter what I say, isn't he?" Keating mumbled.

"Run? Oh yes, run. Run? Mmm. Not know. Yes, 'magine maybe, sir."

Keating smiled. "Let's see. Steerage back to Canton is three hundred dollars. Ask this fella if he has that kind of money, Ying-Chiao. See if he's got three hundred dollars."

Hok-Ling was relieved to hear something spoken in his own language and he smiled unintentionally as Ho Ying-Chiao related the question. "Master Keating wishes to know if you have the money for passage. It is three hundred dollars."

"Yes. Tell him I do. I have sufficient money, and I do not ask for more—other than what I am owed for my few days of work this month. Tell him this." Hok-Ling began to breathe easier. So they are talking about passage now. This is good. The white boss will be pleased that I do not ask from the railroad more than is due me—that I have saved for my own passage.

"Hok-Ling say have money. Does not ask more from rairroad. Only work pay."

Keating leaned back in his chair with the cigar in his fingers. He looked intently at Ho Ying-Chiao, as if to avoid Hok-Ling's eyes.

"You tell this man that, as far as I'm concerned, he is still under contract with the railroad. He will *not* be discharged until the track is laid up past the Cabinet Gorge on the Clark's Fork of the Columbia. The Cabinet Gorge—do you understand me?"

Ho Ying-Chiao's eyes grew wide and fearful. "Yes, Mas-ter Keating."

"You can tell him in the street. Now get out." Keating carelessly pointed toward the door, then caught himself and drew a loud, short breath. "Oh, and by the way, Chinaman, what did this man pay you to bring him here today?"

Ho Ying-Chiao stared at his hands.

"Well, what was it? Five? Ten? Twenty? Damn your hide, speak up!"

"Ten dollar, Master."

"All right, then. Ten dollars. That's all I wanted to know. Now you listen to me. Take all of your men to the river tomorrow. I want them to bathe, and bathe well."

"Yes, of course," replied Ho Ying-Chiao, bowing quickly and starting for the door again.

"And I want you to see to it that this man loses his three hundred dollars or whatever he has. Do you understand me? Find his money and bring it to me directly. We'll hang on to it until his services are no longer needed." Keating squeezed a half-smile over the black butt of his cigar. Ho Ying-Chiao stared at him with bulging, incredulous eyes.

"Do you understand me, Ying-Chiao?"

"I un-stan," he whispered.

Hok-Ling watched Ho Ying-Chiao bow, then bowed himself without looking at Keating. He followed the crew boss quickly down the hallway.

"What did he say? What did he say?"

Ho Ying-Chiao seemed to hide behind his thoughts. He walked swiftly across the street, then half-ran, bent at the waist. His shoulders were stooped as though he carried a great invisible weight, and when he arrived at the wagon he mounted it so suddenly that Hok-Ling feared he would be left behind. He hurried to the opposite side, sliding his fingers along the rough leather traces.

"What did he say, Ying-Chiao? You must tell me!"

The crew boss frowned contemptuously. "Get in. He said you cannot go, not until the tracks are laid to the Clark's Fork. Did I not tell you this would be the way?"

Hok-Ling's strength melted away. He pulled at the side of the wagon but could not lift himself. Trying a second time, he just managed. His desperation and disappointment pinched his lungs and his throat burned with each shallow breath. What are the gods trying to tell me? First, Yee Tai-Hui is killed in my place. Now this!

It was several minutes before he could speak. "It is not just. I have worked three years, Ying-Chiao. I am entitled to go."

"It is the railroad's position that you are not," answered Ho Ying-Chiao ingenuously. "Not until the rails are laid to the foot of the Rocky Mountains." The horse initiated its labors before Ho Ying-Chiao could free the reins from the brake post. He cleared the reins and held them, still knotted, in his two hands. This time, Ho Ying-Chiao was not as careful to stop for every white person in the street, and leaving much to the horse's discretion made for a quicker trip. The wagon rattled past the last house within the limits of Spokane Falls. The two men listened to the sound of the hooves and wheels sloshing in the mud. Their shoulders bumped inadvertently over the rutted road, but they did not look at each other. Only after a long and difficult silence did Ho Ying-Chiao add, "There is something else I must tell you, Hok-Ling."

"What is it?" Out of his misery, Hok-Ling felt a measure of pity for Ho Ying-Chiao, and wondered how this was possible. He stared at the man's narrow face, the lined forehead and sharp, brooding eyes. Ho Ying-Chiao's thin black hair had been parted in several places by the wind and rain, and the seven-twisted queue that hung at the back of his neck sagged from neglect.

"*Well?*" urged Hok-Ling. "What is it?"

"It is about your money," Ho Ying-Chiao whispered. "Master Keating has told me that I must return your ten dollars to you at once. I will do so as soon as we arrive at my tent." Ho Ying-Chiao leaned over his knees and stared vacantly ahead.

Hok-Ling smiled, and a short, hollow laugh rode the end of his breath. "No, Ying-Chiao. It's all right. You keep the money. In this way we will cheat the American, just as he has cheated me."

6

J ason McQuade looked up from his reading, yawned, and began to rub and twist his neck and to roll his head, until he was distracted by an unbroken succession of dust clouds drifting past the windows of the law office. He sat up. A rigid figure was framed within the full-length oval glass of the door. It was Lester Carpenter, the tobacco merchant, standing on the opposite side of Sandpoint's Main Street, his legs spread, his hands rolled into fists on his hips. He was planted in front of the open entrance of his store, staring fiercely down the street. A group of long-legged boys with flushed faces ran in front of him on the street, and behind them came two men, running, and a third man, who held his Stetson in his hand and did not run, but seemed to fight the temptation to run with every step. Jason heard a faint rumbling in the distance. He rose to his feet and stepped out onto the sidewalk, squinting, working his fingers over the small of his back. Carpenter nodded.

"What is it, Les?" Jason shouted. The attorney's apprentice peered down the sunny street. In the distance, through a rising veil of dust, he saw a slow-moving parade of men and horse-drawn wagons. It turned east at Bridge Street, presumably crossing the Sand Creek Bridge and bound for the boat landing. Jason moved to the edge of the sidewalk. His view was obstructed by the crowd of onlookers gathering excitedly along the procession route, marking a wide arc from one side of the street to the other, but he caught glimpses of a multitude of small, dark men—some with round, pointed hats, most burdened by enormous rucksacks piled high above their heads—moving past the crowd.

"It's the Chinese!" yelled Carpenter, swatting the air. "Heading for Hope. Christ! There must be a million of them!"

"Well, I'll be," Jason muttered. He shut the door behind him and set out down the street.

"That's all we need around here!" Carpenter called after him.

Jason was only too happy to step away from the torpid writings of a certain Justice Barstow of the Supreme Court of Virginia. This was something he'd wanted to do for the last hour. Before that he would have sold his soul to rid the world of a certain prolix Justice Albert Hale of the Court of Appeals of Ohio. But he would return to both. He had their opinions, and seven other cases, to read, plus a paper to write, by four o'clock that afternoon.

On my word, I'm glad this is almost over, he thought, dragging an athletic hand through his dark, wavy hair, and letting his eyes blur the image of the crowd ahead. In a few weeks, with any luck, I'll be admitted to the bar, and done with all these damned assigned readings. This is getting to be a bit much. What does Emory want from me anyway?

Tramping down the dusty street, Jason was glad to feel the stiffness go out of his legs, and soon, too, the sun's insistent warmth eased a tension out of his broad, muscular shoulders and open, youthful face. He breathed in organic mountain air tinged with the familiar scent of the nearby lake. With each step another dull axiom of contract law fled his conscious mind. But in place of these came uninvited the parts of a distant memory: of endless, swaying columns of blue-clad soldiers, their footfalls marking a slow beat on the cobblestones of a Boston street, of the numbing confluence of unsynchronized regimental drum corps, of cheers in the street and echoes emanating from somewhere above, of the color and press of a Boston crowd. Yet most clearly he remembered—could not forget—the strange fixity and homogeneity (a quality of unforgetting, he later realized) evident in the eyes of the young soldiers, his heroes, Boston's heroes, the Massachusetts Maulers. Why so joyless in victory, he wondered at age seven from his perch on the gnarled tree overhanging the street. Surrounded by smiles, greeted with waves of applause and whooping from both sides of the street, these young men seemed by their dull, weary expressions to blunt the very bayonets that passed inches from Jason's bare feet.

Jason's childhood memory of drums and soldiers passing beneath him faded and gave way to the dolorous squeaks and groans of axles, the swishing of dry, dusty pant legs, and the shuffling of bare feet and hooves over the hard ground. These rose distinctly from the din as he neared the wall of onlookers. He stepped into the crowd and touched its electricity.

"*Ching Chong Chinamen! Ching Chong Chinamen!*" snarled one man, who spit over his wife's shoulder and nearly struck one of the Chinese. It was Dak-Wah—still perpetually cold, wearing his blue mandarin coat buttoned all the way up. Dak-Wah did not turn his head, but walked past, keeping up with the others. Hok-Ling and Soo-Kwan were not with him.

"Buster James, you stop that!" the woman snapped, laughing self-consciously. Jason glanced around at the men and women who stood nearby. The same excited and self-conscious smiles were frozen on their faces.

"Oh, what the hell!" exclaimed the round-faced man, Buster James, winking at the crowd. "These slant-eyed varmints can't hear me—don't understand a word I'm saying. Hey, China-boy! Hey there! You!" He held an arm out and snapped his fingers. "See there?"

"That's enough, Buster," his wife warned. Buster James laughed just the same. The procession moved on, but each new Oriental face rubbed him sideways until he couldn't hold himself back any longer. He whistled loudly and called,

"Hey, Johnny! Where's your eyes? You asleep?" A low sputtering sounded through the crowd, laughter pressed against the decency to refrain from laughter, a small rupture.

"I believe that's how *you* was looking last Saturday night, Buster!" someone shouted from the sidewalk, and, close upon the words, came more snickering.

Buster gave a look of surprise. Then he stared into the sky and lifted his hands toward heaven. His face bulged with enthusiasm. "As God is my witness, if that's true, I swear I'll never take another drink!" he shouted, and the crowd at once unleashed a roar of laughter.

Jason stared with the others, but did not share their merriment. The ever-moving Chinese did not raise their eyes to Buster James, or to the jeering and laughter around them. They marched on, expressionless, their eyes fixed on the ground, their dusty pants whispering. The rucksacks on their backs bore blankets and pots, long, heavy woolen coats, and black military-style boots with no memory of polish or oil. Their plain blue shirts were rolled at the sleeve, opened at the collar, and stained with perspiration.

They were small men, and wiry, and their long, slender pigtails hung out like braided snakes, or were tucked away. There was not much to distinguish them just now, one from another, save vague hints about lips and noses visible beneath the rims of their hats, or particulars of carriage and gait to which little significance would attach. But remarkable and general to them all was their indifference to the roistering around them.

"Yoo-hoo! Chinaman!"

"Hey! Look at that one. He's got a pigtail three feet 'r more. Let's see you swat a fly with that tail of yours, Chinaman."

"But can he take a bit?"

"God a' mighty! There's a regular army of them. Look at that! They just keep coming."

"You fellas dance any?"

In the midst of the crowd's jostling and abuse, Jason and the majority of the onlookers stood transfixed, staring in wonder at the downward-looking, deliberate men, men on foot and crowded in the wagons, pressing on like a convoy of a thousand ships consigned to the storm-tossed sea. Where have you been? he thought. What corners have you turned only to face another challenge? What distances have you traveled together? What sights seen? What is it like to be one of you—marching through this strange town of ours? Are you afraid? Is this a scene oft repeated? Do you hear taunts and abuse everywhere? Do you gain courage and strength from each other? From your number? What does it feel like to be here, a Chinese so far from China, without resources?

Such questions sprouted involuntarily in his mind and flourished without answers for a time, for the sight of these men left him envious, and hungry for adventure.

Suddenly, the man standing next to him whistled and called, "Hey, look! That there one looks like your behind, Buster!" Jason awakened again to the involuntary laughter around him. He'd seen and heard enough. He wanted to intercede, to put a stop to the mindless taunting, but how was that possible? How could anyone save these townspeople from themselves?

He was turning to go when he caught sight of Esther Langston, the sheriff's daughter, huddled with a group of onlookers in the shadows of the awning in front of Pend d'Oreille Printing. He was sure she was looking at him, shading her cerulean eyes with a long, pale hand. But the moment their eyes met, Esther's lips twisted up, as though she were wrestling a thought, and her attention, still framed beneath the flat of her hand, shifted very elaborately to the spectacle of the Chinese procession. Of course, in this she gave a false impression. Jason smiled. Now here is an adventure of a different kind, he said to himself. His hand went up. "Hell-o there!" he cried.

Esther's cheeks and her delicate chin already shone with the heat and excitement of the day, but in the next second some red appeared in them that had not been there before. She managed, with an effort, to have not heard him. He began to make his way through the crowd, and when Esther saw this she covered her mouth with the tips of her fingers. Her eyes began to dart left and right, the more so the closer he came. Finally, she turned toward him with eyes widening and made a preemptory face. She glanced sidelong, jerking her head up and to the right and grimacing in a manner that signified exactly nothing to him. He proceeded apace, leapt up onto the sidewalk, and took up both her hands. She seemed so discomfited by this that she gasped audibly. Her eyes rolled as if there were some question in her mind where her next breath would come from.

"Why, Esther Langston," he smiled, too relieved at the diversion to notice Esther's hands tugging gently to free themselves. "Fancy seeing you here!"

At five foot four, Esther was seven inches shorter than he, and at twenty years of age, six years younger. She was a pale, erect, pretty girl, well developed, with a strong, narrow nose, graceful hands, and sharp, glinting eyes—crystalline sister ships cresting the waves of her milky cheeks. Her smile was a little wide, yet at all times gentle and self-possessing. She had long blond hair which he'd never seen except in shoulder-length ringlets gathered beneath a brightly colored ribbon at the back of her head. Today, she wore a lilac dress, tight-fitting at the waist, with flounces and a small bustle. The bodice had a triple row of purple buttons, forty-eight in all, and buttons of the same color anchored the chin straps on her bonnet.

Two blotches on Esther's cheeks, and a line running the length of her nose, were sunburned, but these disappeared with her blushing. She withdrew her hands and made a half-turn toward the young man standing behind her.

"Mr. McQuade, I . . . "

"And all gussied up. Look at you!"

"I . . . "

Jason touched her elbow playfully. "Do you know, I was just thinking that I should like to pay my respects to you and your father tonight. I wonder if I might? I had a wonderful time at the picnic last weekend." He winked, but Esther, who was busy turning one way and another, didn't see. Jason, meanwhile, was not thinking of the picnic at all, but of the walk they had taken two days later.

The walk that was not a walk. For the benefit of Esther's father, and anyone else who might have spotted them, it began innocently enough, their slow, theatrical steps over the wagon road bespeaking an aimlessness bordering on a reluctance to move—and with much turning back, teasing, and laughter. But they managed somehow to gain the edge of the wood to the west of the Simpson farm, and then to put two or three turns behind them, so that they were able to leave the road altogether, undetected. When they emerged from the thick, sweetsmelling pines an hour and a half later, and set about whisking needles and small branches from each other's clothing, Esther remarked, "Mother used to say a woman's reputation is like a fragile vase that holds all her happiness. She was very wise about such matters, don't you think?" Jason had hesitated only long enough to get the point, then answered that he thought so, yes. When Esther stopped whisking and looked into his eyes, having found something unsatisfactory in his response, he threw in two "most assuredlys" and a final "absolutely." But even this was not enough. Jason threw his arms out in exaggerated protest. "Land's sake, Esther. If touching one breast is such a dratted crime, you'd think I'd be in hell by now." It was an unfortunate formulation, one that he regretted in increasing increments until Esther's carefully forged pout melted away before his eyes and she covered squealing laughter with her hand.

The strange noise of shouted cursing crowned with laughter brought Jason back to the present. "This is awful, isn't it?" he said, gazing out over the heads of the crowd.

"Jason, I would like you to meet Joe Patterson," Esther said in a voice just audible. She turned. "Joe, this is Jason McQuade. I told you about him this morning, remember?" She turned back and stared at her feet as the two men locked hands. "Joe and I—"

"Oh, sure," Jason interrupted. "Hello, Joe. Your father owns the Patterson Lumber Company, doesn't he? Good to meet you."

Joe Patterson was a dark-complected man of twenty-eight, of medium height and slight build, with black hair and eyes the color of pine knots. His hard, bony hands gripped with a genteel firmness. He had pleasing smile that faded rather quickly. "The pleasure is mine, Jason," he said quietly.

"Joe has just returned from three year's study in Europe," Esther said, still looking down, but not keeping her eyes still for a moment. "In Berlin, I think."

"Oh, that's splendid. Friedrich Wilhelms University, was it?"

"Yes, that's right," said Joe. "How did you know? Have you been . . . ?"

"To Berlin? Yes, in '75. I, uh, liked it there very much. Friedrich Wilhelms has a fine reputation, Joe. You must have enjoyed yourself immensely."

Patterson hesitated, then glanced wistfully at Esther. "Well, not so much really. I didn't want to go, you see. It was my father's idea." He looked at the ground and laughed in spite of himself. "I would have stayed here if—"

Esther straightened. "Joe and I were just walking back from the cemetery. He wanted to pay his respects to Mama."

Jason nodded at the other man. "Oh, that's right. You weren't here when Mrs. Langston passed away, were you?" He looked down at Esther for a moment. "It's been almost a year now. It was a terrible loss."

"A terrible loss," Patterson agreed. "We shall all miss her—those who knew her well." He set his hands on Esther's shoulders. She smiled sadly, then squinted into the street with an air of detachment.

At last she said, "Have you ever seen anything like this before, Jason?"

"No. Never." Jason turned, but from the corner of his eye he saw that Esther had twisted somehow, naturally enough, effecting the removal of Patterson's hands from her shoulders. She smiled up at him in a compensating way. "Have *you*, Joe?"

"No. Huh-uh. It's really something, isn't it? There must be a couple thousand of them."

Esther shaded her eyes again. "It's the entire Northern Pacific grading crew from Spokane Falls. There was a town meeting with the railroad people about a month ago. Do you remember, Jason?"

"What? Oh, yes, of course." But what he remembered was that he and Esther had fled to the lakeshore that night, under a full moon. He glanced at Esther and she rewarded him with a tight-lipped smile.

"Mr. Keating was here. He's the superintendent. He said the Chinese will be perfectly well behaved, and that we have nothing to worry about. They're supposed to stay out at Hope, except when they're working on the track. And, of course, then they're always supervised. Daddy told them he doesn't want any of their coolies coming into town without a supervisor, and they said, 'Fine, that's the way we'll do it.' Said probably the only time we'll see them is when they march through like this, or riding on the construction train, once the track gets up here."

"I see no one said anything about *our* people being well behaved," Patterson sighed.

Jason looked at him appreciatively, nodded, then looked back into the street. Esther's other suitor rose very much in his estimation.

"Mr. McQuade is apprenticing with Mr. Morse," Esther said, changing the subject quickly. "He's reading for the law."

"Oh, is that right?" Joe Patterson colored slightly. "Well, I guess we can always use another good lawyer around here." Joe appeared to wait for one of the others to speak, but not for long. "You've got a good teacher in Mr. Morse. He's top notch, isn't he?"

"Oh, yes. I'm fortunate there." Jason smiled, ignoring for the time being the ingratitude that had informed his thoughts less than a half hour before. The two men fell silent and looked out at the ongoing procession of Chinese. Even with the jeering and taunting of the townspeople, it had all become a picture of sameness. Their steps were rhythmic, like the ticking of a clock. The waving arms and twisting and straining townspeople were like grasses blowing in the wind.

Esther, Jason, and Joe all began to speak at once. They laughed. It was Esther who continued, blushing. "Jason's father owns a textile company back East." She looked uncertainly at Joe for his reaction.

"Oh."

"Yes, in Boston. That's where Jason's from."

"I see."

"He has an older brother, Andrew, who's an accountant." She spun around to face her subject. "And your mother's name is Mary. Isn't that right?"

Jason opened his mouth to change the subject, but she went on. "After he graduated from Harvard, Jason could have taken a position in his father's firm, but that didn't suit him. He met Mr. Morse at a gala reception put on by Mr. Henry Villard, and then . . . "

Jason looked sheepishly at the other man. The inference to be drawn from Esther's knowledge of him was plain.

Joe blinked and turned a cool eye to Jason. "I trust you have not been bored here in Sandpoint?" he said, full of insinuation.

"No, no, not at all," Jason replied, reddening. He glanced down at the top of Esther's head—for she had turned away, suddenly realizing her mistake. "No, this is a charming place, really. Besides, I'm far too busy now to be . . . "

"Yes, I'm sure you are," Joe mumbled as Esther's blue eyes flashed up self-consciously at Jason.

"What in tarnation . . . !" cried Joe. "Esther! Look! Isn't that your father? Down there!" Joe pointed down the street. Esther took hold of the stanchion and leaned out. Jason leaned out beside her. A block to the south, in front of the Carson Hotel, an enormous swirl of dust was rising over the street. There was a great commotion. A chorus of angry and excited shouts, cries of alarm, and the sound of a whip snapping in the air drew their attention. Dozens of onlookers rushed forward. Many pushed through the line of Chinese.

In the center of the dust cloud they could see the sheriff, Roger Langston, his body twisting and turning above his wheeling horse. The horse's black head bobbed, backed, and turned against the constraint of the reins. Its hide glistened in the sunlight. It faltered, then spun again, kicking up more dust with each crack of the whip that curled above its head and lashed into the surging, knotted crowd.

"Goddam heathen! I'll teach you to look at me like that!" Langston bellowed. The end of the braided whip found his target, the side of Soo-Kwan's neck, and opened a long, jagged gash. Soo-Kwan shrieked and fell to the ground. He covered the wound with his hand. Crying out uncontrollably, his body pitched and squirmed in its agony. The crowd formed a circle around him. Blood flowed between his fingers and spotted the ground. The whip circled and snapped again above the sheriff's head, and the other Chinese men pushed back, afraid, beyond the radius of the weapon. They gaped in horror at Soo-Kwan. The whip turned yet again, and its full force ripped across his back with a loud report. "Goddam good-for-nothing!" Langston shouted, his eyes wide with rage. His gold badge flashed in the sunlight as he turned above his victim. Soo-Kwan writhed in his extremity, crying out pitifully after each torturous stroke. The crowd of townspeople looked on. A few turned and walked away with heads shaking. Others seemed to relish this new entertainment.

"What's he doing?" Esther asked helplessly. Her voice cracked with emotion.

"Christ Almighty!" cried Patterson. "It looks like he's whipping one of them!" He's shouting something. I can't make it out. Holy mackerel! Look at that!" There was alarm and compassion in his tone.

"It's got to be one of the Chinese," he continued. "I can hear somebody screaming. Listen! Do you hear it?" His gaze was upon Esther now as she squinted to see her father's violence in the distance. The color had drained from her face, leaving only the spots of sunburn on her pallid skin.

"He must have caught one of them doing something terrible," she said weakly, pulling herself back onto the sidewalk. "He told me he expected trouble." In the time it took Joe to ask "What kind of trouble?" Jason recalled the stories Esther had told him of her father's collapse after the death of her mother, of his drinking at all hours, of his newfound but little considered righteousness and intolerance. These, it seemed, were alive in her, as well, as she turned on Joe, frowning. "He didn't say. Just trouble, I guess. Maybe all kinds. Daddy knows what he's talking about, Joe."

"Sure."

Esther turned her back on her father's brutality and stared long and hard at Jason. Her look seemed to say, "He's going to kill one of them. He's drunk again." The oppressive cracking of the whip brought tears onto her lashes. At last, she stared dolefully at the ground. "What did they do to make him so angry?" she moaned.

Jason looked away, torn—even deflated—by the choice implicit in Esther's reaction. "I'm going up there," he announced. "I'll see you later this evening, Esther, if that's all right." He jumped down into the street and set off, walking at first, then half-running toward the scene.

Esther stepped down and began to follow him, but Joe jumped after her, catching her arm. She turned, and her eyes flashed with anger and confusion. "Let go of me, Joe!"

"Esther, don't. Stay here. There's nothing you can do."

"You're hurting me! Let go!" But Joe only pulled her closer, and with tears wetting her cheeks Esther gave up the struggle. She allowed his arms to envelope her. "They *did* something!" she cried, pounding his chest with her fist. "I *know* they did!"

Joe held her close. "I know." He looked up over Esther's fragrant hair to the clouds of dust still rising and falling in the distance. In the midst of the confusion, the sheriff spun and bobbed above a frightened horse, above the heads of a pressing crowd. Spinning, spinning, he struggled again and again to direct his whip. The vulgarities issuing out of him, one chasing the other, were cut off by the sudden pivoting of the horse so that only pieces could be heard from any direction.

Soo-Kwan lifted himself to his feet in front of the sheriff, then staggered, his head striking the animal's breast at one point, knocking him back to his knees. He scrambled up again, his face twisted with pain. His cheeks shone with the moisture of tears. He held his right hand over the back of his left, where the whip had flayed across the tops of several bones. The gash on his neck was a brown-black patch of blood and dirt with a thick bead of shining red blood trailing under the collar of his shirt. He circled frantically for a few seconds, disoriented, then steadied himself and began to bow before the sheriff, stumbling backwards, uttering something in a low, piteous whine. He inched toward the semicircle of his countrymen. But the whip came down on him again, this time catching his shoulder. The others retreated a step. Soo-Kwan groaned and bowed again, and again the whip flew out at him.

"*Kao kao lei! I beg of you, no more!*" he pleaded.

"What's the point of this, Sheriff?" came a voice from the crowd. It was Simon Walters, the liveryman, a short, dirty, black-haired man with cocked eyes and a full, uneven, unkempt beard. Langston gave no sign of having heard the challenge. The liveryman's face grew red, darkening the effect of his black beard, and he stepped through the wall of Chinese men. "That's enough, Sheriff!" Yet the flogging continued, growing more rapid and more vicious.

"I'll teach you, you son of a bitch!" Langston choked, nearly out of breath. He drove clinking spurs into the horse's flank, and the animal reared, then Soo-Kwan raised his hands to his face. He cowered beneath the bulging, white-ringed eyes of the horse as it strained against the steel bit in its mouth. The whip circled in the sky above its head, then descended over him like black lightning.

"Ayee-gh!" The whip encircled Soo-Kwan's neck this time. His eyes rolled skyward. His knees began to fold under him as Langston backed his horse a step and gave a mighty pull. But Soo-Kwan did not fall. In the short, murky interval between fear for life and resignation to death, when pain is swallowed up by an indifference to pain, which is the last defense of all living things, the hands of a friend were about him. It was Hok-Ling.

In an instant, Hok-Ling had uncoiled the end of the whip from Soo-Kwan's neck while answering the pressure on its stock with his other hand. He watched Soo-Kwan stagger backwards and fall into the arms of the other Chinese. Their eyes met. Between the two friends, in that twitch of time, passed the fullness of human love and companionship, unabbreviated. Roger Langston was, at first, stunned by the sudden intervention. His rancor turned like a heavy, cumbersome cannon toward Hok-Ling. But it turned too slowly. He pulled to free the whip, but Hok-Ling only glared at the man who strained, red-faced, his forehead furrowed with surprise and uncertainty. With little effort, Hok-Ling snatched the whip out of the sheriff's hand, and, when he did so, the sheriff slumped forward, exhausted.

He watched through shadowy eyes as the Chinese began to coil the whip about its stock. The sheriff's chest heaved with labored breathing. He turned a dazed look on the crowd, then shook his head and rubbed his eyes as if to clear them of an apparition. Thick eyebrows dipped ominously as he stretched his neck toward the bold Chinese, really seeing him. Slowly, a smile formed and his hand dropped down over the handle of his revolver, but he could not draw it. He tugged, then looked down to find Simon Walter's wide, strong hand covering the hammer and the cylinder, holding the pistol in its holster.

"We don't need that now, do we, Sheriff?" Walters said softly.

Another man had stepped out of the crowd: Bart Isaacson. He'd squared himself over his heavy, leather boots, spit a long, brown streak into the dust, then wiped his mouth with his sleeve. "Stay out of this, Simon," Isaacson warned. When he spoke it was through one side of his mouth, past a single row of uneven, yellowed teeth. "This here don't concern you none."

The livery man didn't take his eyes off the sheriff. "We don't need a dead Chinese now, do we, Bart?"

"You let the sheriff decide that!"

"No, I'm afraid I can't do that," growled Walters, reddening, forcing something like a confident smile under his beard. "This Chinaman here, he's unarmed. That'd be cold-blooded murder—wouldn't it, Sheriff?" He pulled the pistol up slowly. Langston released his grip.

"There ain't no law against killing a Chinaman!" protested Isaacson. But he fell quiet as soon as the sheriff was disarmed, and no one else spoke. The sheriff frowned miserably, and began searching the crowd—even the Chinese—for supportive faces.

Hok-Ling wrapped the tapered end of the whip around the coil and tied it with a half-hitch. The crowd was silent, sober, watching. The yellow dust had risen out of the street, or settled back to earth, and a blueness drifted over the afternoon as though evening were advancing ahead of schedule. Jason arrived at the back of the crowd, but couldn't see. He stepped along the perimeter to get a better look at the Chinese who had interposed himself.

From afar, Esther turned, pulling a lock of blond hair away from her eyes. She stared in disbelief at her father, a pitiful, beaten man—stared at him as one who seeks to penetrate a wall of doubt, or who dares not look away, fearing she will lose something that cannot be regained. Her eyes did not wilt from the sight of him, even as Hok-Ling, with a mighty step, hurled the coiled whip onto the roof of the Carson Hotel.

Hok-Ling swung Soo-Kwan's arm over his shoulder and lifted him to his feet. "Come along," he said, pulling Soo-Kwan into the crowd of Chinese that had begun to move once again toward the bridge. After a long silence he whispered to his nearly insensible friend, "Let us cross this bridge and be away from them for good."

7

Hok-Ling and Soo-Kwan squeezed onto the crowded deck of the *Henry Villard*. The way was cleared by murmuring passengers who twisted this way and that to view the face of the luckless one as Hok Ling carried him along. Word of the injured man's encounter with a giant green coat—a giant lawman—wielding a whip in one hand and a double-bladed axe in the other had raced ahead of them.

"Away with you!" shouted Hok-Ling to those who nosed in too close. He guided his friend along the starboard rail of the 149-foot stern-wheeler. He lifted him up a short, steep companionway then nodded toward a spot near the wall of the pilothouse. The men standing there gave way. He lowered Soo-Kwan to the deck. Soo-Kwan sat with difficulty, grimacing, but almost at once an expression of weary relief began to settle in his eyes.

Hok-Ling dropped down beside him. He patted Soo-Kwan's knee, then folded his own legs, spreading his hands over his ankles. Fear and dread were not far behind, he knew. He threw his head back against the pilothouse wall, shutting his eyes. Oh! Great spirits! Did that really happen? Now this will be the end of me! The end of me!

His mind replayed bits and pieces of the incomprehensible scene until the sounds of men crowding in around them began to intrude. He blinked open his eyes. Seeing that he and Soo-Kwan were safe, he closed them again and gave over to listening. The movements and chatter of his countrymen grew lively—for wasn't their long march nearly over?—and the men laughed at themselves a good deal for the lightness they felt over their backs and shoulders when they had lowered their rucksacks into the lazaret. The smells that came off the water were a feast to them all, and the lake breeze seemed to carry their words and make their intercourse more pleasant. But the weariness of the men was not lost to them, either, and so the men gradually lowered themselves, as Hok-Ling and Soo-Kwan had done, to the wood-planked deck, and their voices fell off, too, and their laughter aged, and what had come dressed in cheerfulness was revealed as relief.

Hok-Ling did not open his eyes for an hour or more, until he heard the call and answer of the boat's crew and then a low rumbling in the bowels of the vessel. The *Henry Villard* began to move, almost imperceptibly. He listened to the rising baritone and felt the ship shudder beneath him. "Yes. Here we go," he whispered to Soo-Kwan in a low, ecstatic tone, for he sensed a flight of spirit that he assumed—quite incorrectly—was shared by his companion. He opened his eyes and saw the faces of the coolies who still lined the dock. They gaped at Soo-Kwan as the vessel eased out. Hok-Ling eyed each with a strained, inexplicable suspicion. It was all he could do to restrain himself from broadcasting threats and curses to the whole company. Where were *you?* And *you?* Why weren't you there to help him? he wanted to know. He was glad when the last piling of the dock was cleared.

* * *

Their bare feet stretched before them on the planked deck, where a cool breeze and a blade of afternoon sunlight worked at cross-purposes over the tops of their toes. There was a perfume of pine and smoke and algae in the air, and the *Henry Villard,* steaming rhythmically, penetrated invisible pockets of warmer air where these odors were intense and putrid; but, as often, the boat would pass into spaces where the air was cooler and fresh smelling, and the half-sweet, pungent odors would drain from the mind. There were some forty men packed onto the forward weather deck alone, their black, braided pigtails shining out of the shadow of the pilothouse. All of them, it may be said, noticed the alternating smells and took pleasure in them. And the murmur of the bow wave coupled with the distant splashing and churning of the stern-wheel was more sedative than sound.

From the corner of his eye, Hok-Ling watched Soo-Kwan probe the skin around the open wound on his hand. "Why did he do it?" Hok-Ling asked, but when he saw Soo-Kwan's look of despair and bewilderment he turned away and stared toward the water as if he had not spoken.

Now and then a small limb or a shard of bark slid past them. There were large tangles of glistening seaweed floating on the surface, too, with the arched bodies of dead bottom fish, and brown rotting leaves and pollen caught up in them. All these were come upon in the steady approach of the *Henry Villard.* All were passed unceremoniously. All were tumbled and dunked by the vessel's wake, and left to bob in her vibrating chop. Hok-Ling held his eyes up, away from his companion, and at last he covered his eyes and squinted over the prow toward a distant city of tents and lean-tos and crude shacks sprawled above a pale gray beach.

He commanded himself to draw a great breath as his mind traveled ahead to this place, now to analyze its size, now to figure its contours, its layout, now to imagine where the railroad would go, and how it would cross the mountains that loomed above the beach so magnificently. They are monstrous, he told himself, raising his eyebrows to disguise a sudden rapture. He had never seen a place more beautiful.

In his mind, he began to compose a letter to his father, and in a few days he would pay the scribe Xu Feng to write:

"Hope, of the Idaho Territory, is a tiny, unlikely place. The waves of a great lake run past it, parallel to the beach, south to north, so that only small, peripheral, degenerated wavelets are ground up among the flat and rounded stones. Mysteriously, the lake fails to wash itself. There is often a filmy ribbon of debris—mostly greenish-yellow pollen, and dead fish, and twigs, and pieces of bark—which float only a few yards from shore.

"It has one road, a straight road. It rises from the beach and returns again a mile away. It is like a dusty eyebrow over the camp. At its highest point there are tall, splendid pine trees gripping patches of orange earth. Their branches hang out over sharp, granite precipices and earthen embankments parched by sun and wind. And it is here above the road that the forest begins.

"Father, I must tell you of the steepness of Miner's Mountain, for this is the first charac-teristic that a newcomer is forced to consider. I cannot walk here according to my will. I must choose between the road, which is a long and gentle traverse, and therefore very time consuming, or one of the three footpaths connecting the beach to the apex of the road and the offices there. These are steep and treacherous. In places, the footpaths are replaced by wooden ladders or stairways that have been built over the rock cliffs (these shake constantly). All horse and wagon traffic is relegated to the road.

"The smallness of Hope was most visible from the boat, for there I could see the enormity of Miner's Mountain and the other peaks that lock arms high above the surface of the lake (they cast their dark green hue over its surface in a most remarkable way). Now I am on the hem of the mountain and cannot see it!

"What I have called "the offices" are, in fact, a handful of whitewashed wooden buildings tucked into the side of the mountain very near the apex of the road. Their backsides are barely a hammer's swing from dark, dripping walls of stone and moss, but their faces are bright, flat surfaces protruding from the mountain's edge, and in some cases, they seem to hang in defiance of gravity. The Birch Hotel is there. It is the largest of the buildings. Its railed balconies are ornate and beautiful, much like the British hospital at Howloon, I think. A market is in the corner of this hotel, but it is not open to us. There is also a livery, six two-story homes, a barn, a small church and school building, and then the railroad office. We are allowed to enter there, but don't go unless . . . "

As the *Henry Villard* steamed closer, Hok-Ling considered the comforts and possibilities of the place before him. He wondered what fish might be caught in the lake, and how. And would it be cold living so near the water? These things he pondered slowly, for there was a vast and overwhelming serenity about this place that had begun to affect him. At first, this feeling troubled him and mixed uneasily with his state of mind, but as he gazed over the blue surface, into the flank of the mountains and up to their lofty horizon, he thought, perhaps Shangdi, the king of all gods, is here—and this thought alone consoled him, for he knew how happily he would submit to the predeterminations of the supreme ruler. He felt a weight lift from his shoulders, the weight of self-consciousness. For a long time he did not take his eyes off the mountaintops. The rapture lingered in his chest, although it began to evanesce when self-awareness seeped in. Look! This is like the Middle Kingdom! What power do I have to demand or assume, even to desire anything here? he thought. I only have to exist—and see. And having thought this, the rapture returned fully to his chest and to his head, and he forgot himself again.

Thinking of Soo-Kwan, sitting in pain next to him, he said to himself, have I not brought on this terrible day? Wasn't it I who was supposed to die in the basket instead of Yee Tai-Hu? With my impertinence alone I've disrupted the peace of heaven, and now I've nearly caused the death of my friend. But then, while he stared down at his feet, an idea formed that was new to him. Perhaps, he thought at last, this was not a punishment at all, but a redemption. Although the green coat may hunt me down and kill me now, I have been given a wonderful opportunity—a chance to display my loyalty to Soo-Kwan, to follow the *Sacred Edict*, and therefore to assuage the gods whom I have offended. I have saved Soo-Kwan, and proven that I am Han. Perhaps the gods will smile upon my honorable ancestors, in whose eyes I am so unworthy. Hok-Ling took a deep, grateful breath and leaned back against the wall of the pilothouse to let these ideas sink in. After a while, he began to look at the men around him in a new light. A calm settled over him, and the ache in his heart was gone. Yes, he told himself, it must be so. By saving Soo-Kwan's life, I have restored my family's honor.

* * *

Hok-Ling stepped over the gunwale onto the blond, unseasoned planks of a newly built dock. He stretched on his toes to see the shore and the camp over the heads of his countrymen. "Look. It is quite peaceful here," he said to Soo-Kwan.

Soo-Kwan muttered something behind him, but when Hok-Ling turned he saw that his friend was staring back past the gently swaying stern of the *Henry Villard*. He had tilted his head toward Sandpoint, a gray fragment of shoreline visible through a haze seventeen miles to the west. "Of course, *that* place looked peaceful to me. What do I know of this land, Hok-Ling?"

Hok-Ling gently caressed Soo-Kwan's shoulder. "You are feeling better. Good!"

"And you?" Soo-Kwan turned. His eyes glistened with tears.

"Me? I am fine. Why do you ask how *I* am doing?"

"I don't know," Soo-Kwan replied, dropping his eyes and shaking his head.

"What is it, Soo-Kwan? Why are you . . . ?"

"It's just that . . . well, perhaps he . . . he will come here . . . the green coat. He may seek you out and kill you. Yes, I'm sure he will. And while this will mark a most honorable end to your life, I will be powerless to avenge you, for I have no weapon." He grasped Hok-Ling's arm as though to brace himself against a far more dire prospect. "I will live on and lose face before the gods and my ancestors." Hok-Ling made a face at him and started to speak, but Soo-Kwan interrupted again. "Wait! There are the pickaxes! I will hide one under my bed. Yes, that will do it. A pickax." The light of relief shone in Soo-Kwan's eyes.

Hok-Ling laughed out loud, but he saw that Soo-Kwan did not laugh. "You worry about nothing, Soo-Kwan. I think we will never see that devil again. Come. Let us find a suitable place. It is everyone for himself. Here, let me help you."

"No, no. I am able to walk now. Thank you."

The two friends navigated through the milling crowd on the dock and recovered their bags from a growing pile of rucksacks and supplies opposite the cargo hold. After a feeble attempt at tug-of-war over who would carry Soo-Kwan's bag, which Hok-Ling won easily, the two made their way toward the shore. Soo-Kwan pulled a crooked cigarette from his shirt pocket, lit the twisted nib of paper at its end, then wedged it at the corner of his mouth. "Where is Dak-Wah?" he asked, puffing.

"I don't know," was Hok-Ling's answer.

Soo-Kwan sucked methodically on the end of the poor cigarette, making little popping noises as he limped along. "He was ahead of me two days ago, and then we were together yesterday. He met up with an acquaintance, a loudmouth from Fatshan. They began to talk at once, arguing over the honor of their fathers and the fathers of their fathers, for, as I understand it, their families were once great enemies." Soo-Kwan stopped and looked at Hok-Ling as if to make a confession. "I grew very weary of it, Hok-Ling."

"Yes, I can imagine." The two friends were walking again.

"So I slid back into the bushes and waited until they had passed."

Hok-Ling tilted his head back and laughed. "You did what? Ha! Dak-Wah, and this friend of his, did they see you?"

"No. They kept arguing. They did not see me."

"It must have been tiresome to hear them."

"Yes. And I thought you were ahead of me, too."

Hok-Ling regarded his friend warmly. He shook his head and smiled. "No." Hok-Ling was thankful that he had fallen back to help with the off-loading and reloading of a supply wagon whose front axle had splintered in a boulder field north of Rathdrum, for that circumstance alone had allowed him to come upon Soo-Kwan in his time of need.

A wry, pained smile played across Soo-Kwan's face now, while his lips turned inward to hold the glowing cigarette. A tortured calm had settled into his eyes, and Hok-Ling sensed that his friend was preparing to laugh at himself for his misfortune. However, the weal of the whip still angled above his collar, descending from the back of his neck to the front, and a jagged cut had not closed completely beneath his Adam's apple. A white speck of bone was also visible at the base of the cut over the top of Soo-Kwan's hand. It was not time to laugh at anything.

Soo-Kwan stopped at the top of a small, dusty incline that opened onto a long, flat, sandy field. A sea of tents and shacks and lean-tos spread before them, and there were hundreds of Chinese wandering among them. Squares of white and gray canvas reflected the deepening color of the afternoon sky, and their many juts and angles were thrown to the ground, or laid up against each other, in long, black shadows. "It appears we may have the pick of things over there," said Soo-Kwan, pointing.

"Yes. Exactly."

"Look there," he said, as they walked to a large, crudely built shack near a stand of mature cottonwood trees. "That one has a tin roof."

"Hmm. So it does," replied Hok-Ling. "It is large enough for many men, though. We would be squeezed into corners there."

"But it has wooden walls, Hok-Ling. Look. Such a cabin would be much warmer than a tent."

"That's true." The two men smiled at each other with their eyes, for they both knew that Soo-Kwan would have his way. They moved toward the crude knock-down together. "But I see that many of the boards are loose or broken. I would not choose to be inside that poor shack in a strong wind. And Soo-Kwan, my friend, have you ever listened to the rain pound against a tin roof? It is the sound of a thousand drums. It makes sleeping impossible. I'll tell you what. Let's find a good tent as far from this shack as possible."

"What? Are you mad?" Soo-Kwan let his voice rise up and he spoke quickly, for in truth, each man had chosen this moment to conceal his preoccupation with what had happened and with what might follow because of it. "I have heard the sound you speak of many times. It reminds me of how well I am being kept dry. It is music to my ears, Hok-Ling. Very soothing. It puts me to sleep just thinking about it, whereas the thumping of rain against canvas is a menacing sound, and I am constantly feeling the canvas to see if the rain is coming through. Inevitably, it will, you know."

Hok-Ling laughed. "It will? Well, then, don't think about it now. There is much to consider besides rain. And look! There is no window." The two men stood outside the doorway of the shack. Hok-Ling dropped both bags and walked this way and that, surveying the tin roof with its many dents, scars, and rust streaks running from the heads of nails, and then he looked up beyond it to the Birch Hotel and the other buildings perched high above the encampment. He saw the brilliant oranges and reds of the sunset in their windows, and against their flat, white sides. "Look at that," he whispered, turning to Soo-Kwan. But Soo-Kwan was disappearing through the open doorway of the shack, and Hok-Ling saw that he was bent over his injured hand, shaking it frantically. Hok-Ling stepped close to the doorway, but he could not see Soo-Kwan and there was no sound from inside. He poked his head inside and spoke to him through the darkness. "Dak-Wah will like this place for its warmth. That much I can say."

8

Hok-Ling did not regret Soo-Kwan's choice of the knock-down with the tin roof. There were only five shacks in the camp, and this was the sturdiest and largest of them all. He'd established himself in a corner of the room farthest from the doorless entrance, beyond its ability to admit sunlight. Even on the brightest Sunday this place was a dim semblance of familiar shapes and dimensions where he could sit or lie down, free of intrusion, to nap or think. His possessions—his satchel, his iron cooking pot, the packing crate wedged between the cot and the wall, his wooden box filled with miscellany, his thin, coverless pillow, and the round silk skullcap that he hung by a nail above the crate—these, at best, were mere shadows in the corner to the other men. This suited him.

Soo-Kwan and Dak-Wah had each taken another corner, and seven more cots lined the walls or jutted into the room at right angles to the walls. Fifteen men lived here. Five of the men were anchored to the puncheon floor near the doorway each night. They'd long ago sold their cots and mattresses to feed opium habits or had lost them to gambling. They slept on cushions of self-pity, Hok-Ling thought.

There were not enough tents or shacks or lean-tos to accommodate all of the coolies stationed at Hope, so scores of faceless forms sprawled under blankets and newspapers beside smoldering campfires, or huddled beneath the limbs of the pine trees just above the camp. When it rained, and sometimes when a cold wind swept in from the lake, some of these men were absorbed into the shelters, and backs and shoulders were squeezed against walls and corners to make room. But there were outcasts and bumblers who could not worm their way in. These men slept on the soggy ground, buried beneath blankets. And the rain and the night enveloped them, and wore on them, and delivered them as crumpled, sagging heaps of humanity in the gray light of morning.

* * *

Ho Ying-Chiao, the crew boss, balanced himself on the upturned roots of a fallen cedar tree and squinted toward the lone figure standing behind a tripod in the distance. The rising sun lit Ho Ying-Chiao's lips and they were dark and dry. "Down three and one-half feet!" he droned in the peculiar way men have of transposing distant signals into words. The man in the distance, a surveyor, waved his hat above the scope of his transit.

"*Here!*" Ho Ying-Chiao shouted impatiently, his eyes flashing at a man in a basket hat who stood nearby. "Mark that stone!" He pointed toward a boulder rising out of a mulch of broken twigs and leaves. "Down three and a half. Be quick about it!" The obedient coolie scampered toward the stone as if the forest floor were on fire. He wiped the surface of the granite with the palm of his hand, then with a piece of blood-red chalk drew an arrow pointing down and four small circles beside it. The last circle he bisected, filling half with color. Then he filled in the other three. His right hand was stained, and there was a long streak of red running down the right leg of his trousers where he persisted in wiping his fingers. He retraced the circles on the stone to darken them before returning to his place beside Ho Ying-Chiao.

A fourth figure, a tall, pale, full-lipped Caucasian boy of seventeen with red, disheveled hair, and pale, gray eyes leaned over an elevation rod and watched the stone marking through sleep-inspired eyes. When the coolie had finished his work and moved away, the boy raised the long pole and placed it on top of a wooden stake driven at the center of the railroad right-of-way. This stake was marked on one side "CL" for centerline, and bore on the other a series of faded, blue numbers—the left-handed scrawl of an anonymous surveyor's assistant who, more than four years earlier, had steadied a plumb bob and chain over this spot.

The redhead stood astride the stake while, in the distance, the figure of the surveyor in his broad-brimmed hat slouched behind the scope of the transit. The youngster pushed the rod out to the ends of his fingers. He rotated it so that its numbers faced the instrument and then stared as if transfixed, first at the top of the rod, then down at the stake itself. In time the rod grew still. Slowly, the boy raised his head. His dry, puffy lips came together in a rapt expression, and his widening eyes stared out on either side of the slender pole toward the distant figure. Ho Ying-Chiao and a company of 120 Chinese laborers watched in silence, and when the elevation rod had grown perfectly still, Ho Ying-Chiao raised his hand over his eyes and squinted toward the sun as before.

Head and shoulders rose over the brass scope of the transit. Two black arms flapped like tired wings.

"It's good!" Ho Ying-Chiao jumped down from his snarled perch and approached the waiting coolies. They stood or squatted in a thick pack at the shadowy edge of the forest, each facing the right-of-way as though posing for a photograph. Against the gray-green curtain of forest, a dusky reddish-yellow color shone in their sleepy faces. Not a word was spoken among them. They watched the elevation rod fall slowly behind Ho Ying-Chiao and come to rest over the shoulder of the Caucasian boy. Its end flopped violently as the boy thrashed through the brush in search of the next centerline stake.

Ho Ying-Chiao spit a heavy ball of mucous that tipped a broad leaf of devil's club. "You will have this section lowered three and one-half feet by noon. That's five and one-half hours." He looked back at the surveyor, and then at the empty space where the red-headed boy had been. "Move up when you're done. Twenty men here. *You.*" Ho Ying-Chiao pointed into the center of the group. "*You.* And *you* over there. Twenty men. Eight picks. Eight shovels. Four wheelbarrows. The rest of you come with me. Quickly!"

And so it went until there were six groups of twenty men ranged out along a line of wooden stakes.

* * *

It was 1:35. Hok-Ling twisted the heavy pickax in his hand and felt its weight against his sore, swollen palms. Sweat jumped from his temples as he swung the tool over his shoulder. He eyed a point of ground then squeezed back the air trying to rise in his lungs. Determination and strength splashed up like waves colliding. His shoulders squared and his body shook with the force of his blow.

The process began again, and it was repeated seven or ten or twelve times each minute. Up and down the line the picks rose and fell. Shovels plunged.

It was after 2:46. Soo-Kwan's pick stood erect, its bar buried deep in soil. He exhaled heavily, then holding his next breath, he stepped around the pick and pried against its shaft. Fresh blood stained the cloth wrapped loosely about his injured hand. The heels of his boots sank in. He pushed and pried until the earth erupted, and up came its clods and stones and its thick, musty smell. The tool swung out on its arc and its handle shook.

It was nearly 4:30. Bits of earth and roots and speared leaves splashed over the heads of the Chinese crew, and the wheelbarrows clanked over berms and trampled bushes and squeezed a juice from their leaves. Dak-Wah tipped his wheelbarrow sideways at the place designated for "fill," and his load spilled out and traveled down the edge of a small ravine without his stopping for more than a second or two. The earth shrugged and shook, and the percussion of the picks and shovels, and the clanking and squeaking of wheelbarrows, echoed against the forest walls on either side.

Hok-Ling and the others stared at the shadowy ground without seeing it, lost in their thoughts. It was past six. They ignored the tall, sun-capped clouds that boiled in the blue sky above them, and the white-crested eagles drifting through the late afternoon in wide circles above the ridge. They were ignorant of the coming and going of the wind, and even as the light drained from the sky, they toiled unaware of it.

When Ho Ying-Chiao's pistol reported and echoed twice, it was 7:42. They stopped, all at once, and a dim light grew in their eyes as they walked beneath the first and brightest stars. They shuffled down the gentle, dusty incline toward the water wagons—dim gray boxes tucked in under the limbs of two cedar trees—and once there, they fell into lines without speaking. They inched forward and smelled the green water in the barrels. Long-handled tin ladles plunged down, pushing the skim of pine needles and dust to the side. It was the cool water at the bottom that was lifted and felt and swallowed.

There was little talk on the way back to camp, but much was said with few words and gestures as they jostled in the back of the wagons. The tired men stared gently and unabashedly at each other, or picked at the heels of their boots. The wagons bumped along. The smell of smoke and rice and salted fish from the noontime meal came out of their clothing, and there was a tendency among the men to bury their hands in their sleeves and sleep.

* * *

William Keating turned away from the rain-streaked window of the railroad office, swallowing the last of his coffee. "Let's just be glad we're not one of them."

Across the room a young man with pale blue-green eyes and a heavy whisker stubble looked up from a map emblazoned "Northern Pacific Railroad, Lake Pend d'Oreille Division" in bold, black, ornate letters. He was the chief section surveyor, Matthew Skidmore. He stared at Keating for a long time, and although he told himself to say nothing, he heard himself say, "Yeah."

"Have you seen those bastards lying out there in the rain?" Keating poured himself more coffee, then waved the pot toward Skidmore. "More?"

"No. Thanks." The surveyor stroked his coarse beard as his attention settled back onto the map in front of him. Keating returned to the window and stared out at the gray dawn, at the muddy road and the cluttered encampment far below. He saw movement beneath one of the blankets and eyed it intently for several seconds, seeing or thinking of nothing else. A sudden surge of rain against the roof roused him to a recollection of himself.

"Like two thousand dogs," he muttered. "It's a kennel down there."

"I'm sorry?"

"This business. Having to work with these heathens. It's like working with two thousand dogs. They don't understand what you're saying. They can't think beyond their goddamn noses." Keating's face colored, and it was as though he could not stop himself when he added, "They don't wear shoes half the time. They sleep out in the goddamn rain, for Christ sake!"

Skidmore hesitated, letting the heavy, gray morning blunt the fierceness that flashed in Keating's eyes. He looked at the map again. "They seem to give us a fair day's work. From what I've seen, anyway."

"Most of the time," Keating grumbled. "But they're well paid for it, too—by their standards. A dollar sixteen a day now. Hell, that's a lot less than an Irishman will demand. Come to think of it, your Irishman ain't no smarter either! Do you think?"

The surveyor looked up again, and he began to roll up the map. "I don't know much about that, Bill. I s'pose if Irishmen and Chinese are like everyone else, there's some of them bright enough, and some of them culls."

"Culls?"

"Yeah. You know, like a logger's cull—rejects, dullards."

"Ha!" Keating laughed. "Culls. That's a good word for it. I dare say we got mor'n our share of culls, all right."

"Course there's always you and me to think of," Skidmore said, smiling darkly. "I don't s'pose either one of us is a frontiersman by choice. I know I'm not. Shit, I haven't seen my wife in eight months."

Keating turned back to the window and lifted his cup to within an inch of his mouth. "True. But we're not here because we're stupid, either. That's the difference. The new board of directors of this railroad, good old Henry Villard and the others, and all those goddam little German investors he dredged up, with their poodles and their whist parties—now that they're out of the red, they want this thing finished overnight. Well, I'll tell you something, Skidmore. This damn thing's got to turn a dollar, so it's got to be done right. And we're building it right, by gum. Now are you going to tell me that we're a couple of culls, mate?"

Skidmore smiled awkwardly and looked down. "Well, it's crossed my mind."

Keating laughed out loud, and the gold surrounding his teeth sparkled in the light of two heavily embossed brass store lamps hanging from the ceiling. "Well, damn my hide," he chortled, "I guess it's sorta crossed my mind, too." He laughed again while Skidmore shook his head and forced a broad smile. The surveyor wondered if his contempt for this man showed anywhere on his face. "Hello!" sang Keating, "Here comes a cull if I've ever seen one!" He swung the door open and stepped heavily out onto the small wooden porch. "Ying-Chiao! Hey, Ying-Chiao! Get up here!"

Skidmore stepped to the window next to Keating's desk. He spotted the crew boss standing on one of the planked landings about halfway up the steep embankment. There were two other Chinese with him, one with water buckets suspended on a long pole across his back, the other hunched beneath an enormous bundle of sticks. All three had turned and were looking up toward the railroad office with frowning faces, their heads and shoulders drenched. Ho Ying-Chiao nodded repeatedly and waved toward Keating, and when his mouth moved, his high-pitched voice climbed up the hill ahead of him. "Hel-lo! Hel-lo! Coming Mas-ter!"

Keating stepped back into the office and closed the door. "'S'pose we could trust one of these heathens to pick up our mail for us?" he asked, still flushed with amusement. "I can't see sending Ned Johnson off to town every week. He's behind enough as it is!"

Skidmore stood looking past the remnants of his reflection in the window. "I wouldn't know, Bill. That's your department. I just pound stakes in the ground and draw maps to remember where I put them."

"Yeah, yeah. Okay," Keating laughed. "But I'm going to try it. Wouldn't take much more than a cull to do it anyway. Townspeople'll squawk, but that doesn't worry me."

"Townspeople? Why would they care?" asked Skidmore.

"Oh, I don't know. They seem to have gotten pretty riled up about these Orientals. They think they're going to steal their kids and make soup out of them, I guess. I told them a couple of months ago—hell, it was before we moved the camp up here—I said, 'Hey, don't worry about our Chinamen. They're tame. They're not going to cause you no problems, not the way we ride herd over them. Hell,' I said, 'you won't even see a Chinaman unless you're out there on the line somewhere tramping around, or you're over here paying us a visit.'"

"Or at the post office," Skidmore muttered under his breath.

"What's that?"

"Nothing."

Keating pulled a cigar from the pocket of his coat and rolled it in his mouth. Ho Ying-Chiao climbed the last switchback on the footpath then disappeared beneath the lip of the road. The rain had stopped temporarily and the sky's mottled clouds lay spent and flat over the lake. There was a visible silence beyond the window, a frozen, immutable silence that was sleep-like and reminiscent of night, and the morning's light shone over the area as if by a mistake of nature. There was very little activity in the Chinese camp, and the *Henry Villard* and the *Mary Moody* floated stiffly above their reflections at the dock. Skidmore watched the top of the stairway until he saw Ho Ying-Chiao's head rise into view and then he turned to see Keating once again at the window near the door. Keating held the cigar between clenched teeth, as though no part of his lips should touch it. Then he stepped to the door and swung it open. Ho Ying-Chiao stood over the threshold as if caught there, his hands folded at his stomach.

Keating stared at the crew boss without seeing him. "Say there, Skidmore," he said, "what say you let me have a word in private with this old cull? No secrets, you understand. I've just got a bit of a bone to pick with him."

The surveyor tucked the rolled map under his arm. He pulled his gray frock coat from the coat tree near the stove and stepped toward the door. "Excuse me," he mumbled, and he nodded at the quick but respectful obeisance of the crew boss.

"Yes, Mas–ter Keating," choked Ho Ying-Chiao after a long silence. "What may I do . . . to serve you?"

Keating pulled a burning stick through the door of the stove and held it to the end of his cigar. "Come in and close the door. Has he figured it out yet?" he mumbled, drawing the flame to his cigar with heavy breaths.

"What, Mas–ter?"

"Goddam it! Don't play stupid with me, Chinaman." He tossed the stick back into the fire and slammed the stove door closed. "Did this man find you out, or not? What's his name, Hok something?"

"Hok-Ling?" whispered Ho Ying-Chiao.

"Yes. Hok-Ling. The man whose money you stole." Keating stomped across the room, trailing two roundish puffs of cigar smoke. He sat at his desk and pulled out a sealed, bulging envelope from a compartment beneath the roll-top. He waved it menacingly at Ho Ying-Chiao. "Remember?"

"Yes . . . member," stammered Ho Ying-Chiao. His eyes were dark and fearful.

"Does he know who took it?"

"Hok-Ling and his com . . . panions believe I have taken . . . yes. This I have heard from many—"

"All right," interrupted Keating. "I've been thinking about this. If they think you took it, they probably think it was because I told you to, right?"

"This is—oh, I see. Yes. This I do not know, Mas–ter."

"What do you mean you don't know? What are the men saying?"

"Men believe rair-road cheat Hok-Ling. Many say Chin-ee should strike. Hok-Ling is very brave. Has saved life of friend, Soo-Kwan. No more work, they say, until Hok-Ling receive voucher and all money."

"Shit." Keating stood up and moved to the window. Then he turned to face Ho Ying-Chiao. "It would be a terrible shame if the men struck again. Do you follow me? That would just about be the end of things for ol' Ying-Chiao, wouldn't it?"

"Yes, Mas—ter," Ho Ying-Chiao gasped, stiffening and averting his eyes.

"Yup. That'd put you in the chopped celery category. If there's a strike, or the men slow down, I'll replace you quicker than you can skin a cat."

"Oh, Mas—ter! This is—Ying-Chiao will not . . . ! I would not . . . !"

"Never mind that!" Keating snapped, derailing the Chinese's importuning and obsequiousness, and bringing an unexpected hum out of the stove pipe as well. "I expect you to make sure that any rumors about my involvement in this whole affair are squelched. I'm talking about this man's money now. We don't want any labor problems around here. No strikes, do you understand? Christ, J. B. Harris employs these coolies. If they wouldn't issue this fella a voucher, they must've had their reasons."

"Yes, yes."

"In fact," Keating interjected as though a new idea had occurred to him. "Here's what we're going to do. You're going to take this man's money and hide it in your tent." He marched back toward his desk, shaking his finger and nodding to himself.

Ho Ying-Chiao gasped inaudibly.

"Yes," Keating continued. "That way, if it's found, there'll be no question about Northern Pacific involvement. Besides, he's here now, right? He's working. He knows he can't get anywhere without the voucher, so I think he'll stay put." He tore the envelope open, took out the bills, and proceeded to count them out loud. "There's $500 here," he declared. He produced a new envelope from his desk drawer, slid the bills inside, licked the flap, and sealed it carefully. Then he tossed the bundle to the crew boss. Ho Ying-Chiao caught it against his chest clumsily. "Keep it hidden until we've laid the rails past the Cabinet Gorge—do you understand? Then give it back to him or put it back, I don't care which. I'll make sure he gets his voucher at that time, as well. So, you get the picture?"

"Yes. Un . . . stan." Ho Ying-Chiao bowed.

"Good. Now listen up, Chinaman. There's one more thing. I want one of your coolies assigned to me every Wednesday, starting this Wednesday. I want him standing here at the doorway by 7:30 sharp!"

"Ah, yes. Wednesday," replied Ho Ying-Chiao. "I un . . . stan, Mas-ter, but . . . " There was an involuntary quavering in his voice and he stopped. Keating might have mistaken this difficulty for guilt, but it was not guilt. Ho Ying-Chiao had long since triumphed over his conscience in matters pecuniary. It was not a question of right, but of possession. Still, once he had delivered Hok-Ling's money to Keating, as ordered, he had never dreamed that the American would give it back to him for safekeeping.

He wondered what price Keating would exact from him next. What complicity was expected of him. He placed himself some distance away and imagined another Ho Ying-Chiao, a less opportunistic man, refusing the money. It occurred to Ho Ying-Chiao that this would be an educated man, a man more noble than himself. He simmered at the thought.

"It is better, Mas–ter," said his imaginary alter-ego, smiling comfortably, "that you keep all money. Here." And all of a sudden his Cantonese was not a barrier between them, and he spoke quickly. "I have loyalty only to you, Master. I understand there are deeply rooted suspicions about. They are greater than either you or I could have imagined, but, as yet, no one has found the money, nor do they have the slightest proof of their suspicions against me. Now they must ask, 'But if Ying-Chiao has taken the money, where is it?' and there is no answer. This talk of striking will pass, for the men are desperate to earn money for their families. They will begin to doubt themselves and, in time, they will doubt their beliefs and even each other. This I am certain of. As a crew boss, I may gain greatly from this, for the mind that is sharpened through distrust will often embed itself in harmless distractions. Distrusting men resign themselves to me, and their ties and confidences with the others are quickly and silently dissolved. They jump at my command, and they will work as though their whole spirit is absorbed by the work itself. They are driven to great accomplishment so that their bodies will not get in the way of their spinning imaginations. I have seen this. This, you will agree, is reward enough for a humble crew boss."

Ho Ying-Chiao was lost in this rumination and could not bring into focus the face of William Keating. "So you see, Master," continued the educated, noble, far-more-comfortable Ho Ying-Chiao, "I have gained by these events. And I will continue to gain, even though you will have all of Hok-Ling's money for yourself. If I were to take even a part of this money, I would lose much more than I have already gained, for I fear the suspicions of the men will somehow be confirmed. I cannot say how. I must respectfully say 'no.' You keep the money. Does this please you, Master?"

"Chinaman!" shouted Keating, and the thunder of his voice shook Ho Ying-Chiao from his illusion. "Are you listening to me? Wednesday at 7:30. This man will fetch the mail in Sandpoint. It must be someone trustworthy. Do you understand?"

"Yes, Mas–ter ," answered Ho Ying-Chiao, shamefaced. "I will find such a man. Thank you, Mas–ter Keating," he said, and he placed the envelope under his shirt and turned to go without bowing.

Keating gnawed at the butt of his cigar and gazed vacantly at the white light beyond the threshold. He remembered the recent strike by four hundred Chinese near Umatilla, demanding a pay increase of five dollars per month, and the general exodus of Chinese laborers at Bolles Junction following a violent dispute between a Chinese timekeeper and a white foreman. "Sure as hell can't afford another work stoppage," he grumbled to himself as he turned and walked to a large map pinned to the wall. "I've got ninety miles of track to lay by October. These damn Chinese will strike over anything!"

Suddenly, Ho Ying-Chiao appeared in the doorway again. He bowed deeply. "Mas–ter. Excuse, please, but I have just an idea. This man who is to receive mail . . . will he be paid the same money as men working in field?"

Keating thought for a moment. "Yes, I suppose so. Why?"

Ho Ying-Chiao smiled. "May I suggest, then, we give this task to same man, Hok-Ling. Would it not be seen as a fortunate assignment? To be paid not to work? The men would hardly suspect that he was other than most favored by you."

"Well, I'll be." Keating's brows shot up. "By God, you might have a point there. That could be just what we need to defuse this thing." He pulled the cigar from his mouth. "Good thinking, Ying-Chiao. I owe you one."

Ho Ying-Chiao smiled as he had not smiled in years. "Thank you, Mas–ter," he said, backing up. "Thank you. Yes, yes, this will work." He bowed twice without saying more, then trotted down the steps of the porch and across the road to the platform. Upon reaching the platform he turned again and bowed very deeply. Then he descended the stairway that led over the rampart of the road to the serpentine footpath and the Chinese camp below.

9

H ok-Ling stood at the end of the Hope dock, turning the folded burlap mail sack in his hands. He listened to the noises of the camp behind him: the snapping of fires, the rattling of chains and shovels hoisted onto wagons, the shrill barking and chiding of the crew bosses. These sounds rose in long crescendos as the companies mustered and began to move slowly out of the camp. A metallic grinding came from the overburdened axles, a cadence from the planked portions of the roads pointing north and south. A half hour later the camp was silent.

Hok-Ling squatted and stared grimly over the lake. The *Henry Villard* steamed off Bottle Bay, with only its dark stack and a plume of white smoke visible above the false horizon of a silvery mirage. The vessel seemed not to move.

He thought on the camp itself, on the work of the railroad. Many of the Chinese had begun to feel at home here. The steep, shadowy terrain reminded them of the mountains that held the Pearl River and its tributaries in the heart of Guangdong Province. The weather, too, was similar, favoring them. And most of all, there was a welcome remoteness to the place.

This was very different from the camp at Spokane Falls. The lake was a great divider. It quelled the infrequent temptation to intermingle in white society. The Caucasians, for their part, rarely visited. There was skepticism about the seaworthiness of these narrow wooden ships supplied by the railroad, and, more generally, a fear that the Chinese lay in wait for them, tormented and frenzied, as it were, by overuse of opium and an insatiable appetite for treachery. Such an attitude worked to the advantage of the Chinese, and here there were no marauding bands of cowboys, no drunken schoolboys, firing rounds into the camp at night, looting, roping, spanking the awakened and unsuspecting coolies, stripping them of their hats and clothing. There was much peace and quiet here, all to the good.

The work of the railroad was progressing ahead of schedule. The crews found soft, sandy soil and few troublesome stones in the rich delta of the Clark Fork, where the earth's surface was a wide, flat plain, colored with deciduous trees and populations of strawberry and Oregon grape and long, golden-stemmed grasses. It was an east-west valley, just what the railroad wanted. And each day the valley breathed the fresh, rejuvenating air out of the Bitterroot Mountains. The sun lingered there, until eight o'clock or better, long after the recesses of the surrounding mountains were carved and shaped by shadow. So the crews worked long hours. And were productive. In the last weeks of June, the white survey parties were compelled to bivouac east of Lightning Creek, working dawn to dusk, so close were the Chinese grading crews to overtaking them.

In early July, Soo-Kwan and Dak-Wah had been assigned to a party of thirty men, with the English-speaking crew boss Shao Lu-Jin and four American engineers. They traveled by horseback and wagon to a place twelve miles east of Hope, taking axes, augers, cables, a dozen rifles, and other provisions. They would build the trestle at Holiday Creek. Already Hok-Ling missed them.

* * *

He jumped onto the dock at Sandpoint before the crew of the *Henry Villard* could set her lines or swing her crude gang-plank amidships. Hurrying past dozens of dark oil-soaked barrels and coils of rope, past a lean-to that housed night lanterns, gaff-hooks, and boxes of nails, past the silent, empty *Mary Moody*, he gripped the mailbag with a sweaty palm and made for the shore. The sun-heated planks scorched his bare feet, and when he reached the shore he stopped for a minute to wade in a small circle of shaded grass.

Then he walked quickly over the sand and gravel road leading to the Sand Creek Bridge. When he reached the bridge, he began to trot over its rough-planked deck. The clock in the belfry of the brick schoolhouse nosed toward ten o'clock. He crossed Main Street at an angle and slid into the shade beneath the covered sidewalk on Church Street. There were few people about, but he was careful to look at no one. When two men and a woman approached, he jumped down into the street and began to trot, and when they passed he pretended not to notice them. He continued to run, holding the folded mailbag against his stomach. Drops of perspiration slid down his chest and strands of black hair clung to his temples and neck. Ho Ying-Chiao's directions to the post office were recounted in his mind. He jumped back onto the sidewalk, trotting past black, glazed windows. He did not dare to look in. He looked instead at his feet. The shaded, gray wood was cool and smooth, and he marveled at how quietly and quickly his legs surged beneath him. "I could run as fast as a leopard on these boards," he thought, still pushing his thoughts inward to efface himself. He allowed a few steps at an increased speed—a test of sorts—and then he resumed his trot. His back stiffened and his arms began to slide forward and back, in the way of full running. He made a breeze for himself and felt its coolness against his face. The cool planks drummed beneath his feet.

* * *

There is a valley east of Spokane Falls that is really the northern part of a great inland plain that covers much of the region, and here the plain reaches a finger between pine mountains until its character as a plain is strained and muted and depleted. The newly laid Northern Pacific angles through this valley, in a series of long, nearly flat courses, and there are hundreds of stiff, slender telegraph poles supporting two sagging lines that run east and west with the track until the whole thing—all that is forced upon the land—is swallowed up at the tree line near Rathdrum. Here, too, is the road into the Idaho Territory.

On the side of this road, near Oscar Cooper's potato farm, stood a lone figure dressed in loose black trousers, cloth slippers, a wide-sleeved blue jacket, and a round, pointed bamboo hat. Tiny, alabaster hands were pressed together as in prayer beneath the chin of the stranger as a horse and wagon approached from the east, bouncing and rattling ahead of a tall, slanting cloud of dust.

"Ho there, Eddie! Lookie yonder!"

Eddie Rogers sat up in one of the new pine coffins stacked three deep in the back of the wagon. His forehead was etched in red where his rolled shirt sleeve had been slung over it to blot the sun.

"What is it, Johnnie?" he asked through a fog.

"Lookie there."

The two men, one sitting up in the coffin, the other on the wagon seat, stared silently at the strange presence in the road. Saying nothing, they revealed no less than what they knew. Johnnie Fry, a diminutive fellow without a brain, with parchment for skin and a great, wide, frothy mouth, argued with himself that this was either a scarecrow, curiously placed, or the stump of a tree. Eddie Rogers knew it was human enough, being the smarter of the two and a cemetery caretaker, trained in the human form.

A hundred yards from the object Johnnie Fry eliminated both scarecrow and stump. "Shit. Lookie there. That's a Chinaman, isn't it? *That's a Chinaman!*"

"What's that? A Chinaman?"

"Yeah. It ain't no scarecrow. I thought it were at first."

The caretaker shifted in his casket and felt an aching in his hip. He whispered hoarsely over the driver's shoulder. "I got my rifle right here, Johnnie. Just keep a-going. If he makes a move, I'll plug him."

Johnnie Fry laughed nervously and little clouds of saliva pulsed at the corners of his mouth. The figure stood motionless in the road next to a tan bag, head bowed, face obscured by the wide brim of the hat. The horse saw it late and shied, snorting over the bit. Johnnie tossed the reins and chirruped, "Get along, there!" But a second later he took the slack from the reins and pulled to a stop. He set the brake. Eddie Rogers lifted his hand from the breech of the rifle. "Lookie there," he heard Johnnie say. The two men gaped over the wagon wheel.

Eddie had lost the strength to sit erect, and sagged against the headboard of the coffin.

Wide, sloping eyes—feminine eyes, their deep brown irises sparkling—stared steadily up at them, out of the shadow of the hat. The face was small and pretty, its smooth, soft-looking skin stretched over high cheekbones and around a small, perfectly formed chin. The tips of the tiny, praying hands were pressed lightly against a mouth that seemed more painted on than real. A veil of dust slid over them just as the woman in the road prepared to speak. She bowed deeply and rose again when the air had cleared.

"Please . . . to . . . San-poing," she said, and she bowed again at the waist, this time without rising. Mei-Yin waited, half expecting to hear the cocking of a gun, or if not that, angry words. When she heard neither, she repeated in her mind the

English phrase Tai-Hing had taught her: "Please . . . to . . . Sand-poing." Was she remembering it correctly? She remembered Tai-Hing standing over his steaming pots of rice as the ship swung from side to side. She tried to see once again the way his mouth formed the words. "Please" and "Sand-poing"—she was sure of those—but what was the verb? Somehow "please to Sandpoing" seemed insufficient. She was forgetting something—but what?

"What'd she say?" asked Johnnie.

"She wants to go to Sandpoint," said Eddie Rogers sternly. "Can't you hear nothing?" Although he could not see beyond her hat, Eddie continued to see the young woman's face in his mind. Never before had a woman's expression, the set of her eyes, the play of her lips as she spoke, so affected him, so torn him free of his moorings. He sensed something like the bobbing of waves in his head.

"Well the hell with that!" the driver said in a strident, mocking voice. He smiled awkwardly out one side of his mouth, as though preparing to laugh, then leaned self-consciously over his knees and stared at the horse's head. "Huh! She wants to go to Sandpoint. It'll be a cold day in hell when she rides with us, huh Eddie."

They're talking about it, Mei-Yin realized, hearing what sounded like "Sand-poing" coming from each man's mouth. Her heart grew stronger. At least I'm on the right road, she told herself.

The caretaker in his coffin was silent while his companion twitched and bled with embarrassment. Mei-Yin finally straightening, dropping her hands to her sides. There was the beginning of a smile in her eyes as she gazed gently at the driver's hands. Johnnie Fry glanced at her then jerked his head around. "Jesus! Get up here, Eddie! Get the hell out of that damn coffin and get up here!"

Johnnie had never spoken to Eddie Rogers like that before, never without respect, but Eddie didn't seem to notice. He lifted himself out of the coffin and jumped clumsily to the ground.

He pulled his shirt down over an immense bare stomach, and when Mei-Yin turned to face him, he quickly ran his dirty right hand through his hair.

"You . . . want . . . ride . . . Sandpoint . . . ma'am? Yes?"

"Oh God," moaned Johnnie. "Eddie! That's an Oriental. She ain't riding with us."

Eddie Rogers turned and pointed a finger up toward the driver. His eyes were slits, and the skin of his face was stretched tight and red so that his uneven stubble stood on end. "Shut up, Johnnie!" he shouted. "You hear me? *Shut the hell up!*" Eddie turned back to Mei-Yin and saw that his shouting had alarmed her. "Now, don't you worry," he whispered tenderly. "He don't know nothing."

She tried to remember other words Tai-Hing had taught her—how to offer them money, for example—but her mind was suddenly blank. She held her hands beneath her chin again and, with eyes downcast, supplicated, "Please . . . to . . . San-poing." She looked up as far as Eddie's knees to await his answer.

"Sure!" Eddie replied. "We live—" Eddie stopped to point to himself and then at Johnnie. "We *live* in Sandpoint. I'm the caretaker there. Johnnie's my helper." He lifted the tan bag from the road and placed it in the wagon. Mei-Yin inched toward the wagon and Eddie's fingers encircled her waist. "Up you go," he said, lifting her onto the seat. His mouth went dry.

* * *

Hok-Ling turned onto Second Street, scurrying past the open doors of Simon Walter's livery. The post office lay ahead of him, half of its white facade darkened by shadows. The building seemed to crouch beneath the outstretched limbs of an enormous maple tree, but a wedge of its tin roof sent a blinding flash into the street. Hok-Ling let the mailbag unfurl at his side as he ran, raised it, and threw his fist against its rough seam, opening it. The stenciled initials 'N.P.R.R.' were faintly visible on one side.

He jumped down from the sidewalk and the warm, powdery dust of the street climbed between his toes. Slender spears of sand and dust shot out in front of him and angled back to earth. He stirred their cloud-trails with his legs. A tall man in a denim coat and trousers hurried past him on the sidewalk, staring straight out beneath the sweep of his Stetson. His pale, sunken eyes shone like tiny choked wicks, and his jaw jumped with a chewing. His step was purposeful. He paid no attention to Hok-Ling.

Hok-Ling stopped in front of Anthony's Lockers and stared inanely into the mailbag as a buckboard approached, its newly varnished parts shimmering in the sunlight. When it passed, he trotted in half steps across the road. Suddenly, six long-legged boys darted out from behind a shed opposite the meat lockers. The threshing of their legs through the tall grass startled Hok-Ling and he stopped. The youngest two did not advance beyond the edge of the street. Their faces were pale except for a nervous ruddiness about their cheeks.

"What the hell we got here?" exclaimed the largest youngster. He was round-faced and his thick blond hair curled up over his forehead and shimmered white in the sunlight. He was sixteen years old, but with a man's broad chest and powerful shoulders. He stepped in front of Hok-Ling, blocking his way.

"Goo mo-ning," Hok-Ling whispered, nodding.

Jake Prescott rolled his stubby fingers over his hips and balanced a teenager's defiant glare over Hok-Ling's nose. Hok-Ling looked deep into his eyes. Gold and green flecks floating over the blue reminded him of debris floating on tide pools. He saw beyond the pupils, where there was innocence and desire and strength, each thing half-eaten by the other, and he smiled gently, remembering the fires of his own youth. Then he looked at the other three boys who stood behind this one. The strength of their number put a dull shine on their faces. He looked over at the two boys at the side of the road. They were fitted in oversized trousers and their skinny arms dangled at their sides. The smallest hid his hands in his pockets. Hok-Ling shook his head and looked down at his feet.

"I thought them heathens wasn't s'pose to come around here," said one of the boys. Hok-Ling did not look up. He sensed the meaning of the words.

"Hey, you! Hey!" The white-haired youngster pushed against Hok-Ling's shoulder. Hok-Ling looked into his eyes again. His smile was gone. The youth's face contorted, and his mouth opened over uneven, tobacco-stained teeth. "What the hell you doing here? You got no business."

Hok-Ling moved back, then stepped around the boy, but one of the others stepped up to block his path. He stumbled and nearly struck Hok-Ling. Hok-Ling stepped to the side once more, and again he was stopped. "We don't like Chinamen around here," the third youngster croaked nervously, and his face colored at the sorry sound of his voice. Hok-Ling stared at the ground.

"He don't know a lick of English, Jake," said the fourth boy in the street. "Let's leave him be."

Jake Prescott stepped around Hok-Ling, inspecting him. He poked at the end of the tightly braided queue as if it were a snake capable of biting him. "Ma told me these critters weren't allowed in town. That's all. Said they're all a bunch of thieves and no-goods."

But the fourth teenager said, "Come on, Jake, let's go down to the creek like we planned. This ain't right."

"Aw, Jesus, Marcus. *You* go down to the creek if you're so chicken. This fella can't hurt us."

"Yeah? What about the club. We're supposed to be sticking together, remember? And your ma'll thrash you good if you make trouble, Jake."

"Go on. Get out of here. This Chinaman is going to learn a lesson." He spread his open hand over the side of Hok-Ling's face and pushed it violently. Hok-Ling's head sprang back and he looked into the frightened eyes of the boy who stood directly in front of him, who had not touched him. Hok-Ling's nostrils flared and his lips were drawn in tight. An L-shaped vein bulged at his temple.

"Damn you, Jake," shouted the boy named Marcus. "Look. He's got a railroad bag there. Says right there—see?—he's on some kind of railroad business. Maybe he's picking up mail or supplies or something. Let him be, or we're all going to get in trouble."

"Ma told me these critters is hateful. We got to protect Ma and this town and everybody around, including *you*. Ma said at that meeting they had with the railroad people that no Chinamen was supposed be running around the streets. Said 'Sheriff Langston made sure of that.' Now look." Jake Prescott drew a deep breath. "If you're so worried about it, Marcus, go tell the sheriff. Let's see what he says."

"All right, I will." Marcus turned and walked quickly toward the corner.

Hok-Ling stood motionless, his eyes wide and dark and angry. He did not look at the older young man despite his provocations. The other, standing in front of Hok-Ling, had spoken only once, and then feebly, yet he absorbed the sharp, sure, fearsome glare of the foreigner that spoke of experience and agility and strength and survival. This was an imbalance that gnawed at all the youths, and it worsened the impasse and made the skin on their forearms and elbows and above their eyes sting with the need to remain still. Jake scowled after Marcus. "Get going, damn it! *Run!*"

Marcus complied without looking back and the two younger boys scampered after him. "Hey! Marcus! Wait up! Wait for us!"

The smaller boys caught up to Marcus as he reached the door of the sheriff's office. "Now you two shut up!" Marcus said. He twisted the doorknob one way and then the other. It was locked. Marcus pounded on the door. "Sheriff Langston! Sheriff, you in there?" There was no answer. "Damn." He turned to the younger boys. All three were pale from running. "He's not here."

"Maybe he's over at the courthouse."

Marcus hesitated. "All right. Listen. You go over to the courthouse, James. If he's not there, ask around. Nathan, you run out to his house. Maybe he went home." The boys glanced excitedly at each other, then jumped into the street and set off running, elbows high. Marcus breathed deeply, buried his hands in the pockets of his brown denim pants, and set out for the Copper Penny Saloon. "Where else?" he said to himself confidently.

The door to the saloon was held open by a wide-mouth spittoon, but none of the brightness of the morning passed the threshold. The oak bar, its near end just visible, tapered into blackness. Three oil lamps hung above the bar, but they seemed to cast no light at all beyond their soot-smeared chimneys. Only the white, gartered sleeves of the bartender flashed sporadically below them. Marcus listened to the voices and peals of laughter that burst out into the street.

"What do you want, Marcus?" There was no anger in the voice, but a little impatience. The bartender turned, and his white-shirted torso came toward Marcus out of the darkness.

"Oh, uh, excuse me. I'm looking for Sheriff Langston sir," answered Marcus, squinting. "Is he in here?"

The bartender didn't answer, but slapped a wet rag over the end of the bar and began to rub vigorously. Marcus ventured two steps in and let himself be swallowed by the gloom. Shapes and features slowly began to appear, and the amorphous obscurity became depth and space. Faces evolved above the small tables along the side and at the back of the saloon. The bar acquired a beginning and an end. Marcus could see the outline of a man supporting himself on his elbow over its flat, shining surface. He looked back at the bartender and saw his face and knew him at once. "Is the sheriff here, Mr. Buck?"

Dan Buck smiled. "He's in the back, son. He's busy. What do you need him for?"

"One of the Chinamen's loose. He's got a railroad bag or something, but Jake Prescott has him squared off. Fixing to give him a whipping, I think."

The bartender chuckled, then shook his head and grinned absently. "Better Jake than his pa, I guess," he said at last. "Ol' Tiny had more kick than a mule." His eyes seemed to ride over something distant and comical and then they were serious again in the present. "Did you ever know Jake's pa, kid?"

Marcus lifted a memory out in the meager light. He remembered old Tiny, all right, a huge, square man, flaming red hair, freckled hands. A mountain man. Logger. High-pitched voice like a woman's. Always gone though. A huge man. Marcus swallowed. "No. I mean, I seen him now and then, as a kid. He's dead, ain't he?"

"Oh yes! Shit yes! Dead two years now. Never forget though, one time—God, five, maybe six years ago—"

"I need the sheriff, Mr. Buck," Marcus interrupted. "Jake's going to fight him sure!"

"What? Oh. Yeah. Sure, kid. I'll get him."

10

Marcus walked a half step behind Sheriff Langston across Main Street, around the corner toward Emory Morse's law office, and along the planked sidewalk skirting Church Street. The ascending sun reached in under the awning and lit all but a thin margin of sidewalk. It was bright on the sheriff's waist and legs. Marcus was conscious of the sheriff's arm swinging next to him. Behind the moving shadow a double row of brass cartridges glinted out of miniature leather pockets on his gun belt. Marcus caught up with the lawman, looking up. Moisture shimmered at the corners of the man's mustache, and his forehead and temple were ashen below the rim of his hat. His left eye was bloodshot and tear-soaked, staring out between thick lashes with a fatuous and sluggish bearing.

"Where're they, Marc-us?" he slurred.

Marcus felt shame and excitement, a terrible feeling, and his buttocks and hams began to prickle as he marched with exaggerated steps. "Over there, Sheriff," he answered, pointing. "By the lockers."

They turned the corner together. Marcus jumped down into the street and pointed toward Jake Prescott and the others. "There!" he declared, almost triumphantly. The tone was a surprise to Marcus, for some ways back he had begun to feel a dreadful ache in his stomach, and it had grown worse as they approached, and now it was stronger than ever—now that they were within view of the bizarre stalemate. The sheriff stepped off the edge of the sidewalk, misjudged its height, and nearly fell. He straightened, adjusting the heavy pistol at his hip. He was in no hurry. He removed his hat, wiped his forehead with a handkerchief, then, with eyes closed, seemed to swallow back something awful from inside.

"Agh. Goddam it!" He spit and wiped his mouth. A pained grimace distorted his face as he lumbered forward.

Marcus didn't follow. He shaded his eyes and squinted at the scene, the lone Chinese squatting in the street now, his back to them, his arms folded about his knees. The mailbag covered his feet and was splayed over the ground. Marcus's friends, Jake Prescott and the others, were lording over the Chinese, giggling, pushing, and challenging each other. Globules of their spittle shimmered in the Chinese man's hair. Marcus felt a churning in his stomach. He had disappeared around the corner by the time Sheriff Langston drew close, pulled up his gun belt, and said, "What's going on here?"

* * *

Hok-Ling looked back over his shoulder. His eyes met Langston's. Fear cut through him and he looked away. He saw two older women watching from the porch of Anthony's Lockers, and three men and a woman gathered beyond the circle of shade that darkened the post office. Their sun-lit faces were the color of the dust in the road.

Simon Walters appeared out of the blackness in the doorway of the livery, wiping his hands on a limp, soiled rag. He stuffed the rag in the back pocket of his overalls, and brought one immense hand up over his eyes. Jake Prescott grinned up at the sheriff with one eye closed against the sun. "Howdy, Sheriff." His voice crackled with the effort to unite bravado with officiousness and familiarity. "We caught this here Mongolian running around town. He got no business running round like that, do he?"

The sheriff rubbed his mustache with his thumb and fore-finger. "Hmm. Don't think so." Suddenly, his pointed boot flew into Hok-Ling's buttock, knocking him forward into Jake Prescott's knee. "Get the hell up!" Langston shouted. An ago-nizing pain swept through Hok-Ling, like ripples spreading in circles over water. His eyes filled with involuntary tears. He did not understand the sheriff's command but fear and instinct drove him to his knees, and he skittered around to face the sher-iff and bowed before him with his hands clasped.

"Look at that," said Jake.

The sheriff looked around at the stern and somber aspects of the bystanders. His mouth began to twitch at the corners, and his eyelids sagged down over reddened eyes. An intense pressure was pushing in all directions from the center of his head.

"What're you going to do with him, Sheriff?" Jake asked.

Langston looked at the boy as though recollecting him, and then down over the black, pigtailed head. The white spittle had vanished. "I don't know. Maybe nothing," he said.

"Nothing?" chorused Jake and two of his companions. "But Sheriff," cried Jake, "these kind ain't s'pose to be around here. You ain't going to teach him a lesson, or nothing? Them rail-road people promised there'd be no Chinamen running loose. You were there, weren't you?"

"Ma said 'twas you made them promise," one of the younger boys offered.

"Yeah." Jake spoke with emphasis, and his eyes pivoted slightly, but purposefully, toward the two women who watched from the doorway of Anthony's Lockers. "They said any of their

Chinamen that got out of line would have to stand for punishment, too. Just like anybody else."

"That's the fact, Sheriff," said one of the women in a trembling voice. The sheriff turned, and Hok-Ling looked up from his vulnerable position, not knowing what the woman had said but hoping she would intercede on his behalf. Her small, dark eyes were fixed disapprovingly on the sheriff and her mouth, a thin, gray, horizontal wrinkle, quivered rapidly, subconsciously, as though she were forever chewing a seed or a morsel of food. Her companion stared down and to the side, and when the first woman spoke again, she inched away and began to fidget with the handle of her basket.

"These Chinamen are nothing but criminals and heathens, Sheriff. No better than an Indian, or one of them Negroes. They got no culture, no religion, *nothing*. The whole lot of them's rotten. Why, I've heard tales of incest and rape and thievery and such . . . "

"Edda!" said the other woman.

"Where'd you hear these tales, Miss Farlan?" demanded Simon Walters sarcastically from across the street. "That sounds like something you might of picked up in church."

"Why! Of all the—" the woman stammered. She took hold of her skirt as if preparing to make a show of leaving. Just then a commotion erupted inside the stables, punctuated by the beating of hooves against a wooden stall and a loud whinnying. The liveryman turned on his heels and ran back inside. Edda Farlan watched his departure with chin lowered and eyebrows arching heavenward. "I suppose," she began, after a measured pause, "that I know less about the world than *some* people, Sheriff. But I can tell you this. You will not find a God-fearing Christian among the riffraff out there at Hope. Not one!"

"That's right, Sheriff," Jake said, and the second woman, too, looked up at the conclusion of this remark as if compelled to affirm it. Still her lips parted and her pale eyes rounded with uncertainty.

Langston lifted his hat, letting a little air inside. "You folks think I don't know about these heathens? You think I want them here?" He looked over to see if the men and the woman who'd been standing near the post office were still there. They weren't. He whispered orders to the boys to take "the Chinaman" behind Anthony's Lockers, "as soon as Miss Farlan and Miss Conrad leave." Then he turned his back on the scene and took cigarette paper and a pouch of tobacco out of his shirt pocket. He began to roll a cigarette, and when he stopped and nodded at the two women and said, "Good day, ladies," his meaning was not lost on them. They were soon hurrying on their way, whispering to each other excitedly.

A blond dog—which had lazily watched all this while lying on his side in the street in front of the post office—sat up, yawned loudly, and rose to his feet. He walked stiff-legged through the tall grass behind the sheriff and the others, as though he were obliged to accompany them. When they reached the back of the building, Hok-Ling was pushed under a canopy of tree limbs and overgrown blackberry vines. The soles of his feet were punctured by sharp needles and stems, and a tangle of coarse green tendrils nettled his ankles and the tops of his feet.

The dog stopped at the corner of the building and sniffed it intently, but he abandoned this when the sheriff and the older boys, rolling up their sleeves, ducked under the leafy dome after Hok-Ling. The dog's mouth fell open and its pink tongue bounced over its canines and leathery lips. There were sincere dog questions in his eyes, but he blinked and gave them up to faith, as dogs will. His tail thumped the weathered side of the building then stopped suddenly. His mouth closed again. His head tilted and he jumped back, startled. He swallowed nervously. Then his forepaws began to churn the earth. The dog questions returned. Suddenly he bounded, turning away from the scene and back again. A harsh, frenetic barking erupted inside him and it spilled out in an unrelenting succession of loud crisp reports.

Only when the sheriff and Jake Prescott and the other boys emerged did the dog stop barking. He dropped to the ground. His lightly panting face smiled up at them and his tail stirred the grass as they walked past. They paid no attention. The sheriff rubbed his right hand. Jake Prescott and the others brushed bits of leaves and needles from their clothes, too swelled with the heat of battle to notice the thorn cuts on the backs of their hands. And the dog looked after them, listening to the whoosh-whooshing of their pants through the tall grass.

They were gone a full minute when the dog rose and wandered in a serpentine path, head down, sniffing, toward the silent, outstretched figure beneath the leafy, tangled dome. His nose glided over one still arm and the crumpled mailbag still clutched in the man's hand. In the same fashion he examined a long, black pigtail that lay twisted in blackberry vines beside his head.

* * *

All that afternoon the sun baked Black Rock Mountain. Its pine trees, dusty cedars, and skeletal tamarack were ablaze with shimmering light hour upon hour. White butterflies flitted over the tops of huckleberry bushes, and the forest buzzed with the shrill songs of harvest flies.

At day's end, the sky over Black Rock Mountain was a lustrous alloy, not the searing sky of day or the cold blue-black of night, but their confluence—a pearly blue. A troupe of clouds, like weary dancers exiting one stage for another, limped westward. Behind and above them the heavens began to darken.

Jason sat back. His knees were tangled in the wrinkled fabric of Esther's yellow dress and he could feel the softness of her inner thighs through his pant legs. He looked down over her hips and abdomen, shapes visible through the soft gingham, and at her rounded breasts pointing skyward. She stroked his hand and stared at him, her pale eyes gleaming through dark lashes. Her expression was humorless, passionate. She did not smile, did not try to, until Jason looked into her eyes. Then they both smiled desirously.

Jason leaned forward and held himself over her. Her hands rose up and touched the sides of his mouth. "Jason," she whispered. "I want you to know—" His mouth fell over hers and her words were caught in the sweet breath that she inhaled. Her lips pulled at his, but her arms slid weakly out over the blanket until only her fingers encircled his rigid forearms. Through their clothes, he pressed his hardness against her once, twice—by the third time her abdomen rose to meet it. He lifted his right hand over her breast. She shuddered, but did not resist. His mouth slid to her cheek, and then her eye and her forehead. She turned his head with the force of her nose and kissed his cheek, and then her lips found his again. He felt a throbbing beneath his hand and suddenly Esther's pelvis rose up against him, so fully, so desirously, that the breath fluttered out of him and his lips quivered. He could not restrain a gentle groan. He pulled away slightly.

"I want to, Jason . . . I do . . . but . . ."

"I know." He gazed down over her face. Her eyes were closed now. When she opened them again they flashed with the whiteness of the clouds overhead. "God, you have beautiful eyes!"

"It is you who have beautiful eyes," she answered softly, inhaling, then closing her eyes and tensing rapturously.

Jason smiled back playfully, conscious of her ecstasy. "You have beautiful teeth, then, and your smile is . . . is heavenly!"

She laughed weakly.

Their gentle continuous rocking lit a fire between them. Wordless whispered overtures—intimations of sweeping ascendancy, of reward and glorious, precipitous escape stirred red in the pit of Jason's stomach. He sat back on his heels again. It was too much.

Esther's eyes opened wide and were even fearful. She seemed to study the man who loomed above her, whose face was suddenly dark and tinted by the orange-red light of the sunset. His blue eyes, fierce and bottomless, stared off as though he were lost in a distant memory. A curl of dark brown hair tossed in the wind over his forehead, and the rest of his hair shook forlornly against the cold indigo in the east. "I love you, Jason," she ventured.

11

J ohnnie Fry's oblong face was drawn and vacant and dusted the color of corn husks. With his thin, dry lips pressed tight, and his small eyes staring fixedly inward, he leaned over his knees, swaying and bouncing. He had become one with the wagon and even its sometimes violent movements seemed to make no impression on him. When the wagon rumbled over the planked deck of the bridge at Laclede, neither the sudden, hollow drumming of the horse's hooves nor the bright, lustrous flash of the river beneath could rouse him from his torpor.

Eddie, too, was silent, but his was a frenzied, fretful silence. He sat on sore hams in the top, center-most casket, his back squeezed against the head end. His large hands were knotted through the rope handles on either side. He braced himself with these. Beads of sweat dripped under his rolled sleeves and cut trails through the dust on the backs of his hands. His

131

eyes were fastened on the woman seated next to Johnnie—upon Mei-Yin. He measured her size again and again, helplessly. His gaze scoured her narrow, rounded shoulders and back, and the wonderful bevel of her hips. Now that she had taken her coat off and placed it on the seat next to her, he could smell her, and her odor was delicious to him. He sucked the air quietly but intently to draw it in. He watched her bounce and sway, and the movements, he thought, were graceful beyond belief, alluring, dance-like. When she shifted in the seat, and once when she set her arms back, and her fingers went curling over the back of the cushion, Eddie trembled at the fierceness and beauty of the dance. All of the new turns and starts and vibrations that came of it were, to him, agonizingly sensual. All of this was within Eddie, and without him there was a silence and shame that Eddie could feel against his face.

* * *

Mei-Yin stared absently at the road ahead as her body pitched and bounced with the movements of the wagon. She became aware of the shallowness of her breathing and willed herself to draw a deep breath, to stay vigilant. One man seemed anxious, the other oddly attracted. She was not used to men looking at her.

She was grateful that Wu Tai-Hing had agreed to teach her some English. She remembered "thank you" and "please." And when the time is right, she thought, I will point off in a direction and ask "railroad Chinese?" Hopefully, they will know what I mean. But I must wait until we arrive at the town to do this.

"Pay." It came to her. That was the word she hadn't been able to remember! Yes, I will offer to pay them. I *must* pay them, she thought.

Mei-Yin looked down at her dust-covered hands and frowned. I must bathe, too, and soon, she thought. She couldn't imagine how her face and hair looked. She pictured Hok-Ling walking past on the road. She stared at him, but even in her imagination, he did not recognize her. Perhaps her mask of dirt made her look like the villain in a Chinese opera.

The mare slowed as she began to pull the wagon up a long incline. Halfway up the hill, the shadows of tall yellow pine trees darkened the road and lifted the travelers' spirits.

"Do you have everything?" Mei-Yin smiled at the memory of the ship's cook Tai Hing acting the part of a solicitous uncle or older brother on the streets of Tacoma. He rested his hand on her elbow as he shifted to let a group of businessmen pass. She remembered the cacophony of sounds, people chattering, nickering horses, and their burdens of squeaking and knocking wagons and buckboards passing swiftly along the sunny, windswept street. The heavily loaded dray and its team of four Percherons waiting nearby. "Do you have your money?"

"Yes, Tai-Hing."

Tai-Hing looked nervously at the two well-dressed men standing with the consolidator, Mr. Stanfield Johnson, under the awning of the North Pacific Transport office. He turned his head and strained to hear their conversation while watching a fourth man attach a nosebag to the wagon's right wheel horse. Mr. Johnson owed Tai-Hing a favor or two. He didn't want him talked out of this one. He breathed easier when he heard Mr. Johnson bellow, "That's when I told Burke he could kiss my cherry red ass," followed by laughter.

Mei-Yin marveled at how unusual Wu Tai-Hing looked in Western clothes. "You look very handsome in this outfit." She kept her eyes up, away from the confusion of tattoos poking out from under both sleeves of his jacket.

"Listen to me. These men will take you as far as Spokane Falls," Tai-Hing explained, ignoring her observation. "I've talked to my friend. He's reliable and he's promised me that his teamsters are reliable. You'll ride on top of the cargo and sleep under the wagon, do you understand? They're taking extra food for you. You'll be safe. Once you get there, you must ask the devils how to get to Sandpoint. Do you remember how to do that?"

"Yes, Tai-Hing. Go I . . . Sand-poing.'"

Tai-Hing frowned. "I am going to Sandpoint."

"I am . . . go-ing . . . to Sand-poing."

"Right. Then 'Can you help me, please?'"

"Can . . . you . . . help me, please?"

Tai-Hing nodded then touched his mouth in a characteristic way. He looked toward Commencement Bay. "I have to get back to the ship."

"I know," Mei-Yin smiled.

"The wagon won't leave for another hour and a half. You're sure you have everything?"

"Yes, Tai-Hing. Thank you. Can I ask you something?" Mei-Yin looked directly into his eyes, then turned and stared out at the expanse of blue water. Three sailboats in the distance, two large, one small, broke the long double line of gray and green that was the southern shore of Vashon Island. "Why have you been so kind to me?"

"What?" Tai-Hing fidgeted. Mei-Yin remembered the shock that had run through her on that fateful morning five weeks earlier, when Tai-Hing, wrapping himself in a red blanket, had turned to her in front of the shipmaster and mate and said in Cantonese, "The master has agreed to let you sleep with me in the cookhouse. You will help me prepare all meals and clean up. And you will sew for the crew. You will be the seamstress you say you are."

Sleep with you in the cookhouse? Does he mean . . . is he going to beat me and rape me? Will I become his slave? These questions, understandable at the time, had not even a toehold in reality. By the end of the first day following her release from the cordage locker, Wu Tai-Hing had taught Mei-Yin how to stoke and monitor the ship's stove, how to prepare a vast quantity of tuna and cabbage soup, and the names of the three stately masts that towered above the cookhouse. More important, he had quietly retrieved Mei-Yin's belongings from the sleeping deck and cleared a cupboard shelf in the cookhouse for her exclusive use. His sternest words were reserved for the final quashing of Mei-Yin's objections when he insisted that she sleep in the hammock within reach of the stove's warmth, while he spread a blanket in front of the cookhouse door. He took a cleaver to bed with him.

By twilight of the second day, after the crew and passengers had been fed and the dishes cleaned, Tai-Hing could be seen and heard nailing a makeshift sign next to the cookhouse door. It read, in Cantonese,

> DO NOT PASS THIS DOOR WITHOUT
> PERMISSION OF WU TAI-HING.
>
> EXPERT SEWING IS AVAILABLE
> SHIRTS: TWENTY-FIVE CENTS
> TROUSERS: THIRTY-FIVE CENTS
> COATS: FIFTY CENTS
>
> *BEST RATES IN TOWN*
>
> BY APPOINTMENT WITH WU TAI-HING
> ONLY.

Wu Tai-Hing had resolved to limit his "no-charge" pledge to English speakers in general, and to those who had heard him utter it in the master's cabin in particular. That left him nearly two hundred potential paying customers.

Mei-Yin was the author of this idea. She had elicited from Tai-Hing the details of his assurance to the master that her father would be waiting for her in Tacoma with twenty dollars. "But what is to happen when he discovers there is no father in Tacoma, and no twenty silver dollars?"

"The master ordered me to pay it, but, as you say, you will be earning this money by sewing in the weeks remaining before we reach Gold Mountain. In terms of your getting off the ship, you needn't worry about that. I will take care of it." Her amazement and appreciation had no bounds. She viewed the idea of earning this money through seamstress work a most propitious one, so much so that she told Tai-Hing, "This must be done, without any question," and that the voice in her head that had urged her to utter "seamstress" in the first place was that of her great-grandmother Wong Xin An, whom she had known only as a young child, but who continued to watch over her.

A gust of cool wind swept down the Tacoma street, and Mei-Yin's long hair, tied with a piece of twine at the back of her head, was pushed up over her shoulder. A few loose strands angled over her eyes, as well. She pulled them away. "Can you tell me this, Tai-Hing, before you go? Why have you been so kind to me?"

Tai-Hing bit his lip and looked away for several seconds. "When I was growing up in Jilong, I had a twin sister who was my favorite playmate," he began. "We did everything together. But when we turned twelve, my father sold Jing An to a farmer who lived on the other side of the village. This man abused her from the start, making her work like a slave in his fields until all hours. He beat her constantly and degraded her publicly, in the market and in the street. I could do nothing about this, even though I heard her cries, even though she got messages to me on three occasions before she died. I could do nothing." Tai-Hing paused. His voice deepened. "I am older now. I have traveled the world. I can do things now. But I still miss Jing An."

Tai-Hing was subdued as he made his final farewell. When he was gone, Mei-Yin found her way to a bench outside a bank where she could keep an eye on the dray. She felt the stares of people entering the bank or passing on the sidewalk. The realization that she was alone and vulnerable produced a hardness at the base of her throat. This is the same thing I felt standing in line waiting to board the ship, she told herself. As then, she recalled Lai-Ping's words: "There is room for your fear, Mei-Yin."

Mei-Yin turned the phrase in her mind. She forced herself to look into the faces of a man and woman walking toward her. Their expressions changed slightly, but the variations were not threatening. The woman even looked down as she passed, as though, Mei-Yin thought, to acknowledge something shared by them in spite of the distance between them. Mei-Yin followed the couple with squinting eyes as they walked down the sunlit street. When they disappeared in a crowd, she sat back and had the odd sensation of sitting taller and breathing more easily. She set her hands flat on the bench on either side of herself for a moment, then quickly put them back on her lap and folded her fingers. She felt a slight surge of energy. She reached down and positioned the bag that held her belongings between her legs. Then, sitting up again, she put her hands back on the bench beside her—flat again. She let her fingers dance over the polished wood. The hardness in her throat began to melt. Something she could not name had closed in around her and was making her light-headed. She shut her eyes and breathed it in: freedom.

* * *

A doe and fawn standing at the side of the road brought Mei-Yin back to the present. She watched them over her shoulder as the wagon passed.

She began to imagine herself sitting with Hok-Ling, recounting the details of her long voyage. Many times she had thought of this, of the need to satisfy his curiosity. How would he react to the fact that she had traveled over seven thousand miles to find him?

"The captain was very angry, Hok-Ling. He flew into a rage, and I was sure he would order his men to throw me overboard. At that point, I was ready to die. I had begun to address the spirits of my ancestors, seeking their understanding . . . "

Eddie coughed. The very thing that had transported Mei-Yin to this reverie—the steady clop-clopping of the horse's hooves—seemed to bring her back to an awareness of the present. She felt the coolness of the approaching evening on her face, and was again conscious of the two men who traveled in the wagon with her.

She found it odd that they had not spoken to each other all this time. I must pay them, she thought. Perhaps this is why they have not spoken. Because they have forgotten to demand payment from me, and now they are embarrassed. But who is to say? she thought. These men are very different from Tang people. Grandfather could have spent an hour listing the differences. He would have concluded, "Do you see how different we are? Our differences define us, just as theirs will always define them. We are not meant to live with them." He had taken pains to identify what he called "defining oppositions": man/woman, wise man/fool, parent/child, son of Han/foreign devil. It was not until she was a teenager that Mei-Yin began to understand the practical significance of these dichotomous descriptions, for as he explained, "It is only through defining oppositions that we can know ourselves. I am old and ugly," he would laugh, "but if everyone were the same age, and looked like me, would I know this?"

The wagon crossed the rutted intersection at Lakeside Road, a few miles from Sandpoint, and the lading of caskets thumped and shifted beneath the caretaker. The horse stopped. Johnnie flicked the reins gently over its rump and called out, "Ho, there! Sssst! C'mon!" Johnnie sat up, revived. The wheels began to turn once again.

From the windows and open doors of the houses that at first dotted, then lined, then crowded against the road, there came a slick golden light. It was bright, in some cases, where it shone past walls blackened by the pall of the twilight in the east, and it was pale and watered down in others, where it competed with the halo that lingered in the west—this light clung stubbornly to the white sides of the houses.

"This here's Sandpoint," exclaimed Eddie from the back of the wagon. His eyes were fixed on the top of Mei-Yin's head, where a bluish luminescence wavered over the black strands of her hair. "Yup, by God. We made it."

Mei-Yin turned and her eyes fell quickly away from Eddie as she bowed her head. "Yes . . . Sand-poing. Thank you." She pulled a small leather pouch from the pocket of her coat. The coins inside clinked softly as she held it out. "You . . . want . . . to pay?" she asked.

"Pay? Oh, no. God, no. No pay. No pay." Eddie snickered, "Did you hear that, Johnnie? Do *I* want to pay?" Mei-Yin knew from his tone that she had misspoken. But how? She turned back and stared down at the road that was passing quickly now beneath the horse's hooves. What did I say wrong? she wondered.

Meanwhile, Johnnie answered Eddie by shaking his head up and down at first, then sideways. "Let's get rid of her 'fore somebody sees us."

Mei-Yin struggled to remember. In her mind, she could see Wu Tai-Hing sitting on his three-legged stool, his face etched with shadow beneath the swaying lantern in the cookhouse. She could see his amused eyes looking at her as she struggled to learn. Then it came to her. She had used the word "want." This is not the place to use the word "want," she concluded. She turned back to Eddie. "No . . . to pay?" She extended the purse closer to Eddie.

Eddie shook his head and gently pushed the purse away. "No. No to pay."

She turned to Johnnie, holding the purse in both hands. "To pay . . . San-poing?" The innocence and confusion in her tone made Eddie swallow back a sudden tide of emotion. Johnnie just shook his head and would not look at her.

"Ain't she the prettiest thing you ever saw?" asked Eddie innocently.

"*What?* God a' mighty, Eddie!" Johnnie spit loudly over the wheel.

"I mean it. She can't understand me. Don't do no harm to say it."

"I'm worried about you, Eddie. Maybe you been touched by the heat."

"Go on." Eddie was staring at Mei-Yin's diminutive torso. Her pale face flashed and flashed again as she looked eagerly left and right, down cross-streets and alleys, and her lips seemed to move quickly around words that were mouthed without sound. Eddie repeated to himself the words he had spoken, then added, "She *is* beautiful, damn it. Oriental or no. If you can't see that, Johnnie, then I . . . I feel for you."

"Shhhhee," wheezed Johnnie.

"I mean it. You had a good look at her?"

Johnnie sniffed. "I'd rather look at this here horse's put-too."

Eddie glanced quickly at Mei-Yin, embarrassed. His frustration simmered, and he pointed a finger at the driver. At last he said, "Shit, *you're* the horse's put-too around here, Johnnie Fry. Biggest, ugliest goddamned horse's put-too I've ever know'd." To Eddie's way of thinking, this denunciation was ideally conceived and perfectly suited to the occasion. He delivered the deathblow. "Next to your mother, I mean."

The homeward horse commenced to jog rhythmically, drawing its burden beneath the outstretched arms of the cottonwood trees. In the distance, another wagon, a large dark hay wagon hitched to a pair, pulled slowly onto the road. It approached and passed them in a flurry of rattles, clanks, and thumps, and the nodding man and the wagon and the team were all black like shadows, even at the moment of passing. The odor of hay was strong in their wake. Eddie, from his roost in the back of the wagon, looked up at the first stars visible over the road, and over the rooftops, and when the horse and wagon turned onto Church Street, he threw his head back and watched them turn in the sky.

Suddenly, Mei-Yin whispered, "Thank . . . you . . . please," and Johnnie eased the reins back. The horse halted, then shook its head, bringing a ringing music out of the tack. A flood of night sounds enveloped them: a dog barked and another answered, doors banged shut, crickets sang allegretto from the gardens.

Johnnie's eyes grew round and dark as if to allow for the failing light in the sky. Mei-Yin put on her coat, turned toward him, and smiled. Her almond-shaped eyes, which did not rise above the level of his shoulders, were exceedingly grave and appreciative. Johnnie looked straight ahead and blinked wildly. He licked his lips and the corners of his mouth, as if some part of his former tranquility might be found there. Mercifully, Mei-Yin turned away. She climbed down to the hub and then jumped to the ground. She pulled her tan bag out of the wagon bed while Eddie Rogers watched. It happened too fast for him. She was on the ground now, alone, and the bag hung from her coiled fingers. She stepped back and the wagon jerked violently beneath Eddie before Mei-Yin cold ask them for directions to the Chinese camp. She bowed her head.

Eddie watched her over his shoulder, dumbstruck. His muscles tightened all of a sudden, as if he might bolt over the rail himself. His hands even went swiftly to the edge of the casket, but he moved no further. He felt heavy and clumsy, inadequate. He looked around as Johnnie slid to the center of the bench. The driver was sitting up tall now, his shoulders back, his elbows bouncing in the air. He had pushed back his hat, and crimped and oily forelocks drooped over his temples and forehead like straps of leather. Eddie stared helplessly at his friend. His only need was to hear the answer to a silent plea. Johnnie! Johnnie! You've gotta help me, Johnnie! You've gotta! He looked back again, twisting in the coffin until his knees held him. Mei-Yin had turned and was looking after them. Her pale face shone above the dark street like the moon. She was beautiful. Beautiful. And Eddie wanted to hate himself. He decided he would do that, for he had to do something.

* * *

141

The quartered squares of light at the end of Church Street were the windows of the Carson Hotel. "Look. There are people in the street," she whispered to herself. "Someone there will know." But when she reached the hotel, the street was dark and empty. She looked around. An eruption of boisterous laugher and piano music came from the open door of a saloon a few doors down. Mei-Yin climbed up on the sidewalk and walked slowly toward a golden swath of light angling over the planks. Her heart began to pound. At the last moment, her courage failed her and she jumped down into the street to avoid the light.

"Ugh! Hold on there!" She was staggered by the collision, then held fast by two powerful hands. Her eyes met the bottom half of a man's face revealed in the muted light from the saloon. He wore a Stetson so low over his eyes that its shadow crossed the tip of his nose, obscuring everything above it. A thick speckled mustache hid his upper lip. "Just you hold on, Miss . . . " The whiskey-soaked words garbled and caught in his throat. His mouth hung open and points of light shimmered out of the featureless hole. The fingers loosened about her arms, and she backed away quickly, bowing. The smudged gold star he wore over his chest flashed dully, then vanished.

"Please . . . to . . . rail-road Chinese?" she stammered, pointing weakly in one direction and then another.

"What the hell," the sheriff growled as he stepped toward Mei-Yin.

She turned and ran as fast as her feet would carry her. When she reached the corner at Bridge Street, she stopped and looked back. She saw the dim outline of the man staring after her. He had moved no further. She felt a shudder of fear, more sudden and violent than their collision. Suddenly the night felt cold around her. Would he follow her? She lifted the bag at her side and felt the hardness that ran along the seam at the bottom. Her fingers followed it until she felt the point of the blade. Only then could she be sure she still had the knife that Wu Tai-Hing had given her.

She walked quickly at first, then ran in short, rapid steps toward the bridge. She crossed it, hearing her own shuffling footsteps against the gritty planks. She stopped again and listened for other footsteps. Now she was moving toward a greater darkness, and when she stopped at the other end of the bridge, she turned back and saw a range of lights from the buildings of Sandpoint, and a doubling of those on the flat surface of Sand Creek. The bridge stretched out behind her. It was empty. She stood trembling, waiting for the sense of danger to leave her. But her heart raced.

Ten or twelve minutes passed, then twenty. It was only a scare, she decided at last. I startled him. He meant no harm. She peered over the thick, wooden rail and noticed that tall grasses and plentiful weeds grew beneath the bridge. "I can bathe there," she whispered aloud. She descended the embankment, bracing herself on the rough-hewn pilings until she reached a small margin of flat land near the water's edge. It was black beneath the planked bridge deck, and she grew afraid again. She crouched over the ground and waited for several more minutes, listening and watching intently, making sure nothing came out of that black space. Suddenly, a whistle like a boat's whistle sounded in the near distance—one long blast. Its fade and brief echo struck a lonely chord in the night. A few minutes later, Mei-Yin heard the approach of footsteps scampering over the wooden bridge deck. Someone was running in quick, short steps, either in bare feet or sandals by the sound of it. Mei-Yin lunged behind a bush. She looked up in time to see a Chinese man in a long coat, trousers, and conical hat, obscured in shadows, running toward the sound of the whistle. He must be a coolie, she thought. Her heart nearly burst with joy. I'm so close! she thought. I've done it! The camp is within reach!

A few minutes later, there were no sounds but the distant laughter from the saloon and the nearby whistling of crickets. Mei-Yin moved closer to the pilings and looked around in a final effort to get her bearings and ensure her privacy and safety before bathing. Finally, she undressed and slid, goose-pimpled, into the black, silent water.

12

The night wind was gentle and cool after the day's oppressive heat, and it came in little whispering gusts through the streets of Sandpoint. It was a wind more irksome to a woman than a man, for it was enough—and just enough—to provoke a woman to don a scarf or to cast a second blanket over a sleeping child. It would not bother a well-fitted Stetson. It was a harmless enough breeze, but it had a bite.

Mei-Yin turned her back to the wind. She set her heels in the mud and knelt until the warm, flat water of Sand Creek skimmed over her shoulders. Then she moved further out. Flaccid fingers of bottom weed danced over her feet. She cringed and made a dreadful face, and crossed her arms beneath the surface. But gradually she grew used to the sensation and divorced it, and then the tensions of her journey began to ease out into the gentle current.

The Chinese labor camp must be nearby, she thought, looking about. She began to rehearse in her mind how she would approach the next white devil, in the morning, with American coins flashing in her cupped hands. "Please . . . to . . . railroad Chinese." Yes, that will do, she concluded, with another sudden thrill.

With childlike curiosity she regarded the pale image of her hands beneath the surface. She began to move them in short, sweeping strokes, feeling them glide effortlessly at her sides. They were unreal to her, and she touched them to her stomach to make them real. She became lost in dream-thoughts, rubbing the dirt and smell from her body. She bent her head forward and lifted handfuls of water against her face. Then she leaned back and scrubbed her hair, letting the current rinse it. Its coolness crested on her forehead. She stood up, dizzy, steadying herself against a piling. And her eyes closed, blotting the night. "How will I find him?" she wondered, but instantly the vision of Hok-Ling standing on a sun-drenched beach came to her. She imagined him running into the lake to meet her, to carry her from a boat even before it could land. His face was bright and pink from the sun, and drops of water clung to it from his splashing. A wide, careless smile—like that of an over-tired child—pushed her cheeks round above the soothing flow. Oh, Mei-Yin, she thought, there is no longer time for worry. This is surely the eve of your greatest day. If you doubted this why are you not this minute at your father's home, or at the home of the water carrier, whoever he was? Is not the love you once felt for Hok-Ling waiting to be reborn? You have believed it. You have—

Suddenly, there was a threshing noise in the grass behind her. She started and turned. Her eyes flashed open, but she saw nothing, darkness. She reached for the piling, but in her haste slipped, and the current pulled her back with unexpected force. Her fingertips brushed the piling—her fingernails caught. She righted herself and pulled, and the noise continued, drawing closer. Her heart beat frantically. She placed one hand against her chest and struggled to breathe. Silently, she crouched down. Only her head was above the surface now.

Oh no! she thought. *Please*, no! She leaned out past the edge of the black column. Her angular eyes were wide with the need to see. But she could not see. There was an uncertain hissing in the grass, then silence. Mei-Yin's fingernails penetrated the algae-softened skin of the piling. She closed her eyes, and, wincing, set her forehead against it. "No-o-o. Please *no!*" she breathed without sound.

There was the minute rasp of clothing being turned and wadded, and the dull whish of it being thrown back over the ground. A thief! thought Mei-Yin. He has come upon my clothing and my bag. The wind gushed and checked her breathing. She blinked back the helpless formation of tears. He may take my bag, even my money, but he must not see me! *He must not see me!* There was another interval of silence. Mei-Yin slowly moved one eye past the edge of the piling. Suddenly, both eyes grew wide, and her lips parted in front of clenched teeth. A faint high-pitched whimper rose involuntarily in her throat.

The man's pale body was visible, ashen, ghostlike in the darkness. He stood at the edge of the water, no more than ten feet from her, leaning out. His raised head moved about in starts. A darkness that began at his chest angled sharply downward and fell like a shadow over his body. It grew wide between his legs, and it was there that his right hand circled and moved in rapid successions. There was the same darkness above his mouth. His bare legs were slightly bent at the knees.

There was a sudden, sharp pain in Mei-Yin's chest. Her arms and legs had grown cold and stiff, and the mud and bottom weed that encased her feet seemed to bind them perversely, inextricably. She freed them with difficulty and pushed slowly away from the piling, breathing silently. She set her legs and held herself against the current, keeping the piling between herself and the figure on the shore. She could see the dim outline of one of the man's ghostly white legs. The water brushed her chin. He moved. Mei-Yin sank slowly, so that only her nose and eyes were above the surface. She could see him now—all of him. He held his erect penis in his hand. Mei-Yin lifted her feet above the bottom weed and drifted in the current until once again a piling stood between them, blocking his vision. She held herself there, but there was a sunken log, slick with algae, pressed painfully against her ankle. She reached instinctively for the log, to find her way over it, but her hand struck a thin branch above the surface. It cracked loudly behind her.

The man on the shore stepped quickly toward the noise, stopped, then moved again closer to her. He had seen her! She rose suddenly, drawn out of hiding by an impulse of resignation, by a strange desire to have it over with, even a fear of her own black hiding place. Her arms hung weakly at her sides as she faced the man who stood naked in front of her. The wind gusted, and the skin of her torso was tight and cold. Spears of hair angled across her face and droplets of water darted down the contours of her body, and leapt from the nipples of her breasts into the pool below.

"To railroad Chinese," Mei-Yin cried. "Hok-Ling. Hok-Ling to railroad Chinese." Her voice was gentle and apologetic, but edged with fear. The man stood silently at the edge of the water. She could not see his eyes in the darkness. "Please. Please . . . to . . . pay," whispered Mei-Yin, raising her hand and pointing into the black shadow beneath the bridge. *"Kao kao lei! I beg of you!,"* she begged, "Hok-Ling . . . *hai?* . . . to . . . railroad Chinese. *Please?* Hok-Ling . . . Mei-Yin . . . Hok-Ling . . . Mei-Yin."

"Shut up!" the man hissed angrily. He looked up toward the white, almost-lucent railing of the bridge, then back again. "Come 'ere, you little bitch!" He stepped into the water and extended his hand toward her. "It's all right. *Come 'ere!*" He waved her toward him, while his other hand closed over his penis as if to hide it.

"No. Kao kao lei! Kao kao lei!" Tears streaked from her eyes. Her head tilted sideways under the strain of her pleading. "No

. . . please," she begged, trying to whisper. The naked man ambled slowly through the water toward her.

"To pay . . . Hok-Ling . . . to railroad Chinese . . . To pay . . . *To pay!*" The water splashed white in front of his legs. His stiff penis, now free of his hand, wagged wildly. Mei-Yin slunk back and drew a deep breath, but when he drew within a few feet of her, she raised herself upright. Anger rose in her throat. She thrust her arm out, pointing to the place where her clothes and her bag lay. "To pay!" she shouted, in a tone fit for the reproof of a child. "To pay!" The muscles of her jaw bulged as she drew another breath. The air hissed through her teeth. "To p—"

Roger Langston's lips fell over Mei-Yin's open mouth and he caught the rasp of her muffled plea against his throat. His broad hand pushed her slender body against his, and he shuddered with the first sting of pleasure as his hardness pried upward against the top of her cold, wet stomach. He brought his right hand to her breast and crowded his fingers over her nipple. A deep rattling moan vibrated inside him.

Mei-Yin twisted her head away from him. Her fingers dug into the soft bulge of his stomach. *"No! Please! Kao kao lei! Kao kao lei!*

* * *

The figure of a man nearly doubled over at the waist, holding his left side and favoring his right leg, emerged all of a sudden from the shadows behind Pioneer Paint Store. He made for the corner of Main and Bridge Streets, a distance of 130 yards. Although he moved with a broken and grotesque gait, he moved quickly. Near the end of his transit, a dray turned onto Main Street two blocks away. He grasped his left thigh and began to run. He plunged headlong into the blackness between the smoke shop and the Wilson Brothers Bakery, and he waited there, with his back to the bakery building, until the wagon had passed. His buttock and thigh began to cramp and fresh blood trickled from the cut on his lip. He looked down at the empty, folded mailbag that he carried in his right hand. A bottomless sense of dread began to overtake him, eclipsing his pain. It is late, he thought. What if the last boat has left? What will they do to me if I do not return? Perhaps it is better. I have failed—I have no mail. He touched his swollen face. The demons have beaten me until I can take no more. They will kill me now, I know it. This is my fate.

The wind whistled over Hok-Ling as he hobbled back into the street, pushing up a cloud of dust with the foot that dragged behind him. Oh! It is the end for me! he lamented, raising the mailbag to his eyes and pressing the fabric to his forehead. The wind and dust poured over him. I did nothing, he declared in his thoughts, imagining Ho Ying-Chiao standing before him. They would not let me pass—the boys and the green coat. You must believe this. They attacked me, and there were old women who watched, and, by their words, seemed to offer them encouragement. They must hate all Chinese, Ying-Chiao. Don't you see? It is as I told you before. And the green coat. It was the one who whipped Soo-Kwan. I cannot return there. They will kill me next time. You must tell Master Keating these things. He imagined Ho Ying-Chiao shaking his head gravely, agreeing.

The wind subsided as Hok-Ling staggered onto the Sand Creek Bridge. There was a new sound, the low murmur of a voice beneath the bridge. It was a man's voice, a whispering broken by deep, angry tones. The words were garbled in the windswept hissing of the grasses along the bank. Hok-Ling stood, listening, his eyes intent on the railing at the far end of the bridge, for the sound seemed to come from there. Would this man—whoever it was—suddenly appear over the railing to confront him? Was it safe to cross? Had his footsteps been heard already? Would he be beaten again? He moved silently, breathlessly, walking only on his toes. The half-whispered soliloquy continued beneath the bridge.

Then he has not heard me, Hok-Ling concluded. But to whom is he speaking? He listened for another voice, but it was only the same voice over and over, very low. Perhaps this is an old drunk, he thought, and such an idea suddenly seemed very plausible to him. Perhaps he whispers, knowing that his wife will be out looking for him. Hok-Ling felt a slight smile turn the corners of his mouth. He breathed normally and began to move more surely.

Then there *was* another voice. It was no more than a muffled whimper, there and gone, but it sliced through Hok-Ling's brain like a bolt of electricity. He stopped at the center of the bridge—indeed, it seemed for a moment as though his knees might be incapable of supporting another step. He was filled with a sudden and inexplicable foreboding, and an icy shudder swept through him. He covered his heart and strained to hear the sound again.

A loud chorus of laughter came all at once through the back door of the Copper Penny Saloon, and Hok-Ling turned to see the silhouette of a man staggering out onto the balcony. The door closed behind him. It shut off the light and most of the sound from inside. The man's cigarette became a glowing point of orange-red light in the darkness, rising and falling, rising and falling.

Hok-Ling knelt low and, despite the onset of stabbing pains in his arms and legs, scrambled on hands and feet to the railing of the bridge, where he laid down flat, out of view. There were no sounds beneath him now, except for the gentle gurgling of the stream past the many pilings and cross-braces. He looked up. The cigarette rose and fell again and again, flaring to a bright orange in front of the man's face. Certain that he had not been detected, he let his body relax, for there was nothing to do but wait until the man on the balcony disappeared again. The aching throughout his body was exquisite.

Suddenly a voice sounded beneath the bridge again, startling Hok-Ling. It came from the opposite side of the bridge, on the embankment below. It was a man's drunken whisper, and now Hok-Ling could hear the slurred English words. Although he could not understand them, they portrayed a mischievous, disdaining, even hateful quality. He looked again toward the stationary figure standing on the saloon balcony. This man had not heard the voice, apparently, for he puffed the cigarette twice more at a leisurely pace, flicked the burning butt from the porch, and then turned away, giving the saloon door a mighty jerk. As it swung shut again, the man entering the saloon was pulling up his dungarees with force enough to lift the heels of his boots off the ground.

Quickly and silently, Hok-Ling moved to the other side of the bridge. He knelt again and peered between the bottom two white planks of the three that comprised the railing. He was at once taken aback, for he saw the figure of the naked woman lying there, her legs and arms splayed awkwardly in the blackish grass. Her head was turned away from him and the contours of her face were obscured by the tall grasses tossing in the wind. She lay motionless, as if dead. It was only when she lifted her left forearm and dropped it weakly over her forehead that he knew she was still alive. He saw dark patches of blood over the pale skin of her thighs.

"Get up, bitch," came the voice beneath the bridge. The top of the man's head and his round, broad shoulders suddenly appeared directly below. Hok-Ling retracted swiftly, and he would have cracked his head against the upper rail had it not been for the thick trunk of his pigtail.

"You ain't hurt," the man snarled as he moved closer to the woman. He stood over her, buttoning his shirt, tucking it into his pants. He reached down into the open crotch of his pants and squatted, adjusting himself. "Come on, come on, come on," he coaxed, his voice suddenly playful, as if he were addressing a child.

The woman did not move or utter a sound. Hok-Ling could not see either of them clearly. Only their forms were visible, particularly that of the faint-skinned woman. The man stood over her now with his broad hands resting on his hips. His anger seemed to leave him. "It's just a little blood. Better wash it off. Hey!" He prodded her with his foot. "Hey! Get up."

He waited a few seconds, and when the woman did not stir he snorted and said, "Well, go to hell then." He ambled to the water's edge and squatted. He splashed water on his face and over the back of his neck. He stood up, turned back to the woman. "I guess you don't mind very well, do you? Maybe I should teach you another lesson." He got down on his hands and knees and squeezed her rib cage while planting a kiss between her breasts. The woman's body jerked violently. Her arms rose up out of the grass like cobras, her hands latching to the sides of his head. The man reeled back, and the woman rose up with him. Her head turned.

Hok-Ling's eyes opened wide. The woman clung fiercely to her attacker, lunging at him with her face, as though it were a weapon. Her teeth shone. She growled like a ferocious animal. Hok-Ling leaned closer, not believing what he saw. Oh, Great and Almighty One, he cried inwardly, Say it is not her! Say it is not!

Hok-Ling jumped to his feet and stumbled, for he felt as if he were weightless. Turning. Going blind. He closed his eyes and shook his head. His stomach rolled—and vomit surged over his lips. And behind his disbelieving eyes it was still, *"No! It cannot be! No! Not her! Not her!"* With each painful running step toward the end of the bridge, and each leaping footfall through the grass and weeds on the steep embankment, it was a silent scream, *"No! Please, no! This can't be!"*

Mei-Yin cried out. Hok-Ling felt his heart breaking in his chest. It is her! Oh, Great spirits, it *is* her! No! The world was suddenly cold and silent.

Only Hok Ling moved, and his motion was strange and distorted. His legs felt as if they had never run before, and yet here they were, running beneath him. His eyes burned, and the combination of anger and panic within him created a bizarre illumination, fringe flashes of light behind the bridge pilings, behind the stems of grass, behind the buildings across the creek, behind everything that was black—a thin wisp of milky white.

The man lay over Mei-Yin, his left forearm pinning her to the ground. Her arms were again outstretched in the deep grass, twisted as if she had fallen to her death from a great height. He had buried his face against her neck and was kissing her and laughing in turns. His right arm fumbled with his belt in the little space between them.

Hok-Ling instinctively approached from the far side of the bridge. It was a greater distance by the width of the bridge, but it allowed him to descend to the level of the creek unnoticed. He ran into the black recess beneath the span, his hands outstretched and groping in front of him. He could not see Mei-Yin's clothing, nor the sheriff's gun belt, which lay nearby, but his bare foot did strike the hard blade at the bottom of Mei-Yin's cloth bag. He dropped instantly to his knees, staring fitfully and still disbelieving at the dim figures sprawled in front of him. He lifted the bag and stretched his hand inside. The knife fell surely and comfortably against his fingers, as if passed to him by a confederate. He stood up, and the blade winked silver at his side. The strange whiteness was gone.

He drew a hissing breath as he ran the four leaping steps through the grass, his teeth clenched, the knife raised above him. He lunged, eyeing the right side of the man's rounded back. The blade entered, but in that instant Hok-Ling felt the muscles in his arm go soft and weak, suddenly debilitated. His hand shook, and he was unable to hold the hilt tightly as before. He tried but could not push the blade further, and then, suddenly and without thought, he threw his chest—thus, all his weight—over the hilt and the blade sank completely into the man's torso. He lay over the back of his victim with his eyes shut tightly, and when he opened them, at last, reluctantly, he was face-to-face with Mei-Yin. Their noses were nearly touching. The horror that was engraved on her face was fixed, unchanging, death-like. Her eyes were open, but he knew she could not see him.

There was the sound of blood spilling from Langston's mouth to the ground. It stopped suddenly. The sheriff moaned, not painfully, but rather as if in sleep. His body moved under Hok-Ling, slightly at first, then in a great rolling motion, and he rose to his feet. Hok-Ling held on tenaciously, piggyback, still feeling the knife's pommel against his chest. His arms and legs were wrapped tightly about the man's body. He cried out with abomination and fear, for it seemed suddenly as if he were riding the back of the devil of devils, the tormented one, the unconquerable evil. He drew the knife out of Langston's flesh and drove it in again. His strength had returned. Langston spun twice, like a cat chasing its tail. His arms circled randomly, groping in front of him. He staggered toward the bridge. Hok-Ling stabbed him again and again, and became lost in the stabbing.

The sheriff moved stiff-legged through the grass, and when he reached the bridge he extended an arm and balanced himself against one of its pilings. His body rocked gently with Hok-Ling's unflagging attack, but he uttered no cry or complaint, and he made no move to repel his assailant. His free hand hung limp at his side. He stared into the darkness, silent, enduring, and then at last he muttered, "All right. It's over. You can stop."

Hok-Ling did not understand, and, worse, the calm monotony of the sheriff's voice heightened his fear. He swung the knife with frenzied repetition until there was no sensation of its penetration left. The sheriff shuddered and his head fell forward. Slowly, Hok-Ling straightened his legs and stepped away, leaving the knife implanted in his victim's back. He stared in horror at the sight. It had all happened so fast. With a hideous gurgling, the knife drooped from the pulpy wound and fell to the ground. Hok-Ling froze. Now he was certain that the wounded man would turn and retrieve the weapon. But *he* could not move, could not approach to remove the weapon himself.

He stared helplessly at the slumping man, fearing him, awaiting a terrible vengeance that never came.

Langston raised his head and shook it weakly, as if to dispel an unthinkable dream. He slumped to his knees. His body spun and fell forward, and a low murmuring escaped from his throat. He lay in death, twisted around the base of the black piling like a sleeping animal. His right hand was still lodged against it high over his head.

Hok-Ling bent at the waist and stretched to see the face of the dead man. He gasped, and his face turned upward as if to beseech the gods to erase the vision. He shut his eyes against the silvery stars and the ghostly clouds. It *is* he. No! No! A thousand no's! Let it be another. A thief. A vagabond. Let it be *me.* But as he thought this, he knew the absurdity of it and was wrenched from his prayers by his own angry denial. He stood benumbed over the dead man.

His senses slowly returned to him. He felt his breathing again and wondered if he had breathed at all since he had stood upon the bridge. The wind surged ominously. He felt its cold edge against his face and hands, and at the tips of his fingers. Feeling it was good to him. He heard the grasses swishing at the top of the bank, and although he did not turn, the thought that someone had come upon them was formed, then dismantled, for it was only the wind, he knew. And then a voice such as his own came to him, speaking faintly within him, unemotionally. "As there is separation between all things," it began, "between sun and earth, between ocean and sky, between thought and the spoken word, so, too, there is separation between the soul and the flesh that holds it. You have killed a man by your right hand."

Hok-Ling gaped forlornly at the twisted body of the sheriff. He was unaware that Mei-Yin had crawled to him and knelt behind him in the position of a kowtow, that her arms were wrapped loosely about his foot, or that her tear-soaked face was pressed against his ankle, wetting it.

13

The wind gusted and cried out with a zealot's hoarse voice. Across the creek, the shutters on the windows at the rear of the smoke shop began to clap, and above the rooftops three gulls glided diagonally, their wings minutely testing and adjusting. Their undersides carried the light of Main Street.

Mei-Yin dressed in silence. Her legs and abdomen ached with cramping as she lifted first one leg and then another past the waistband of her trousers. But she hurried nonetheless and was thankful when her nakedness was covered. She glanced uneasily at Hok-Ling. He stood in the relative light of the open air, his feet spread, his arms hanging loosely at his sides. He did not speak, and the strange shadows over his face made him seem unfamiliar, heartless, a stranger to her. But she had no fear left. She knelt and groped for her bag and found it a few feet away, where Hok-Ling had dropped it. Instinctively, she felt along its bottom seam. The knife was gone. She looked up at Hok-Ling, breathless, her heart pounding. It had been her knife! She moved quickly to the body of the sheriff. His shirt, wet with blood, rippled beneath her groping, outstretched fingers. It sickened her to feel his size again, his flaccid muscles. Even the smell of whiskey lingered about him and twisted up into her nostrils as before.

Her fingers plunged into the pulp of his wound, and she withdrew them with a startled cry. Then silver flashed in front of her, in the grass next to the piling. She lunged toward it, over the sheriff's sprawled legs. She patted the thick grass frantically, then stopped, and when she rocked back on her heels she was turning the bloodstained knife in her hands.

She crawled to the edge of the creek and plunged the knife into the water, driving the blade into the soft mud at the bottom, rinsing it once, twice, three times, until it shone along its full length. She held it only inches from her eyes, inspecting it, then dried it in the grass and dropped it into her bag. She looked carefully at her fingers, front and back, then rose and walked out of the night-shadow of the bridge toward Hok-Ling. Lifting her eyes to him slowly, she was startled. What she had thought were shadows cutting across his face were, in fact, large bruises. In the dim light she began to make out a swelling around his eyes and lips. And what she had thought was a sprig of hair over his forehead was the thick line of a cut.

She raised her hand toward his face, but he turned away from her. She withdrew her fingers and placed them near her own mouth. Hok-Ling did not speak, but pointed and nodded toward the top of the embankment. He started ahead of her, stumbling, half-running, then climbing, pulling himself up by the tussocks of fescue and sedge. When he reached the top, he crouched and looked around nervously. Finally he extended his hand to Mei-Yin, who was struggling and slipping below him. She took it.

Oh, great spirits! she sighed within herself. His hand is so warm and strong! I have disgraced him. I am defiled and no longer deserving. But his hand is so warm and strong, and it consumes mine! I do not remember such strong, safe hands!

She could not take her eyes from him, but when she stood finally at the top of the embankment, he released her hand and waved with his head toward a dark line of forest in the distance. He set off ahead of her at a limping trot. She stood, staring after him. His body bobbed in the dimness, and although he was hampered by injury, she recognized traces of the sturdy gait she remembered from their past. He was a boy, only a boy then, she thought, and now he is a man—with very strong hands. The vision of Hok-Ling running away from her left her weak and resigned. Is there no better fate for me? she lamented. What terrible evil has brought us together this way?

She followed him through the forest, to the edge of a road on the other side. There, at last, was the great lake. They had stopped within sight of the dock and the *Henry Villard*, her engines rumbling, her topsides all plumb and right angles.

"Here!" Hok-Ling snapped, taking a folded green silk cap from the pocket of his shirt. "Put this on. And braid your hair—quickly! Three twists."

Mei-Yin leaned close to see the harm that had come to Hok-Ling's face. Her brows knotted. "Dear one, what—"

"Hush, woman! Do not speak. Do as I say. There is no time." Hok-Ling looked around them in the darkness.

Mei-Yin was stunned. Why is he treating me this way? she asked herself as she reached back, capturing her hair in her left hand. But her movements were too slow for him. He stepped around her, taking up her wet hair, weaving the braids himself. "Three twists," he muttered impatiently.

"You're hurting me!"

"Shhhh!" Hok-Ling stepped back to face her when he had finished. "Take the mailbag. Keep it folded. No, wait. Open it. Here, place your bag inside. Hurry!"

"What are you doing? Stop it!" she cried, refusing, at last, to let go of her satchel. Hok-Ling grabbed her forearms and held them rigid, like two sticks. He stood before her, unmoving, then he turned and peered into the forest, as though he were reliving in his mind what had happened beneath the bridge. His eyes glinted angrily, but when he turned back they held only questions for Mei-Yin—questions that he could not ask.

It is the first time you have really looked at me, she thought. Talk to me, Hok-Ling! Tell me what I should do! You mistreat me with your orders and impatience.

As if afraid to speak, he wetted his fingertips and rubbed a smudge of dirt from her chin. The blood she had washed from her mouth, but her upper lip was still rosy and swollen where her assailant had struck her. Instinctively, he touched the swelling with his fingertips. "Ooo-oo!" she cried out.

"Shhhh!" Hok-Ling nodded. They stood in numbed silence for a minute or more, their disbelieving eyes finding each other's battered faces in the black shadows that fell across the road, until the sound of heavy-soled boots pounding and scraping over the gravel drove them back into the forest. They crouched close together behind a small bush. Hok-Ling looked at Mei-Yin with a finger held to his lips. This time it was she who nodded.

It did not occur to either of them that this man, whoever it was—it was a man, to be sure, mustachioed, dressed in a dark shirt with sleeves open and loose at the cuff, dark dungarees, and a cocked derby on his head—might have witnessed Roger Langston's killing, or happened upon his body, and feeling its warmth, be in pursuit of his killers. Even as the demon came to a stop near their hiding place and tarried in the road to catch his breath before stumbling forward, this did not occur to them, and therefore it was not with a sense of danger that they observed him.

"This is the last boat," Hok-Ling whispered, as soon as the man was out of earshot. They stood up together, quietly. "He is trying to catch it." Mei-Yin started to speak, but Hok-Ling would not be interrupted. "Listen to me! It will leave soon. We must take this boat to Hope. Do you understand?"

"Hope?"

"Where the camp is."

Mei-Yin's eyes widened, and the flames from the *Henry Villard's* deck lanterns shone as pin-points of light in them. "This is the boat to the camp?" she asked, turning toward the vessel without waiting for the answer. The once-cherished dream of her arrival, of Hok-Ling running into the water to meet her, to pull her from the deck of a boat, of his uncontainable joy, of the sun bright against his skin, of the smell of flowers and the sound of their laughter, replayed in her mind. So it was on this boat, the *Henry Villard*, that she would have stood, waving with proper constraint, but wanting to jump and scream and wave with both hands high above her head. She had anticipated it so clearly. But could she ever feel such joy again? Her reverie was broken by the urgency in Hok-Ling's voice.

"You must go aboard as me, Mei-Yin. Those on board do not know me, but they saw me this morning, so you must be careful." He took her satchel, which she now relinquished, and dropped it in the mailbag. "This will be the mail. You must not open it. Do you under—?"

"But what will you do?" Mei-Yin interrupted.

"Never mind that. I will find a way, but you must go directly. Here." He guided her left hand into her right sleeve. "Keep this hand in your sleeve. It will hide your bosom. Carry the bag in this hand—high, like this. Take large steps, like a man. If you are spoken to, do not answer. Shake your head, but do not answer." Mei-Yin performed the movement to show Hok-Ling that she understood. "Yes. Good. Now you must go. Walk quickly, and step onto the boat as if you own it. If you don't, you will raise suspicion. Do you understand?"

"Yes."

"Go directly, then. Inside you will find a passenger compartment. There are many wooden benches. Sit on one of them and pretend to sleep. When the boat lands, walk quickly to the shore and wait for me behind the first shed you come to. It will be on the left."

"The first shed on the left," she repeated, nodding.

"Go! Quickly!"

Hok-Ling watched her venture bravely down the road and move into the open. He followed a few steps behind, darting from one cover to another, crouching here and there in the black, spotted underbrush, disappearing behind oily barrels, or piles of refuse. He glanced warily behind them for others on the road. Just as she reached the landward edge of the dock, Mei-Yin turned to face Hok-Ling, wanting nothing more than to see him once in the enhanced light. But he had crouched very low, hiding his face in the shadow of a dense bush. She could not see him as he spoke to her in a whisper.

"Go, Mei-Yin. Quickly." Mei-Yin tried to smile, but swallowed back tears instead. She turned and walked with exaggerated steps out onto the dock. Once again, she was required to board a vessel disguised as a man.

As he watched her, Hok-Ling felt his heart pounding at the base of his neck, and he could not breathe in the tiny spaces of time it provided. Oh, Great One! he pleaded. Oh, Great One! Do not let them see her! He watched her move along the starboard companionway and disappear through the door of the passenger compartment.

Ten minutes later, Hok-Ling pulled himself over the railing on the port side, where the *Henry Villard's* long, graceful sheer dipped to within two feet of the surface of the water. He stumbled, exhausted, along the port gangway, then ducked into a shadowy crevice near an open storage locker. After a moment's respite, he stepped out again. He tiptoed silently toward the window of the passenger compartment and peeked in at its edge. Mei-Yin and the man they had seen moments earlier on the road were alone in the cabin. It is good that this is the last boat, Hok-Ling thought. Mei-Yin sat in the center of a polished mahogany bench, her head bowed, her eyes closed, her legs crossed at the ankles. Her back was to the other.

Her features were obscured in the penumbra of a lantern that burned low over her head. It was the only light in the cabin. Its feeble flame danced and threatened to go out in the draught from the open doors. The man in the derby got up to close the doors and Hok-Ling took a step back, pressing himself hard against the cabin wall. When it was safe to do so, he again peered through the window at Mei-Yin. Her arms were folded and she held them high against her breasts. She pretended to sleep, but her tongue dabbed incessantly at the bulge on her lip, and in the short while that he watched she winced a half dozen times.

Hok-Ling stepped away, unable to believe any of this was happening. He stood for a minute staring down at the water, unseeing, but a noise on deck roused him. He quickly climbed up the side of the vessel to the quarterdeck, and from there he made his way to the flat roof of the crew's cabin. The *Henry Villard's* long, black smokestack rose up out of the center of this cabin. Hok-Ling lay on his back beside it, for there was a warmth radiating there. And when the *Henry Villard* began to move, he felt the pulse of the great, distended billows of smoke racing past him.

For several minutes, he could not think, could not fix his concentration on a single idea, for ideas beyond number were leaping into flight like startled birds flushed from hiding. He turned one way and then another, as though seeking a more comfortable position, but it was rather to avoid thinking at all that he did so. At last, he lay back again. His mind reeled. With a forearm slung over his forehead, he gazed up unseeing at the hissing white-gray plume that raced sternward, at the stars, frozen and indifferent, beyond the stack. Did this really happen? he asked himself at last. No, it couldn't have. It couldn't have! The wind that tossed the wet cuffs of his trousers and shook his dripping shirt sleeves freshened with the ship's steady advance. His body trembled with cold. How could she have come? I couldn't have killed him. Could I? Was it him? Was it the green coat? Yes, it had to have been! There was the same gold star on his shirt. Oh, Great Spirit, No! And Mei-Yin? Is it really her? Is she really here, on this boat, below me now? How could this be? It can't be! This is impossible!

And the rush of the wind filled his ears.

But it is her! I know it. How did she get here? Why is she . . . ? Who would've . . . ? Suddenly, Hok-Ling covered his face with his hands. He let out a terrible cry, one that he could not stifle completely. Ahhheeee! She is defiled! He raped her! The demon green coat raped her!

* * *

Moments before the *Henry Villard* docked at Hope, timed to synchronize with the two blasts of its whistle, Hok-Ling sprinted and jumped into the water from the roof of the crew's cabin. He disappeared beneath the surface and did not reappear for nearly a minute and a half. When he surfaced, he was beyond the range of the deck lights, and only twenty feet from shore. It was he who waited for Mei-Yin behind the shed, instead of the other way around.

He led her along a deserted stretch of boulder-strewn lake-shore to a point approximately a quarter mile south of the Chinese encampment. He was silent during this time. She walked several paces behind him. At no time did he turn or slacken his pace, although he knew from the sound of it that she stumbled twice over the loose rocks, trying to keep up. When at last he did stop, he looked around, but only long enough to see that the fires in the camp were out of sight. Then he turned back and set off up a short, steep embankment. Soon he disappeared into the woods. Mei-Yin redoubled her effort to keep up, clawing the embankment with her tiny hands, grimacing but otherwise ignoring the intense pain between her legs, in her shoulders and chest, deep in her left thigh, over her face, and at the back of her head.

She ran to catch up with him. A few moments later, she stepped onto a dusty wagon road and found Hok-Ling waiting there. Hok-Ling crossed the road and pointed into a ghostly stand of young cottonwoods. "In here," he whispered anxiously. Mei-Yin understood. She moved past him and stepped down off the shoulder of the road into a low, flat area where dozens of slender, leafy trees flourished. Her careful steps carried her between their outstretched limbs and over a carpet of dry, crisp leaves, until at last she found a suitable place and sank to the ground in a squatting position. She did not look up to see if she might still be able to see Hok-Ling on the road, but bowed her head and waited for him to speak through the darkness. "I will find a tent and some food," he said. "I will be back." Still she did not look up or speak. A moment later she was listening to his fading footsteps on the road.

Despite her best efforts to be brave, Mei-Yin felt the onset of a sudden and indescribable terror. She heard noises. Was there something there? Someone? She wanted to scream, but her heart began to thrash against the walls of her chest, and for a time she could not breathe. She started to rise up, as though she must spring animal-like from this black, unfamiliar place or be killed at once, but then she checked herself and by a force of will resumed her squatting position. Think of something else, she commanded herself, closing her eyes tight. She held on to the trunk of a small tree beside her. The world was spinning. Think of something else. A moment later, she rolled forward onto her hands and knees and wretched violently. Although her stomach was empty, she continued this for two minutes. When it was over she crawled away and lay on her side holding her knees. Tears streaked across the bridge of her nose reaching her left temple before dripping onto the forest floor.

Now she heard nothing but the sound of her own mouth-breathing. It was raspy and ragged at first, but slowed bit by bit until, five minutes on, with one deep breath, and then a second, she inhaled through her nose the forest smells again, the redolent cottonwood, the loamy soil, the pine, fir, and cedar. Sniffing once, she began to assess her situation in the quiet of her intellect. I should not have come here, is that it? But what kind of life would I have had if I hadn't? If I had gone away with the water carrier to pay my father's gambling debt? This man would have raped me, too—raped me again and again, for I would never have given myself to him willingly. Never! For all these years my father has known that I have been promised to Hok-Ling and that my heart is with him. I think the water carrier might have killed me, or had me killed. Yes, I'm sure of it. I would be dead by now! So I would never have seen Hok-Ling again. At least now I can say I have seen him—with my own eyes. Oh, but Hok-Ling has killed the demon who raped me. What if he's caught? They'll kill him! Surely they will! Why did he have to be there tonight? Why did he have to see this? Why?

Mei-Yin began to construct a different ending in her mind. It was not Hok-Ling who killed her attacker. It was she. When her assailant approached in his nakedness and reached for her, she imagined herself deftly pulling herself free and scrambling for her bag and the weapon inside. She knew exactly where it was. She pulled it out cleanly as he approached. As he lunged for her, she saw herself lunging at him with even greater force and single-mindedness. The blade, now an extension of her clenched fist, would sink smoothly and unmistakably to the center of its target. She would marvel at her surpassing, life-affirming power and strength. His arms would droop to his sides and then she would let out a terrible growl of insatiable rage. She would thrust the knife into his bulbous abdomen again and again. Stepping back momentarily, she would see that his penis had begun to weaken. She'd hold the blood-stained knife up to his disbelieving eyes and then lower it, making sure his eyes met hers. "You will not defile me, you devil!" she would cry, spitting every word. And then, plunging the knife into the side of his neck, she would kill him with the cool efficiency of an executioner.

She cherished this version and replayed it over and over in her mind. Its only changes were toward greater redemptive violence on her part. She took a perverse comfort in the evolving story.

A half hour later, Hok-Ling returned with a tent and blankets and a generous amount of food and water that he carried in a wheelbarrow. He called for Mei-Yin as he approached beneath the stars, and she emerged on the road several hundred feet ahead of him. His heart swelled and thumped ponderously when her dim, once familiar outline first came into view. Yet with each step he told himself in ever firmer tones to deny all feeling and thought about her, about her presence, about everything that had happened or seemed to have happened since he awoke lying in the weeds behind Anthony's Lockers. In a word, he did not trust himself to feel or think anything further on this day, and then, too, the question had crossed his mind, "How much of this will be real in the morning?"

Now they walked silently up the hill until they reached an old abandoned mining road. It climbed further into the pines above the ridge, and would lead eventually to a series of small, weary, black holes gouged into the granite near the top of the mountain. Hok-Ling put his weight into the work of pushing the wheelbarrow up the road. He tried not to think about the thing that would not leave his mind, the scene below the bridge. Mei-Yin's footsteps sounded lightly behind him.

When they had gone a few hundred yards, the road switched back and began to ascend much more steeply. Hok-Ling lowered his head and gave the barrow a mighty push. His sore hams and feet commenced to run over the rough ground, but the weight of the wheelbarrow seemed to double in his hands. He could not advance it at a run, perhaps not at all. His feet slipped. The wheelbarrow teetered. He struggled to right it, cursing under his breath. He had nearly ground to a stop when he lowered his head again and gave another thrust. The wheelbarrow lurched forward. Once again, he tried to run, but this time he did not gain more than a few feet before he came to a stop. He leaned over the handles, exhausted. His lungs burned. I will wait here a moment, he said to himself.

Suddenly the wheelbarrow began to inch forward in his hands. He looked up. In front of him, ghost-like in the dim light of the stars, he saw the woman's back, her queue, her small, pale hand reaching back, squeezing the edge of the wheelbarrow. She was nearly doubled over in front of him, facing forward. Hok-Ling at once redoubled his effort—pushed with all his might. The wheelbarrow moved slowly but certainly up the hill. Its wheel wobbled over the stones and gullies in the road.

Hok-Ling pulled back on the handles when they had gained the top of the hill. "Over there," he said. He nodded toward a clearing in the distance. Mei-Yin straightened. She felt a soreness across her back such as she had never felt before. Struggling to catch her breath, she stepped to the edge of the road. She stood for a minute or two with her back to Hok-Ling, looking down at the lake, a ghostly sheen stretching out for miles, and at the fires in the Chinese camp below, which were just visible above an intervening ridgeline. Finally, she looked up at the stars. She wiped her brow with her sleeve, and turned back to Hok-Ling.

This is so difficult for you! she thought, seeing his outline against the dark, mottled mountainside. Look at you! You do not even have three words to say to me. I am Mei-Yin. Do you remember me? You stand there so stiff! Can't you say anything, Hok-Ling? Can't you speak to me? Even if it is to curse me?

But Hok-Ling did not speak. He pushed the wheelbarrow past her, over the shoulder of the road, and onto a narrow deer path that traversed the steep hillside and led, eventually, down to a remote clearing below. Mei-Yin frowned and wondered that he did not whistle to himself. She followed him, fighting the need to cry again.

After putting up the small bivouac tent, he placed the blankets and larder inside, and set two earthenware jugs of water just beyond the flaps. Mumbling to himself, he looked around to see what else he might do. Mei-Yin slipped around him and disappeared into the tent.

"Where are you?"

"In here," she answered.

"Oh." Hok-Ling spun around. He began to lower himself in front of the opening.

"I will be all right here," Mei-Yin said miserably.

Hok-Ling thought for a moment, then said, "You must forgive me, Mei-Yin. I cannot digest all of this—your being here, what has happened this night. I cannot think straight. Perhaps tomorrow I will wake up and none of this will . . . "

He checked himself. There was no sound inside the tent. "Well, never mind," he concluded. For several minutes he sat squatting on his heels, his head resting in his hand.

"Listen to me, Mei-Yin," he said at last, rising to his feet. "You must do exactly as I say. Tomorrow afternoon, just before sunset, walk into the camp along the road we have just taken. Do you understand? Do not be frightened. Ask for Soo-Kwan. Remember that name. You will be told that Soo-Kwan is encamped with the bridge engineers at Holiday Creek, and that he will not return for several days. Tell whoever you speak to that you are Soo-Kwan's sister, and that two months ago—do you understand, *two months ago*—you came to the Gold Mountain to join him, to labor as a wash woman and seamstress in his camp. He has been uncertain of your safety, so he has required you to camp up here, alone and unannounced, for the last three weeks. Do you see? Next, ask for me. Tell them you know of me from correspondence received by your family. I will be summoned as soon as I return from the field. At that time, I will make it known to all that I have taken charge of you and will help you situate a more convenient distance from the camp. Do you see? All of the men will be warned against disturbing you. I will send a message to Soo-Kwan by way of the provisioners. He will gladly uphold the ruse on his return. But remember, you have been on Gold Mountain two months, and you have been here, hiding, for three weeks."

Hok-Ling waited for some response, but none came. "Did you hear me, Mei-Yin?" he asked impatiently.

A quiet sniffle sounded in the tent. "Yes. Of course. I will do as you say."

* * *

It was well past 1:00 a.m. when he stepped from the old mining road onto the main wagon road and turned toward the camp. The wheelbarrow glided easily before him and gave no trouble, for it carried only his silk hat and the empty mail bag—folded again. He quickened his pace, readily following the road's strangely luminous track through the forest. A fog-like trail of dust rose up behind him. He stopped for a moment on a hillock at the edge of the camp. Black, lumpy, twisted mounds of humanity were spread over the trampled ground before him, crimped and prone and supine, weary even in sleep. The silence and the cold seemed to hover above the coolies, to lord over them, to reduce them. They were helpless against the night, and the night seemed intent upon them.

He raised then quickly dismantled the idea of pitying them. Their inaction irritated him. Even the fires among them were flameless and spent. Here and there embers gave off ash-muffled pops, but otherwise silence reigned. The tents and shacks were blotches on the landscape, ruinous of it, and they seemed to brew stale odors. For a moment, he hated them all. Hated them for their lowliness—stillness. They turned his stomach, and he may have forgotten that he was Chinese himself, for he hated all Chinese. That was easy here. Separated from them by the day's events, he could not remember them, did not know their difficulties in this place. And worse, it seemed as if he had never known them, that he was a stranger here and would never again feel as they felt. No, he was someone larger, greater than they. His desperation—unlike theirs—was a fuel, bright with burgeoning flames, and his mind raced—as he knew theirs never would—through a cross-fire of hopelessness and hope, of self-doubt and self-exaltation. He was alive! He sensed a power about himself that horrified him.

The whoosh of an owl passing close overhead left him seeing the darkened landscape again. He picked his way carefully
over the rough ground and left the wheelbarrow by a felled tree
where firewood had been freshly cut and stacked. With the mail
satchel and his skullcap in hand, he descended into the sleeping
camp. He passed the first clearing and crossed the footbridge
at Gold Creek without hearing its gurgle or smelling the dank,
organic perfumes that flow perpetually on a rivulet of cold air
above it. He was suddenly very tired. Half-running and zigzag-
ging around obstacles, he emerged from a drapery of willow
shoots and stopped suddenly at the sight of a campfire burning
brilliantly in front of his shack. There were four men squatted
about the fire, staring in on it, with hands clasped about their
knees. The one facing Hok-Ling was Ho Ying-Chiao. His face
glowed like the full moon, and the other three were set about so
that their faces were quarter moons in the distance. He did not
recognize them.

The flickering light threw shadows against Hok-Ling as
he approached. Ho Ying-Chiao stared absently at the glowing
hollow in the center of the fire until Hok-Ling came to stop a
few feet away. When he looked up, Hok-Ling knew that the
crew boss had watched every step of his approach. "You have
come back, Hok-Ling," said Ho Ying-Chiao ingenuously, "and
thus proven my friend Wah Sang a luckless gambler." Ho Ying-
Chiao looked up, but the mocking glint in his eyes quickly
vanished. "What's happened to you?"

Hok-Ling ignored the tired smiles that lingered on the
faces of Ho Ying-Chiao's companions. "Does your conscience
not permit you to sleep these days, Ying-Chiao? Or are you here
with a purpose?" Hok-Ling stepped closer to the fire, then, realizing the state of his clothing, he withdrew.

Ho Ying-Chiao frowned at Hok-Ling's evasiveness. "My
purpose should be obvious to you," he growled. "Where is
Master Keating's mail?" Ho Ying-Chiao lifted a hand from his
knees and pointed to the empty bag dangling from Hok-Ling's

hand. The other three heads turned, and the firelight flickered in the wet corners of their eyes.

Hok-Ling, too, looked down at the burlap bag as if to see it for the first time. He lifted it in both hands, and it drooped over his outstretched arms like a lifeless body. Then, without approaching, he squatted over the dirt and ceremoniously laid the bag on the ground. He remained there in a squatting position, pointing to it frequently as he told Ho Ying-Chiao of the confrontation with the boys in Sandpoint. The sheriff was never mentioned, nor Mei-Yin, of course. It was all the ruffian boys— eight of them, with sticks and clubs, as he told it.

When he finished, Ho Ying-Chiao looked up from the fire as if surprised, then lowered his eyes and poked gently at the fire with the end of a long stick. "And did these boys throw you into the lake when they had finished with you?" he asked.

Hok-Ling looked down to see bits of bottom weed clinging to his pants. He struggled to think of another explanation, but, when none occurred to him he was compelled to answer, "Yes. Exactly. They took me for dead, or they hoped I would drown. I do not know." He paused, then added with a smile, "But the water only revived me."

"Mmm. Yes, I see," said Ho Ying-Chiao softly still without looking up. The other three watched Ho Ying-Chiao, and adopted his unruffled manner. One set his chin over his right knee and closed his eyes as if to sleep. He opened them abruptly and closed them again, startled by Ho Ying-Chiao's next words. "It is true, then? You have no mail for Master Keating?"

"No. As I have spoken—"

"Yes," muttered Ho Ying-Chiao, interrupting. "I heard you." He continued to poke at the fire, and the flames grew higher. "I was afraid of this. When you failed to return with the mail by the noon boat, I sent Yee Chun-Wah here into town to find you." One of the men nodded at the rejuvenated fire. Hok-Ling didn't recognize him. Ho Ying-Chiao continued, "He spent hours looking for you, but you were nowhere to be found."

"I had been beaten . . . "

"As you say."

"Then you will explain this to Master Keating? I cannot go back there. It is unsafe."

Ho Ying-Chiao studied Hok-Ling over the dancing flames. His yellow teeth shone dully between thin dark lips. He smiled, and then the smile vanished, and he spoke with gloom and resignation. "I will tell him whatever you wish. But you have lost face, Hok-Ling, and I, too . . . I, too, am disgraced by your failure." Hok-Ling looked up sensing the threat in the crew boss's tone. "What will come of you is uncertain, but, as the heavens control your fate, perhaps it will be made good, with prayer. I, on the other hand, am less fortunate. It is my unhappy lot to answer directly to Master Keating, up there." He nodded toward the dark offices above the camp. "I have never failed him before, and it troubles me that my failure this day has been assured so many miles away in my absence. What punishment do I face, Hok-Ling?"

Hok-Ling did not answer despite Ho Ying-Chiao's long, questioning gaze. The fire popped loudly and sent a cluster of sparks spinning high over Hok-Ling's shack. Ho Ying-Chiao began to smile awkwardly. "I must have your queue, Hok-Ling. Does this surprise you? I will take it with the empty mail bag and lay them both before the master. I will, of course, explain to him that among the Han this is a sign that one has lost face—or worse. He will know of your failure. But I will tell him of the beating, just as you have described it."

Hok-Ling's eyes grew wide, and the heat of the fire seemed to scorch them. "Is my honor lost this day, Ying-Chiao? Do I count for no more than a week's mail received a day late? Can it not be retrieved tomorrow, by another coolie?—or by a demon?"

"That is insignificant," sputtered Ho Ying-Chiao angrily. "Tomorrow will be guided by tomorrow's thoughts!" The crew boss's brows knitted. "You speak of *your* honor, Hok-Ling. This surprises me. Why would a Tang person speak in such terms?

Is it not the honor of your family and your clan that matters? *Humph!* In any case, you cannot undo your failure. You have no value to me—none!—but your duty is only to your employer." He shook his head, then smiled into the fire. "It is a strange thing, but you may have unwittingly done yourself a great favor." His eyes flashed up again, meeting Hok-Ling's glare. "The men have threatened to strike on your behalf—did you know this?—and Master Keating is very worried. He gave you this assignment for only one reason, to curry favor with them. Now that you have failed, and have been beaten in town, he will most assuredly take pity on you and arrange for the return of your money—assuming he has it, I mean. And I suspect that he will assist in securing your voucher, too. Now you can return to the Middle Kingdom. Is that not ironic?" Hok-Ling didn't answer. Ho Ying-Chiao's eyes flicked to the men squatting beside him. "I have brought them here to ensure that I will leave with your hair."

The three accomplices sprang to their feet and quickly surrounded Hok-Ling, leaving the fire and Ho Ying-Chiao unobstructed in front of him. Hok-Ling stood up abruptly, and the three men inched closer to him. The muscles of his arms and legs twitched and went soft again, and prickled with soreness. Ho Ying-Chiao produced a gold-bladed knife from his sleeve and stood up.

"Save your strength, Ying-Chiao," cried Hok-Ling. He stepped toward the fire and extended his open palm through its heat. Ho Ying-Chiao froze. Uncertainty clouded his eyes. He turned his head slightly as if to measure some part of Hok-Ling he hadn't seen before. "Yes. Give it to me! Come!" snapped Hok-Ling impatiently.

The knife went slowly into Hok-Ling's hand. He turned it and its blade flashed with the tongues of fire that licked the air beneath it. He found a queer comfort in the fact that the blade was golden. This was much different than the other knife— lighter, stouter at the handle, but shorter-bladed. This strange reassurance lingered in Hok-Ling even as he returned the knife to Ho Ying-Chiao with one hand and held out his slender coiled queue in the other.

* * *

Word of the arrival of Soo-Kwan's sister spread quickly among the Chinese at Hope, generating a fervor. Day and night, lonely and inquisitive men came in search of Soo-Kwan, to bribe him, or to cajole him with talk of their pedigree and family wealth. "She would be most fortunate to marry me," they would say, "for indeed, I would have the pick of much wealthier women—women of my own station—back in the Middle Kingdom. So, what is your answer, Soo-Kwan?" Others babbled accounts of dreamed encounters with Mei-Yin, insisting that these were prelibations of Buddha's will. "Will you defy Buddha, Soo-Kwan?" they would ask breathlessly. Always, he told them she was his sister from Kwangchow. She had come at his invitation and under his promise of protection. She had remained hidden for three weeks at his demand. She was betrothed to the son of a Chinese merchant in San Francisco and would be married within the year. Now that he had allowed her to enter the camp, she would live nearby and do laundry and seamstress work at a fair price. Any man who touched her would plead for a thousand different ways to die.

Hok-Ling grew used to Soo-Kwan's scowls and sidelong glances. "Will you ever forgive me?" he would ask, unable to control a sheepish grin. Soo-Kwan would answer ruefully, stretching his collar down to expose the scar left by Sheriff Langston's whip on the day of their arrival in Sandpoint. "Is the blemish gone, my friend?" Soo-Kwan knew, as did Hok-Ling, that the scar was permanent, and thus Soo-Kwan viewed his indebtedness to Hok-Ling as everlasting. "But tell me, Hok-Ling," Soo-Kwan would add. "Why do you grow so quiet when the woman is mentioned? Why do you not speak of her yourself?"

Mei-Yin passed through the camp each morning in quick, short steps, stopping to pick up the soiled and torn clothing left by the men outside the entrances to their dwellings. Each pile was marked with stones in the manner prescribed by Soo-Kwan: one stone on top of the pile meant "clean only," two stones meant "mend only," and two stones stacked one on top of the other in front of the pile meant "clean *and* mend."

With her eyes to the ground, Mei-Yin went about her business, ignoring the stares of the men around her and speaking to no one. No doubt she would have chosen to wait until all the men had gone from the camp, were it not for the fact that Hok-Ling had not come to her since the first day. Despite her disappointment, she'd told herself at first that this was all right—"he is afraid, after all. He needs time to think"—but one day's absence had become five, and five, eight. She could wait no longer. A terrible wretchedness—a mingling of guilt, shame, anger, and fear—scratched at her heart. I must see him, she told herself at last. I must make him see me! Surely, he needs only to look at me again, to look into my eyes, and then he'll remember—won't he? Yes, of course, he'll remember all that we had planned, all that we had hoped for! He'll see that everything can be made right.

She walked unmolested through the camp, carrying the men's clothing in two large canvas bags. Although she was seldom spoken to, she was received warmly by the men there. They turned solemn or playful or longing eyes on her, and when she passed, their eyes held these expressions so that the men giggled and were uncomfortable at the sight of one another. Being ill at ease, they spoke up, remembering something of their work or a word of old news—something beside the point—until finally, eventually, and always they spoke of Mei-Yin and shook their heads. "Did you smell her? What a marvelous rose she is! Did you see her handsome figure? She tries to hide it. She smiled at me! Did you see?"

14

Jason McQuade lifted the second page and blew against the shiny scrawl of his signature. He read the letter over.

July 25, 1882
Sandpoint, I. T.

Dear Bernie,

My pleasure at receiving yours of June 20 is in no way reflected by this delay. If I have an excuse, it lies somewhere between the number of questions you asked—a few of them literate—and how busy I've been since becoming a full-fledged attorney. (Yes, from now on, when you write "Esquire" after my name, it won't do for humor. I shall continue to write "M.D." after your name, however. Let the boys in the mail room at The Hartford figure it out. If it dawns on them that it means "Most Demented," I shall reward them with a bottle of Jameson.)

I'm pleased to hear about you and Miss Sally Williston. You've always had a hankering for Sally, whereas I've labored under the unshakable knowledge that she could do much better. But seriously, heartfelt congratulations, Bernie.

Here are a few answers to the questions you've put to me in the style of a Boston police examiner:

(1) Yes, as mentioned, I've finished my studies with "Uncle Emory"—am now admitted to the territorial bar.

(2) Yes, I like the work. He's a fine boss and a great man, as you know.

(3) He's doing quite well.

(4) No, he hasn't mentioned anything to me about coming out to Boston this fall.

(5) My health is excellent. Mrs. Stewart, with whom I board, is a superb cook. You'd like her. She reminds me a great deal of your Aunt Joyce. Keeps an excellent garden.

(6) No, I don't hear from my father. I've written a letter or two—maybe more. Mother writes, of course.

(7) Yes, still seeing Miss Langston on occasion.

There's unpleasant news on that front, by the way, and I might as well tell you about it. Her father, the local sheriff, was found stabbed to death last week under one of our bridges. Who did it, or why, is a mystery. No witnesses have come forward. The town's in an uproar. Esther, as you can imagine, is completely inconsolable. She lost her mother last year to consumption, and the sheriff had pretty much lost himself in the bottle since.

I hate to close on bad news, but must get back to work, old friend. Give my best to Sally and to any of the old boot-lickers from the rowing team that you run into.

Anticipating your next correspondence, I
remain
Your friend in spite of it all,
Jason

He had carefully replaced the cork on the ink bottle and was wiping the nib when Emory Morse entered the office. "Good morning, Emory."

"Yes, indeed! A very good morning. Better than you think!"

"Oh?"

Tyler Forbes walked in behind Emory. Forbes, the other attorney in town, was a man in his early forties, bald on top of his head, with pink, delicate-looking skin and large, quizzical eyes. He wore thick silver-rimmed glasses that magnified his blue orbs indelicately. His face was flushed as he turned to shut the door with care, as though trying to protect someone's sleep.

"What's up?" Jason asked.

"We got him!" Emory exclaimed. "Just this morning." Forbes walked to the coat tree and peeled his coat off as if it were on fire. His demeanor was unusually intense and uneven. Emory left his coat on. "What do you think of that?"

"Who? The killer?"

Forbes dropped into Emory's swivel chair. "A Chinaman." He looked at Emory. "It was one of the Chinamen all along," he chuckled, turning and stacking his feet over the window sill.

Jason's mouth fell open. "A *Chinese*? Are you *sure*?"

Emory let his bushy gray eyebrows rise up and nodded.

"Who is he?" Jason asked.

"A fella named Wong Hok-Ling. He's over at the jail right now."

"Damn," sputtered Jason excitedly. He looked at Forbes, then Emory. "*God*damn. You fellas did it! How . . . ?"

"There was a bunch of us. Deputy Lambert arrested him."

"How'd you figure it out? And why'd this guy do it?"

Emory strolled past him and sat thoughtfully on the corner of the reading table. He propped one foot on the edge of a Windsor chair in which Jason had logged countless hours, day and night, over the past two and a half years. "The sheriff and a bunch of boys beat him up pretty good—kind of a one-sided fight, I guess." Emory looked at Forbes for confirmation. "Left him for dead, damn near."

"Yup," nodded Forbes. He removed his glasses and had a good look at them. "The railroad sent one o' their Orientals into town to pick up the mail. It was this fella. They knocked him unconscious and when he came to, he went after Langston."

Emory stared soberly at Jason. "We talked to Keating this morning. He's the superintendent out there at Hope."

"Right," Jason nodded.

"This Hok-Ling came back on the last boat Tuesday night, four or five hours late, *without* the mail. One of his crew bosses showed up first thing the next morning holding the empty mail pouch in one hand and this fella's pigtail in the other, asking for forgiveness, that sort of thing. According to Keating, the Chinese'll cut those things off as a punishment."

"What? You mean the pigtail? Did Keating keep it?"

"No. I don't know." Emory paused. "What does that matter?"

Jason shrugged. "Probably doesn't. Just curious." Jason sat quietly, staring at the toe of Emory's boot. His mind travelled back to the afternoon of the Chinese procession. He remembered the expression of horror that came over Esther's face when she saw her father's brutality—his tortuous struggle to bring horse and whip to bear on a defenseless man. They hadn't spoken of it since. "I suppose I oughta tell Esther," he added at last. "I don't know. It may do her more harm than good right now."

"Why's that?" exclaimed Emory, surprised. "Hell, she'd want to know. You want me to tell her?" Jason looked up, struck by Emory's passion, but his thoughts were still mostly in the past. "I don't mind," Emory added.

"No. That's all right. I'll do it."

* * *

Mei-Yin was awakened after midnight by the sound of approaching footsteps. "Mei-Yin! Mei-Yin, are you there? It's us, Soo-Kwan and Dak-Wah."

"Yes. Just a minute," she replied, reaching over to place the knife back in the corner of the tent. She stepped out into the moonlight, wrapped in a blanket. "What is it?" she asked, holding her chin up to the cold air and squinting drowsily.

Dak-Wah answered, "It is bad news. Very bad."

Mei-Yin's eyes opened wide. "Tell me!"

"The demons have taken Hok-Ling, arrested him," said Dak-Wah. They came to our work site this morning. They're accusing him of killing a green coat . . . at least that's the rumor that quickly spread. I got there as it was happening. I saw them shackle him and place him in the back of a wagon. I went over to him but there was nothing I could do."

She had covered her mouth with her hand, and from that point on she saw the two men dimly, through sparkling, moon-lit tears.

Dak-Wah continued. "He told me that I was to tell you of his arrest, and to instruct you of his most earnest demands. Therefore please listen. You are to say nothing and do nothing concerning him. You are to remain here as Soo-Kwan's sister in name until you have saved passage for your return to the Middle Kingdom. Then you are to leave at once." Mei-Yin clamped down on her lower lip painfully. "You are to marry or be sold to a master according to the wishes of your father, as it should b—" Dak-Wah stopped and recoiled slightly. "What? Why do you look at me this way? This is what Hok-Ling has instructed," he exclaimed.

"I don't believe you!" Mei-Yin croaked, her voice breaking. She turned away and covered her face with her hand and a cor-ner of the blanket. When she turned back, she spoke as one who herself has brought a message. "He is afraid. He's trying to protect me—don't you understand?"

"What do you mean?" Soo-Kwan and Dak-Wah asked at once.

"I . . . I don't know what I mean . . . but I know it's true. We must help Hok-Ling."

Dak-Wah spread his hands. "What can we do? They've taken him. We don't know where he is. He's probably in jail, or . . . " He stopped himself mid-sentence and looked down.

"There must be something," Mei-Yin cried. She looked up toward the top of Miner's Mountain, to the dark line of trees poised beneath the Milky Way. A falling star flashed and disappeared in an instant followed by another. "Ho Ying-Chiao!" she cried at last. "We must ask Ho Ying-Chiao to help him. He speaks English. He can help Hok-Ling explain his innocence—that he didn't kill the green coat. Without him, Hok-Ling is helpless."

Soo-Kwan spoke from another, more distant thought. "Ying-Chiao is half devil himself. Before we came here, in late spring, he stole Hok-Ling's money. This was after Hok-Ling had asked the railroad for his voucher to return to the Middle Kingdom. Master Keating put him up to it, we're sure of it."

Mei-Yin held in one bittersweet instant the image of Hok-Ling trying to get his voucher, trying to return to her, but the image lacked verisimilitude and vanished as her breath caught in the chill air.

"It is therefore unlikely that Ying-Chiao will do anything," Soo-Kwan continued.

"What's that?" Mei-Yin asked, collecting herself. "How much money?"

"According to Hok-Ling, it was $500," said Dak-Wah. "Enough for passage and more."

"Did you look for it?" asked Mei-Yin.

"Yes, but he doesn't have it," insisted Soo-Kwan. "We've looked everywhere. We looked again after the camp moved here. Either he gave it to Master Keating, or he sent it home to his family."

Oh, he will need money for bribes, Mei-Yin thought touching her fingers to her lips. "We must look again," she blurted, facing Dak-Wah and then Soo-Kwan. "We must! He will need this money to bribe the judge, don't you see?"

"But Hok-Ling told me that you were to—"

"No!" cried Mei-Yin. She hesitated, softened her tone. "I know he said that, Dak-Wah, but he didn't mean it. You must believe me." Then she said as if to herself, "Ho Ying-Chiao has Hok-Ling's money. I know he does." After a few seconds, Mei-Yin looked up at Soo-Kwan and Dak-Wah. "We must do more. We must prepare an alibi for Hok-Ling. When do they say the green coat was killed? Was it early in the day? Was it late?"

"According to the story going around, it was in the evening on the day Hok-Ling went into town to get the mail," replied Dak-Wah. "Why?"

"Listen. We must say that Hok-Ling returned on an early boat. That . . . that he came back here because he'd failed to get the mail—or he'd lost it! Yes! It was taken from him by a white devil, so he took an early boat back and spent the afternoon here with us . . . with me."

The embers outside Mei-Yin's tent were stirred and rekindled and the three squatted before the fire. Mei-Yin made tea. What plans could be forged were. By sunrise Mei-Yin lay awake in her tent, and Soo-Kwan and Dak-Wah were back in their shack, asleep in their places.

* * *

Mei-Yin turned back to Ho Ying-Chiao emphatically. "You must believe me!" she pleaded softly, so as not to be heard by the men nearby. "It is I who is at fault. This man Hok-Ling was with me on the day the green coat was killed. I met Hok-Ling on the beach. He was very discouraged—this was about noon or one o'clock. He'd come back from town, but had had the railroad's mail stolen. He didn't know what to do. I brought him to my tent and made tea so that he could think. He was afraid of what you would say. He was ashamed. Hok-Ling is a kind man. He expressed great concern that you might lose face because of his failure . . . " She watched Ho Ying-Chiao's expression as he sat rubbing an oil-soaked cloth over the heel of his boot. He would not look up. "This is the day the green coat was killed," she added. "This is why he couldn't account for his whereabouts. He was with me, you see, all afternoon."

"Young woman, you waste my time!" Ho Ying-Chiao cried. He spit into the mound of black ashes where countless fires had been set. "What you say is nonsense. Besides, there is nothing I can do. Tell Soo-Kwan he should not send a woman to do his bidding! Now go about your business. Leave me alone."

"But you must help him!" Mei-Yin cried, a little too loudly. A few men turned, and she avoided their stares. She shielded her mouth with her hand. "He cannot speak their language as you do. He cannot help himself."

"Go at once, I tell you!"

"But—"

"Go!"

With a pale face, she rose slowly, bowed, and started off.

The silence that Ho Ying-Chiao demanded left him alone with his thoughts. He stopped oiling and watched Mei-Yin's departure, her short, rapid steps. She seemed to wipe tears from her eyes. He spit again into the ash heap then looked down at his wiggling toes. "I can feel the change of season coming," he muttered to himself.

* * *

The hoo-hooing of an owl startled Soo-Kwan and drew his eyes to a silvery vein of moonlight that streamed through the branches of a cottonwood tree above Ho Ying-Chiao's tent. Crouching in the dry, trampled grass, he made sure nothing human moved around him then scampered on hands and knees to the far corner of the tent. He looked up at the brightly lit window of the railroad office. A figured passed inside. Ho Ying-Chiao is still meeting with them, he thought. He looked out at the dim outline of the camp and the ashy glow of spent fires. His heart was pounding in his ears as he sat back again.

He listened to the sounds of Dak-Wah's groping inside: clothes and bedding being turned and probed, boxes moved, a case opened, its effects jostled. A moment later, he plunged toward the flaps. "What're you doing in there? Hurry up!"

"I can't find it," Dak-Wah whimpered. The noise of his searching continued.

Soo-Kwan thought of going in to help. No, one of them had to be on the lookout for Ho Ying-Chiao's return. He looked up at the moon and sighed. Had there ever been a more still night, he wondered? Hmmm. There is the smell of dew already. It is very late.

"Wait. I've found something," whispered Dak-Wah. Soo-Kwan spun around and threw open the flap. The rippling of paper emanated from the darkness. A moment later Dak-Wah's large form appeared, crawling out into the moonlight. He stood up and looked down at a white envelope in his hand. He fingered the money inside. "Yes. This must be it," he whispered.

He caught Soo-Kwan's approving stare, and bobbed his eyebrows in salute. Soo-Kwan smiled and slapped him on the back. "Good job! Now let's get out of here!"

* * *

The deputy's shadow swept across the white plaster wall opposite the cell door. It was a morose, elongated shadow, barely human in form, with an overlarge head and a great, protruding nose. It leaned forward at an impossible angle, then shrank and fell toward the ground. Through the lighted doorway came noises of monotony and routine, a rustling of papers and the infrequent opening and closing of a desk drawer. There was, for a time, a spirited whistling of a medley of tunes—Yankee Doodle, Dixie, Camp Town Races—and when these were finished, the deputy called out in a seriocomic voice, "ev-ery-body!" and he began whistling them again, alone. When he quit there was a long spell of silence.

Hok-Ling sat forward on the wooden frame of the bed, holding a tattered blue blanket about his neck. The smell of his own urine and feces rose from a bucket in the corner of the cell. Urine was escaping through its rusted seams. He tried to limit himself to shallow breaths, but still the pungency burned his nostrils and left him dizzy and convulsed. He tasted bile at the back of his mouth. He began to rock and speak inwardly. It is a strange time. Strange time. Too many men and demons. Too many ideas. Too many desires. Father, I never should have—

The sound of something striking, then sliding, over the floor jarred Hok-Ling from his dreaming. He looked down. On the floor in front of him was an envelope. Was this his money? At first he was frightened and disoriented. He couldn't move. Then he sprang to the window and called out in a hoarse whisper, "Soo-Kwan! Dak-Wah! Are you there? Is it you? Come back! Come back!" He pressed his face against the rough iron bars. "Dak-Wah!" He peered into the darkness. The world was airless and silent beyond the window. He could make out the shapes of buildings and trees against the faint glow of Main Street. Nearer, there were strange contrasts of shadow hinting at the random boards piled in a grassy margin behind the jail. But he saw no one. "Dak-Wah! Soo-Kwan!"

Hok-Ling turned to retrieve the envelope but his breath caught with a sudden start. His brows shot upward. There in the hallway stood the deputy, Alexander Lambert. The contours of his face were sharp with the light of a kerosene lantern which he held up in his left hand. The barrel of a rifle glinted fiercely through the bars. It was a third eye pointed at his face.

"What the hell's going on in here?" The deputy raised the lantern until its wire cage struck the bars. Hok-Ling commanded his eyes not to look down at the package lying on the floor between them. He realized that the deputy had not seen it, and yet he could scarcely believe it. He raised his hands and spoke rapid Cantonese around a crooked, nervous smile.

"I came from Kwangchow three years ago. Did you know that? I am the son of a fishmonger. Did you know that?" He waved his hands in front of his face, inching toward the deputy and the envelope. "I have two sisters. They are quiet and beautiful. I have no brothers. Do you have any brothers, sir?"

Lambert winced at the strange cackling.

"Do you know my sisters are often mistaken for twins, but, alas, seven years separate them. Have I already told you that?" Hok-Ling felt the lump under his feet. He stopped and bowed, saying, "Ask me anything."

The deputy's mouth hung open and his eyes were arched with wonder. "What the hell kind of dribble is that? You people really understand that?"

"The daughters of my mother's brother are homely. They have many warts." Hok-Ling smiled and bowed again, as if to signal that an accord had been reached between them.

The deputy frowned and withdrew the rifle. "Jesus, what a stink in here!" He pulled a large key from his hind pocket and jammed it noisily into the lock. "Maybe that's what you was talking about," he muttered under his breath. Hok-Ling watched in horror as the deputy swung the door open. Had he seen the envelope after all? His body stiffened. His smile vanished. The deputy walked toward him, then past. He picked up the bucket in the corner and turned his head. "Whew! Hey, give a call or something when this happens, huh? Understand?" He held the bucket at arm's length as he walked past. "Call. Hey! Hey! Like that."

Hok-Ling nodded uncertainly as the deputy carried the bucket into the hallway and closed and locked the cell door behind him. He muttered softly, "Hey, hey," and stared at the deputy.

Lambert looked up and smiled. "There you go. Now we're talking."

"Hey, hey," Hok-Ling repeated, smiling and nodding. The deputy lifted the bucket and walked away quickly.

Hok-Ling swooped down to pick up the envelope, and stuffed it under his pillow. Then he lunged toward the window. "Soo-Kwan! Psst! Are you there? Dak-Wah!" He stared out at the black, still landscape. Suddenly, from the corner of his eye, he saw a crouching figure emerge from a thicket of bushes next to a shed behind the feed store. It dashed in fits and starts across a vacant lot cluttered with stumps and debris. A second figure emerged from the same thicket.

Hok-Ling extended his right arm through the bars. "Soo-Kwan! Dak-Wah!"

"Yes, Hok-Ling! Shhhh! It's us." The two men emerged from the darkness and took Hok-Ling's hand. "Are you all right?"

"Yes."

"Did you get the money?"

"Yes," whispered Hok-Ling excitedly. "How . . . ?"

"I saw the shadow on the wall," explained Soo-Kwan breathlessly. "It startled me and I dropped it."

"How did you . . . ? Where did you find it?"

"It was hidden in the false bottom of a wooden box in Ying-Chiao's tent," Dak-Wah answered.

Soo-Kwan nodded. "You'll need it to pay the judge, Hok-Ling, and if you need more—"

Hok-Ling put a finger to his lips and looked behind him. "What news do you bring? Have you spoken to Mei-Yin?"

"She is desperate, Hok-Ling," sputtered Dak-Wah. "I have told her everything, just as you told me to on the first day. I told her she must deny any knowledge of you, and that she must continue to pretend to be Soo-Kwan's sister until she is able to leave this place for good. These things she knows. But she is determined to help you. There is—"

"She must do nothing!" cried Hok-Ling, pressing his face against the bars. Soo-Kwan and Dak-Wah shrank back a step.

Hok-Ling stared out past his two friends, at the image of Mei-Yin being arrested, being placed in the white man's jail. When he began to conceive of the demons placing a rope around her neck, he pushed the picture away with a low, bestial growl. "Listen to me, both of you! She is to say she arrived at the camp four weeks ago. That she came to find you, Soo-Kwan, to work here under your protection, to make money washing clothes and mending them. But now she wants to return home as soon as possible. Tell her that! Do not fail me!" Hok-Ling's face shook behind the iron bars. "Tell her again and again if you have to! She is a woman! She must obey me!"

There was a sudden stirring in the sheriff's office, punctuated by the sound of boots striking the floor. The deputy's swivel chair squealed, but it didn't knock, which meant he had gotten up, but not in a hurry. A drawer was opened and slammed shut again. Once again the deputy's shadow crossed the wall opposite Hok-Ling's cell. It fled the golden glow of his lantern as he ducked into the hallway.

"What the hell's gotten into you tonight?" asked Deputy Lambert.

Hok-Ling sat on the edge of his bed, with his hands folded in his lap. The stark shadows cast by the cell bars moved over his face. He looked up at the deputy and said nothing.

"Hey, hey?" inquired the deputy, with a sudden earnestness. He pointed the barrel of his rifle awkwardly toward the spot on the floor where the bucket had been. "Hey, hey?"

Hok-Ling saw the kindness in his eyes. He smiled and nodded slowly. The deputy smiled and said, "All right then," and he walked out to retrieve the bucket that he had left in the street. In the meantime, Hok-Ling jumped to the window of his cell and looked out. In the stillness of a summer's night, no man was ever more alone.

15

Circuit Judge Essex Simmons leaned out the window and let a long string of tobacco-stained saliva slide from his lips. He stepped back into the room, working his tongue and wiping his mouth with a soiled handkerchief. "Are you ready to proceed, Emory?" The jurist playfully rapped the corner of the counsel table as he walked back toward an elevated farm table and high-backed oak office chair that would serve as "the bench." He stepped up onto a low, wooden platform recently nailed together for the purpose. "It's about ten o'clock or better," he said as he took the black robe that was slung over the back of the chair and began to put it on.

Emory looked up from a sheet of paper on which he'd been rapidly scribbling notes. "Yes, I'm ready, Your Honor." He sat with Jason at one of two counsel tables. Behind them, a crowd of townspeople filled the benches that had been brought in and compressed into the south end of the room. These people had grown quiet since the judge appeared and walked down the aisle toward the head of the makeshift courtroom. They were a study in simmering anticipation.

"Very well then." The judge settled into his chair and threw his arms out to free his hands from the robe.

"But, uh, Mr. Forbes is missing," Emory observed. "I don't know if . . ."

"Yes. I was informed this morning he won't be joining us," said the judge nonchalantly. He opened a file and began a desultory search of its contents. "Apparently," he continued, "he's stuck in a trial in Coeur d'Alene, and, on top of that, his mother's quite ill. He'll be leaving for Ohio as soon as that trial's over. Let's, uh . . . let's bring in the defendant."

Jason sat upright. What do you mean "bring in the defendant," he thought. If his attorney's not here, the matter should be continued. Jason gave Emory a sidelong glance.

Emory winked and nodded. "Your Honor," he said, standing. "Before we get started, let me introduce a new member of the Idaho bar. This is Jason McQuade."

"Hello, Mr McQuade. I thought I recognized you. I believe we met last year at the mining law conference in Kellogg."

Jason stood and buttoned his frock coat. "That's right, Your Honor. If I . . ."

"It's good to see you again, young man. Welcome to the club."

"Thank you, sir. But . . ."

"Go ahead and be seated and let's get started. We're here for the arraignment of this Chinese fellow—what's his name, Henry?"

The bailiff, Henry Sours, also a traveler of the judicial circuit, was a slender wisp of a man with a thin, assiduously maintained mustache and heavily oiled hair that bore the arrow-straight furrows of the comb. His duties included keeping minutes of the proceedings. He answered without looking up from his notepad. "Wong Hok-Ling."

"Wong Hok-Ling. Bring in Mr. Ling if you would, Henry."

A few moments later, Hok-Ling appeared in the doorway of an anteroom followed by Deputy Lambert, who had him by the arm. Hok-Ling was handcuffed and walked with his head down. Next came Ho Ying-Chiao, dressed in a gold silk shirt with a black and gold skullcap and black trousers. He had his hands folded in front of him and bowed quickly as he crossed the threshold. The prisoner and Ho Ying-Chiao were told to sit at the defense table. Deputy Lambert asked someone to move in order to take a seat in the gallery behind them.

The bailiff walked back to his desk. Standing at attention beside his chair, he called out, "Hear ye! Hear ye! The territorial court of the Territory of Idaho, First Judicial Circuit, is now in session, the Honorable Essex Simmons presiding."

"Thank you, Henry," said the judge, putting on his glasses and looking out. His only greeting for the audience was a quick, perfunctory smile. "This is the matter of the People of the Idaho Territory versus Wong Hok-Ling. This is the arraignment hearing. Hold on here a minute." He shuffled some papers. "Okay, here we go. No, that's not it."

Jason leaned over and whispered to Emory. "He can't be arraigned without his attorney present—*can he?*"

Emory raised an eyebrow. "It's a bit unorthodox, but—"

"Ah!" the judge interrupted. "Here's what I was looking for. We have an interpreter for the accused today." He looked over his glasses toward the defense table. "Which of you is which?" he said. When no response was forthcoming, he raised his voice and said, "Which of you is Po Ho Ying-Chiao?"

"I am Ho Ying-Chiao," said the crew boss jumping to his feet.

The judge waved him back down. "All right, all right. Sit down. Now listen. You're going to translate what we say to the accused, and then we're going to ask him if he wants to plead guilty or not guilty—do you understand?"

Jason tapped Emory's arm and whispered excitedly in his ear, "He can't do that. This isn't right."

Emory rubbed one eye and turned his head pretending the movement was involuntary. He was incapable of whispering, but uttered in suppressed tones, "Let it be, Jason. Forbes isn't available. This happens sometimes."

"Is there something I can help you with, gentlemen?" The judge aimed a look of mild impatience in their direction.

"No, Your Honor," replied Emory, clearing his throat.

"But listen, Emory," whispered Jason excitedly, "the law's clear that you can't—"

The older attorney held his hand up. "Your Honor, may we have a moment?"

"Certainly."

Emory lowered his head. "What is it, Jason?"

"In *Hester v. The United States,* the Second Circuit held that once an attorney has been identified to represent a defendant in a felony case, the accused can't be arraigned until he's had a full and unfettered opportunity to meet with the attorney. Forbes has been in trial in Coeur d'Alene the last two weeks. He left the day after Hok-Ling was arrested. This arraignment is improper."

Emory scraped his teeth over his lower his lip as he thought. "Why didn't you mention this yesterday?"

"I thought Forbes would be coming back for this."

Emory glanced out the window for a few seconds, then turned back and spoke in a soft gravelly voice. "We're not the Second Circuit here, Jason. There are only two attorneys here, and sometimes we have scheduling conflicts. I'd argue under the circumstances that Forbes was never formally identified, if the issue ever got that far. I don't think it will. This town is ready to hang this man—as you can see for yourself. At least here he's getting a chance to say whether he did it or not. If he says he didn't, he'll get a trial. If he admits doing it, well then we'll be able to move on." Emory turned back to the bench. "Thank you, Your Honor. We're ready to proceed."

Judge Simmons scratched the side of his head with one finger. "Now hold on there. I heard some of that. You've got me curious, Mr. McQuade. Tell me more about this Second Circuit case."

Jason looked self-consciously at Emory then rose to his feet. He was sure he'd never heard anything as loud as the sound of his chair scraping the floor. His heart beat against the base of his neck as he began. But begin he did, and soon he was overtaken by the unexpected thrill that accompanies the logical construction of an argument in court. After Jason sat down, Emory stood to oppose the argument along the practical lines he'd foreshadowed moments earlier. All the while, Hok-Ling and Ho Ying-Chiao sat silently at the defense table.

"All right," said Judge Simmons at last. "Here's what we're going to do. Mr. Forbes is absent, but we do have a new member of the bar here, so I'm going to appoint you, Mr. McQuade, to represent the accused."

"*What?*" Jason cried.

Emory, who had started to take his seat, rose up again. "But Your Honor, that's impossible. Mr. McQuade is my associate."

"Yes, yes, that's true," said the judge. He looked down and rubbed his chin, then his eyes flashed up over the rims of his glasses. "What do you say, Mr. McQuade? Do you want your first case, or not?"

Jason stood. "I work for Mr. Morse, sir. It would be a conflict of—"

"I can tell you this for sure," interrupted the judge. "This Chinaman is going to be arraigned this morning. I'm not making another trip up here for an arraignment hearing. We can either do it with, or without, defense counsel."

Jason turned and looked at Hok-Ling. None of what was being said in court was being translated for him. Ho Ying-Chiao sat still as a statue, his head down, his hands tucked into his sleeves. Only his dark eyes moved side to side like the eyes of a caged animal. I can just see it, Jason thought, as he imagined Hok-Ling standing up when called and nodding yes to every question put to him—from "Is your name Wong Hok-Ling?" to "Did you kill Sheriff Roger Langston on July 16, 1882?" Jason turned to Emory. "I . . . "

"You could resign, at least temporarily," the judge offered, his eyes going back and forth between the two attorneys. "The Territorial Court would pay you while you work on the case. It wouldn't be much, mind you, but you won't starve."

"Resign?" said Emory.

"Yes. To resolve the conflict of interest problem."

Jason couldn't believe what he was hearing. Resign? he thought. Quit Emory's office and take on the defense of this fellow? Could the judge be serious?

Suddenly Jason was aware that all eyes in the gallery were staring at him. There was a low whispering coming from that quarter. His mouth went dry as he tried to take in all the implications of the judge's suggestion. They were there, of course— the implications. But for some reason they stood each and every one outside his thinking and refused to enter. All he could think of was Hok-Ling. He knew that within five or ten minutes, if he didn't act, this man, a complete stranger to the West and its jurisprudence, would seal his own fate and then be executed outside of town within a matter of days. A second thought began to creep in after that one, the possibility of Hok-Ling's innocence. It had stirred vaguely within him a few days before. And it was tied, not to the fact that Hok-Ling had been beaten up earlier on that day by the sheriff, Jake Prescott, and the other boys, but with the location of the sheriff's body. Under the Sand Creek bridge. How had it gotten there, he'd wondered. Could this small Chinese man really have stabbed the sheriff to death on the bridge or somewhere else, then dragged his body and lifted it over the railing? And why? Why bother?

Jason lowered himself to the counsel table, deep in thought. Take the defense of a hated Chinese laborer. Risk making an enemy of everyone in town. Why would I do that? he asked himself. An answer began to form that would have been no

answer at all for most men. He imagined his father, Robert
McQuade, standing before him, telling him, "Don't be a fool.
Why risk this? You've worked hard to become a lawyer. Now
you're prepared to throw your reputation away? It's lunacy." "In
other words," Jason answered him in his daydream, "play it safe.
Is that the idea? Why risk anything—to hell with right and
wrong. Why fight when you can sell blankets and tents and go
home at night to stand in moral judgment of others. Well, at
least now you'll have a reason to reject me."

The judge removed his glasses. "I'm sure this would be an
inconvenience to you, Emory."

Jason didn't hear Emory's response, which was, "Yes, and a
great deal more than an inconvenience," because he was speaking over him now, with a surging boldness and fixity of purpose. He rose to his feet again. "I'll do it, Your Honor," he said.
"But I have one condition—that Your Honor will authorize me
to hire at once an experienced court interpreter to be paid by
the Territory."

The voices in the back of the room grew louder. The judge
struck his gavel. "Quiet! Emory, what do you have to say?"

Emory turned to Jason. "Do you know what you're getting
into?"

Jason shook his head. "No, I don't have the foggiest idea."

"But this is what you want to do?"

Jason took a deep breath. "I . . . " He looked over his shoulder at the confused and surprised expressions in the crowd
behind him, then at Hok-Ling. "I think it's what I *have* to do."

Emory turned toward the bench. "I guess he's made up his
mind. I won't stand in the way."

"Very well. The Court is agreeable to the hiring of a professional court interpreter without delay. Mr. McQuade, do you
want to take a few minutes to meet with your client?"

My client, thought Jason. Oh God, I've really done this!
Jason was aware of Emory taking his seat beside him. Now
what? he thought. He tried to force saliva into his mouth.

"Your Honor," he began slowly. He turned and walked to the defense table. Once there, he leaned over it, put his hands on the surface and looked down at the dark brown mahogany finish. After several moments in which the courtroom was encased in silence, he stood erect. He inhaled and exhaled a loud, long breath. "Your Honor, the defendant Wong Hok-Ling enters a plea of "Not guilty" to the charge of murder in the first degree, and requests that the matter be set over for trial. What's more, the defendant demands a jury of twelve men."

* * *

On Tuesday afternoon the sky darkened early. Dozens of soaring thunderheads crept north and east out of the deserts of Oregon and Washington. Nervous wind gusts began to darken the lake's surface. For miles around, the air was sticky and smelled of a light, sweet cologne lifted from the skin of the earth.

Jason sat on the porch steps of Esther's house, petting her orange cat as it propped one paw over his lap but could not decide whether to retreat or go further. "You're a fine one, Dolly. Stuck in the middle, aren't you?" he said, lifting the cat to his lap. He began to scratch the base of her ears. Suddenly, thunder rumbled in the distance then rolled across the sky above Sandpoint in a loud crescendo. The cat lurched and ran off, but not before digging her claws into Jason's legs. "Damn!" he sputtered, rubbing the tops of both legs. He scowled over at the animal perched on the railing at the far end of the porch. She glared back at him with wide-eyed recrimination. Esther appeared at the front gate, carrying a large canvas bag filled with groceries. "Kitty wanna die?" Jason called out in a soprano voice. "Kitty wanna go for a boat ride?"

"Jason!" Esther tried to hide her amusement. Jason stood and moved to the side, brushing the seat of his pants.

"Well, the damn thing scratched me, Esther. Both legs. Tried to kill me, I think."

She ignored him, handed him the groceries, and went directly to the cat's aid. "Come here, Dolly." She picked up the animal and held it snugly against her bosom. "Is that bad man being mean to you?" Her pleasure at seeing Jason shone in her eyes as she lifted the cat and planted a comforting kiss on the back of its head. "Poor little thing. Mama's got you now. I'll protect you."

Jason opened the door, stepped back, then followed them in. "Mama and kitty wanna go for a boat ride?" he growled under his breath. Esther, giggling, led him into the kitchen. When she'd deposited the cat stiff-legged on the floor, she turned to him, smiling wearily. Jason set the groceries down on the wood countertop. Esther spread her arms and embraced him.

"I'm glad you're here."

Jason closed his eyes and set his nose in the thick of her hair, breathing deep to capture the familiar lavender smell. He felt her shape and a surge of pleasure followed. Esther held on tenaciously. "Every time I turn around, someone's telling me they're on their way over here to look in on you. You doing all right?" He could feel her nodding.

"It's going to storm out there," he added. "I can feel it."

"Uh-huh."

"Listen. Don't you just love the sound of distant thunder?" Esther was quiet. He pulled her shoulders hard against him and closed his eyes. "It's such an awesome and foreboding sound," he whispered, "but not frightening, really, do you think?"

She nodded.

"You do? Oh well."

When he opened his eyes the light in the adjoining parlor dimmed so suddenly that everything he could see in it seemed to move. The piano, the settee, the austere daguerreotypes on the wall—Roger and Rebecca Langston on their wedding day, Esther's grandparents, aunts and uncles, cousins in their infancy and youth. The room looked cold and comfortless cast in the gray light, as though it were death's own chamber. He looked away and buried his face at the side of Esther's head.

"I've missed you," she whispered at length. "Terribly."

Jason took a shallow breath, pinched with sadness. "I've missed you, too, Esther," he heard himself say. His throat constricted as he swallowed.

"You know," she went on, "those things you said to me after the funeral were some of the kindest, most thoughtful words ever spoken. I mean that. I'm sure I shall always be grateful to you." His hands caressed her back, but when she looked up, and he straightened, she saw that he was not preparing to speak. His eyes held a gentle, unassuming smile. "I truly shall," she added. She squeezed him tightly again and held on for another two minutes, which seemed to Jason ten. At last, she released him. "I bet you're hungry. Can I . . ?"

"I'm awfully hungry," he agreed. "My stomach's even been growling."

Just then the sky above Sandpoint rumbled ominously. Her eyes narrowed with a smile. Jason nodded. "There it is," they said together.

Jason chuckled. "See?"

"I guess so," Esther laughed. "I'll get us some cookies and milk. Why don't you sit down."

"Great. I've got something I want to talk to you about anyway." He peered into the gloom of the parlor as Esther walked to the icebox. "I'll tell you what, I'll take the blanket from the settee and meet you out on the porch."

"That sounds fine," Esther called out over the sound of cupboards opening and closing. A few minutes later she appeared on the porch with a tray bearing a plate of cookies and two glasses of milk.

Jason sat back in one of the porch chairs until its back came to a rest against the front of the house. He chewed absently, watching the first giant raindrops splatter on the weathered railing. Esther sat next to him with the blanket over her legs. She watched him and smiled secretly. "I wrote home the other day," he said vaguely, after swallowing.

"Your parents?"

"No, Bernie Page. A friend."

"He was on the crew team with you, wasn't he? I'd like to meet him someday."

"Yes. Oh my, these are good." He stalled by reaching for another cookie.

"Daddy used to pay me a penny apiece for my oatmeal cookies, when I was little, that is." She began to tear up. "He would say I could get rich making them and selling them to strangers." Esther sniffed and foraged delicately through the plate until she found the smallest morsel. She held it in front of her mouth. "When they were still warm from the oven, he'd smell them on the table and shout, 'Come and get em! Esther Marie Langston's Grand Prize Oatmeal Cookies!' 'Hot-damn,' he'd say. 'Hot-damn.'" Esther smiled and daintily bit her cookie. Jason chuckled. A sharp clap of thunder peeled and rolled over their heads.

"It's moving in," Jason observed.

"So what did you write to Bernie about? Did you tell him your good news? About getting your attorney's license and all?"

"Yeah. Sure. Thought he oughta know."

"Well, of course he should."

Beyond the rail, the rain surged. Its silver droplets pummeled the earth noisily. Thunder followed the lightning again, and a hissing squall bent the tops of the trees. But the dark porch was dry and commodious, and it smelled of summer dust.

"I wanted to tell you what happened this morning." He stared out at the yard. Esther pinched a crumb off the blanket and put it in her mouth. "I wanted to tell you about the arraignment of this Chinese fellow. He was formally charged and . . . "

"I don't want to talk about that!" She sat bolt upright. "Please! Don't talk to me about that!"

Jason's chair banged forward and he stood up. "I've got to, Esther."

"No you don't!"

"But—"

"Stop, Jason! Please . . . "

"I'm going to represent the Chinaman."

Esther blinked. The color drained from her face.

"I'm going to defend him, Esther. I'm going to represent this Chinese fella."

"The man who killed Daddy?"

Jason glanced to the floor of the porch, then back. "The man they've charged with the crime," he replied, nodding. The downpour beat against the roof above them. Its low, riotous drone filled the silent spaces between their thoughts.

"But why?"

"There was no one else to do it, for one thing. Forbes was supposed to do it, but he didn't show up and he's leaving to go back east to see his mother soon. The whole thing was in danger of being handled wrong—as though a conviction and a hanging are foregone conclusions."

Esther's eyes darted as if she were looking for a way out of a maze. Eventually, they found Jason again. "*You* work for Emory. How can you take a case against him?"

"I don't anymore, Esther. That's the other half of the news. I quit. I had to, at least for a while."

"What does Emory say about this?"

Jason smiled wryly. "It surprised him," he said, and then he thought for a minute and added, "Surprised everyone, I guess."

Esther looked hard at the gray rain. "Oh, Jason, this is horrible! Doesn't Judge Simmons know about . . ? That we're . . ? How could anyone be so heartless?" Jason peered back at her, questioningly. "Didn't he discuss this with Emory before appointing you?"

"Esther, no. You don't understand. He didn't appoint me at all. That's what I'm trying to tell you. This guy comes into court totally helpless. They're just ticking off the steps before they can hang him. Even Emory's going along with it. Don't you see?" Esther's eyes widened. She looked past him, to the other end of the porch. "They're ignoring this man's rights. He has rights, Esther—constitutional rights, just like anybody else. And it doesn't matter whether he's guilty or not, or whether he's a foreigner—he still has rights. You believe that, don't you?" She faced him again, startled by the question, but her stone-like demeanor persisted. "I think it's even more vital that his right to a fair trial be protected because he *is* Chinese," Jason continued. "He's helpless in this culture. And he's hated. Everybody around here hates the Chinese. Damn near everybody." Jason was acutely aware of her silence, and he saw in her frozen countenance the dimension of her dissent and disappointment. It angered him and stirred in him the slow poison of his own doubts. "Damn it, Esther, he's got rights!"

"You volunteered," she whispered, as if to herself.

"He's entitled to a fair trial, isn't he?"

"You volunteered."

"Yes, I volunteered! What difference does that make? I'm not saying he's innocent. I'm not. But he's entitled to a defense. God, why can't you understand? What did I do that's so horrible?" Esther eyes were still and blank, like eyes probing darkness. Jason spread his hands. "This is why I studied this stuff, Esther. I can't turn my back on it now. That's what Judge Simmons is doing. He's turning his back on his oath, on the constitution, *everything!* Seems like Emory is, too. But I won't, dammit, I won't.

"The court is an adversary forum. Fine. That's what it's called and that's what it is. Emory is the best around. He'll present his case for the prosecution and I'll present mine for the defense. That's all it'll be. He'll probably tear me to pieces, just like that. This Chinese fella, he probably *is* guilty. He'll be convicted and it'll be over. But, there's gotta be a fair trial. That's all I want. Really. That's all I'm after." He waited for the word or the change of expression that didn't come. He chuckled nervously, "You're really upset with me, aren't you?" Esther stood up and shook the blanket as calmly and indifferently as she might have had she been alone on the porch. She folded it over her arm and started for the door.

Thunder rolled overhead. Jason moved toward her, his arms extending toward her waist. "Oh, Esther. For God's sake, be reasonable. I—" His head was twisted by the force of her sudden slap. His lips tingled and the side of his jaw burned painfully. Esther's mouth trembled.

"Get away from me! How dare you! Go! Do you understand? Go away and never come back!"

He backed to the top of the stairs, touching the side of his face. Esther shook her head, then faced him and sneered savagely, "I hate you. I've always hated you." Her eyes were wide and bright and fierce. "Get off the porch, Mr. McQuade. Get off my father's property!"

Jason turned and walked down the steps and into the slanting rain.

16

T he next day Jason arrived at the office before eight. Emory was sitting at his desk. Jason shook off his coat and hung it where he always did, on the hook beside the clothes tree. "Good morning," he said, but Emory didn't answer. Jason hesitated, pursed his lips, then stepped past him. He lit the lantern above his desk and sat down. After a moment's reflection, he withdrew a piece of paper from the center drawer. As he readied his pen and ink, he was certain Emory was preparing to start in on him. He fought the urge to glance sidelong at his mentor. Ten seconds passed—twenty—forty—a minute—two minutes. He heard the scratching of Emory's pen, and now and then a faint whistle in his breathing. Then again, maybe he wouldn't.

No matter, he thought. He dipped his pen and stared intently at the blank sheet of paper in front of him. But nothing came to him. He was so distracted he'd forgotten why he'd taken out the pen and paper in the first place. Finally, he remembered. He dipped his pen again and wrote at the top of the page "People of the I.T. v. Wong Hok-Ling. Things to do." To this he appended a looping arrow which pointed to the bulk of the page. He turned to look at Emory again and found him bent over his desk, reading. "All right, Emory," he said, laying his pen down and sitting back in his chair, "we're going to have to work something out here."

The old lawyer continued to read for a few seconds, then marked his place with his finger and looked up. "What's that?"

"I said we should work something out."

"Work what out?"

"On the office. You know, timing, that sort of thing." Once again, Emory did not answer. "Look. I know it's presumptuous of me, but I need a place with a desk and some books, a place to work. Just for a month, until this thing is over. Then I'll make other arrangements." He wiped the corners of his mouth. "If you don't want me back here."

Emory removed his reading glasses. His face darkened. "Are you saying you expect to use my office?"

"I'd like to, yes. I need a place."

"You need a place." He laughed. "Boy, you're full of it, aren't you? A real comedian." Emory used his letter opener to mark his page then closed the book. "Listen, my friend—"

"Okay! Forget it, Emory!" Jason interrupted, thrusting his hands up. "Just forget it." He rose to his feet and began to collect his papers. Emory watched his fumbling at length.

"You think you're ready for a murder defense?" he asked.

"Hell, no. I told you that already."

"Neither do I."

Jason proceeded through the desk drawers, pulling out letters, a dictionary, his outlines and study notes. He went to the bookshelf and removed a folded shirt which had collected dust for nine months. "But I guess I admire you for what you're doing," Emory added. Jason's hands stopped. "You've got pluck."

He looked over at the old man. "I'm scared to death."

"Yeah. I know. And that means you'll work your tail off trying to beat me." Jason smiled self-consciously. "I've been there. I used to take some pretty fair bites out of the apple myself."

Jason looked around the office until he spotted an empty wooden box in the corner. He walked over to it. "Do you mind?"

Emory waved his hand. "Go ahead." Jason balanced the box at the corner of the desk and began to fill it with his papers and effects.

"I'm not going to negotiate a damn thing with you," Emory said, rising and walking toward the door. He put on his coat and hat. "And I won't answer any questions unless talking to you will help me get a conviction. Got that?"

"Sure."

Emory nodded. His eyes seemed small and sad, his color gone. He opened the door and adjusted the hat over his forehead. "This is it," he exclaimed from the threshold. "I'll be gone this morning until eleven. From here on, you get the place Tuesdays and Thursday afternoons after one. And Saturdays. The rest of the time is mine. Alone. You so much as look sideways at my desk when you're in here and I'll break your neck myself." Emory stared in after his threat as though glad to be rid of it. "When this man of yours hangs, we'll talk about what comes next. Right now, I'm inclined to say you're out for good." The door slammed behind Emory and Jason braced for the glass to crumple to the floor. It didn't happen.

Jason was alone in the office. "You old goat!" He looked down at his desk and slapped it cheerfully. "You damn old goat!"

What he didn't need, he left in the box and set it on the floor beside the desk. He sat down with the paper marked "Things to do" and began to write, mouthing the words. "One. Get interpreter." His hand shook with anticipation and the tiniest measure of optimism. This made him laugh at himself. "Two. Go to Hope. Three. Find out what I can about Judge E. Simmons."

* * *

Nine days later, on a brilliant afternoon, Jason sat with his elbows propped over his knees at the edge of the elevated sidewalk in front of Carpenter's Market. It was a Wednesday, not one of his office days, and it was hot in the street. Flies buzzed all around him. He produced from his shirt pocket his "to do" list, which now numbered twenty-four items, and began to study it.

"Master Mc . . . McQuade, please?" A Chinese stood on the sidewalk directly behind him. He was a small man, very straight, thirty-five to forty years old, with pale, yellowish skin and eyes that seemed to peek at him through a louver. He was dressed in a green tweed suit and a crisp, black hat. He carried a large suitcase in each hand.

"Yes? I'm Jason McQuade." He smiled suddenly and climbed up to the sidewalk. "Are you. . . ?"

"Lei Chi-Man," the man answered softly. He dropped a suitcase in order to take Jason's hand, then bowed perfunctorily. Jason returned the gesture.

"You are my interpreter, then?"

"Yes, of course."

"Lee Chee . . ?"

"Lei Chi-Man," rattled the Chinese. He picked up his suitcase again. "Call me Charlie, Mr. Mc . . . "

"McQuade," Jason laughed. "Charlie?"

"Yes. My friends call me Charlie. And my clients." Lei Chi-Man smiled humorlessly. His eyelids shut tight. Crow's feet spread over his temples, then vanished. He bowed, then straightened, looking serious again.

Jason wanted to laugh out loud, but only smiled, showing his white teeth. "Charlie it is, then. Call me Jason." Lei Chi-Man bowed again. "Good heavens, am I glad to see you! You got the money?"

"Yes. But you sent too much. I will return a portion to you."

"Nonsense."

"No, it is not nonsense, Mr. Mc . . . Ja-sawn. There can be no generosity between strangers. Only mistakes. As my father would say, 'give your riches to respected friends. Pay me my fee and expenses and let me sleep.'"

"All right, all right," said Jason, "We'll talk about that later. C'mon, Charlie. I've reserved a room for you at the hotel. I want to get started right away. Here, give me one of those."

"Thank you." They walked down the sidewalk leaning opposite the pull of the heavy suitcases. "We will meet your client today?" Lei Chi-Man asked calmly.

"You bet we will. First thing. You wash up and get out of that heavy suit. I'm going to wait for you in the lobby."

"Yes, yes. Understand. What is his name again, please?"

"Who?"

"Your client."

"Oh. Hok-Ling. Wong Hok-Ling"

"Hok-Ling," the interpreter repeated. "Yes, thank you."

As they approached the double doors of the Carson Hotel, Jason reviewed the visit he'd had with the hotel proprietor, William Carson, the day before. At first, Carson had made a show of his aloofness toward the young attorney, but when Jason produced and began idly stacking and restacking five fifty-dollar gold pieces, the conversation took a more confidential turn. Soon, both men were leaning heavily on the hotel's mahogany counter. The sign over Carson's shoulder read,

$$ROOMS\ \$2^{\underline{00}}$$
$$BATH\ \$0^{\underline{50}}$$

"You say this fella's an Oriental, huh?"

"That's right, Bill. He's a writer, too—writes for a Chinese newspaper down there in San Francisco."

"Is that so? And what's he coming up this way for anyway?"

"Well, I've hired him, Bill. That's the long and short of it."

"Oh?"

"Yup. He's going to be my interpreter on this law case up here. You knew I was handling the case of that Chinaman, didn't you?"

"You know, I guess I did hear something about that, yeah." The hotelier kept his eyes above the gold pieces by widening them and blinking excessively.

"Yeah. And I got to get him situated once he gets up here. Man's got to have a place to sleep."

"Well, I suppose that's true."

"Yeah. You know, it's the kind of thing where a person's got to make it worth someone's while. Strikes me it's one of those kind of things, you know what I'm saying, Bill?"

"Well, uh, sure. I know what you're saying, McQuade. It's gotta be, I reckon. I guess money's money, if you look at it that way."

"There you go. That's what I'm getting at. You and I are thinking the same thing now."

"I mean, business is business. That's what I've always said. It ain't nothing more elaborate than that."

With his room quickly arranged at the front desk, Lei Chi-Man thanked Jason, refused further help, and carried the suitcases up the stairs and out of sight. In less than two minutes he returned, running down the stairs with remarkable quiet and agility. He bowed quickly as he approached Jason, "I am ready, Ja-sawn. Thank you." He had removed his hat, coat, and tie, but still wore the green tweed pants and the same white shirt with its stiff, upright collar buttoned at the top. His black suspenders looked enormous over his narrow shoulders. Jason opened the door for Lei Chi-Man and looked at the interpreter's head as if to see it for the first time. He did not have a queue, but wore his hair lightly oiled and combed to one side. Lei Chi-Man smiled and exclaimed, "I was born in San Jose. I'm afraid this is as close to a pigtail as I'll ever get."

Jason pointed them toward the sheriff's office, and, as they walked, he told the interpreter as much as he could about the case. Lei Chi-Man asked no questions. His narrowed eyes were fixed straight ahead with his listening.

Jason stopped with his hand on the doorknob of the sheriff's office. "Last week, the deputy found an envelope with $500 under Hok-Ling's mattress. We don't know how he got it. Judge Simmons ordered the funds be held by me in trust to defray the expenses of trial, including our fees. Maybe we can get to the bottom of this, as well. We'll ask him where he got the money, what it was for—that sort of thing."

* * *

Hok-Ling sat on the floor in the narrow space between the wall and the end of the wood-frame bed. He wore no shirt. In the dim light his skin was glossy and dark. His arms were stretched out over his knees, and his fingers dangled like the points of spoiled autumn leaves. He did not look up despite the twice clanging of the door.

"Good luck," said Deputy Lambert, after shaking the cell door to test the lock. "He's been like this for three days. Refuses to eat an' everything. Never says a word 'less it's to tell one of us to fetch the bucket over there. Say, I've got to step out awhile. I'll be back in about ten minutes."

"That's fine, Deputy Lambert." Jason waited for the sounds of the outer door opening and closing. "Come around here, Charlie," he said, indicating with a tilt of his head without taking his eyes off of the prisoner. Jason moved closer to Hok-Ling. A foul smell filled his nostrils, but he stayed his ground to get a better look at the man. Never had he seen a more melancholy sight—a man bereft of hope and vitality, bent and death-like, resigned. But more startling still was an unmistakable evenness about Hok-Ling, a perverse grace, a sense of the whole man turning inward and shutting out his accusers. Jason looked for a hint of fear, certain that it would show in some way in an innocent man. It was not there. He cringed, thinking of the hurt he'd caused Esther, of the damage that had been done to his relationship with Emory, of the looming prospect of his own humiliation.

"Introduce yourself to him, Charlie. Tell him that I am Jason McQuade, an attorney. That I will be representing him when he is tried for the murder of Sheriff Roger Langston."

Lei Chi-Man cleared his throat and began. Hok-Ling looked up. The whites of his eyes shone like ivory against his dark eyelids. Jason's persistent stare brought a glance from him, but he was most intent on the interpreter. Hok-Ling answered, beginning with the interpreter's name, Lei Chi-Man, just as the interpreter had begun his communication by addressing the prisoner by name. It would be so each time they spoke.

When he finished, Lei Chi-Man turned to Jason. "He says he does not want an attorney—he is prepared to die."

"Tell him the deputy confiscated his $500, and the court has ordered that the money be used to pay me, and to pay you, as well. Now we have no choice but to work for him."

Hok-Ling started at the mention of the $500. He answered excitedly at first, but then his tone became monotonous as though he were reading something etched in memory. Charlie nodded then turned to Jason. "He insists this is not his money. Whoever delivered it probably meant well, but the money belongs to the sister of a friend of his, Soo-Kwan. He says he was keeping it safe for her in his lockbox at her request, for she lives alone and separate from the camp. He doesn't know her name, only that she is Soo-Kwan's sister, and that she is saving money in hopes of returning to the Middle Kingdom. He was doing this as a favor to Soo-Kwan. The woman he speaks of is a washerwoman and seamstress at the camp. He asks that you return it to her. Please. He is very insistent. He does not want an attorney, and asks that we do no work for him."

"Why did she ask him to hold the money and not her brother?" Jason watched as the question was put to the prisoner.

"He says he has the best lockbox money can buy. You see, he, too, saved money for his return passage, but this spring his money was stolen. So with his next paycheck he went to town and bought the best lockbox he could find. It is that simple, he says. Oh, and he adds that the woman is preparing to leave Gold Mountain very soon, and needs her money now."

"How did it end up here in his cell—the money, I mean?"

"He says someone dropped it through this window while he was sleeping. It landed on his feet and woke him up. He didn't see who this was, but thinks it was someone who stole it from his lockbox after he was arrested—then was overtaken by guilt."

Jason sat at the edge of the bed. He stared at the opposite wall and then at Charlie. "Tell him that I will give the money back to this woman, but only if he will cooperate. He must answer truthfully all questions. Tell him and make him promise."

"Very well."

Hok-Ling did promise, but falsely. In answer to the questions that followed, he readily admitted killing the sheriff in retribution for the beating he had received earlier in the day. He said he dragged the sheriff's body over the bridge with the intent of hiding it in a thicket near the lakeshore. When he heard voices, he became alarmed and rolled the body over the railing. He said it surprised him when he did not hear a splash, for he thought he was still over the creek. But he did not look down. He simply ran to the boat and returned to Hope. Jason asked him where the weapon had come from, and he answered that he always kept a knife in the waistband of his trousers. When Jason asked whether or not Hok-Ling returned the mailbag that night, he declared that he had, that he had given it to his crew boss along with his severed queue.

"His trial is scheduled for early next month," said Jason, standing and moving woodenly to the cell door. Lei Chi-Man advised Hok-Ling of the date. "Say, Mr. Lambert! Are you out there?"

"Yeah! I'm back."

"All right. We're ready."

Lei Chi-Man closed the door to the sheriff's office and trotted to catch up with Jason in the middle of the street. Both men by the lightness of their steps evinced gratitude for the daylight and fresh air.

"What do you think?"

"Think?" Charlie contorted with his smile again. "Interpreters don't think, Ja-sawn. They interpret."

Jason laughed ruefully. "Yeah. Okay. I guess that's fair."

"Did I tell you that Hok-Ling requests the Four Treasures of the Writing Table?"

"No," answered Jason, surprised. "What are the Four Treasures of the Writing Table?"

"Pen and paper. He is literate."

Jason turned. "Pen and paper? That's two things, isn't it?"

"In China it's four," explained the interpreter flatly.

Jason stopped, knotted his brow skeptically, then set out again, shaking his head. "This should be interesting. What did you tell him?"

"Why, I told him that you must decide. It's not my decision."

"What does he want to write?" Jason asked, then he ventured to answer the question himself. "Maybe a letter to his father. Or to a woman back home."

"Yes, a woman. Mei-Yin."

Jason looked down at the interpreter. "Is that her name? Did he tell you that?"

"Yes, he said a young woman named Mei-Yin awaits his return. Their fathers have approved their marriage."

They stepped up to the sidewalk in front of the Carson Hotel. Jason waited for a man and woman to pass before speaking. "Tomorrow, we'll go to the railroad camp at Hope. We will try to find this Soo-Kwan, or the woman—Soo-Kwan's sister—or anyone else who knows Hok-Ling. Understand?"

"Yes, sure."

"Okay. See you tomorrow then, Charlie. Oh, and take some paper and a pen to Hok-Ling, will you?"

"Sure." The interpreter bowed.

Jason jumped into the street and started off. He turned within a couple steps, and Lei Chi-Man, who had started for the door of the hotel, saw him and turned and bowed quickly in his direction. "Glad you made it today, Charlie."

The Chinese's head bounced somewhere between nodding and bowing. "Yes, sure," he replied. "I'm glad, too. Now."

* * *

Hok-Ling stretched out on the mattress and slid his hands under his head, reminding himself of the loss of his queue. He stared up at the cracks in the ceiling of the jail. A pair of flies buzzed overhead. Tears began to form in his eyes. He blinked them back. He labored to think under the weight of a great, lowering despair, to right himself in a turbulent sea of emotions, but with little success. What am I to do? he thought at last. I am helpless! He thought of sleeping as a means of escape, but then an avalanche of panic swept over him, threatening to suffocate him. He sat up with a violent start. He looked around him. His heart was pounding. Suddenly a verse from the *Book of Songs* sprang to his lips.

> "In your secret chamber even you are judged.
> See you do nothing to blush for,
> Though but the ceiling looks down upon you."

Yes, of course! he thought. I must bear my shame honorably, and without complaint! That is my duty.

He rehearsed the verse in his mind, drawing several relieved breaths. "Yes, this is the way!" he whispered triumphantly. The poem was one of hundreds he'd studied in elementary school, and now he gained a moment's comfort recalling his favorite teacher, the elderly and stooped Ah King, pacing, ever pacing in and out of the slanting shafts of sunlight that splintered the head of the small classroom. He remembered Ah King's surpassing wisdom, his keen wit, the power of his gentle, croaking voice to penetrate youthful minds and inspire them to a new and unfamiliar eagerness for knowledge.

"Remember, my pupils," he would say, "it is man that makes truth great, and not truth that makes man great. See you do nothing to blush for. The true man must exercise complete moral discipline. He must put in order his own personal conduct and seek nothing from others, no matter what the circumstances. Only the foolish man complains and takes to dangerous courses. When he does so, then the whole country is plunged into disorder. All of heaven is disrupted. Harmony is lost. What has Master K'ung instructed us? That is what you must ask yourselves! And the answer? Why, it is the same always. Remember the five universal obligations, and the moral qualities by which they are carried out, which number three. Do you remember them, class? Of course you do. The duties Confucius speaks of are those between ruler and subject, between father and son, between husband and wife, between elder brother and younger, and between friends. The moral qualities that are required are what? Why, you already know this! They are wisdom, compassion, and courage."

He felt a sudden jolt. Is this really happening? Am I really here, in this cell? He looked into the corner of the ceiling. I can't believe this! It is like a dream! But it's true. They're going to kill me. I'm going to die in this foreign place, here on the Gold Mountain, away from my family. He let his head sink back into the cushion. I came here to earn money. That's all. I came to work for three years, and I worked three years and more. But they would not let me go. Why? And now this.

Why did she come? I wouldn't have permitted it. Never! None of this would have happened had she stayed in the Middle Kingdom. What impertinence! Did she not think I would return eventually? Certainly, she knew—I had promised it after all. She knew I would not break my promise. Now look what she's done . . .

How in the world did she do it? Disguised as a man? Is that possible? It is one thing to do this on a dark night, for a two-hour journey across a lake, but on a ship for weeks on end, how could she . . . ? Hok-Ling scowled. It is not meet for a woman to be so independent. Now my fate is proof of this. They are going to kill me.

Oh, forget that! It's not her fault. I have seen the omens. The death of Yee Tai-Hu and the others in the explosion on the palisades, the whipping of Soo-Kwan, the theft of my money. And now Mei-Yin's rape. The gods foretell by these omens that I must die here. This is their will.

Still, all of this seems so unreal. Hok-Ling closed his eyes. They are going to kill me? Kill me. It's all so unreal. I can hardly believe this is happening to me . . . hardly believe . . . I'm still here . . . when I should be in Kwangchow.

Hok-Ling was soon asleep and his anxieties were swept into a dream. He awoke a half hour later, remembering.

"Look, Hok-Ling!"

Of course he recognized the treble of Wong Wai-Sung, but he could not spy his diminutive childhood friend through the swarms of people who crowded the narrow street near the Flowery Pagoda. It was a market day. "In a minute!" Hok-Ling turned back to the old, bent, toothless woman who held out three coppers.

"These frogs are small and not worth a penny more, young man," she screeched. "You have only young frogs here. Or per-haps they are old and sick, like me." This last she said with humor, turning a bright and duplicitous eye to a droopy-eyed man standing beside her. He was not interested in Hok-Ling's frogs, nor in the antics of the old woman. He had stopped, only waiting to get by, and as soon as an opportunity presented itself, he moved away.

"Hok-Ling!"

"Coming!" Young Hok-Ling frowned and reached down into the barrel, pulling out an animal. "These frogs are not sick, old woman," he insisted. He held the frog down on a piece of ship's planking that lay over the top of the barrel and with a single, practiced motion, he struck off the frog's head with a knife. He scraped the head to the ground and threw the body, legs still moving, into the old woman's basket. "I caught them myself, early this morning, by the light of the moon," he continued. He moved very rapidly. Two more frogs followed the first into the basket. "There."

He knew why Wai-Sung had hailed him. It had to do with whatever was going on in the public square. A large crowd had been gathering for some time. Twice he'd heard shouts echoing down the narrow, shaded street, gushing like a wind over the heads of the shoppers.

Hok-Ling turned to look at his father, who sat smoking behind his brightly painted fish barrels. "Go ahead, son," the man said. "I'll watch the frogs."

He stopped at the niche where only an hour earlier Wai-Sung had spread his coarse burlap and arranged upon it dried insects and pieces of smoked fish. The place was empty. There was no sign of Wai-Sung. Again, the voice of a crowd animated by some shared excitement or agitation rolled up the street.

He set off in a hurry toward the public square, certain that he would find his friend there. More and more, people stopped what they were doing and moved in that direction. A block from the square, hundreds of people moved as one great animal and there was little spoken in the street. All at once they had about them a silence and a purposefulness. Hok-Ling was not far from the square when he reached over, without thinking, and seized the arm of a small, neatly dressed boy who ran beside him. The boy turned to him, offering no resistance. He had a cherub's face and wore new black slippers, black cotton pants, a brocaded shirt, and a green silk skullcap fitted with a false queue. He was heavily perfumed. Hok-Ling knew the costume of a courtesan, and he released the boy immediately. The youngster started to run again, but a second later Hok-Ling called after him, "Hey! Tell me what is it? What's going on up there?"

The boy cried over his shoulder, "Don't you know? It's an execution."

A low murmuring rumbled through the crowd, and it appeared that those nearest the center of the circle up ahead retreated a step or two, forcing the others back upon the themselves. Hok-Ling instinctively sought a vantage point. He bounded across the street and climbed to the top of a ladder that leaned against the wall of a warehouse. From there, his view of the public square was unobstructed.

Near the far side of the circle of onlookers, a constable wearing a blue uniform with a full-length skirt and cloth slippers stood over the slumped, decapitated body of a male child of no more than twelve or thirteen years. The pale, unblemished body was naked, save a loose, white loincloth. In the position of death, the child's small buttocks pointed skyward, as though he had only just then put his ear to the ground to listen. Blood poured freely from his neck around his detached head. His shoulders were forced back unnaturally, and his lifeless limbs were twisted up, bound to a backboard. The backboard, no doubt intended for a larger victim, extended upward, a foot or more past the child's elevated buttocks.

Hok-Ling tasted his vomit at the sight of death, yet he found he could not look away.

The constable kicked the end of the backboard with his foot, causing the body to roll onto its side. Hok-Ling held on to the ladder with both hands, and by force of concentration kept his knees from buckling. Out of the corner of his eye, he spotted Wai-Sung, standing with his brother near the front of the crowd. They were not ten feet from the dead boy, and Hok-Ling felt pity for his friend, for having witnessed the moment of death, and at such close quarters. Just then he heard a piteous wailing, and when he covered his eyes to block the sun he saw—through a copse of steel-tipped flintlocks—the faces of the condemned man, and his wife, and their two remaining children, a round-faced girl of fifteen or sixteen, and a boy of five or six. Each was fastened with hemp to a dark, narrow, bloodstained backboard. The girl was being pulled out into the open by one of the guards, and forced to her knees near the body of her brother. Evidently, she had chosen to die with her family rather than be enslaved. The younger male child, not having reached puberty, would be emasculated for his father's crime. But first he would watch the rest of his family perish. It was in keeping with the ancient custom of familial extermination, Hok-Ling knew—a rare punishment reserved for acts of treason or official corruption. Hok-Ling could not read what was written on the backboards of the condemned prisoners.

While the girl was being positioned for her execution, Hok-Ling stared at the older prisoners. The woman's face had fairly come apart with grief, but her husband's was stiff. It bore deep parenthetical lines and a false and concentrated air of detachment. He flinched only slightly at the sudden flash of the long sword. He did not look—would not. Thus, he did not see his daughter die.

17

"It is very beautiful here," Lei Chi-Man exclaimed as he stepped from the deck of the *Henry Villard*. He was not looking at the water, but at the steep side of Miner's Mountain.

"Yes, it's nice all right. There's the camp, over there," Jason said, pointing. "All those tents and shacks. Up there is the hotel and the railroad office. The railroad right-of-way goes along this shore, and it turns east down there ten miles or so. From there it follows the Clark's Fork into Montana and the Rocky Mountains."

"And these are houses for the Americans," Lei Chi-Man added, still squinting at the buildings perched high on the flank of the mountain above the arching road.

"Yes. That's right. Some of them. Looks like the camp is pretty empty. Let's see who's here."

The path leading from the dock had been beaten to a powdery dust. It spread like water beneath their feet. They climbed to the edge of the camp, running up the last little hill.

Lei Chi-Man plucked a grass stem and twisted it in his fingers. "The Chinese leave their homes and families, crossing the sea to reach a land of fortune and happiness. They send almost every dollar home and live like this. Where is the fortune and happiness?"

Jason set his hands on his hips and looked around. Even in the bright sunshine there was a gloominess about the cluttered camp, an aura of meanness and struggle and loneliness. For a moment, he was glad the faces of its inhabitants were missing. What he saw in his mind's eye depressed him: a throng of thin men, of brown bodies—as brown as Hok-Ling had appeared to him the day before—bent and lethargic, hair and queues slick with unwashed oils and dirt. Two thousand sets of small, pinched, eyes—brooding eyes—mouths shut, two thousand men breathing slowly through their noses, their heads turning slowly to see him.

In front of the tents and the doorless shacks there were scattered piles of driftwood, like the bones of strange creatures, ends worn round. Blankets of all colors, faded reds and greens, tattered, multicolored blankets stretched over tent lines here and there. Their colors were like blisters in the heat and dust. Their limp corners cast shadows, black and still, against tent walls or over the ravaged ground. Wisps of smoke climbed out of the ashes of campfires, and there were spoiled bits of food and rusted cans thrown about, and charred, overturned kettles.

They walked slowly into the heart of the camp. Lei Chi-Man stopped suddenly, as if startled. He craned his neck and pointed toward the last row of tents, toward a spot thick with deciduous trees. "There is someone!" he cried. "Over there. A man with an umbrella." Jason looked up, but saw nobody. "He is behind the furthest tent now," Lei Chi-Man explained.

Jason looked around, wiping sweat from his forehead. "All right, Charlie. Go talk to him. Ask him if he knows Hok-Ling. Don't tell him anything, just ask. If he can help us, come and get me. I'll be over there." He pointed to a large open area at the center of the camp, ringed by fire pits and old, broken-down tables and chairs.

"All right." The interpreter stutter-stepped around a network of ropes that anchored two opposing tents then quickened his pace, angling toward the place where he'd seen the man with the umbrella. He stretched his neck intermittently as he wove his way among the crude habitations, around debris and woodpiles and campfires, straining to keep his eyes on the black tent in the distance. Jason watched for a time, then moved toward the clearing. As he approached from the rear of a large, rectangular tent and rounded its corner, he was stopped, not by the force of his own will, but by the effect of utter surprise.

A few yards away, a woman stood in front of a gray, weathered shack, its tin roof heavily streaked with rust. She wore faded, oversized dungarees and a green silk shirt with tiny flowers of red and orange brocaded on its collar. Her hair was pulled back and tied with a piece of string, its length unbraided. Two long spears of black hair escaped capture. These drooped wing-like as she bent and straightened and bent again, lifting and sorting soiled shirts and trousers from a jumble of wadded clothing on the ground. She placed the clothing into two large canvas bags at her sides.

Her eyes were grave with introspection, her mouth dour. Twice as he stood watching her, her brows furrowed. She lifted one of the sacks and pushed its contents to the bottom. When done, she wet her lips delicately and guided a long, bothersome forelock over her ears. Her face, when she bent low again, was the color of tarnished gold.

He had never seen a Chinese woman before, only artists' depictions. How different this woman was! Her nose and eyes were larger, her chin stronger, than any he had seen depicted on canvas. Her bearing spoke (to him) of a self-possession and rectitude tempered by storms, corporeal and otherwise, such that one who was never there might never know her. But where was "there" exactly? And what is she doing *here*? Jason coughed—a single sharp, involuntary cough. At first, he was not aware of it, but the woman jumped at the sound and gasped softly. Her eyes grew wide and fearful. It was this that prompted him into an awareness of himself.

"Hello—oh, I'm sorry. Did I frighten you?" Mei-Yin's dark eyes met his. He smiled uncomfortably. She blindly groped for the drawstrings of the two bags and stepped back. "I did, didn't I? I'm very sorry." He extended his hand. "My name is Jason McQuade."

Mei-Yin backed away quickly, dragging the two bags. "Please believe me," he begged. She turned and, despite her unwieldy burden, ran between two tents and disappeared. He ran after her, shouting, "Hey! Don't go! Please! I want to talk to . . . " But when he reached the end of the passage through which she had fled, he saw only the two bags lying on the ground and row upon row of tents and shacks and lean-tos, and the silent frozen clutter of the camp as before.

He found Lei Chi-Man sitting in the shade near a talkative brook, which the Chinese called Gold Creek. He held a long, blond stem of ryegrass in his mouth. With his chewing its tassel darted and danced in front of his face, bee-like. Sitting next to him, leaning against a tree, was another Chinese, a skinny old man with weathered skin and retreating, rheumy eyes that glinted out of the shade. This man's right arm was splinted, and poorly so, for there was a grotesque curvature to the forearm visible through his wrappings. Jason moved under the tree with an outstretched hand, but when the Chinese did not return the gesture—but spurned him with a dismissing wave of his gnarled fingers—Jason leaned out of the shadow and spit, something that he had not done in years.

"Is this the man you saw?" he asked Lei Chi-Man.

The interpreter, sensing his employer's irritation, sprang to his feet. "It's him. Yes."

"What does he know?" Jason withheld his look from the old man, hoping to slight him. He couldn't help noticing, however, when the injured man raised an earthenware jug that had been half-concealed in the tall grass near his hip and drank from it thirstily.

"This man has heard of Wong Hok-Ling but does not know him. He has heard that Hok-Ling was arrested for killing a sheriff, was taken to Sandpoint, tortured, and killed by the white demons."

"The white demons?"

The interpreter smiled and looked away from Jason's eyes. "Demons, yes. Don't worry about that. In China, all foreigners are demons. Only the Chinese—Tang people—are civilized." He looked back at Jason in earnest and waved his hands about. "Good white men, bad white men, all are demons to the Chinese. Do you see?"

Jason gave the man with the splinted arm a wintry smile. "Does he work with Hok-Ling?"

Lei Chi-Man turned and scowled at the man, who wiped a dripping excess of rice wine from his lips. He put the question in an angry voice.

"No. This man works with a tunneling crew. He fell from a scaffold three weeks ago. Hasn't worked since."

Jason looked out into the sunlight. "Damn. Ask him if there is anyone else in the camp today, anyone who has worked with Hok-Ling?"

"He says the men have all gone. There are some sick or injured about, but they are asleep in the tents. He doesn't know them."

"When will they get back? The others, I mean." Jason had to concentrate to avoid watching the man as Lei Chi-Man repeated the question. He spit again.

"He says not for three days. The men are working several miles east. They're building shacks and cutting firewood for the winter. They'll be back Thursday or Friday."

Jason rolled his eyes. "Great! We've wasted our time coming here." He started to walk into the open, then turned. "Tell this man I saw a Chinese woman in the camp, a young woman picking up clothes. Ask him who she is. See if that's Soo-Kwan's sister." Now Jason looked at the old man. When the question was put to him, the old drunk smiled with his toothless mouth and sodden eyes. He put his good left hand over his crotch and shook it so violently that it pained the other two men to watch. The man was fairly squeezed shut with silent laughter and did not breathe or utter a sound. Finally, he stopped the incredible waggling and revived himself with four great, wheezing gasps of air. Lei Chi-Man listened to the old coolie's excited conclusion then turned to Jason and swallowed before speaking.

"This man is an imbecile."

"I have no doubt. What does he say?"

"He says . . . "

"Go on. Well?"

"He says this woman is the hole into which the men of the camp crawl in their dreams. He says he personally has . . . " Lei Chi-Man stopped.

"Has what?" Jason scowled.

"Has lain with this woman many times. That he sneaks into her tent at night. That she cries out with pleasure at the sight of him. He warns us, 'Do not tell Soo-Kwan,' for she is his sister, and he would not understand their lovemaking." As the interpreter related this, the old letch watched eagerly and giggled, drooling over reddened gums.

"He is imbecile, Ja-sawn." Lei Chi-Man turned his back on the old man. He held his chin high and folded his arms at his chest.

Jason said, "And then some. I have seen the woman. Let's go."

Lei Chi-Man ducked under the birch boughs and stepped into the sunshine ahead of Jason. He mumbled a string of Chinese curses under his breath. Jason watched him, then looked down at the simpering drunk. The Chinese's eyes were half-closed, but they peered up at Jason as if to implicate him in his secrets. Jason bent over suddenly and snatched the neck of the jug. The old man lurched sideways onto the grass in a poor attempt to prevent it, and his brown fingers groped the matted grass. Finally, he twisted around, and looking up at Jason again, his eyes opened wide. He smiled puckishly, then nodded and pointed to the earthenware vessel. "*Yam! Yam!*" he cried.

Jason winked and smiled, and this brought the tongue out of the old man. His shoulders and his eyebrows flew up with uncontrolled fancy. "*Yam! Yam!*" He pointed a shaking finger at Jason.

"Let me guess," said Jason. "*Yam* means 'have a drink'—am I right?"

Lei Chi-Man said he was.

Jason, still with his eyes on the old man, pointed at the jug and then at himself, questioningly. "*Yam?*" The old man nodded, ecstatic. "Why, thank you." Jason stepped away into the sunshine. He took a long stride and hurled the jug into the air with all his strength. It sailed on a high arc, twisting, spitting its clear liquid in all directions. Near the end of its flight it struck a tree and exploded. "Y-a-a-a-m!" Jason shouted, spreading his arms. Shards of clay scattered over the ground like hailstones. The old man tried in vain to stand up. His good arm and his splinted one both stretched out toward the wine-splattered tree. Jason turned to him again. "Thanks." He stomped away, brushing his hands. Lei Chi-Man fell into step with him and together they set off for the landing.

"The woman you saw must be Soo-Kwan's sister," Lei Chi-Man volunteered after a long period of silence.

"Yes. And tomorrow we will find her again and return her money."

"Tomorrow? You don't want to wait for Thursday or Friday, when the men will return?"

"Nope. Tomorrow. She's not safe here."

* * *

"Charlie?" Jason faced the door at the end of the hotel hallway. He knocked again. "Charlie? Are you in there?" There was no answer.

The door of the next room opened with a screech. Lei Chi-Man leaned out. He had only his black pants on. His suspenders were attached and hung in loops over his thighs. "Good morning, Ja-sawn," he said, scratching his head.

Jason glanced quickly at the door in front of him then scampered toward the interpreter, waving him back into the room. He slipped through the door and closed it gently behind him. "Wrong room," he whispered, grimacing, then signaling for quiet. He set his eyes as if listening for a sound beyond the door.

"No one there," declared Lei Chi-Man flatly.

"No one is staying there?"

"I don't think so," Charlie answered, and then he stopped and seemed to listen himself. "No. I don't think so."

Jason straightened. "Oh, good. Say, I thought you said your room was at the end of the hallway?"

Lei Chi-Man looked at him, then moved to the open suitcase on the dresser top and took out a white shirt. He put it on then stared out the window, buttoning it. "It was, until last night."

"What happened last night?"

"The manager knocked on door. Using pidgin English, he told me to move. 'Chinaman move,' he said. 'No want Chinaman in window fac-ee street. Bad for business.'"

"Oh God."

"I told him I wouldn't look through the window—that he could close the curtains as far as I was concerned." Lei Chi-Man turned and pointed angrily toward the adjoining room. "He said 'No, no good. Chinaman move butt. Now!'"

Jason sneered and shook his head. "Yeah, the bastard."

Lei Chi-Man's face darkened, then he scoffed and shook his head as he pulled his suspenders over his shoulders. "It was shameful for me," he said.

18

Mei-Yin emerged from behind a tree holding her stomach and wiping her mouth. What am I to do, she asked herself as she looked up to get her bearings. There was her tent and, just beyond, smoke rising rhythmically in modest, inward-turning puffs from her morning fire. Both—the tent and the column of smoke—were bisected by bright slanting sunlight and forest shadows. I've made a terrible mistake, she thought. I've come so far only to have the gods punish me at the last moment. Why couldn't they have let me die on the ship? Or taken their revenge on the long road to this place? Instead, they waited until I was within an arm's length of Hok-Ling, until our very fingertips were within reach. What a cruel fate. If only I had stayed back and waited until daylight to enter Sandpoint. Yes, that's what I should have done. I would not have been raped. I had money to pay my way onto the boat. The reunion I dreamed of was meant to happen in the daylight. Instead, I was impatient. So impatient.

Mei-Yin stared at the teapot hanging over the fire. When steam began to rise out of it, she reached over with a dew-soaked rag and picked it up. She poured the boiling water into her cup and black tea leaves swam and circled riotously. I am lost here without Hok-Ling, she admitted to herself as she picked her way over the loamy soil and sat on a granite outcropping that commanded an expansive view of the lake. She was up before the cicadas, but nuthatches and black-capped chickadees were awake and conversant in the pines over which she set her gaze. I can't go back to Kwangchow—even if I had the money. I can't stay here either. I don't speak English and I am hated here, as are all Tang people. There will be nothing for me here if . . . She closed her eyes. If Hok-Ling is executed, then it is clear what I must do.

A tear rolled down her cheek, and she wiped it with the palm of her hand. "I am the cause of it all," she said aloud. Then to herself again she said, because of my impudence, Hok-Ling is in grave danger. Perhaps they have killed him already, or at best he is suffering in a jail cell and may soon be put to death. And then I will have no one.

She stared down at the tea for a few moments and then raised the cup to her lips. As she drank it in, a new thought occurred to her. What about the choices *I* have—to try to save Hok-Ling? To admit to the killing myself, if necessary?

Another idea presented itself. What if the $500 Dak-Wah and Soo-Kwan recovered and delivered to Hok-Ling is insufficient? The system, she thought, must be the same here as in Kwangchow, at least in outline. A payment is made to one, but it gets spread out—and up. There are the suggestive, oblique glances between officials, and insinuative hands stretch out in the odd upticks and pauses of the day. Rather than sit and worry, I will help Hok-Ling by raising more money. I will double my efforts. There is almost no limit to the number of shirts, pants, and socks the men want washed or mended.

* * *

One long blast of the steam whistle meant the *Mary Moody* was leaving the Sandpoint dock. The echo that returned from Granite Mountain a mile and a half to the southeast simulated a double blast. It swept over the vessel as a deckhand, pulling the dripping stern line through a hawse pipe and coiling it on the aft weather deck, exchanged lighthearted banter with a man standing with his dog at the end of the dock. "Good days" sealed their conversation over the rapidly expanding, churning, bubbling space of separation.

In the bow Jason and Lei Chi-Man leaned comfortably over the rails. Staring down into the silent "moving water," each noticed—it was impossible not to see—hundreds and then thousands of blades of light that angled obliquely beneath the surface and disappeared at a depth of five or six feet. Jason recalled the memory of those glinting bayonets that passed beneath his bare feet as a child, whose unsmiling owners, in parade formation, held forth so general and inscrutable an expression. He snorted at the absence of his father from that regiment or any other, then looked up. He turned and put his back to the rail.

"I don't know much about you, Charlie," he said, setting his gaze to a receding series of mountain peaks far to the north. The wind created by the accelerating vessel began to toss both men's hair.

Lei Chi-Man glanced up at the tall, twenty-six-year-old from whom, less than six weeks earlier, he had received an unexpected letter, in which the young attorney had introduced himself, taken pains to explain his role in the upcoming defense of Hok-Ling, and left no doubt about the urgency of his need for professional interpretive services. Lei Chi-Man's expression registered the depth of his surprise that the attorney would now ask questions about the details of *his* life. "What do you mean?" he asked.

"Well, what your life's like, how you ended up living in San Francisco, that sort of thing. I know you're a certified court interpreter. You come highly recommended by the clerk of the California Supreme Court."

"Yes," Lei Chi-Man mused. "Now that Tang people can testify."

"You once wrote for a Chinese newspaper, *The China News.*"

"Mmm."

"But I don't know much else."

"What else do you want to know?" Lei Chi-Man asked self-consciously, again focusing his eyes on the "moving water."

"Well, are you married, for example? Do you have a family?"

"No. I'm single. I thought I would be married two years ago, but our fathers ended up in an argument. That was that."

"Your English is perfect. Where did you learn to speak it?"

"I was born in Oakland. My parents insisted that my brother, my two sisters, and I all be tutored in English from the age of three on. They hired students from St. Ignatius College to tutor us and paid them very well."

"What does your father do?"

The questions came in this fashion thirteen to the dozen and touched on subjects as far-ranging and innocuous as the size of Lei Chi-Man's family and the spark that lit the interpreter's interest, at age twelve, in California mission architecture. Lei Chi-Man submitted to the interrogation with calm perseverance, pausing after each question in a characteristic way. Only once or twice did he raise his eyes from the water to find an answer in the distance.

Jason finally let a little silence in. "May I ask a question of you now?" asked Lei Chi-Man, turning his head.

"Sure."

"This case. Can you tell me, why did you take it?"

"What do you mean?"

"What do you expect of it? It seems you've taken a case at the very start of your legal career that places you at odds with almost everyone here—certainly all the white people. Even your mentor. This man Hok-Ling has admitted killing the sheriff—although not publicly. He had both motive and opportunity, as the courts say. He's Chinese. I'm curious why you'd take the case. Or perhaps you didn't have a choice?"

"No, of course I did. An attorney can't be forced to represent someone against his will."

"Then why, if I may ask?"

Jason seemed almost to welcome the implication. He turned back to face the south and sniffed loudly, collecting his thoughts. "It's bigger than me," he said at last. "It's a long shot all right, but if I can win . . . " He choked over the word, then paused a long time, his eyes widening as a curtain opened in his mind and distant memories, painful ones, jostled for his attention. "If I can win," he repeated, "then people will see that . . . "

Jason could not, or in any event did not, finish the sentence before Lei Chi-Man interjected, "Yes, yes, Ja-sawn. I understand. The law protects all men."

* * *

In the heat of an airless afternoon Mei-Yin stood up to her shins in water a few feet from the shore. Her loose black pants were rolled to her knees, and the sleeves of an oversized blue work shirt—a man's shirt—were rolled above her elbows. She was bent over at the waist near a pile of clothing that rose out of the shallow water like a mountain isle. Taking a garment from this pile, she scrubbed it with a bar of lye soap, her hands and arms churning the water like pistons. Each article was carefully wrung out, unfurled, inspected, then tossed onto one of two stacks on the pebbled shore (depending on the presence of open seams and tears needing mending). Feverishly she labored, stopping to wipe her forehead with the back of her hand only once in the time it took Jason and Lei Chi-Man to walk from the landing, along the crest of the bank, among leafy young cottonwoods and devil's club, to a place opposite her, and from there, to inch their way over the rocky shore, undetected. A trail of grayish water and bubbles stretched south from where

Mei-Yin stood, and it seemed neither to dissipate nor to run ashore. Lei Chi-Man called out to her on a signal from Jason.

Mei-Yin turned, startled. She held a dripping gray work shirt in her hands. She glanced first at Jason, but spoke to the interpreter. "What do you want?"

"I am Lei Chi-Man," he said, bowing. "This is Ja-sawn McQuade. He is an attorney, a *leuht si*. He is responsible for defending a coolie named Wong Hok-Ling, who has been charged with murder. Do you know this man, Wong Hok-Ling?"

Mei-Yin looked at Jason. Her eyes narrowed distrustfully. This is the same demon who approached me yesterday, who frightened me.

"Please do not be afraid," Lei Chi-Man added. "We are looking for the sister of a friend of Hok-Ling's, a man named Soo-Kwan. Are you this woman?"

Mei-Yin continued to stare at Jason, transfixed—her body so still, in fact, that the water beneath her flattened and reflected the twin pillars of her legs.

Mei-Yin's gaze evidently disarmed Jason as well. He cleared his throat. "Tell her about the money," he managed at last. Mei-Yin's eyes widened at the sound of Jason's voice. "And tell her not to be afraid," he added.

"I have said that," the interpreter answered calmly. He bowed toward Mei-Yin again. "We are sorry if we frightened you. Are you Soo-Kwan's sister? If so, we have your money."

Hok-Ling's attorney? she thought. Then there is hope. She wiped sweat from her nose then lowered her eyes and stared blankly at the water's edge where it reached in among the rocks. What has Hok-Ling told them? she wondered. Do they know what happened that night? What do they want with me? What does he mean "my money"? And who is this Tang person who speaks for the attorney?

Neither man disrupted her puzzled silence. She began to space her questions and in the interstices answers began to dawn. Is Hok-Ling still alive? Yes, he must be. What have they done with him? If this man defends Hok-Ling then he awaits trial in Sandpoint, as a prisoner. Have they seen him there, visited him, talked to him? Yes. Of course! The Tang person would not know of Soo-Kwan and Soo-Kwan's sister except by Hok-Ling's mouth. But what money are they talking about? Hok-Ling's money?

"What do you want with me?" she asked gravely, looking up at Lei Chi-Man then down again.

"She asks what you want with her," he told Jason.

"If this is Soo-Kwan's sister, tell her we have the $500 that Hok-Ling was holding for her in his lockbox. Tell her that the money was stolen from his lockbox after his arrest, but that someone returned it—we don't know who—and delivered it to him. Tell her our client has instructed us to give it back to her."

Lei Chi-Man complied with these instructions.

"I don't think she believes us," Jason said. He pulled the envelope out of his coat pocket and held it up for her to see.

Mei-Yin glanced at the envelope then turned to the interpreter. She needed time to think. "Please ask the demon why he is bringing me this money."

Why did you do this, Hok-Ling? The money Soo-Kwan and Dak-Wah recovered and delivered to you was for bribing the judge. Why have you told this attorney to bring it to me? I'm so confused!

"This money was found by a deputy green coat," answered Lei Chi-Man. "It was turned over to the court. The judge gave it to Mr. McQuade to pay for Hok-Ling's defense. However, Hok-Ling has explained to us that this was never his money. It was money he was holding for you at your request. He asked that it be returned to you. Your brother is Soo-Kwan?" Mei-Yin nodded hesitantly. "Of course. And thus we have brought it back to you."

"Why did he choose to return it?"

"The attorney?"

"No. Hok-Ling."

"Have I not just said? That is all I know."

Mei-Yin dropped her shoulders wearily and bent over to immerse the shirt that she still held in her hands. She began to scrub the collar, then stopped. When she straightened again with the tattered garment dripping in her hands it was clear that she had used this time to collect herself. There was a firmness in her eyes and her face seemed to darken with resolution. She tossed the shirt back onto the island of soiled clothes, then looked up at Lei Chi-Man, shading her eyes. "You are very kind to bring me this money. A reward is in order." She stepped toward them, then halted and bowed. "Please. Take what money is fair for your trouble."

Lei Chi-Man started to translate. Jason declared, "Tell her, no. No re—"

"Yes please! Please take!" Mei-Yin interrupted. She blushed at her boldness and then, realizing but hardly believing that she had spoken in English, she closed her eyes and bowed, if only for the moment's escape.

Jason stared at her nonplused, but Lei Chi-Man smiled as if he had discovered a friend in disguise. "You speak English," he laughed. "Oh!"

"No. Only a little," explained Mei-Yin in her native Cantonese. She continued to look into the water, embarrassed. At last, she added, "What I know I have learned from an English-speaking cook aboard the *China Sea*, the ship that brought me here. It is not much."

"Oh my! Oh my!" exclaimed Lei Chi-Man, nodding and smiling warmly. His enthusiasm caused her to look up and smile with her eyes. For a long time Lei Chi-Man's teeth flashed, and his eyes were all but shut. There were the crow's feet at his temples again. "Even a little English is wonderful. It's a difficult language to learn, isn't it? I'm impressed."

Mei-Yin tipped her head to thank him. She spoke again in Cantonese. "Please, sir. Take as much money as the two of you desire. I will consider myself most fortunate whatever the remainder."

"You are most generous, sister of Soo-Kwan, but we are not interested in a reward. We wish only to talk to you about this man Hok-Ling. Will you come out of the water to speak to us?"

Without answering, she walked toward them, toward a point between them. When she reached the shore, she unrolled her pant legs and her sleeves. She took the envelope offered by Jason then bowed gently, first with her face turned toward Jason, then toward Lei Chi-Man. "Let us go this way, please. I must make tea."

She led them on a narrow path over an incline covered with sharp stones and hemmed in by stinkweed and thistle. When they reached the edge of the camp, where virtually all vegetation had been eradicated except for a few stunted dandelions, her pace quickened. She turned in and out of the various campsites so abruptly and effortlessly that Lei Chi-Man and Jason looked at each other in wonder and were pressed to keep up. They entered the large open area where Jason had encountered her the day before. She stopped before the same weathered shack. This was the knock-down occupied by Hok-Ling, Soo-Kwan, and Dak-Wah. Jason stepped to the door and peered in. The afternoon sun lit a small wedge of its floor, but beyond that the interior was dark and obscure, and gave no hint of itself from the outside. Ten steps from the open door, the remnants of a fire burned low, its flame almost invisible above the charred sticks and billets and whitish ash. The woman took several pieces of driftwood from the pile beneath the eaves and laid them over the flame. She stepped into the shack and reappeared a few moments later carrying a celadon porcelain teapot, which she inspected, then blew into and shook upside down as she passed them and walked toward the water barrel.

"Hope there aren't bugs," Jason quipped. Lei Chi-Man did not answer, but stood by impassively. By contrast, Jason seemed to watch the young woman's every move with unbounded interest until, becoming aware of himself, he sat down on a log beside the fire. Mei-Yin produced a long, rusty iron rod from an assortment of rods and implements leaning up against the wall of the shack. Slipping the bail of the teapot over its crude hook, she lifted the rod and guided its free end into a crevice between two large stones adjacent to the fire pit. In front of these was a third stone, a fulcrum, over which she carefully laid the rod, suspending the teapot over the flame. She backed away from the smoke and gently lowered herself to the ground. Sitting upright, on her ankles, with her hands settled over her knees as gently as seashells come to rest upon the ocean floor, she looked at neither man, but gazed steadfastly, serenely upon the fire. It had begun to surge a little beneath the teapot.

The heat edged up to Jason like a tide, and he drew his legs in and covered his ankles with his hands. Mei-Yin and Lei Chi-Man were both closer to the fire than Jason, and when they saw Jason's reaction they looked at him with prolonged curiosity. "The demon is suffering," said Mei-Yin. "Why doesn't he move?"

Lei Chi-Man snorted, suppressing a laugh. Mei-Yin pressed her lips together and looked away.

"What did she say, Charlie?"

The interpreter looked up, surprised. "Oh, nothing. The tea is almost ready." He raised his head and squinted over the steam rising from the brim of the teapot. "Yes. Almost."

Mei-Yin rose suddenly and fluidly and leaned over the fire to check the teapot herself. This attorney is too young, she thought. He is not old and wise like the *leuht si's* of Kwangchow. He is nervous and inexperienced, and very emotional. He fidgets— and he smiles too much. What chance will Hok-Ling have with a smiling attorney? It's good that Hok-Ling has an English-speaking demon to speak for him in court, but this *leuht si* is just too young!

Mei-Yin arranged three ceramic bowls on the ground and poured the steaming liquid into each. Her smile blossomed, lifting the corners of her eyes. Using both hands, she lifted one bowl at a time, handing one to each man. Jason and Lei

Chi-Man took theirs and when she had had taken one up as well, they drank. Only when they began to drink did she sip her own. She watched the interpreter for several minutes. When he paused and signaled his refreshment by laying his bowl on the ground, she said to him, "Soo-Kwan and the others are away for two or three days. When he returns, I will tell him of your visit. He will have many questions." Lei Chi-Man nodded. Mei-Yin measured off a pause, then continued, "First, he will ask, 'How is my friend, Hok-Ling?' He will ask this."

Jason divined the meaning and smiled at her. "Hok . . . Ling . . . is *fine*. Fine . . . O-kay."

She turned and shook her head mechanically but her eyes betrayed bewilderment. "O-kay?"

"Yes," offered Jason. "Okay—fine. Same thing." Jason drew an arc in the air to illustrate the connection.

Lei Chi-Man coughed into his hand. "The man Hok-Ling is in good health. He is held in a cell in Sandpoint, but is not mistreated. We are told he has not eaten in many days, but this is by his own choice." Lei Chi-Man looked at Jason and grinned. "Let me answer, please, Ja-sawn."

Jason reddened with frustration. "Yes, of course. All right, Charlie. Ask her if she knows Hok-Ling herself. If they've met."

The interview lasted more than an hour. Mei-Yin remembered what Hok-Ling had instructed, and succeeded in hiding the truth by offering half-truths, and in some cases lying. She told them, for example, that she'd first met Hok-Ling only a week or two before his arrest. That she knew nothing of his past, or of his family, except that he had mentioned his father once or twice. He was an eel vendor, she thought. When she was asked if she knew anything about the woman who waited for him in China, Mei-Yin hesitated and stared at her hands.

"Her name is Mei-Yin," Lei Chi-Man said.

Mei-Yin's heart seemed to swell dangerously. She felt a weakness in her neck but managed to raise her head to see if the two men had detected her reaction. They seemed not to have.

"How do you know this?" she whispered to the interpreter, for the first time signifying a desire to speak to him privately.

"He told us. This is the woman he came here for. He said her name. I remember. Mei-Yin."

She stared at the small patch of earth between them. What has Hok-Ling done? she thought. Why has he used my name? Has he changed his mind? Can I tell the truth now? About that? Oh, it would be wise! Should I tell them it is I they speak of? Yes, oh yes, and be done with it. Have you given them my name so that they can find me, Hok-Ling? So that I can tell the attorney that you are good and gentle. That you . . . ?

Her eyes began to climb up to meet Lei Chi-Man's stare. But wait! If this is true, why didn't he tell them that *I* am Mei-Yin, not Soo-Kwan's sister? Why did you give them this money to give to me? Oh, my head! I can't think! Did you use my name mistakenly? Oh, Hok-Ling, what do I do now?

"Do you know of this—"

"What? Oh. I'm sorry, Lei Chi-Man," she whispered. "What is her name again?"

"He calls her Mei-Yin."

"No," she explained, shaking her head. "I have never . . . I know nothing of this woman."

19

The house was as quiet as sleep itself. That is not to say it was perfectly still. Like a sleeper, it breathed through an open window in the living room. The white margins on the pages of *Harper's New Monthly Magazine* fluttered softly beneath the billowing curtains, so it was that loud. And in the kitchen, between draining boards still damp from washing, the faucet dripped a heartbeat. And from the warming stove there came sharp, irregular snaps like the snaps of knee and ankle joints. It was that loud. And there were the soft sounds of Mrs. Stewart's puttering—her slippers on the stairs, the door of the china closet opening and shutting, the sweep of her broom in the kitchen and on the porch. These, like little bowel sounds, could be heard. But it was quiet on the whole, as quiet as sleep.

Jason awoke a few minutes after seven. He staggered to the dresser, poured cool water from a white enamel pitcher into a matching pan and splashed it over face and hair, then examined himself blindly in the mirror as he toweled off. He was oblivious to a shock of yellow and white roses mingled with leaves that winked at him from a glass vase beside the mirror. He peeled off his nightshirt and dressed hurriedly in the bracing air. Clean socks awaited him in the top drawer. He looked at his watch and whispered the time to himself in a mannered, clipped voice while anchoring the fob in a buttonhole of his vest and tucking the silver instrument into his pocket. Then he crossed the room to pick up his black shoes.

"Is that you, dear?" Antonea Stewart wiped her hands on a towel as she looked up at the closed door at the top of the stair. It was dark but for two thin vertical lines a door's width apart and a third suggestion of light above the casing. "Breakfast in five minutes."

"Thank you, Mrs. Stewart," Jason called out. He sat on the edge of the bed and loosened the laces of his shoes. His thoughts traveled back to the image of Soo-Kwan's sister standing in the water, shading her eyes. How suddenly and unexpectedly this pose had revealed the fullness and perfection of the Chinese woman's breast, even the hint of a nipple. It surprised and delighted him more than he would have guessed possible. Here I am still thinking about it, he said to himself as he put on one shoe and then the other, and then tied them. I guess a Chinese woman is like any other in that regard. Had Lei Chi-Man noticed, too?

He sat up, remembering the moment of their leave-taking. The long, uncomfortable silence broken by the *Mary Moody's* ten-minute warning. He'd stood, brushed the back of his pants, then offered his hand to Mei-Yin, but she didn't take it. He remembered being startled by the pallor of her face as she clambered to her feet. Her full, rose-colored lips trembled slightly as though some important message were trying to escape. She bowed but did not make eye contact with him.

"Please tell your brother Soo-Kwan and Dak-Wah that I— that *we*—will return to ask them a few questions," he'd said.

"It's very likely that I will want to call them as character witnesses at trial." Jason had turned to Lei Chi-Man, who nodded his understanding. When the interpreter was done, Jason had added, "And thank you very much for the tea." Being somewhat dumbfounded by her expression, he'd put his hands on his thighs and bowed his head. "Thank . . . you."

"Thank you," she'd whispered, imitating his movements. He and Lei Chi-Man, with jarring steps, then walked down the steep, well-worn path to the dock. But for Jason there was an invisible pull in the opposite direction.

Mrs. Stewart reached over his shoulder and placed a steaming bowl of oat porridge before him. Two-day-old bread, butter, and strawberry preserves shared the oilcloth-topped table with three skittish black flies. "No eggs this morning," she said, setting a cup of coffee down beside the porridge. "Don't know what the hens are up to."

Antonea Stewart was a sixty-three-year old widow who'd moved to Idaho from Neosho Rapids, Kansas, in 1867—as the world believed, to honor a secret dream of her late husband's, but as she knew to relieve herself of the recurring obligation to visit his grave Wednesdays and Sundays with his increasingly exasperating mother and twin sisters. His war ended at Baxter Springs on October 6, 1863, but hers, she realized, might never end. Her active, round, blue eyes were the telltales of a kind and at times shrewd disposition. She had a round face and densely freckled arms.

"Oh, that's fine," Jason said. "This is going to fill me up."

"I went next door to see if Margaret had any to spare," she continued, "and—strangest thing!—she didn't come to the door. I know she's home. I saw her pass by the window upstairs as I was going through the gate."

"Huh. Indisposed maybe," Jason said between spoonfuls of hot oats.

Mrs. Stewart poured steaming hot water into the pan she'd used to cook the oats. "Perhaps," she said. "I'll go over there and check on her later." A hummingbird buzzed at the open window as Jason slathered butter on a piece of bread. Mrs. Stewart propped open the kitchen door with a ten-pound lead dumbbell that had belonged to her husband, then took a seat at the end of the table. "There's something else I'd like to talk to you about, Jason—this party that Mr. Villard is throwing next week when he and his entourage arrive. It's bound to be the biggest event ever seen in these parts."

"Oh, yes, if he has anything to say about it," Jason chuckled. "Henry Villard doesn't do anything in a small way."

"No, I realize that. That's why I wanted to talk to you. It was very kind of you to ask me to accompany you, but, having thought about it, I'm not one for lavish parties. Never have been. I think perhaps you should ask someone closer to your own age. Esther Langston, maybe."

Jason looked up in the middle of chewing. He took a sip of coffee to help him swallow. "Esther?" he choked. "Are you kidding? Why, she would no more consent to—"

"You hurt her feelings, Jason," Mrs. Stewart said as she wiped her hands on a towel. "That's all. She wasn't ready to hear that you'd taken on that Chinese man's case."

"No, I know that, but how did you . . ?"

"It felt like a betrayal to her. She doesn't understand how lawyers work."

"Well, yes, I suppose," Jason answered. "But how . . ?"

"This is apt to be the social highlight of her life, a chance to meet not only Mr. Villard and his wife, Fanny, but journalists and dignitaries from the East and from Germany as well. She'll want to make these memories with you, Jason. I don't know if you can understand that or not, but it's important to a woman to . . . "

Jason stopped listening. Wrapping both hands around his coffee, he saw behind inward-searching eyes the vision of Esther dressed in a maroon evening gown turning to face him. And then it was not Esther, but Mei-Yin. She walked toward him, smiling, both hands extended. "I've been waiting for you," she whispered.

The inflection in Mrs. Stewart's voice interrupted his thoughts. "You two need to resolve your differences. This trial will soon be over and then things can return to normal around here. I wish Mr. Villard were coming a week after the trial, not the week before. But that can't be helped. I just want you to do right by Esther."

Jason took a last bite of bread, followed it with a gulp of hot coffee, and rose from the table. "I'm running late this morning. Thank you for breakfast."

"Please don't take offense, dear."

"No, no, none taken," said Jason, turning at the door. "I think you're right. However, I want *you* to come to the reception with me. I've elicited your promise, and unless you object adamantly, I intend to hold you to it."

Mrs. Stewart reddened and slapped Jason on the shoulder with her dishtowel. "Get out of here. Yes, all right, I'll go with you. Now get along."

Turning the corner on Lake Street, Jason saw William Fitch in his front yard pruning a large cherry tree. Fitch stood near the top of a tall ladder, wielding a rusty bow saw. He seemed to be looking directly at Jason as he pulled one of the cut branches loose from its entanglements and tossed it to the ground. Jason waved. "Morning, Bill," he said. "Looks like you've got your hands full this morning." But Fitch didn't answer. He turned and commenced sawing another branch. His wife, Dolores, who evidently had been watching her husband from the porch, entered the home and closed the door behind her.

A few minutes later, Mrs. Alda Hendicott, wife of the Presbyterian minister, was approaching Jason on Oak Street. The normally loquacious woman crossed the street and quickened her pace, avoiding eye contact with Jason as she passed.

So this is how it's going to be, Jason thought. Not only are Esther and Emory upset with me, the whole town is.

* * *

Dak-Wah took a deep drag from the long brass smoking pipe and handed it to Mei-Yin. She took it but held it away from her mouth, listening to Soo-Kwan tell a story of home. When he had finished, she took two short puffs of tobacco and passed the pipe. They sat in a long, companionable silence on a rocky outcrop that jutted into the lake.

Soo-Kwan and Dak-Wah were both covered in dirt from the day's toil. Between streaks of black soil, their skin took on some of the reds and oranges from the sunset. A fish jumped nearby. Dak-Wah pointed the mouthpiece of the pipe at the circles widening on the surface of the lake. "I'll get you yet," he joked. Their laughter and teasing banter could be heard by the men in the camp a quarter mile away.

But they grew serious again. "What about the money, Mei-Yin?" asked Soo-Kwan.

"I've hidden it near my tent. They said Hok-Ling told them to give it to me. But this was wrong. He should have . . . "

"I know," said Soo-Kwan, taking the pipe offered by Dak-Wah. "He should have used this money for bribes. This is what we thought, as well. But now that he's given it to you, you must understand. He wants you to use it to return to the Middle Kingdom. You will need a trustworthy escort, of course—"

Mei-Yin raised her hand to shield her eyes. "Return? I do not wish to talk about this. I will not leave here while Hok-Ling is in prison." She saw that both men were startled by her unyielding and therefore unladylike tone. She held each man's gaze and then, in her own time, turned to look at the sunset.

Dak-Wah lay back with his hands behind his head. He nodded at Soo-Kwan. "It's been a long day," he said.

Mei-Yin searched the depths of the blood-red clouds. They speak of returning as though it were walking home from my uncle's fields outside Kwangchow! Return? To my father? Is that what they mean? To the water carrier? Do they know what awaits me there?

Hok-Ling had enough money. More than enough to pay for passage home. Why had he not left this unhappy place? He knew we—*I*—waited for him. He promised and yet . . .

She reached down and touched the smooth granite surface of the outcrop as she had touched the seat of the bench outside the bank in Tacoma. She drummed her fingers lightly, remembering freedom.

* * *

It was Saturday night. Lei Chi-Man, dressed in a dark suit and tie, sat alone in the corner of the hotel dining room surrounded by three empty tables. The remaining tables were full, and a small crowd of people stood near the door waiting to be seated. The three tables closest to the interpreter had been offered and rejected so many times that the waiter stopped referring to them. Diners averted their eyes from the Chinese man as they got up to leave the dining room or were led to their tables.

Lei Chi-Man ate a dinner of mushroom soup, creamed potatoes, lettuce salad, venison, and Yorkshire pudding. A glass of claret accompanied the meal. About the time he had finished and set his silverware on the plate, a piano player near the windows began a medley of songs from *H.M.S. Pinafore*. This touched an appreciative nerve in the room. Lei Chi-Man smiled with the others and kept time to the music with one foot. He ordered another glass of claret. Then he produced a diary from the inside pocket of his suit coat, along with a pencil. The hotel owner, William Carson, served the second glass of claret. "Say there, Mr. Lee. We've got people waiting over there, as you can see."

Lei Chi-Man saw that many of the people crowded at the door were looking at him. "Yes."

Carson ignored the empty tables that surrounded him. "We're going to need you to finish this up and move along."

"I'm sorry?" said Lei Chi-Man, pretending either that he couldn't hear over the music or that he didn't understand the request.

Carson leaned over, red faced. "Drink this and get the hell out of here so I can get these people seated," he snarled.

It was not Carson that drove Lei Chi-Man to his room early that night. Carson had kept his voice very low so that only Lei Chi-Man could hear his menacing order. And it was not the continual glaring of the people standing impatiently at the door, waiting to be seated. What did it were the other diners who, one after another, began to turn in their seats and stare at him. How odd that he had thought a community had formed—not of music lovers writ large, but of people bound together by the humorous genius of W. S. Gilbert and Arthur Sullivan.

20

The banner stretched across Main Street read:

WELCOME MR. H. VILLARD

THE RAILROAD KING!

American flags were draped in store windows and hung from dozens of flagstaffs mounted on the stanchions holding up the sidewalk roofs. Red, white, and blue bunting was festooned beneath the windows of the Carson Hotel. All morning the front and back doors of the community hall were propped open so that bouquets, table settings, silver pieces, pies and other pastries, and chairs and side tables could be brought in in preparation for the gala reception. Strangers began to arrive and check in at the Carson Hotel from as far away as Coeur d'Alene, Rathdrum, and Spokane Falls. They walked in their finest up and down the shady side of Main Street.

The Chinese camp at Hope was quiet by comparison as the men stretched out and let the heat of a late summer's day sink into their tired muscles. It was an unexpected but welcome day off. Men fished from the dock beside the *Henry Villard* or bathed in the warm backwater south of Hope. They gambled or shaved each other's foreheads in the open sunshine. Their conversations did not exceed in intensity the gentle, nearly inaudible coursing of windless waves amongst the pebbles on shore, or the lazy slap-slapping of green, clear water under the aft overhang of the *Henry Villard.*

Preparations of a different kind were underway at the ranch home of Silas Penn seven miles north of the Chinese camp. Penn's son J.R. and his ranch hands Clive, Joseph, Benny, and L.T. were toasting each others' health in the shade of an oak tree with two bottles of Old Charter when Jake Prescott, Lamont Ferguson, and several other young men arrived by horseback. They did not ease their horses in past the gate, but cantered through like a battalion under orders. J.R. looked at the line of dark, sweaty animals through drunken, bleary eyes. "Christ! You were serious," he blurted to Jake Prescott, waving a half-empty bottle at him.

Eight days earlier, Prescott had loosely raised, around word of Henry Villard's arrival, the possibility of a raid on the Chinese camp. The white supervisors and camp bosses would all be in Sandpoint for the festivities, "so it's our chance to let the Chinamen know what we think of them." J.R. had laughed out loud at the time and touched Jake Prescott's tin cup of whiskey with his own, and other cups clinked in the corner of the hayfield on the outskirts of town where a group of young toughs had congregated. But from that moment to this, J.R. had forgotten all about it. A rush of excitement ran through him as he considered the happy coincidence that his father was away on business.

* * *

A short man in a green tweed frock suit with reddish blond hair meandered through the crowd and announced with a heavy

Boston accent that Mr. Villard's stage would arrive "out front" in five minutes. A murmur of anticipation preceded a crescendo in the volume of chatter and laughter as the crowd pressed toward the door. "Isn't this exciting?" exclaimed Mrs. Stewart, who had taken Jason's arm and was pushed close to him, closer than he would have liked.

"Yes, of course," he said. He saw up close the efforts made earlier in the day to brighten and highlight her facial features. From a distance she looks twenty years younger, he told himself. He turned away as though gallantry required this of him, but was glad she was so enthused, and could feel her excitement through his arm.

"Just think, on top of everything else, the owner of *The New York Evening Post*," she said.

"There's not much that Mr. Villard doesn't own, or hasn't from time to time," Jason quipped. He turned in reaction to a gentle push from the crowd and saw that several people converging behind them were strangers, while others he knew or recognized. The latter were at pains to avoid making eye contact with him.

"Once a pariah, always a pariah," he whispered to himself.

When they'd made their way through the foyer and out onto the lawn, the crowd dispersed then reformed in a knot near the road. Jason and Mrs. Stewart hung back at his prompting. "We'll have a chance to meet him," he assured her. He began to scan the faces in the crowd for Emory. He wondered if this odd episode—attending a second Villard reception three years later, more than half a continent away—would give them respite from the estrangement that had been forced on them by his taking Hok-Ling's case. He leaned over to whisper in Mrs. Stewart's ear, "Have you seen . . . ?" But just then Emory's hand came to rest on Jason's shoulder. "There you are," Jason smiled. "I was just asking Mrs. Stewart if she'd seen you. You know Mrs. Stewart, of course."

"I do, indeed," said Emory. "Antonea, you look lovely this evening."

"I've been told that by two lawyers now," she said, "but not a single honest person has so much as broached the subject." She laughed heartily and slapped Emory's arm with the back of her hand. "You don't look so bad yourself, Emory," she continued. "Jason tells me you know Mr. Villard—that the two of you attended one of his receptions back East three years ago."

"That's right." Emory tilted his head back to look at Jason through his glasses. "It has been three years, hasn't it?"

"June of '79," Jason replied. "Right after graduation."

"Ah, yes. I don't know him very well, mind you. I worked for the Oregon Railway and Navigation Company for a time, and then he sent me up here to do some legal work—negotiating and drafting easements, that sort of thing. I fell in love with the place and cut the cord at that point. You watch though. He'll say he remembers me. He's a regular politician, that one. Never forgets a name."

Jason chuckled but his smile was arrested by the sight of Esther Langston standing less than twenty feet away. Why hadn't he seen her before? he wondered. She was looking away and evidently hadn't seen him either. She was dressed in a floor-length lavender dress and matching waist. Two columns of white pearl buttons accented her figure. The garniture of her dress was a single white bow above the bustle, and a ruching of miniature pleats harmonized the hem and the ends of her sleeves. Her golden locks were balanced expertly on top of her head, held in place by a host of unseen hairpins and a single white ribbon tied in a bow at the back of her head. Her blue eyes were turning back and forth between her two childhood friends, Elaine Parker and Mary Silverton, who evidently were discussing something that inspired ardency and friendly disagreement. Esther began to giggle at the histrionics employed by her friends until all three melted into laughter.

It was a laughing Esther who first set eyes on Jason, but the laughter was cut short. She gave him a very somber nod. Her friends saw the change and pulled Esther around, putting her back to Jason.

"Go over there and talk to her, Jason," urged Ms. Stewart, sliding her hand away from his arm. Emory glanced over at Esther and sealed his neutrality by running his fingers over his mustache.

"I probably should," Jason whispered, but just then there came the distant snap of a whip followed by the drumming of horse hooves and the jangle and squeal of carriage suspensions under stress. Looking north, the crowd was silenced by the sight of three overlarge stagecoaches, one after another, turning south onto Main at speed. Each was pulled by four spent-looking black horses, their sweaty shoulders and hindquarters flashing silver as they jostled and sidestepped through the last tight, sun-suffused corner. Coming out of the turns, the wheel horses struggled to regain the rhythm of the leads as the coaches, still swaying precariously, were swallowed up in the late afternoon shadows along Main. The on-rushing sounds intensified second by second. When the first carriage passed under the welcome sign, up shot a giant flag of the United States that nearly doubled the rig's height overall. A cheer went up from the crowd. The stars and stripes waved mightily as the stages advanced in a line toward the community hall. More speed, and more, was being pressed from the horses. Again, the snap of a whip and calls of "Yah! Yah!" could be heard. Slanting clouds of summer dust sprang above them, up and out of the shadows of the buildings on Main Street, so it appeared that gold dust overhung the spectacle. Henry Villard had his entrance.

* * *

"Get your horses ready now," said Jake Prescott to the eleven young men and boys who stood in a loose circle. "We ride in five minutes."

"Go over this thing again, Jake," said J.R. Penn, clearly encumbered by liquor. "We're not going there to kill anybody, right?"

Jake threw aside a piece of ryegrass he was chewing. "That's right—like I was saying before. We're going to scare the hell out of them, but we ain't shooting or hanging nobody. When we get close, we'll light some torches and burn some of their tents, but any shooting will be up in the air. Got that? And some of us brought whips. Those are all right, too. Stick together! We'll ride down on them in a pack and then back up again. We'll meet up at Trestle Creek. Don't nobody take off from there till we're all accounted. Now, get saddled up!"

* * *

The advance man in the green tweed frock suit managed to form the crowd into a long serpentine receiving line. Thus, Henry Villard could shake every hand and cement his celebrity in every eye. His thick German accent seemed to find a place in his laughter as well as his words, so it was easy to know where he was at all times. Beside him stood his wife of sixteen years, Fanny Garrison Villard, the daughter of the famed abolitionist William Lloyd Garrison, and their twelve-year old son, Harold. Villard greeted the townspeople like old friends. When the last of his entourage had disembarked, the three stagecoaches, whose doors were marked "Northern Pacific R. R." in gold leaf, were led away at a walk.

Jason stood between Emory and Mrs. Stewart, watching the approach of the mustachioed Villard, listening to bits and pieces of his banter. "Oh, I agree," he bellowed. "Prettiest spot on the whole line. No doubt about it. That's why I wanted Fanny to come see it. Fanny, this is Mr. Les Carpenter and his wife Ruth."

With the hundreds of others who eavesdropped, waiting their turn in self-imposed silence, a kind of suspended animation developed, an anticipatory contentment that found them looking in on their own lives. Perhaps to find the thing they would share with the honored guest if asked, the thing they were most proud of. Jason found himself doing this, rehearsing for the famous German émigré, Civil War correspondent, confidante to President Lincoln, and now railroad magnate. "I had the good fortune to meet you at the reception you gave at the Parker Hotel in '79. Since then, I've traveled out here to Idaho at the invitation of Emory Morse, and have read the law under him. I'm a lawyer now myself." It did not occur, though, for as he let these words unfold in his mind, his eyes traveled over the head of the famous visitor to a woman at the back of his entourage. He could see only the back and one side of her head at first, but something about her movement drew him in. As he continued to look, Esther looked at him, and she followed his stare to the woman at the back of the line. Suddenly, this woman turned to address one of the other women waiting there. Jason's mouth fell open. Could it be? Just then, Josephine Carter looked up and a wide smile crossed her face. Her hand and arm went up in an excited wave.

"Jason! Hello, Jason! Over here!"

Esther turned to look back at Jason. Their eyes met, although Jason could not hold on. He turned back to Josephine. An expression that spelled neither horror nor joy, but parts of these, landed on his face.

"Impossible," he whispered.

"What is it, Jason?" asked Mrs. Stewart.

"Excuse me," Jason said, stepping out of the line. He walked toward Josephine, who had picked up the train of her dress and was walking toward him.

"Josephine? What on earth?" The next thing he felt was her body pressed close to his, her lips on his neck.

"Oh, Jason!"

Jason pulled her arms down. "What are you doing here?" he exclaimed. "I can't believe you're here."

"Are you mad, Jason? Don't be." She touched the side of his face with delicate fingers. "It's so good to see you."

"Josephine, how did you get here?"

"Oh, I know I should have written, but I wanted to surprise you. It was awful of me. But when Henry and Fanny asked me to accompany them, to play along the way—well, I couldn't say no, especially after they told me that Sandpoint was one of their stops."

Josephine straightened her dress as she looked around at the crowd, most of whom were still focused on Henry Villard and his family. If she noticed Esther Langston staring at her with tears forming, she gave no sign of it. "I thought you'd be happy to see me," she pouted.

"Of course I am," Jason lied. "It's just that I . . . Well, I can't believe you're here, that's all."

"So this is Sandpoint," Josephine said, looking over her shoulder. "It's a far cry from Boston, isn't it?"

"Yes."

She took a deep breath. "But it's beautiful. I couldn't believe how beautiful the mountains were as we approached town—and the lake."

Jason tried to avoid looking at Josephine's tantalizing figure, and the old familiar hunger that dwelt in her eyes. "You're lucky you arrived in one piece. After seeing the way the reinsmen took that last corner, I wouldn't wonder if—"

"Oh, I know. They warned us about that. Henry insists on something memorable at every stop."

"Very impressive, if you can keep the carriages upright."

Josephine laughed and touched her fan to her mouth. "Oh, Jason, if you only knew how much I've missed your sense of humor."

"Come with me, Josephine. I want to reintroduce you to Emory. Do you remember him?"

"Of course," she smiled, gathering the train of her blue and white striped satin dress.

"And I want you to meet Mrs. Stewart, my landlady."

She took Jason's arm. As she moved, he breathed in the familiar odor that encased memories of youthful sexual exploration and discovery, and undifferentiated moments of unfathomable delight.

* * *

Mei-Yin emerged through the doorway of the knock-down with a tin salt shaker. She squatted over a sizzling pan of perch and crappie, preparing to turn them, when she heard the first gunshot followed by a series of whoops and cries. A second shot rang out and then a third. Her heart jumped into her throat. She stood up and ran behind the shack. She was met there by Soo-Kwan, Dak-Wah, and several other men. They could hear but not see what was happening. One of the men ran to a different vantage point and yelled, "Over here!" As a group they ran, Soo-Kwan, Dak-Wah, and Mei-Yin among them, and from this place they could see up the hill to the upper edge of the camp.

Mei-Yin's breath caught as she witnessed the white demons on horseback riding over the tents and lean-tos, setting scores of half-dressed Chinese running in all directions. Great clouds of dust were rising from the skittering, charging, turning horses. One of the riders was chasing down a coolie, whipping him. Gun smoke rose up like chalk strokes on a painting, and then a more ominous column of gray smoke began to form. One of the tents was on fire.

The hollering continued and the marauders slid down further into the camp. Tang people emerged from their tents, running in all directions.

"What do we do?" cried Dak-Wah.

"We must grab our valuables and run," shouted one of the men and a second later he disappeared around the corner of the knock-down.

"They're killing people!" shouted Soo-Kwan. "We have no arms. Come on. We have to get out of here!"

Mei-Yin watched in horror as mounted men torched tent after tent and fired their guns in the air. There was no one to stop them. She saw a coolie chased down and struck with a machete. He screamed. Another man tried to intervene, but he was kicked out of the way, and the then the horse was turned and run over him. Loud whistles added to the cacophony, but Mei-Yin could not tell where they were coming from. Suddenly, a horse at full gallop rounded a tent near her. The rider, with a red handkerchief over his nose, saw her and stopped. He turned the horse in a circle, shouting, "Over here!" Before she could react, he raised a pistol and fired into the dirt a few feet in front of her. Now she ran as fast as her feet could carry her. She ran though open spaces crisscrossed with panic-stricken coolies. She dodged between tents, hopping over tent lines and around clotheslines burdened with clothes. The zing and whistle of bullets, the snap of a whip, the screaming of men filled the air. Mei-Yin dared not look back. Where are Soo-Kwan and Dak-Wah? she asked herself as she ran. She spied a pile of firewood near a copse of cottonwood trees and veered toward it. She dove behind the pile, scraping her hands and knees. The white demons were circling now near the lakeshore with loud war whoops. On a signal from one of them—the rearing back of his horse on two legs—they charged back up into the camp and whipped their horses up the hill to the road, firing into the air. Once they gained the road, they circled again. A few of the men fired randomly into the camp, others into the air. Then, at a gallop, they rode off to the north.

* * *

"Our goal," said Henry Villard, standing at his place at the head table, "is to make sure the people back East know the beauty of this part of the world, and the economic opportunities that are now available. Take my word for it, we will be sending you new neighbors, new friends, opening up new opportunities for all—from here to Tacoma. Thank you."

When the applause had died down, Villard continued, "As a way of showing our appreciation for your wonderful hospitality, Fanny and I have arranged for one of our country's finest pianists to accompany us. She has agreed to perform for us tonight. Miss Josephine Carter."

Josephine rose from her place to great applause. She bowed, then raised her hand. "Ladies and gentlemen, the piece I would like to perform for you tonight is one I wrote several years ago in honor of President Grant. I performed it for him at his fifty-first birthday party in Philadelphia. And I'm happy to report that he rather liked it." Josephine laughed along with the crowd, then raised her hand again. She walked to the spinet piano at the head of the hall, then made a dramatic turn. "As an artistic work, it was not fully realized—cannot be, in fact—without the addition of a second piano, a fact I came to understand a few years later. I have since rewritten the piece for two pianos."

Jason closed his eyes and slowly began shaking his head. "Oh my God, no!" he whispered to himself.

"Now, what you may not know is that you have right here in Sandpoint a former student of mine, with whom I have played this piano duo many times. The last time we performed it together was also at a reception put on by Mr. Henry Villard, that time in Boston's Parker House Hotel. Do you remember this, Henry?"

The guest of honor beamed. "I do indeed."

Josephine continued. "I've asked our advance man, Mr. O'Sullivan, to arrange for a second piano tonight, but, alas, I see only one piano." Josephine pouted elaborately at Mr. O'Sullivan, who was seated at a side table. He rose on cue and raised a triumphant finger in the air as if to say, "Now hold on there. All is not lost." He disappeared momentarily into an adjoining room and came back a few seconds later pushing a second wheeled spinet to the center of the room. The audience applauded the effort, as did Josephine.

But then Josephine's smile seemed to grow serious. "Ladies and gentleman, I fear I may need your help in gaining the cooperation of your own Jason McQuade. Would you join me, Jason, in playing *Two Roads to Appomattox?*" She extended her two hands towards him and set her head at an angle.

Jason felt the eyes of the room upon him, but only Mrs. Stewart offered verbal encouragement. "Go on, Jason. I had no idea you played."

"No. I . . . I can't."

Mrs. Stewart smiled. "Sure you can."

Josephine walked to one of the two pianos and sat down. She began to play. The notes and chord progressions were slow and haunting, suggestive of absence. A theme was discernable, but it gave no satisfaction. Jason recognized it. It was the stirring of exhausted, war-weary soldiers, the silver sun rising through the acrid smoke of a Virginia battlefield, hints of reveille sounding far in the distance—but from whose side? Josephine pressed the keys almost reluctantly, as though even she were, at most, only partly alive to the sonorous effect of her hands' efforts. She looked up at the audience as she changed mid-phrase to a minor key and closed her eyes.

You're trying too hard, Josephine, Jason said to himself. You think you can manipulate the music and make all these people want me to play—want me to fill in the holes and disharmonies you're leaving like crumbs dropped in your path. It'll never happen.

But as Josephine opened her eyes he saw in them the flame of an indomitable fire. She smiled in a triumphant, self-possessed way, the smile of someone who would not be denied. "Ladies and gentlemen, I would like to share with you a unique musical experience, one that captures that fateful day in April 1865 when the Army of Northern Virginia and General Lee surrendered to General Grant and the Army of the Potomac. Jason, if you will do us the honor."

"Go on then," someone called out from the back of the hall. This was followed by a series of similar encouragements and a kind of half-hearted applause. Josephine continued to play a series of soulful chord progressions. The applause for Jason grew stronger. Emory leaned over and said, "Better do it, son."

Jason looked up and caught Esther's eye. She neither applauded nor smiled, but sat stone-like and seemed to look past him.

"Come on, McQuade!"

"Do it!"

Eventually, the room shook with their urging and applause. A couple of men stood and applauded.

Jason took a deep breath. How can this come out well at all? he asked himself. Why is she doing this? He glanced at Josephine. When she saw him, she looked down immediately, as though her playing took all her concentration.

"Go on, Jason," Emory said. "You're for it now."

Jason rose and set his cloth napkin on his chair. He made his way to the unoccupied piano and sat down. He quietly raised the fallboard. Josephine continued to play, looking down at her hands.

She knows, of course, thought Jason as he shook his head. Knows what awaits this room, these one hundred-plus souls. For her, as for him, it was seven minutes of technical musician-ship—the mere ability to draw complex and nuanced sounds from two inanimate objects. But for others?

Jason's hands struck the keys like lightening and climbed from one register to the next with such majesty and urgency that all in the room, save the performers, were left dumbfounded. They were not prepared—they had not begun to digest the enor-mity of this swelling wave of sound when Josephine bounced in her chair and let loose a similar but even grander and more ambitious run. Suddenly, Josephine was no longer playing in the slow, methodical style that she'd begun with. She was at war with the phrasings emitted from Jason's piano. Jason would not be undone. His fingers flew over the keys in perfect point and counterpoint. A mood of great passion soon developed. In time, the room swelled with a soaring, ecstatic theme that none of the listeners had expected—none could have. Four minutes into the piece, women began to weep and cover their mouths with their handkerchiefs. Some of the men began to wipe tears. The heart that let itself be touched by the music was swept away, could put up nothing in the way of resistance. It was transported. It was no longer in Sandpoint—but beat in the long afternoon of an odious, disastrous war, behind the blue or gray cloth of a war-torn uniform, miles from home and hearth on the road to Appomattox Courthouse.

When they rested their hands in their laps, silence reigned in the hall for several seconds. Then a great applause erupted. Bravos rang out all around. Jason, his brows dripping, looked over the top of the spinet at Josephine. She sat with her chest heaving, her eyes downcast. Then he turned to where Esther had been sitting. Her chair was empty.

21

"I'm telling you this in confidence," Jason said over a cup of steaming black coffee. "I don't want you to share this with anyone."

"Who could I possibly share it with?" said Josephine dismissively. "We're leaving in half an hour and I won't ever be back." She removed her tan leather gloves and set them on the table. Two spoonfuls of sugar went into her coffee and were stirred. She punctuated her silence with a sniff.

Jason knew what she wanted him to say. The expression that passed over her face said she knew he knew. He looked around at the sleepy-eyed people seated at the other tables in the hotel dining room. All were members of the Villard entourage. Henry Villard and his family sat in the corner, framed in the sun-suffused light of a dusty window, beyond which one of the waiting stagecoaches and the rump of a wheel horse was visible.

"You asked me how my case was going. Not well. The trial starts Monday and I have nothing to go on. Oh! Let me take that back," Jason whispered, leaning over the table. "I have a client who admits to the murder and wants to be executed. How could I forget that? I've scoured the panhandle for anyone who might have held a grudge against the sheriff. The few people I could find are either in jail or have an alibi. The sheriff was apparently a prince of a guy up until last year when his wife died. Then he turned to the bottle."

Josephine smiled mincingly. "I'm sure you'll figure something out."

"You're very funny. A Chinese defendant—for starters. A dead sheriff. Witnesses who place my client in town. A motive to kill."

"What motive?" Josephine asked, sipping her coffee.

"The sheriff and some boys around here beat him up earlier in the day. Five or six to one. It's a wonder they didn't kill him."

Josephine glanced sidelong at a waiter carrying two plates of eggs and bacon to a nearby table. "I'm going to get crushed," Jason continued. "I can't believe I agreed to take this case. A defense without a defense."

"I'm leaving in half an hour, Jason," Josephine snapped. Her large brown eyes bore into him, pushed aside his self-pity.

Jason cleared his throat. He took an extra sip of coffee. "I know. I'm still in shock that you came."

Josephine waited. "I'm sure you'll get over it," she said at last. "I'm beginning to think it was a mistake." Blotches of red appeared on her cheeks. She brushed lint off of the breast of her carriage dress—lint that wasn't there.

* * *

Mei-Yin dipped the bloody rag into a pail of water and wrung it out. She carefully patted the machete wound that angled over the man's back. He flinched and cried out in pain, then stifled himself with a great effort.

266

"I'm sorry," Mei-Yin whispered.

"It's nothing."

"Lin Shu-Qin did a good job of sewing you up," Mei-Yin said. The man did not answer. Mei-Yin looked over his shoulder at the smoldering ruins of the camp—a swath of destruction left by the marauders the evening before. Men injured in the calamity and unable to work circled around ash piles, kneeling down to pick up what could be salvaged. They stacked belongings according to ownership and left notes under stones in front of items whose ownership was in doubt. Down the length of the camp where tents once stood but were burnt or trampled, the edges of these notes, scribbled on long, thin pieces of red paper, fluttered in the morning breeze.

Is there any limit to the cruelty of these people? Mei-Yin asked herself. Is there any place safe for Tang people on Gold Mountain? She thought of her aunt Lai-Ping and consoled herself that Lai-Ping had no idea about the dangers on Gold Mountain. Surely, she would have not have encouraged me to come, had she known. Go, and happiness will find you there, she'd said. Happiness seemed a distant dream to her now, more distant than she had ever known.

"Thank you, woman," said the man, and he turned and smiled through his pain. "Soo-Kwan has a wonderful sister."

Mei-Yin smiled in turn. "I will be back later."

* * *

"Jason, I'd like to talk to you outside," Josephine said severely, putting her gloves on again. "Can we walk?"

"I don't have much . . . " The flash of her eyes stopped him. "All right. Sure, I guess we can. Let me leave a message for Charlie at the desk." He paid for the coffees and got up to leave. Just then Mr. Michael O'Sullivan, the "advance man," came running in from outside. His fair face was stained a bright red. He glanced around the hotel dining room until he spotted Henry Villard in the corner reading a newspaper.

"Sir!" he cried, stepping quickly around the crowded tables. "Excuse me, sir." He leaned over and whispered something in Villard's ear. Villard looked up at him stunned.

"Who told you this?" Villard demanded.

"Sparling, sir, pilot of the *Mary Moody*. He just arrived with some of the injured coolies." Villard folded his newspaper and threw it on the floor. "Damn it all!" he spat.

"What is it, darling?" his wife said.

Villard stood up. "Listen, everyone! We're going to be delayed. I . . . there's been an incident at the Chinese camp at Hope, some kind of raid."

"A raid?" several people cried out, including Jason. Alarmed utterances and confused questions followed but were nearly drowned out by the scraping of chairs as a half dozen people rose to their feet.

Villard threw his hands up. "I don't know the details. There are apparently injuries. This could delay our progress along the Clark's Fork to Heron and beyond. I will need to investigate. Mike, tell the teamsters we won't be leaving until tonight at the earliest. Probably tomorrow. And have Mr. Spalding hold the *Moody* for me. Is Keating still in town?"

O'Sullivan said he was.

"Let him know what you've told me and have him meet me at the dock in an hour."

The front doors of the hotel swung open and Lei Chi-Man came running in. He was stopped short by the confused and desultory arrangement of the people in the dining room, some standing, some leaning over tables, all bearing expressions of surprise and concern. He sought out one face. Finding it, he nodded as if to say, "I have news. I need to talk to you."

Jason turned to Josephine. "I'm sorry, Josephine. You'll have to excuse me." He didn't wait for an answer but walked swiftly through the maze of tables. "I just heard," he said to Lei Chi-Man. "Is she all right?"

"I don't know," Lei Chi-Man replied. His eyes were wide with concern. "I was instructing Hok-Ling about his demeanor at trial, as you directed, and the deputy came in and told me there'd been an attack on the camp."

"Okay, Charlie. We've got to get out there."

"Not without me." Jason turned to find Josephine standing behind him, her hands poised on her hips. She spoke over the sounds of people rushing to the counter to pay for their breakfasts, and hatching—and arguing over—last-minute plans. "I did not come halfway across the continent to sit in my room."

"Josephine, you don't understand. This is—"

"I don't care, Jason. Truth be told, I don't care. I'm coming with you." She looked out just then through the hotel's double glass doors, as though giving some sign of distraction would work to her advantage.

Jason sighed, knowing the extent of her obstinacy. "All right. We're going now, though." He looked at the clock behind the front desk. "The *Villard*'s just arriving. We can get there an hour before anybody else if we catch it." He took a step toward the door, then stopped. Josephine collided with him. "Josephine, this is Charlie. Charlie, Josephine."

"Happy to—"

Jason was off. Lei Chi-Man and Josephine hurried to catch up.

* * *

They found Mei-Yin sitting in the doorway of the knock-down, mending clothes. She looked up with a needle pressed between her lips as first Lei Chi-Man then Jason and Josephine rounded the corner of the cabin. Josephine, dressed in her dark blue carriage dress and tan traveling hat and gloves, tiptoed forward as though avoiding puddles. Mei-Yin was startled at the sight of the demon woman and removed the needle from her mouth, but said nothing.

"You are all right then?" said Lei Chi-Man. "You were not harmed last night?"

"No," Mei-Yin said.

Lei Chi-Man exhibited obvious relief. He turned to Jason. "She is all right."

Jason swallowed. "Good."

Although Mei-Yin felt the eyes of the demon woman gawking at her, she looked at the interpreter and Jason closely. Their speech is squeezed with concern, she thought. They learned of the raid and have come to see for themselves. But who is this wom—

Lei Chi-Man addressed her again. "And your brother? Was he injured?"

Mei-Yin shook her head. Now she turned to look at Josephine.

"Soo-Kwan is fine," said Lei Chi-Man. "She is confused by the presence of Miss Carter."

"Tell her this is a friend of mine, Josephine Carter. She was visiting when we heard about the troubles here last night."

Josephine smiled and walked quickly toward Mei-Yin with her gloved hand extended. The need for translation evidently did not occur to her. Mei-Yin stood up abruptly and backed into the knock-down. Lei Chi-Man spoke very quickly. "Excuse please, Miss Carter. Chinese women do not shake hands. It is— perhaps a bow would be better." He bowed to Mei-Yin himself as a demonstration.

Josephine withdrew her hand but did not bow. "What are we working on?" she asked, looking down at the pile of clothes just inside the cabin.

"She wants to know what you are doing," said Lei Chi-Man.

"Is it not obvious?" Mei-Yin said, mildly perturbed. She checked herself and whispered, "I am mending torn shirts and trousers." She showed relief when Josephine nodded and withdrew a few steps.

Lei Chi-Man blinked profusely. "I'm sorry."

Jason said, "Do we know her name, Charlie?"

"What is your name please? The attorney wishes to know."

"Fan-Fei," Mei-Yin answered as she exited the cabin and walked in short steps to a nearby woodpile and picked up billets for the fire. "I am Wong Fan-Fei, sister of Soo-Kwan." She placed the billets carefully over the low flame.

"She is Fan-Fei, Ja-sawn."

"All right. Ask her what happened here last night."

As Mei-Yin recounted the disastrous events of the evening before, she prepared and served tea, so that each listener held a cup when she had finished and had found a place to sit beyond the fire's heat. Jason asked, "Do you know why they would have done this?"

Mei-Yin looked evenly at the interpreter. "Because they hate us," she said, but it was clear in the expressions that passed quickly between them that such an answer would not suffice. "No, I don't know."

"She doesn't know," said Lei Chi-Man.

Josephine got up with her tea and walked to the edge of an incline commanding a better view of the camp. "These are miserable conditions," she said, looking out. She turned back to Jason, "Are these people paid *nothing* for their work?"

"Very little," Jason answered. "But it is a great deal to them."

Josephine pondered his answer for a few seconds, then turned away again in silence.

"Would she be able to recognize any of the men who attacked the camp?" Jason asked Lei Chi-Man.

"She says 'no,'" replied Lei Chi-Man after translating.

Jason asked, "Fan-Fei, can you keep yourself safe here?" Josephine turned and fastened her gaze on Jason. She seemed on the verge of speaking, then raised her teacup to her lips and smiled behind it. Lei Chi-Man interpreted the question and Mei-Yin looked up, surprised.

"Yes," she answered in English. "Thank you." Then in Cantonese to Lei Chi-Man, "My tent is a quarter mile from here. I am closer now than when I first arrived, but Hok—.

Soo-Kwan, Hok-Ling, and Dak-Wah found a place that is very private and hidden."

When her answer was translated, Jason nodded.

"Fan-Fei," he began, "we can't tell you how sorry we are that this happened. I fear it may have something to do with the trial of your brother's friend, Hok-Ling." He was adept at waiting for Charlie's relay, but he didn't notice Mei-Yin's body stiffen. He glanced up to see Josephine crossing in front of them, shaking her head. He brought his focus back to Mei-Yin. "The trial starts Monday. Hok-Ling continues to insist that he is guilty, but there is something about the way he talks that makes us feel . . . well, that something is missing. According to Lei Chi-Man, he attributes all his ill fortune to his ancestors. He believes they are punishing him because he came here without his father's true consent."

Mei-Yin listened intently to Lei Chi-Man's translation. With a shaking hand she poured more tea for Jason, the interpreter, and herself. She brought her teacup to her lips.

Jason continued, "We have nothing to go on, you see. We know he was there in town on the day of the murder, and that he'd already had two run-ins with the sheriff. He stopped the sheriff's whipping of Soo-Kwan when the Chinese arrived in town, and then the beating he took on the day of his murder. We need something more. Have you heard anything here in the camp? Surely, the men must talk about this?

Mei-Yin leaned forward to stir the fire. She winced momentarily and stopped. Then she got up and knelt close to the fire and prodded it to life. "It is widely known here that Hok-Ling did not kill the green coat," she began. "It's true he was in town early in the morning, but he returned at midday. He was not there when the green coat was killed." Mei-Yin continued to look in on the fire as Charlie translated. "I saw him myself at about one o'clock. He was despondent, for someone had stolen the mail from him. He had lost face, and had caused Ho Ying-Chiao, the crew boss, to lose face."

Jason sat in silence as Mei-Yin spoke. She made eye contact with no one save Lei Chi-Man, to signal the end of her story.

Jason began, "And do you—"

But Mei-Yin interrupted in hurried tones, "You needn't believe me, for Soo-Kwan and Dak-Wah both know this."

"Was he with them, as well, that afternoon?"

"No—yes, possibly. I don't know."

Mei-Yin closed her eyes. "He came to my tent for tea. He needed time to think."

"This may be all we have to go on, Charlie. Ask her if Soo-Kwan and Dak-Wah will be back this evening."

She answered affirmatively as she rose to her feet.

"All right. Charlie, I need you to stay here till they arrive, and see what you can get on this story. See if there are other witnesses. I'll go back and work on subpoenas. We're going to need these men to testify, and I want Keating's testimony, as well. Also this crew boss, Ho Ying-Chiao." Jason walked up to Mei-Yin, who stood before him with downcast eyes. He ventured to touch her chin and her eyes flashed up to meet his. "I cannot tell you how helpful you've been. Please keep yourself safe here." As soon as he removed his finger her head fell again. He turned to see Josephine staring at him from the corner of the knock-down.

Why did he touch me? Mei-Yin wondered as Lei Chi-Man translated. She turned her head away. He had no right to touch me.

The ten-minute whistle sounded on the *Henry Villard*. Jason turned to Josephine. "We need to get going." Josephine turned and began walking down the path on her own. "Charlie," Jason added, "Walk with us down to the boat, won't you?"

"Yes." He turned to Mei-Yin. "Excuse me. We will say good-bye for now."

Mei-Yin nodded. She moved to pick up the teacups and carry them inside the knock-down. When she returned they were gone. She squatted at the door and stared out at the silent confusion of the camp. Do they believe me? she wondered. They give him so little chance. What will Soo-Kwan and Dak-Wah say? Will they remember everything? Her hand jumped to her throat. "Only the truth can save him," echoed involuntarily in her mind, and she looked to heaven and cried silent tears. Would I dishonor him by telling the truth to save his life? Does he know how alone and afraid I am? Tears fell onto her cheeks. A sense of panic began to stir within. The money! she thought. How can he have any hope without money to bribe the judge? He will die if he does not have it!

Suddenly, she jumped to her feet. They *must* take it back to him—they *must!* I have eight minutes to get it and give it to them. I must try. Mei-Yin took off and ran as fast as her feet would carry her. She flew past tents, and the remnants of tents, past men hobbled and sitting, nursing their wounds. Her legs and arms churned frantically. She had never run so fast—had never tried to run so fast—in all her life. She tore into the woods along the path that wound up through two switchbacks, until at last her tent was visible. A few steps more—she dropped to her knees beside a cedar tree, where the money was buried. Frantically, she dug. At last, she freed the jar from the earth's gentle grip. She rose and tore back down the path, back into the dark margin of pine woods. She emerged at the top of the camp at a speed that nearly caused her to fall. Her bare feet flew over the earth and stones, past tents and fire pits, hopping over tent wires, splitting through clothes hanging from ropes—clothes she had put there herself. She tripped and fell and rose again, as though in one motion "Lei Chi-Man!" she cried out, seeing the three figures in the distance, walking along the dock. "Lei Chi-Man!"

The three visitors turned together. When they spied Mei-Yin running through the camp, they turned and began to walk back toward shore. Jason signaled to the pilothouse to wait "one minute." By the time Jason, Josephine, and Lei Chi-Man reached the bank, Mei-Yin was upon them.

"What's happened? What is it?" asked Jason.

Mei-Yin was doubled over, catching her breath. She tried to rise twice, but each time returned involuntarily to a doubled-over position. "You must," she wheezed, staring at the ground. "You must take . . . "

"She has a jar full of money," Josephine said.

Mei-Yin tried to stand erect again. Her shoulders rocked with her breathing. Jason's eyes widened. "What's happened to you?"

Mei-Yin followed his wondering eyes to her left forearm. Her sleeve was torn and blood-stained, with two rivulets of blood angled over the back of her hand.

Mei-Yin held her arm out. How odd! she thought. I didn't feel it. Still I cannot feel it. She patted the wound lightly through her shirt. "It is a small cut. It doesn't hurt," she said to Lei Chi-Man. He opened his mouth to speak, but she interrupted. "Please, Lei Chi-Man. Listen to me!" Again she doubled over, but this time it was out of time with her ragged breathing. She straightened again quickly. "Listen to me! Please! My brother and I . . . have talked many times . . . about how brave Hok-Ling was to save him . . . from the green coat's whip. You have heard . . . about this, right? We want him to have this money now . . . for bribes. He must have it . . . to save himself." She held the jar out to him. At the same time, she put her free hand—her bloodstained hand—over her stomach. "Please take it!"

Charlie began to translate, but Jason, pointing to the injured hand, said, "Let me have a look at that." He moved toward her, but Mei-Yin jerked her arm away.

"No!" she cried, surprising even herself. She bowed slightly and tried to smile. "No. Please. Not . . . hurt."

"Okay, okay. Better wash it though." He pointed toward the lake. "*Wash.* Understand?"

That word! she cried out to herself. The green coat had growled it standing over her—his hand, circling his stomach—his white, plentiful teeth smiling. "Wash," he'd demanded. "See? Wash. Wash." Mei-Yin swallowed against a searing rage rising in her throat. She uttered the word almost inaudibly, then cast her eyes downward to conceal the hatred that burned in them. "Please," she begged, "take the money. Soo-Kwan and I wish him to have it."

"What shall I tell her, Ja-sawn?" asked the interpreter. "About the money. She is insisting that we take it."

As Lei Chi-Man spoke, Josephine regarded Mei-Yin closely, then turned to look out over the lake.

"Tell her we don't do things that way. That I cannot give the money to the judge. She should keep it."

Mei-Yin's eyes filled with fresh tears. Her face contorted like a child preparing to cry and she drove her fists against her legs, spotting blood on her trousers.

"No!" she cried. "No." She doubled over again. "Tell him! Tell him that Hok-Ling did not kill the green coat." Again, she raised herself. "That he needs this money for bribes. *Please.*"

Lei Chi-Man recoiled. "What do you mean by this, woman? You know only rumors."

Her face contorted with frustration. She pushed the jar into Jason's hands.

Then her eyes widened at her effrontery. She began to feel a searing pain at the back of them. She tried to speak, to defend herself, then only to utter a sound through her open mouth. But she could do neither, and could not raise air from her lungs. Her eyes closed. She set her hand against her stomach again. A terrible pain was erupting there. The world began to spin.

"What is it? What's wrong?" shouted Jason, leaping forward to steady her.

Josephine jumped toward her, as well. "Oh my!"

"I don't know!" the interpreter answered quickly. "What is happening with you?" Lei Chi-Man demanded.

Mei-Yin's eyes opened and seemed to settle on Josephine. She backed away from them, seeking distance, but Jason lunged toward her as her knees buckled and she turned, falling. In the next instant, she lay limp in Jason's arms. He had stumbled to his knees himself, still holding the jar in one hand, and now her head hung backward at his side, her black nostrils pointing to the sky. "What in the world?" he gasped, glancing up at Lei Chi-Man. The interpreter stood stunned and incredulous. "What's happened to her?"

"I don't know, Ja-sawn. She—"

"Help me here!" Jason cried. He pushed the jar into Josephine's hands. He adjusted his arms beneath Mei-Yin and picked her up as he stood. He stared dumbfounded at the unconscious woman. "I've got her," he repeated as Lei Chi-Man sidestepped around him with his arms out, ready to help.

Jason looked up at the buildings to the east, high on the mountain's flank, their white sides blazing in the sunlight above the smell and squalor of the Chinese camp. "Does the railroad have a doctor, do you suppose?"

Lei Chi-Man squinted up in the same direction. "I do not know, Ja-sawn. Anyway, not for a Tang woman."

"No, you're probably right." He looked at Josephine, who simply shrugged and shook her head helplessly. Mei-Yin's lips twitched and her head began to move as if she were denying something in a dream. "Delirium," Jason ventured. "She's probably exhausted." He looked intently at Lei Chi-Man. "Listen, Charlie. Josephine and I will take her to Sandpoint. Dr. Randle will have a look at her. I know him. He won't refuse. You stay here and find out what you can."

Lei Chi-Man looked down at Mei-Yin's face. "But I would like to . . . " He cut himself off. "Hmm-hmm. Yes," he said. And to the retreating backs of Josephine and Jason, with Mei-Yin's limp body stretched across Jason's arms, he called out, "I will see you tomorrow then."

* * *

The screen door swung open and shut behind Josephine. She turned. Seeing that it was Jason, she stood and brushed the back of her dress. "How is she?"

"The doctor's doing some tests. He thinks she's just over-tired is all." Jason climbed down the steps. Josephine joined him in stride and when they reached the walkway she took his arm. "He said he'd take her over to Mrs. Stewart's in a bit. She can rest there, and he'll look in on her in the morning."

"Hmmm," mused Josephine.

"What?"

"Oh, nothing. I was just . . . Never mind."

With the crisis over, Jason smiled inwardly. He didn't pursue the matter. He let the coolness of the approaching evening wash over him. The sun was low on the western horizon now. Long shadows pointed east, in the direction of Hope. He cupped his hand over Josephine's. "It's been really wonderful to see you again," he said somewhat wearily. They turned at Cedar Street and made their way onto the wooden sidewalk at Main. Jason acknowledged by name two men in Stetsons who passed them. They raised their heads but held their tongues, reminding Jason of the price he was paying with the townspeople.

"Not the friendliest men I've ever seen," said Josephine.

The shadows were climbing the front of the Carson Hotel when they arrived. "There are no stages out front," Josephine said. "I'm sure we're leaving in the morning."

"Yes, I doubt the others are even back from Hope." Jason pulled out his watch. "It's just seven." He looked away from Josephine.

"You needn't worry, you know. I'm not going to embarrass you. I know it's time to say good-bye."

He nodded and smiled. "But that doesn't make it easier, does it? Thank you."

She touched his face with her gloved hand. "You've always had a special place in my heart. You always will." She smiled.

"Please be careful, Jason." She studied the parts of his face. "I know you love her—or you think you do."

Jason recoiled. "Who?"

"This woman, Fan-Fei."

"What?"

Josephine lowered her hand. "It's as plain as the nose on your face, darling. Do you mean you haven't seen it yourself?"

Jason stared at her nonplused. He shook his head. "Don't even think about doing this," he stammered.

"Doing what? All I'm saying is be careful. I think she'll break your heart. Actually, no—she won't break your heart. You'll break it yourself if you place it where love can't grow."

"I believe you are quite insane, Josephine," Jason laughed.

"Maybe. But there is something else I think you should know. I could be wrong, but I think you'll find she's with child."

22

"Is that you, Jason?" Mrs. Stewart called from outside. The kitchen door of her boarding house was propped open, bisected by bright, slanting sunlight. It was a splendid, clear morning, and although the kitchen was stuffy, there were filaments of cool, clean-scented air suspended through it. The planked floor was cold, and there were still marked differences in the temperatures of other objects—chairs, cupboard doors, pots, and such—depending on the sweep of the sun through the window above the sink. In this respect, it was like any kitchen in the morning.

"Yes. Good morning."

"Coffee's on the stove, dear."

He appeared in the doorway with a cup already in his hand. "Where's Fan-Fei? She's not on the couch."

The old woman looked up from a chair in the middle of the yard. There was a mixing bowl on her lap and another smaller bowl between her feet. She was shucking peas. "Oh, she's fine—sleeping like a baby now."

"She's not on the couch."

"No. I gave her my bed. She needed a good night's sleep."

Jason cut short a drink. "But I could have slept on the couch, Mrs. Stewart. Why didn't we give her my bed?"

Mrs. Stewart laughed and then her laughter was squeezed off by the inadvertent grimace that she lent to the opening of a pod. "You were already in your room when Doc Randle brought her by, dear. Your door was closed."

"I was reading a book on evidence. I didn't hear them come in."

"You were reading and snoring at the same time then," she chuckled.

"Oh come on!" He moved to the edge of the porch and sat down. "I've never snored in my life."

"That so? When I put her down—it was just after ten—your room sounded like a sawmill."

"He kept her that long?"

"Mm-hmm. Said he wanted to keep an eye on her for a while. Patched up the arm, too."

"Did you find out what's wrong with her?"

"He said he'd know more today, but he thinks she's just tired, overtired. All that running. That's probably why she collapsed." Mrs. Stewart seemed to wait for a smile that was a long time forming on her thin lips. "Funny thing," she said at last, "Doc says he's never seen such a tiny little thing—said she wouldn't make a splash in a bowl of soup."

Jason snickered. "She is awful small, isn't she?" He gulped the last of his coffee then held the cup past his knee, letting it swing on its handle. "Pretty, though," he added without emphasis.

Mrs. Stewart glanced up at him then quickly returned her attention to the peas spilling through her fingers.

Absorbing the morning's easy rhythm one minute, Jason's sleep-swollen eyes were assaulted the next by the bright spangles of dandelions abounding in the yard. A trace of his dream from the night before—the image of his father standing on the porch of their cottage at Cape Cod, looking down at him in the garden—flashed through his mind then vanished. The sun was warm against his face and his bare chest. The muscles of his arms and shoulders flexed and relaxed and flexed again, sending exquisite tremors across his back. He looked up to find Mrs. Stewart inspecting him.

"How are you and Charlie doing with this case of yours?"

Jason gazed into the bottom of his cup. "Not so good, I guess. Say, you don't seem too upset about it all."

"About what, dear?"

"What I'm doing."

"What are you doing?"

"You know. Defending this fellow. I haven't said anything. I figured you felt the same as everybody else around here."

"No, I don't feel that way at all," said Mrs. Stewart. "I'm too old to go judging other folks—you or this Chinese fella or anybody else. Too close to being judged myself, maybe."

Jason stared at the old woman and saw that she avoided his eyes. He said, "You know, I'm glad to hear—"

"Besides, from what I hear, he's guilty as guilty can be anyway. Everyone around here liked the sheriff, or they used to anyway. Liked Rebecca, too . . . poor dear. When she passed, he took it awful hard—got ornery, didn't he? Funny though, folks don't say much about his drinking these days, or about that mean streak of his that came out of nowhere when she died. It was fear, I suppose—fear that he would be next . . . I guess people remember only what's good about you." Mrs. Stewart looked up with hope in her eyes. "That ain't so bad, is it?"

"Morning, McQuade." It was Eddie Rogers, lumbering around the corner of the house. He wore round-toed boots, black, shapeless, patched trousers, and a sleeveless undershirt. His large hands were swinging just above his knees. Eddie worked odd jobs for Mrs. Stewart—chopping wood, pruning, painting—in exchange for meals.

"Hello, Eddie. How are you?"

"I'm okay." His six foot three frame cast a long shadow that climbed partway up the house's stone foundation.

"Haven't seen you in a while."

"Nope. Been gone a week."

Jason was fighting direct sunlight in order to see Eddie. He raised his hand up over his eyes. "Where'd you go?"

"Fishing. Up Bloom Creek. Say, Missus, I'm going to have to take an ax to that gate post. She's stuck but good."

Mrs. Stewart raised her own hand for shade. "It won't come out of there, huh? Did you try digging around it?"

"Sure. Three feet or more."

"It should have come out then."

"She won't."

"It's moving, though, ain't it?"

Eddie nodded blockishly. He squatted in the yard. Mrs. Stewart looked into the bowl and picked up a long, twisted pod. "John and I put those posts in thirteen years ago," she mused. "I didn't think they'd be any trouble."

Eddied rubbed his chin. "Well, I could . . . "

Jason asked, "You need a hand, Eddie?" It had just occurred to him that Eddie was another who didn't judge him for getting involved with the Chinese defendant. That meant something—a great deal, in fact. "Maybe together we could—"

"No," interrupted Mrs. Stewart slowly, as if she had reached a difficult decision. "No, just cut it out, Eddie. We'll have to split another one, but that's all right."

Jason looked at the shining sweat on Eddie's neck and was secretly relieved. "Besides," Mrs. Stewart continued, glancing up at Jason, "you got your hands full with your own doings."

Eddie was impassive. He began fingering the grass in front of his feet. Jason pulled a piece of lint from his pant leg and threw it at Eddie. It landed in the grass between them. Eddie smiled. Jason pretended to find another piece of lint and throw it at him, but this time Eddie didn't see him. His attention had drifted up the side of the house. When he looked up at Mrs. Stewart's bedroom window, it was probably not with anything particular in mind, except that he wanted to look away from himself because he was ashamed.

"That's her," he said. "That's—"

"Don't stare at her, Eddie," said Mrs. Stewart firmly and with a little excitement. But Eddie continued to stare, and his mouth and his eyes hung wide open, as though he had forgotten himself entirely. Jason looked from Mrs. Stewart to Eddie, and from there, following the direction of Eddie's stare, to the window.

Behind the grayed, peeling sill and distorted glass stood Mei-Yin. Her face was rosy and puffy with sleep, with the line of a pillow crease impressed on her cheek. Yet her eyes were wide and alert, even grave. She tried, at first, to hide behind the half-drawn lace curtains, but her curiosity brought her face out into the open. She peered down into the yard, intent upon Eddie. Jason looked at Eddie and chuckled. "She's pretty, isn't she? What's wrong with you, Eddie? Cat got your tongue?"

Mei-Yin wore one of Mrs. Stewart's nightgowns. It fit her like a sheet—so loosely, in fact, that she looked like a girl of ten, or about half her actual age. The sleeves had been pushed up in great folds past her elbows, past a swath of bandages on her left arm. Her black hair was thickened and mussed, and, for Jason, at least, the effect of all this was that she seemed profoundly "westernized," to have grown familiar and indigenous over the course of a single night spent under a shared roof. He turned and smiled up at the window again, but it was just as the curtain fell straight and Mei-Yin disappeared.

Eddie continued to stare up at the window, blinking only once.

"She looks okay," said Jason flatly, intent on an air of nonchalance. "Maybe we could give her some breakfast. I'll have Charlie take her back out to Hope this morning."

Eddie finally looked away and gulped. "By God, that's her. That's—"

"She's probably hungry, all right," interrupted Mrs. Stewart.

"That's the woman me and Johnnie brought in from—"

"Sure she is," Jason agreed. "Can we—"

"—from Spokane Falls."

"—fix her something?"

"Of course," said Mrs. Stewart. "I wonder if . . . "

Eddie stood up, and there was a terrible darkness about his eyes.

"Did I interrupt you, dear?" Mrs. Stewart asked him.

Eddie seemed confused. "No, ma'am. It's just that—"

"Well," she laughed, somewhat haughtily, "the way you jumped up, I thought maybe—"

"Oh, no, ma'am." Eddie buried his thumbs in the waistband of his patched trousers.

"—I'd interrupted you or something."

"Oh, no, ma'am." Questions were heaped on Eddie's face. "But remember the Oriental woman I told you about, that woman me and Johnnie picked up on the road a while back?"

Mrs. Stewart lifted her eyes toward Eddie, frowning. "Yes, dear, I remember."

"What's this?" Jason asked, sitting back and resting on his elbows. He looked from Mrs. Stewart to Eddie and back.

"You weren't here," the old woman replied impatiently. "You were out. With Esther Langston, I guess." She stopped and raised her eyebrows as if Eddie's revelation had already been whispered in her ear. Eddie read her expression and nodded eagerly.

"Yeah. That's her." He chuckled nervously and pointed up toward the bedroom. "That's the gal we brought in."

"What are you two talking about?" Jason asked, squinting one eye up at Eddie. "You've seen her before?"

Mrs. Stewart raised both eyebrows and put two peas into her mouth. "Isn't that something!"

"Yeah, sure," boasted Eddie. "I've talked to her an' everything." The giant beamed.

"When?" Jason's tone was incredulous, even challenging.

"I spent most of a day with her, McQuade. Talked to her, too. She knows some English words."

The fanciful lilt in Eddie's voice startled Mrs. Stewart and left her choking on a pea. She recovered somewhat gracelessly, coughing up the green pulp into the palm of her hand and flicking it out into the yard. "Oh, heavens me!" was her apology.

"Now, wait a minute," cried Jason. "This woman is Fan-Fei, the sister of one of the coolies out at Hope there. She's been there three months or more. You're thinking of someone else." He looked quickly up at the window, without knowing why.

Eddie mimicked him, but he kept his eyes elevated.

"Nope. That's her."

"Tell him about Johnnie," suggested Mrs. Stewart.

Eddie lowered his eyes to the ground. "There ain't nothing to tell there," he demurred. "I guess I better get at that damn post."

Mrs. Stewart frowned. "What are you ashamed of?"

"Nothing, missus," Eddie insisted. He straightened momentarily, as though a deep breath held him erect. "There ain't nothing to tell, that's all."

Mrs. Stewart winked at Jason then poked among the empty pods. "Eddie took out after Johnnie Fry that night—gave him one heck of a shiner."

Eddie looked at Jason and spread his hands. "Hey, that don't mean nothing! Johnnie—he got mad when we seen this girl in the road, you see? And he said he didn't want to take her along." Jason looked up to see points of anger surfacing on Eddie's face. "He says, 'No way, don't want no China girl—'" Eddie grimaced and glanced up at the window and repeated "China girl" in a whisper "'—in the wagon.' That's what he said, only real loud. But I said 'Yeah, we're taking her,' and it turns out she can speak a little English, see, and I figures she heard what Johnnie said—got her feelings hurt, and that ain't right. Johnnie—he didn't need to say that stuff."

"Are you *sure* this is the same woman, Eddie?" Jason demanded.

"Yeah, I'm positive." Eddie seemed relieved that his rift with Johnnie did not seem important to Jason. He set off in the direction of the tool shed. There was color to his face. "That's her all right."

Jason jumped to his feet. "Hey, wait a minute!" He ran after Eddie, spinning him around violently. "You said you brought her from Spokane Falls? When was this Eddie? *When?*"

Eddie's eyes were quizzical. "What? Let go of me."

Mrs. Stewart sat up in her chair. "My lands! What's wrong, Jason?"

Jason frowned. "Dammit! When was it, Eddie? When did you pick her up?"

"I don't know." Eddie's shoulders dropped and his eyes turned away from Jason. He was looking for the answer. "It was when we picked up them caskets," he sighed, "six of them. We brought six of them in. That was it! I'm sure of it."

"Okay, okay!" Jason began to rub Eddie's shoulders, as if that would help jog his memory. "Now when? When was that?" Jason glanced nervously up at the bedroom window. An idea too disturbing, too unexpected to have substance or direction was nevertheless taking shape in his mind. *"Hurry, Eddie. This could be important. When was it?"*

The giant looked at Mrs. Stewart helplessly. "I . . . I . . . don't . . . Wednesday? It was Wednesday, I guess. Yeah. I got the wire on Monday. Then Johnnie and me, we went in the next day. Come back the next, so that would have been Wednesday. July 16."

Jason jumped back as if the man had given him a shock. He began to run in a strange side-stepping manner toward the house, but he kept his face turned toward Eddie and succeeded in pointing his finger at him menacingly. At last he stopped, and after a peculiar and involuntary smile came and went, he stared back at Eddie, squinting fiercely down his outstretched arm as if it were the barrel of a rifle. "That's it, isn't it?" he demanded. "The sixteenth! You came back the evening of the sixteenth!"

He turned a maniacal grin on Mrs. Stewart. "Did you hear that?" he howled. "Ha! The sixteenth!" The old woman gripped the sides of the mixing bowl and made a face that was three parts horror. Only after Jason pivoted and dashed into the house did she manage to turn to Eddie and, with a hand at the base of her neck, say, "My gracious! I think he's been touched!"

Jason charged up the stairs three at a time. He stood before the door of Mrs. Stewart's bedroom nodding, whispering, trying vainly to collect himself. "Hello in there. Come on out!" he ordered at last. "Get dressed. You must get dressed! Do you understand? Hurry!" He shouted these things as he bounded into his own bedroom and scooped up his boots and shirt. The house shook with his commands, and he shouted again from the landing, hopping in circles as he struggled to put on the boots, one and then the other. "Hurry, dammit! Get dressed! We must go now, Fan-Fei! Go now! See Charlie! Hurry!" At one point he tottered and slammed sideways against the wall. The boots would not go on. He growled bear-like and pushed with all his strength, until his fingers were pinched and nearly cut by the bootstraps. "Dad *gum-it.*" Finally, when it seemed he had no more strength to lend to it, his heel fell into place. He picked up his shirt and pounded on the door of Mrs. Stewart's bedroom with alternating hands as he put it on. "Come on! Get out here! We must go! Hurry . . . !" He looked down to button his shirt and saw that his boots were on the wrong feet. He gave a gull-like "Shhhh-ee!" He set his heels against the top of the stairs, pried the boots off, switched them, and slipped them on again with relative ease.

So, Fan-Fei arrived in town on the night of the murder, he thought as he fumbled nervously with the collar of his shirt.

That's why she tried to cover it up—all this business about meeting Hok-Ling at noon or one o'clock, fixing him tea. Ha! And the money for bribes. The voice within him was calm and deliberate. It seeped through his frenzied, tremulous excitement like moonlight in a veil of wind-driven clouds. He straightened. A shudder danced across his shoulders. But why? Why did she lie to us? To protect him? To protect herself? Could *she* have killed Langston? I don't think so. And the $500. Whose was it? Did the sheriff have $500 with him? No. Esther would have said something. Besides, there were gold pieces found in his pockets. Hok-Ling claims the $500 was hers, but why would a washerwoman have that much? No. He's lying, too. Damn it, it's all lies. All of it.

He pounded on the door. "Come out, do you hear? Open the door, Fan-Fei! Please. Come out." Nothing. He waited, then set his ear to the door. There were no sounds. He knocked again. He twisted the knob and the length and width of Mrs. Stewart's bedroom unfolded before him. The door thudded. She was gone.

He dashed downstairs, and ran out the kitchen door. He stood before Mrs. Stewart with his hands held away from his sides, fisted. The skin over his diaphragm was pulsating violently beneath his open shirt. His eyes showed an intensity from which the old woman shrank, nearly upsetting the bowl on her lap.

"She's gone!"

"Well, what do you expect? My lands, with all this shouting and carrying about you've probably scared her half to death!"

"You didn't see her come out?"

"Why, no. What's going on, Jason?"

He sprang toward the corner of the house, but when he arrived at the opposite door he found no sign of her. The door was closed. A short distance away, Eddie worked quietly over the hole that he had dug around the gatepost. Behind him, his horse was harnessed to a small dray loaded with old and new fence posts and a glistening coil of new barbed wire. Jason ran toward him. "Hey, Eddie! Did you see her? She ran off. She must have come out this way."

"Nope—didn't." Eddie looked up in slow motion. Kneeling on all fours, with a little mountain of dirt in one cupped hand, he looked like a child at play.

"Cripes, Eddie! She had to walk right past here!"

"Who says?"

"I do, dammit. Mrs. Steward's still sitting there in the backyard. She couldn't have gone out that way without tripping over her. She had to come this way." He turned and spread his arm toward the front door," but Eddie was looking down in the hole and scooping out the next handful when he turned back. "Damn you, Eddie!" He kicked the top of the mound and brown dust flew into Eddie's eyes.

Eddie recoiled and let out a soft bleating. "Hey! Don't! What'd you do that for?" He rubbed his eyes fiercely, and after a while little wet noises came from them. His mouth was stuck open like the arch of a bell tower.

Jason shook his head. "All right, I'm sorry, Eddie—but godammit!"

"What's your problem, McQuade?"

"Let me take the wagon, Eddie. I've got to!"

"Nothing doing. I need it." Eddie was still rubbing his eyes as the wagon moved off. "Hey! I said . . . Hey! Hey!"

* * *

It was not a chase, and in the first minute the speed was bridled out of Eddie's horse. Mei-Yin walked in the middle of the road ahead of him. She wore the same clothes she had worn the day before, black trousers, her blue shirt, sleeves rolled to the elbows. The white dressing on her forearm was bright against her skin and against her clothing. She did not look back.

He was struck by her movement. Her short, rhythmic strides, the set of her shoulders, the constrained swing of arms and hands, as though tethered, the absence of lilt. These spoke to him of independence, of the strength and joyless wisdom of one who had traveled alone. He'd witnessed it first when the coolies marched through town, for it was general to them all. And here, Fan-Fei seemed not merely to proceed, but to evince with her steps the exquisite depth of her soul, of her suffering. He drew back on the reins. *God, she is like a spirit walking! It is her very consciousness that moves! How many miles has she walked? How much of her happiness, her hopes, her dreams has she pressed into the earth with her feet?* He gazed at her blankly, like one who stands at the edge of the ocean to wonder at its inscrutable depths. He was broadsided by a pang of melancholy and loneliness.

Suddenly, as if there had been a loud noise, he awakened to himself. He thought of Hok-Ling, then of the trial and Eddie's revelation, then of Esther, and Emory, and Lei Chi-Man, and then of this woman—who had lied to him, and who in her way now sought to escape him. He thought of Josephine and her strange prediction. *Fan-Fei's not with child,* he imagined announcing to Josephine as she bounced along in a jangling stagecoach bound for Spokane Falls. *That smile! You knew that all along, didn't you? It was just your way of getting under my skin.*

He pulled up beside Mei-Yin. "Whoa." Wagon and pedestrian stopped at once. Mei-Yin stood still, without turning. Her eyes were fixed and forward-looking, but he sensed that she'd been aware of his approach all along. Jason sat in the wagon, benumbed. He wiped his mouth with the back of his hand. He scratched his ankle inside the legging of his boot, but he did no more than glance at her once or twice through the fog of his thoughts, and wait, and she, in turn, did not once flinch or blink or wilt from her steadfastness. *What an iron will,* he thought at last, allowing himself to regard her closely. *How odd that she does not even try to run! She must know that Eddie has told me everything. Look. Maybe she is not afraid, but she doesn't move at all, and she will not look at me. Oh! But she is strong, isn't she? And to think it is because of me that she stands here, frozen in the road.* Finally, he whistled softly, and waved her toward the seat. He smiled gently and nodded. "Come on. Get in."

23

T he bay mare nosed neatly around in the narrow road. The roses and the blue hydrangeas that hemmed the yards and overhung the fences, the freshness of the dew-tinged air that filled Jason's nostrils, and the wagging approach of an old, yellow dog intent on sniffing what odors might be suggested in the wagon's wake—this was all counterfeit and abstraction to him, no more real than the Paris skyline painted on a photographer's backdrop. In these first moments the only thing real to him was the fact that Fan-Fei was, in addition to everything else, beautiful. How had he not seen this before? He glanced at her out of the corner of his eye. Oh my God, Josephine has done it again. She's figured out what I was thinking before I knew myself. No, that's impossible! I can't be in love with a Chinese woman. I don't even know her. He scooted away from Mei-Yin, but in the process quickly glanced up at her face again. Oh God, she's lovely, isn't she?

Only one thing could intrude. It crept over him a few moments later, coming almost as quickly, surely as decidedly, as this romantic rapture. It was the realization that his one alibi for Hok-Ling had vanished in an instant. With the trial starting in two days, now he had nothing—*nothing*. Jason's eyes opened wide to let in the new information. His impending humiliation at trial, and Hok-Ling's almost certain conviction, didn't banish his stupefying contemplation of Mei-Yin's beauty. He was of two minds. He could not set one thing aside for the other. Jason frowned as he reached up to scratch his shoulder. An observer would have seen in the two faces drifting by in that wagon icons of human worry and misery.

Emory has the burden of proof, Jason imagined himself telling the jury as he gazed over the horse's undulating rump. If you find my client guilty, you've got to find him guilty beyond a reasonable doubt. And the prosecution—not the defense—must prove each element of the crime. Hok-Ling can't be compelled to testify, just as none of you could be if you were charged with a crime. And if he doesn't testify, you can't infer anything from that. You can't hold that against him is what I'm saying. Jason gently tossed the reins. It was unaccompanied by a command of any kind and it seemed to make no impression upon the horse. As you're going to see, the prosecution's case is entirely circumstantial. They have no eyewitnesses. At least I don't think they have eyewitnesses. What do you have, Emory? What *is* your case? Me? I have nothing.

Jason turned down the alley rather than risk a reunion with Eddie. Mrs. Stewart was right where he'd left her in the backyard. Tossing aside a pea pod she asked, "Where did she go?" Jason jumped down from the wagon and offered his hand to Mei-Yin, but she refused it and climbed out of the wagon herself.

"Not far. I think she saw Eddie and remembered him. Got scared. Listen, Mrs. Stewart, I need to ask a favor. Would you stay with her? I can't have her taking off again. Plus, you said Doc Randle wants to have another look at her."

"That's right."

"I need to get Charlie," Jason said, adding, "I think it would be best if you didn't let Eddie see her again. Maybe you could close the blind or something."

Mrs. Stewart set the bowl on the ground and walked toward them. She put a reassuring arm around Mei-Yin. Mei-Yin jumped, but didn't move away. "Yes, of course I will," said Mrs. Stewart. "You come along with me, darling." Mei-Yin glanced back at Jason as the two women walked toward the door. "I'll make us some tea."

Jason climbed back in the wagon. "I'll be back. I'm going to the jail, too. I may be a couple hours."

"That's perfectly all right," Mrs. Stewart said, opening the door. "We'll be fine here."

* * *

"What do you make of it, Charlie?" Jason said, staring down at a half-buried log stuck at the bottom of Sand Creek. The two men stood alone at the midpoint of the bridge, their backs to the sun. Each had a foot on the lower railing.

Lei Chi-Man took a deep breath. "I don't know. If your friend Eddie is right, that means Fan-Fei has been deceiving us from the beginning. They all have, in fact, including Hok-Ling. But why?" The reflection of three large V-shaped skeins of Canadian geese—over one hundred birds—passing high over Sandpoint caused Lei Chi-Man to finish his thought looking up. "Yesterday, Soo-Kwan and Dak-Wah told me they returned from work on the sixteenth to find Fan-Fei and Hok-Ling together. They said Hok-Ling explained that he'd lost the mail and returned earlier in the day."

"It's one thing to come up with an alibi for Hok-Ling," Jason mused. "I mean, he saved Soo-Kwan's life, right?"

Lei Chi-Man looked down again and nodded.

"That much I understand. I can see Soo-Kwan concocting a story about Hok-Ling getting back to Hope early. He'd need Fan-Fei to corroborate it—to say *she* was there, because *they* were at work all day. But now to find out that she arrived in Sandpoint on the sixteenth is another thing altogether. It doesn't add up."

"No, it doesn't."

Jason leaned an elbow over the top rail. "What else did you find out yesterday?"

"I interviewed the crew boss, Ho Ying-Chiao. There's talk among the coolies of striking if Hok-Ling is convicted."

"What?"

"Yes. This is Ho Ying-Chiao's main concern, in fact—perhaps his only one. He brought this up many times. Hok-Ling is something of a hero among the workers, not for killing the sheriff but for standing up to him and saving Soo-Kwan's life. Ho Ying-Chiao is terrified of a work stoppage. He implied that his job is on the line if the workers strike."

"I see."

"According to Ho Ying-Chiao, most of the laborers believe Hok-Ling has been treated unfairly. He finished his three years months before the camp moved to Idaho, and he had saved sufficient funds for his passage, but Mr. Keating refused to give him his voucher. Then his money went missing. They're certain Keating stole it."

"They?"

"The laborers. According to Ho Ying-Chiao, the railroad is under great pressure to finish the track through the Cabinet Gorge before winter. Mr. Keating told Ho Ying-Chiao that a work stoppage would be intolerable. He's threatened to fire him if it happens."

"Did you ask him about Fan-Fei?"

"Yes, although I didn't ask him when she arrived in camp. Now I wish I had. He confirmed that she's Soo-Kwan's sister, and that she lives alone on the hill outside camp. He told me Soo-Kwan put her up to speaking to him on Hok-Ling's behalf after his arrest. She asked him to use his English to help Hok-Ling."

"What did he say?"

"He told her he was sorry but there was nothing he could do."

Jason exhaled slowly. "So with Fan-Fei, Soo-Kwan, Dak-Wah, and Hok-Ling, we have four people lying to us about when Fan-Fei arrived?"

"Is it possible that she had been on an errand to Spokane Falls?"

"No. I can't imagine that. A young Chinese woman who can't speak English being sent seventy miles on an errand—alone. Doesn't make sense." Jason turned to Lei Chi-Man. "You don't think *she* killed the sheriff, do you?"

Lei Chi-Man's eyes widened. "No, of course not. You don't believe this, do you?"

"No. It's inconceivable. For one thing, she couldn't have lifted the sheriff's body over this railing."

Lei Chi-Man took a step back and studied the height of the railing. "No. You're right."

"But that doesn't mean the jury wouldn't convict her," Jason added darkly. "Or that she couldn't have been an accomplice to murder."

Lei Chi-Man nodded reluctantly. "Of course you're right."

Jason rubbed his chin and gazed back down at the slow-moving current, at fingers of green bottom weed waving just below the surface. "I don't know, Charlie. If people find out she was in town that night, they're going to assume the worst. They'll demand two hangings instead of one."

"Perhaps, then, this is why they have lied to us and told us that Fan-Fei has lived at the camp for several months."

Jason nodded. "All right. We need to get to the bottom of this. Let's go talk to Hok-Ling."

* * *

They pulled the wagon around to the rear of the sheriff's office and jumped down. A note posted on the back door read, "Out at Darnell's place. Back Sunday at 11:00. Al." Jason knocked. "Al?" There was no answer. He tried the doorknob. It was locked, but the door swung open—the latch had failed to catch. Jason shot Lei Chi-Man a questioning glance. He leaned in. The outer office was empty. "Deputy Lambert? You here?" They stepped into the center of the room and looked around— at glass-covered gun cases, a display of wanted posters above the wainscoting, a year-old calendar on the wall, two cluttered desks with spittoons, a photograph of President Rutherford Hayes. Lei Chi-Man pointed to the green door that led to Hok-Ling's cell. "I'll be damned," Jason whispered, nodding at their good fortune. He went back and unlocked the door, then closed it.

They opened the green door and stepped into a gloomy, unlit corridor. The door closed behind them. There was an abrupt shuffling in the cell on the right side of the corridor followed by a long silence. Jason stepped into the gray light visible between the bars. The prisoner's outline came into view. Hok-Ling's left arm hung at his side. He was staring at the far corner, and Jason could see the start of a new queue at the back of his head. It was an awful stub. He was dressed only in pants—pants that sagged over his narrow, emaciated hips. His face and arms had become astonishingly slight and attenuated, and they were dark and featureless against the light from the window behind him.

Lei Chi-Man stepped around Jason. "Are you ready, Charlie?" Jason asked softly, still staring at Hok-Ling. The prisoner looked up at the sound.

"Yes. Of course."

"Ask him if he knows that his trial begins on Monday."

Lei Chi-Man complied. Hok-Ling nodded.

"Tell him we have Soo-Kwan's sister with us. She fell ill and had to be seen by a doctor. Now she is safe at a home here in town, resting."

Hok-Ling turned and faced Jason and Lei Chi-Man. Then he backed up and sat down on his cot. "Why do you tell me this?"

"He asks why you tell him this," said Lei Chi-Man.

Jason ignored the question. "Tell him that Fan-Fei has been recognized by one of the men who brought her into town. That she arrived in Sandpoint on July 16th, the night of the sheriff's murder."

Hok-Ling's body stiffened and the muscles of his arms protruded as he clenched the edge of the cot. In the next instant, he relaxed them again but his chest heaved with his breathing. "Tell him we don't believe Fan-Fei could have killed the sheriff, but if she is found out by the jury, they will almost certainly take a different view."

"This woman had nothing to do with it!" Hok-Ling cried, jumping to his feet. He took two steps toward the cell door. "She wasn't there, I tell you!"

When Lei Chi-Man had translated, Jason said, "The jury will not believe this. There is a potential witness who places her in town on the night of the murder. We don't know if the prosecuting attorney knows of this witness, or is aware of Fan-Fei, but we will see." Jason felt his heart begin to pound suddenly. He pushed from his mind the image of Fan-Fei being apprehended and charged with capital murder. "But there is also the matter of your lying to us about the money," he continued. "You said you were holding the $500 for Fan-Fei, but it turns out she was not even at Hope until the night of July 16. It was not her money at all, yet you told us it was. *Why?*"

The bang of the outer door startled them all. A second later the green door flew open. "There you are!" Eddie Rogers said triumphantly and with a little threat in his voice. His rotund face had both the darkness of the corridor and the light of the outer office upon it. He held the green door with the side of his foot.

"Hello, Eddie," Jason said.

Eddie glanced at Lei Chi-Man then leaned clumsily to one side in order to see into the cell. He straightened again. His bearing was childlike. "Is he in there? The one that killed the sheriff?" he whispered, pointing and nodding toward the iron bars.

"What do you want?" Jason snapped.

"Huh?"

"I said 'what do you want?' What are you doing here?"

Eddie didn't answer. He lifted his chin. "Mrs. Stewart said you found her."

"Yeah." Jason's face tightened.

"Did she give you much of a run?"

"Look, Eddie—"

"Mrs. Stewart says she don't know what's going on. Me neither. She thinks maybe you're touched." Eddie laughed shallowly. "Are you?"

"You came for the wagon, right? Go ahead. Take it. Go on. I don't need it anymore."

Eddie blinked and stared at Jason as if he had forgotten all about the wagon. He shook a sausage finger in the air. "I'm going to kick dirt in your face someday, butch!"

"All right, all right. You can kick dirt in my face. Now we're busy here, see? You can take the wagon."

"Oh." He looked at Jason, then at Lei Chi-Man. His eyes darted toward Hok-Ling's cell and then confusion and a little hurt showed about his eyebrows. "I guess I'd better get back to that gate then," he said. He stepped back and the green door began to swing shut, its color evolving, darkening. "Hey! Wait a minute!" he shouted past the door. It flew open again and he stepped into the corridor. He started to speak, then was distracted by the sight of a plate of untouched sandwiches just inside the cell.

"What is it, Eddie?"

"I almost forgot, Jason. Doc Randle came by this morning, just after you left. He was looking for the girl . . . says she's going to have a baby . . . figures that's what's making her tired and whatnot."

Jason and Lei Chi-Man stared at Eddie. So Josephine was right, Jason thought to himself. "Are you sure?" he demanded.

"Yeah, I guess so," Eddie stammered. "That's what the doc told Missus Stewart. I heard him. Said she's about six weeks along. What's wrong? You look—*Hey!*"

Jason had grabbed Eddie's arm and was marching him out the door. When they were in the street, Eddie pulled his arm free and brushed his sleeve indignantly.

"Dammit, McQuade, what's got into you? You *are* touched in the head."

"You and Johnnie were alone with her for almost a day. I don't even want to say what I'm thinking, Eddie."

"Well don't then. We didn't touch her. I wouldn't think of doing something like that, and neither would Johnnie."

"No, I didn't think so. Now listen, Eddie. Are you sure that's what he said? Six weeks? Doc Randle, I mean."

"Yes, godammit.

Jason looked off in the distance and exhaled heavily. "All right, Eddie," he said. He brushed Eddie's sleeve apologetically, then slapped him on the shoulder. "All right. Sorry I got so excited there. Hey, and I want to apologize for taking the wagon like that. That wasn't right. You take it now. It's around back. In fact, I'll walk with you."

They walked around the sheriff's office at a companionable pace. "Let's you and I have a beer one of these days, Eddie," Jason said. "As soon as this trial's over, I'm taking you out for a steak dinner and a beer. How's that?"

Eddie's face lit up. "Why, sure. That'd be nice."

"And in the meantime, what I'd like to do is keep real quiet about this Chinese woman and her baby—'specially now that she's having a baby. Do you know what I mean, Eddie? She's been through a tough couple of days, and I'm afraid if people find out about her and start asking questions that she can't understand— well, it'll get her riled up again and that'll hurt the baby."

"Sure."

Jason watched Eddie climb into the wagon. "The trial'll be over by the end of the week, so let's figure the following Monday or Tuesday night for that dinner out, shall we?"

"That sounds good, McQuade." Eddied mounted the wagon. As he turned it and began to pull away, Eddie twisted around and said, "And I was only kidding about that dirt business."

Jason waved. "Oh, I know that."

When Jason entered the sheriff's office, he found Lei Chi-Man waiting just outside the green door. "Did you tell him?" asked Jason.

"No."

Jason reached for the doorknob. "Let's do it. I want him to know."

When he was informed, Hok-Ling hesitated, touched his mouth with his hand, then turned away and moved quickly, as if on the verge of running toward the window. He curled his fingers around the iron bars. Jason and Lei Chi-Man stared after the prisoner, and both were robbed of breath by what they saw. Across Hok-Ling's back—across the whole of it from the top of his buttocks to the nape of his neck—there was an unbroken network of welts and open wounds. The offended skin was white and every conceivable shade of purple and red and pink. The raised skin even cast shadows across his back.

* * *

"It seemed when I first spoke with you, you did not know you were with child," said Lei Chi-Man, averting his eyes away from Mei-Yin. He picked up the salt shaker on Mrs. Stewart's kitchen table and idly turned it round and round in his hands.

Mei-Yin was staring down at the red and white checked tablecloth. "I did not."

In the silent intervals they could hear Jason and Mrs. Stewart talking in the yard.

"Are you married, Fan-Fei?" Lei Chi-Man asked.

"No."

"Do you . . . have someone?"

Mei-Yin shook her head. She sniffed and wiped a tear from one eye.

"May I respectfully ask, who . . . "

"There is no father," she blurted.

Lei Chi-Man stared dumbfounded at Mei-Yin as Jason entered through the kitchen door and walked toward the stove.

"What have you learned, Charlie?"

Lei Chi-Man hesitated. He put the salt shaker down. "Nothing, Ja-sawn. I was telling her about my grandparents."

"All right. Tell her it's not safe for her to be in town, but I need to have her close by during the trial. I may need her to testify. Ask her if she understands this." Jason wrapped a towel around the handle of the steaming teapot and carried it from the stove to the kitchen table. He carefully poured boiling water into four cups. It was dusk, and the light of the oil lamp on the table had just begun to have an effect.

"She understands," said Lei Chi-Man, after translating.

"Mrs. Stewart and her late husband bought acreage with a hay barn a few miles north of town. I need to move you there for a few days, until the trial is over. You'll have food and water. Charlie is going with you. He'll protect you. Do you understand, Fan-Fei? I've been discussing this with Mrs. Stewart. She's agreed to let us use this place. I'll visit you there, as well."

Mei-Yin, her eyes downcast, whispered something to Lei Chi-Man. "She asks if it is possible to see the prisoner beforehand." Mei-Yin whispered something else, and Lei Chi-Man quickly added, "Alone."

* * *

Mei-Yin waited until she heard both doors shut, then she knelt before Hok-Ling's cell and pressed her forehead to the floor. She waited for Hok-Ling to speak. When he didn't, she raised herself up at last. She gasped at the gaunt figure seated on the cot along the opposite wall, barely visible in the dark cell. "Hok-Ling?" she whispered, wondering for the first time if the attorney and his interpreter might have pointed her to the wrong cell. "Hok-Ling? Is that you?"

"What have you told them?" he hissed. "The attorney and the Tang person?"

She was shocked at the weakness of his voice, but this was as nothing compared to the impression on her heart left by his evident lack of affection and concern. "Nothing—only what you told me to say. I did as you instructed."

"You are to say *nothing* to them—do you understand?" Mei-Yin's eyes grew wide with fear. "They are bluffing. It's a trick. No one could have seen you that night. You were with Soo-Kwan the entire time."

"But there is no point in it, Hok-Ling," Mei-Yin said in a resigned and feeble voice. "I have seen this man they speak of. I, too, remember him." She put one hand on the bars. "Is there no other way?"

"No!"

Mei-Yin recoiled at the suddenness of his reply. "But the demons will kill you! Is that what you want? What about—?"

"Yes!" he snapped, cutting her off. He stood up and moved to the window, then turned to say, "I want that. I want that and nothing more! You have brought great shame to me. Why did you not wait for me? There is nothing left for me now. I know this. I have accepted the inevitability of my death. It is the will of the gods." A strange smile revealed his teeth shining in the light from beyond the window. "I have grown to know one of my ancient ancestors. He visits here—not often, but sometimes. He has shown me things that frighten me, and then he asks, 'Why are you afraid?' I tell him that I approach his realm uninvited and unworthy. That I am afraid for not knowing what will be expected of me—of my spirit. To this he replies, 'Your concern is wasted upon me, Hok-Ling. Why does rain fall in the sea? What is the need of it, if it is only sea water returning to its home?' His voice is very strict and gruff when he says such things." Hok-Ling laughed in spite of himself. His eyes began to bulge in the same indirect light. "He is always growing impatient with me."

Mei-Yin lunged for the bars. She tried to shake them, but only succeeded in setting her own diminutive frame in motion. "Stop it! Stop it! Stop it!" she pleaded. A desperate cry escaped her lips. "How could you? I'm having the green coat's baby," she wailed.

For several minutes, the only sound in the dark corridor was Mei-Yin's sobbing. Hok-Ling approached the cell door and stood looking down at her. She leaned awkwardly away from the cell as though she held some heavy object against the opposite wall, but in fact it was her own weight she supported. Her shuddering was violent, and there were shimmering points of light in the trails of tears that drained over her cheeks, diffusing over the rise of her mouth. She looked over her shoulder at Hok-Ling. She had not seen his back, which was just as well, for a wretched torment already clouded her eyes.

She stared at him as if he were a stranger. And wasn't he? she wondered slowly. All her youthful hopes and dreams—the life they would lead together, the love they would share, the sons she would bear him, their glorious old age. Were these ever real? Did they ever really exist? Why had she thought this would work? And this man—who was he? She looked at him miserably.

"Are you sick?" asked Hok-Ling.

"What?" she asked after a long pause. "Sick? Yes—sick at heart. I have no more courage. I am afraid, do you see?" Mei-Yin was speaking in opposites, but Hok-Ling did not understand. Her eyes became active, studying his face. "You are not afraid, are you? No. Perhaps you have seen this outcome in the yarrow stalks. Have you been told already, Hok-Ling? Has this ancestor you speak of told you? How fortunate you are! And how worthy of such fortune you are!"

"I do not understand!" Hok-Ling cried desperately, grasping the bars. "It is *my* death—*mine.* You must leave me to it. I . . . I resent your fear, Mei-Yin. I almost hate you for it."

"May your hatred die with you then," she whispered, and she turned and leaned back against the uneven plaster. "For I will always remember a man who did not hate me—a man who loved me enough to kill another in order to save me. A man of courage."

"No!" he cried, and he veered away from the bars and tore the mattress from his bed and flung it across the room. He stared at the crumpled mattress for a while, then he returned, as in a kind of retreat, back to the door of the cell. He grasped two bars with his arms wide apart. "There is no justice here, Mei-Yin—not for me, you, or any of us. Why can't you see that? You have seen these giant men, how they swagger and speak with thundering voices—haven't you? It is so even among friends. I have seen them entertain each other with brutishness and loud, threatening gestures. They strut like roosters. A celestial is no more than an ant to them."

Hok-Ling continued, "Two months ago I arrived at a camp to deliver food and supplies. It was many days' travel, high in the mountains, and the camp was small and disorganized, and there was much work to be done there. Even the latrines were unfinished. I heard a great commotion as the lead wagon entered the camp ahead of me, and very soon cheering and laughter came back down the trail disguised as the wind in the trees. It lifted my spirits, if you can understand, and I sat up in the wagon. I even leaned out and prodded the tired horses with my foot. I tried to imagine what it was ahead of me that made them laugh and I was so anxious that I even laughed out loud thinking about it. Do you know what it was?"

Hok-Ling's eyes had wandered away from Mei-Yin, but now returned with the question. "They had tied a coolie—a man I did not know—to a large tree. He was naked, and bound hand and foot, and there was even a rope across his forehead, so that he could not hide his face. They had placed a large sheet of paper over his groin, and had written on it, 'Welcome to Smith Creek Camp.' Do you hear what I'm saying? These foreign demons despise us—all of us. And I think pleasure comes from their hatred of us. What room can there be for justice? Don't you see? There is none, none at all."

Mei-Yin slowly rose to her feet. She moved toward him and gently touched the outside of his hands with her fingertips. "I do not believe you," she said. "Oh, I believe what you tell me happened. I have seen such cruelty myself. I have seen more cruelty than that. I, too, know that we as a people are hated. But I do not believe that all demons are vile and heartless and cruel. Many have been kind to me. Many are gentle and good. And this man? The *leuht si?* He is not cruel," she explained, pointing toward the green door. "He wants to help you. He has hired Lei Chi-Man to act as an interpreter for you. And for me."

"Did I tell you that there were ten coolies for every white demon in that camp?" Hok-Ling interrupted. "Did I tell you that our people stood or squatted behind the jeering devils and would not lift a finger to help their countryman?"

"There are dull spirits among all people," Mei-Yin said. "There is also fear and weakness. How different are these things from cruelty?" She paused and stared into his eyes. A calmness had settled over her. "Maybe this is what disturbs you most—the fear and weakness of some of our kind, not the injustice of the demons. Could it be? I know you, Hok-Ling. I've known you since you were called by your milk name. I know what you did for Soo-Kwan when the green coat tried to kill him in the street. Let me guess. You were angry at the others who did not act. Am I right? But Soo-Kwan is a stranger to them, just as he is your friend. You know as I do that among our people it is considered bad luck to get involved in the ill fortunes of a stranger—yet you were angry with them? Yes, and I know why. I know as surely as I know what you did for me when the green coat raped me. You are a kind, brave man, Hok-Ling, and most important, in your heart you respect life. You will always fight the takers of life, for you have a passion for justice." Her smile grew wide and almost interfered with her talking. "Do you know that you would have been a grand green coat yourself? It is true!"

Hok-Ling drew a deep breath and looked away, his thoughts evidently derailed. His face darkened. When he turned back, he squeezed the bars with redoubled effort and a gleam danced over his eyes. "You speak as though my idiocy were a blessing— as though it does not bear consequences beyond what you or I may see. But look at me! Look at this place! Do you not think heaven and earth are affected? Do you not think I . . . "

He could not finish with Mei-Yin's hand against his mouth. "There is more I must say." Her voice became secretive. "You— Hok-Ling of Kwangchow—you have decided to die. You say it is the will of the gods. So be it. Now I, too, must decide between life and death. If I stab the green coat's baby, I will die with laughter."

"But you would never kill yourself!"

She smiled mysteriously. "No? I would have said that of you—that you would never have given up—that you would shun all vanity for truth, and all that is just. How funny that you say I dare not! However, if I am wrong, it is my fault, not yours. I am prone to error, aren't I? Do you remember your mother telling you, 'If you know all things before yourself, the roots of your happiness will be shallow.' How wise she was! When you told me this, I heard its poetry, but not its truth, which is much grander." She paused and a pleasant recollection seemed to brighten her eyes. Whatever it was, she held the thought of it for several seconds, and when she looked up from this memory she found Hok-Ling seated wearily on the frame of his bed with his back to the wall. "So you see," she continued as if there had been no interlude, "I, too, can decide to die."

He did not look at her. Mei-Yin's heart, like a tired swimmer, began to sink in spite of itself. She looked down, seemed to search the dirty floor for a clue as to what to do next, what to think or say next. But it was not for long.

"What do you want of me, then?" Hok-Ling groaned.

"I want you to *try*, Hok-Ling! Take a chance!" Mei-Yin stepped sideways to see him better. "The chance to win, to see justice done, to have you live again!" Her hands encircled the bars. "Perhaps it is a small chance here, as you say, but I want it. I want *them* to have it, the *leuht si* and Lei Chi-Man. Let them try, Hok-Ling! Let them!"

Their eyes clung desperately through the half-light. Mei-Yin continued, "You don't owe me anything—not anymore. As you say, I am defiled. I release you from your promise. But you owe this to yourself!" She blinked back tears and waited. Slowly, almost imperceptibly at first, she began to slide toward the ground. Hok-Ling rose to his feet, frowning. His eyes were round and hard in their staring. At last he approached her, woodenly, as though a part of him resisted. He stopped when Mei-Yin's up-reaching fingers were only inches from his bare stomach. She whispered something that he did not understand, and when he saw the desolation in her eyes, his heart slowed and his blood pounded through the veins of his neck. She slid further and further from him, and when her hand was at the level of his knees, he dropped to the ground but still did not touch her. He closed his eyes and the muscles in his face pulled with the need to cry.

24

T he puddle of beer on the floor vibrated and grew, and sprouted two arms that raced toward an open seam in the planking. The left one, from Jason's point of view, was wide and plodding. It pulled the puddle out of shape. The right one was thin, and growing thinner, but it had a lively head—good for propitious bursts of speed, Jason thought. It had been a good contest. The lead had changed hands three times in ten minutes and now, it seemed, it was a dead heat. With both arms stopped, Jason carefully poured another stream of beer from his glass over the edge of the table onto the floor. He leaned far over his chair to inspect the sinuous streaks. He blinked sluggishly and knitted his eyebrows. "Why, there's not a quiver left in either of them," he said. "Go on then," he grunted. He waited. Neither line advanced. He poured more beer into the puddle, emptying his glass. "C'mon, Harvard," he said. "Pick up the stroke, boys." He sat up. After some thought, he set his fingers in a little pool of beer on the table and swept it toward the edge. The cool liquid splashed over the ground and over one leg of his pants.

"Hey! Don't do that!"

Jason looked up slowly. It was Dan Buck, the bartender. His hips were swiveling through a maze of tables and chairs. "What the hell you doing over here, McQuade?"

"Got a little problem here, Dan. Had a decent race going, but, you see, Yale caught a crab, and Harvard in . . . ex . . . plic'bly just quit rowing." He trained a dark scowl on the table. Then he laughed. "Maybe they're waiting for my father to show up." He leaned over the table again. "It's going to be a long wait, boys!" he said.

"Looks like you're having just one hell of a good time here, McQuade." The bartender bent to pick up the empty glass and wipe the table with his rag. He had a fresh, agreeable smell about him, and Jason decided he was glad for his company. He smiled inwardly. "Can I give you a hand with that, Dan?" The bartender paid no attention, and Jason began to wonder if he'd really asked the question, or had only thought to ask it. He started to wipe a corner of the table with his shirt sleeve.

"Another beer, McQuade?"

"Sure. He'll have another. Bring one for me, too, will you, Dan?" It was Emory Morse. He sat down, removed his hat, and put it on the table. "So, how've you been, kid?"

"Well, fine. I was just . . . I was having a couple beer-ers."

"So I see. Mind if I join you a minute?"

Jason felt liquid on his chin and swiped at it with the back of his hand. Watch what you say! came a voice from inside him.

"I was hoping to find you. I left a note for you, but . . . " Emory sat down. Dan Buck appeared and placed two fresh glasses of beer between them.

Jason picked his up. "I'm too damn drunk right now to read it."

"I understand. I've got to talk to you, though." The older lawyer straightened in his chair, took a long draft. "It's like this,

Jason," he began, leaning forward again. "There's slippage in the system. There's lots of it. That's something we didn't talk much about when you were studying."

"Slippage?"

"Yeah. Room for error. You know, breakdowns. A trial won't always come out by the book, no matter how good you are, or how hard you try. It doesn't have to be your fault either— usually isn't. It can be the damnedest, littlest things—the kind of thing you'd never expect. I lost a case once because my client's boy whipped the jury foreman's boy in a footrace over a ham sandwich. Another time, a juror fell asleep and lit himself on fire with his pipe. He was in the hospital three weeks, and the judge declared a mistrial."

Jason laughed and his spirit rose with his laughter. He missed spending time with Emory. But then the voice inside warned, watch out! Don't relax. Don't talk about the case. Don't say anything.

There was a sudden outburst of laughter from the bar. Emory leaned closer. "There's plenty of examples of it, Jason— some not so humorous. Any lawyer will tell you about the sleepless nights he's had." After a large swallow of beer he continued, "I don't know what you think will happen on Monday, or what kind of a defense you've got prepared—*and I'm not asking either*. But I want you to know something. I believe this is one of those cases with slippage built into it. I can see it coming plain as anything. I can't expect you to recognize it because you're young and, well, too new to this game. It won't be a little thing that causes it—nothing funny, like those boys racing over a sandwich. It'll be hatred, Jason, prejudice, call it what you like. These people here got a dead sheriff on their hands, and your man's a Chinese. We've got a motive, and, of course, the opportunity was there. You hear what I'm saying?"

Jason stared across the table, not hearing the racket around him for the sound of his thoughts. Emory's penetrating gaze made him uneasy. "Seems to me you're saying all you got is circumstantial evidence, and maybe not much of that. I told you I didn't want to . . . " He stopped, completely out of breath.

"Oh, c'mon, Jason. Let's put the swords down for a minute. This is me talking now. Emory. I want you to know it's a loser. I'm not telling you this for my sake, but for yours." Emory smiled as if a hunch had been borne out before his eyes. Jason parried the expression by lifting the latest glass of beer to his lips. He drank it halfway down.

Emory sat back. "You've never even thought about losing, have you, son? I can see that now. Dammit, that's part of this business. That's the bad part. And there'll be times when you'll want to say the game just ain't worth the candle anymore. It happens to all of us. You've got to learn how to keep your balance and let these kind go their way—tell yourself it's just one more case down the pike." Emory paused and studied Jason's face closely. "This town's going to hang that Chinaman of yours," he said. "There's no doubt about it. Ask any man here— hell, half your jury's right here! Look at them! They've had this one decided all along. The trial? The courtroom? You and me? We'll just make it convenient for them—legal—won't change a thing. And you probably don't know about Judge Simmons. I'd wager he's got the execution date on his calendar right now. I mean it, Jason. He's going to make this hanging a publicity event, too. He's told me as much. Wants a photographer there and reporters from every newspaper north of San Francisco. Thinks it'll spur the debate over statehood, show how we can govern ourselves, strict law and order, all that." Emory leaned far over the table, just inches from Jason's nose. "When he heard your man was trying to starve himself, he fussed for three days, afraid that 'that damn Chinaman' would die before he could hang him—said, 'This won't do! This won't do!'"

"I find out one day he sends Deputy Lambert to Bonners Ferry on an errand, and while he's gone, somebody mysteriously gets into the jail and whips your fella and force-feeds him." Jason's eyes narrowed. "You knew about that? Well, no matter.

It's over and done. I tell you, Jason, I've seen it happen like this before. He's going to hang. Of course, this case is a little different because the evidence is there, enough to hang anybody, I wouldn't wonder. I just hate like hell to see you in the middle of it, that's all. That's why I thought I should talk to you."

Jason stared forlornly at his glass. To avoid Emory's innuendos he let his thoughts turn back to Fan-Fei, the way she was the first time he'd seen her, standing above the pile of clothing in the empty camp, unaware of him. How she moved—bending and twisting as though in a dance. Her face and arms sunburned, her forehead glistening with perspiration. He remembered how tiny strands of her hair were pressed to her temples like pen strokes. And he saw again how she scanned the articles of clothing one by one, looking for tears. Her wide, youthful eyes were so serious.

"Are you listening, Jason?"

"What? Oh. Yes, of course."

"Do you understand what I'm saying? Don't let one case consume you. That's the first rule of lawyering. I know you're idealistic. I know you want this man to have a fair trial and I respect that. He's entitled to it. But don't lose sight of what's happening around you. You've got a long career ahead of you— there'll be other cases. Why, I believe you'll be . . . "

Jason nodded slowly, only pretending to hear the rest. He recalled holding Fan-Fei when she'd collapsed at Hope, and how, moments earlier, a storm had raged in her eyes. He wanted to feel such anguish himself, to take a part of it from her, but no, it didn't work that way. He was untouched by her storm, as one standing safely behind a window, looking out. In this dreaming he had to look away from her and he passed a curse over himself.

But her skin had been warm and soft to his touch. Her hair had hung like silk cloth over the back of his hand. She'd sighed and he'd turned back and gulped her breath to better smell it and taste it and thus know her. And the memory of these things delighted him and fed a strange chauvinistic dream in which he could speak to her in English. "You are young and beautiful and your child will be marvelous—perhaps with dazzling eyes like yours. You are very fortunate. Perhaps it will be a girl—a soft, sweet girl, for whose attention men will endure such tortures as you and I cannot imagine." And he imagined that he stroked the straight, thread-like hairs that dangled over her temples as he said this. But in his dream Fan-Fei smiled compassionately. "Do not bother yourself with my despair, Jason McQuade. Save him. Save Hok-Ling."

Jason scowled and looked away. And this side of his dreaming—in a gray, middle, transitory place—he was shaken by her refusal to acknowledge his feelings—not their depth—yes, that too—but their very existence. A wave of desperation swept over him, and then he said to himself, what am I doing? I can't be in love with a Chinese woman. What in God's name has gotten into me? It's someone else's baby. How could I think that I could—

"Would you listen to me?" Emory snapped, reaching over the table and squeezing Jason's wrist. The older lawyer's face moved in and out of a shadow. "Listen to an old man, will you?" Jason struggled to keep his eyes up. "I'm hearing things around here, all right? People are talking. There's been some talk about you, about your quitting to represent this fella. I don't like the tone of it, Jason. People can be damn unpredictable. They're saying you're a Chinese-lover, and now I'm hearing words like 'carpetbagger' and 'Benedict Arnold.' I don't like it. I don't like what's happening to this town. Listen to me, Jason. I want you to *plead* him."

"What?"

"Plead him, I said."

"*What?* What are you talking about?

"To second-degree murder. I've talked to Simmons. He'll take it. He doesn't want to, but he will. The Chinaman will get life in prison. We'll send him down to Oregon, or California . . . maybe a federal prison down there. I don't know. We'll work that out. He'll be out of our hair—we can put this thing behind us. What do you say?"

"I don't understand."

"I'm offering you a plea bargain. Second-degree murder in exchange for life in prison."

"I . . . I don't know," Jason choked. He looked at Emory as if he were seeing him for the first time that night. Out of our hair? What does he mean? Is he really worried for my safety, or does he know about . . ? But how would he know about her? No, he couldn't. *Plead him?* Could I do that? Would I? To save his life? Am I really thinking that? But why? God, I must be drunk! I *am* drunk! Save his life? But how long would a Chinese last in an American prison? Jason took another long drink. How long will he last at the end of a rope?

"Look. I've gone out on a limb, put something together for you. You oughta give it some serious thought."

"I . . . I don't know, Emory. I don't know how I'd . . . "

Emory snatched his hand away and slapped it against the table. "He's your client, Jason. Talk to him about it through that interpreter of yours. You tell him what the chances are and what I told you. You give him the offer and make a recommendation. That's all there is to it."

Jason stood up and his chair scraped noisily over the floor. He pulled a three-dollar piece from his pocket and tossed it on the table. "I'm not saying yes or no, Emory," he said in a loud, broken voice. "I need some time. Just give me some time."

"You're obligated to talk to him about it. You got till eight o'clock Monday morning." Emory picked up the coin and handed it back to Jason. "I'm buying."

When Jason stepped past him, he staggered and caught himself on the back of Emory's chair. He stopped and fixed his gaze on the center of the two swinging doors. He drew a long, slow breath and exhaled it through pursed lips. The sound was of wind sheared by a rooftop.

* * *

"Charlie! Wake up. It's me. *Charlie!*"

"Ja-sawn? Is that you?"

"Yeah. Open up!" Jason pressed his fingers to his temples, against a throbbing pain in his head.

"Coming."

There was a chirping of bed springs. Jason leaned his head against the door, but it gave way a second later. "Oh! Hello, Charlie. Mind if I come in? Say, light the lamp, will you?"

The interpreter moved aside. "All right," he croaked, at the end of a yawn. "What is it? What time is it?"

The room filled with a thin, yellow light that flickered and held. When Lei Chi-Man turned, waving the match in his fingers, he saw Jason staring aimlessly out of the depths of the chair opposite his bed. Lei Chi-Man shuffled to the edge of his bed and sat down. He wore only his underwear. His body was covered with gooseflesh.

Jason's eyes finally focused on the water-stained cream and blue wallpaper above the dresser. "I thought I'd come by . . . by and talk to . . . " His voice trailed off to a mumble

"Is there something wrong?"

"No. Well, yes." He waved his hand in the air, then tried to sit up and sagged back down again. "Where is she, Charlie?" He winced, and touched the side of his head again. "Oh, Lord."

"Who? Fan-Fei?"

"Yes, dammit. Who else?"

"Isn't she still at your . . . at Mrs. Stewart's house?" The alarm registered in Lei Chi-Man's voice drew Jason a step closer to sobriety.

"Oh, yeah," he blinked. "Yeah. That's right. It's tomorrow you're taking her out to that barn, isn't it?"

Sober, he would have remembered his conversation with Mrs. Stewart, decisions made just a few hours earlier.

"It's just that I know Emory's been out there at the railroad camp," Jason had said. "He's talking to people out there."

"Well, I don't wonder," offered Mrs. Stewart. She was taking clothes off the line. Jason lent a hand. "He's going to find out all he can about this Hok-Ling, isn't he? For my money, these people are pretty docile and . . . " She seemed to remember Lei Chi-Man and Fan-Fei sitting at her kitchen table, within earshot, and stopped. Her color deepened. "Well, anyway, I'd wanna know more about what got into this Hok-Ling fellow— why he'd want to go get involved with a bunch of white boys and a white man—a sheriff to boot."

Jason thought for a moment. "Of course you're right, Mrs. Stewart. He'll dig and keep digging. He'll be out there again tomorrow, I wouldn't wonder. There could be talk about Fan-Fei, about this sister of Soo-Kwan who showed up all of a sudden. We don't want him thinking about that, getting ideas."

"You'd better take her out to the farm then," said Mrs. Stewart matter-of-factly. "To the old barn. The place hasn't been worked since John died. But it's secluded, and it's dry enough. It's a couple miles out on the Baldy Road. She can hole up out there until you need her, or until the trial's over." Mrs. Stewart lifted a full clothes basket and shook her head when Jason reached to take it from her. "I think that'll do just fine," she grunted. "We'll send food and blankets out there, of course, and I'll send along something for her to do. She'll be safe." She stopped to pick up a clothespin on the ground. "I wonder if the poor dear can sew?"

"Oh, yes," Jason offered. "That's what she does at the camp."

Sober, Jason would have recalled these details, but now he remembered them only dimly. He looked bleary-eyed at Lei Chi-Man. "You'll take her to the barn, and from now on you'll stay with her at night. I don't want anything to happen to her."

"Yes, Ja-sawn. We've already discussed this."

"It'll only be a couple of days, until the trial is over."

"Yes."

"All right. You probably want to get back to sleep." Jason looked around the room, outwardly indifferent to the gentle, selfless man who shivered before him. He made no effort to rise from the chair.

"Is there anything else?" Lei Chi-Man asked hesitantly.

"What?"

"Is everything else okay?"

"Oh. Yeah, sure. Everything's fine." Jason leaned his head against the worn, yellowed antimacassar. "Everything's . . . " He began to shake his head against an onslaught of troubling thoughts. Lei Chi-Man, compelled by the long, uncomfortable silence, performed his own unnecessary survey of his room, yawned once, and started rubbing the goose bumps out of his thighs. "No," Jason continued at last, "everything's not fine."

"What's wrong?" asked Lei Chi-Man.

"It's . . . I don't know where to begin. I've . . . it's just that I've developed . . . what you'd call . . . or *could* call . . . very affectionate feelings for Fan-Fei."

"For Fan-Fei?"

"Yes."

Lei Chi-Man's mouth fell open. "What are you . . . ? You mean . . . ? I don't understand, Ja-sawn."

"I love her, Charlie. Well, I think—"

"You *love* her? What are you talking about? Fan-Fei? You don't even know her. How could you . . . ?"

"It sounds lunatic, doesn't it? I can't explain it, Charlie, but . . . what if she's the one? I just want . . . "

A shadow crossed over Lei Chi-Man's face. He sat erect and the muscles of his jaw tightened. What appeared as equanimity bore the pull of dark, disinclining forces. Jason, who was searching midway between himself and Lei Chi-Man for his next word, didn't see this.

"I just want her to know, Charlie," Jason said, looking up miserably. "I need to communicate with her—through you. The timing, of course, is terrible, but I have to act now—tomorrow. This can't wait."

Lei Chi-Man looked away momentarily, but when he spoke again he glowered at Jason. "You are speaking nonsense. You're drunk. You must go home and sleep."

"Yes, I'm drunk," Jason answered, raising his voice, "but I know what I'm saying." He looked down. "I wish it weren't true, but it is. Yes, I love her. And I don't care if she's with child. I'll raise the child with her." As he mulled this subject, he felt himself suddenly up on his feet moving arm in arm with someone toward the door. "We'll raise the child as our own." The door swung open. It occurred to him that time was running short with Lei Chi-Man. "And you're going to interpret, because that's what I'm paying you for," he said, vaguely aware that he was racing a shutting door.

* * *

They sat in the "silence" of crickets and frogs. Above, the stars glittered and the moon shone with a fierce light. Mrs. Stewart's knitting progressed in the dark corner of the porch while Mei-Yin sat along the top step with her back to a post. She gazed out onto the front yard, at the serrated shadows of pickets, at dots scattered about, like dull stars—dandelions.

Am I really here? she thought. I can't believe it! So far! Did I have to come so far? Her breath caught and she closed her eyes to the moonlit landscape. If only for a moment, she thought, let me be away from here. Let me be in Kwangchow. In school. I do not want to be pregnant. Yes, in school. A baby? Can it really be so? A demon's baby! She brought her knees up and wrapped her arms around them, hiding her stomach. Her head slumped forward then she turned again to look out at the world. Several minutes passed. Mrs. Stewart's breaths were audible and became for Mei-Yin part of the night's rhythm. This old woman is kind, she thought. She reminds me of Lai-Ping in a way. She speaks her mind. I wish I could talk to her. But I wouldn't talk. I would listen. I would like to hear her tell a hundred stories, true stories about her life.

The frenzied barking of a dog gave notice of Jason's approach. Mei-Yin raised her head. She recognized him at the gate, but there was something unfamiliar about him, as well. It didn't take long to figure out what it was. How many times had she seen her father return home in such a state? Jason stumbled up the walkway and didn't see her until he reached the bottom of the steps. Even then he might not have, but she turned and swung her feet down to the third step, giving him room to pass.

"Oh!" he said. "It's you!"

Mei-Yin scooted closer to the post. Please don't talk to me, she said to herself. I can't understand. Please just pass by. *Please*."

"I didn't expect to see you out here." He sat down on the top step next to the post opposite her. "Beautiful night, isn't it?" He took a deep breath.

What's he doing? Mei-Yin wondered. And what's he trying to say to me? Before she could turn to Mrs. Stewart, Jason added, "The stars are really amazing."

"Good evening, Jason," said Mrs. Stewart.

"Oh! I didn't see you there. Hello, Mrs. Stewart. Everyone's out late tonight." Mei-Yin heard what sounded like disappointment in his voice, in addition to his slurring of words.

"It's a warm night," was Mrs. Stewart's reply. She didn't say anything else, and Jason didn't move. Mei-Yin wondered what would happen next. She was wracked with self-consciousness and humiliation, sitting so close to Hok-Ling's attorney on the porch of a stranger's house—doubly so at night. This is not proper! she told herself. He should not have sat down next to me. And look! He's leaning back now as if he plans to stay here indefinitely. Mei-Yin looked beseechingly at the dim figure of Mrs. Stewart. Finally, she heard the creaking of Mrs. Stewart's wicker chair, and her ample legs came out of the shadows.

"Jason, we're off to bed now. Come along, Fan-Fei."

She is beckoning me, thought Mei-Yin. At last! She jumped to her feet and climbed the stairs. She followed Mrs. Stewart to the door. The old woman stopped and said to Jason, "Good night, dear."

Jason answered from some distant, distracted place, his face turned upwards towards the stars. "Good night."

Mei-Yin knew this phrase "good night." She paused at the door and thought about saying this to the attorney, but something kept her from doing it. She bowed quickly and entered the house ahead of Mrs. Stewart.

25

Mei-Yin followed Lei Chi-Man and Jason and watched bees and grasshoppers race ahead of their threshing feet. They came to a vast tangle of blackberry vines and skirted them until a pathway presented itself. The path, shaded by aspen and birch, still wet with dew, wove in and out, and climbed many rises. At last, they stood near the large, gaping doorway of a barn. The structure was larger than she'd imagined, over twenty feet high, and twice as wide. Inside were shapeless mounds of dark, spoiled hay, and dank, fetid air. Wasps could be heard buzzing in the rafters. The skewed boarded walls were as gray and brittle as old bones.

The two men set their boxes down just inside the door. Mei-Yin did the same. She was aware of a sudden nervous malaise, for she knew she would be left here for at least two or three days to spend many hours alone. She looked up at the hayloft, then into the far corner of the barn where an open plank door revealed a small, exceedingly dirty tack room and workbench with sun-suffused windows painted over with years of dust and cobwebs. She looked into the other corners of the barn. Still, she thought, there is protection from the rain in places. With Lei Chi-Man sleeping out here, I will be safe.

She turned partway to the interpreter and shaded her eyes with an imperfect salute. The false smile of her squinting disappeared, leaving a placid gaze that seemed to attract and surprise him. "What is it?" he asked.

"Nothing," she said, averting her eyes. "I'm sorry. I was thinking of something. You will be comfortable sleeping out here while I sleep in that room?"

Lei Chi-Man glanced quickly at the small room. "Yes, of course," he said perfunctorily. Mei-Yin smiled inwardly, for she knew his answer before he uttered it. She had known other men like Lei Chi-Man—her mother's oldest brother, for one. "There are some men who simply do the right thing, the good thing," Lai-Ping had said to her once, dreamily, for Lai-Ping liked men and Mei-Yin knew she wanted one of her own. This was many years ago. "They don't talk about it, or make a fuss. It's just business as usual for them. My oldest brother, your uncle, is this way." Jason was busy unpacking one of the boxes, and Lei Chi-Man another. When they had finished, Jason started on a third. Then he stood up and scratched his hair. "Charlie, why don't you go down to the wagon and get the sewing, and if you can bring up that last box, grab that, too."

"All right."

Mei-Yin watched Lei Chi-Man disappear down the path. She wondered where he was going and, without knowing why, wished she could have gone with him. She glanced at the attorney out of the corner of her eye then set about organizing some of the articles provided by Mrs. Stewart—potatoes, onions, apples, cherries, bread, cheese, also a cooking pot and utensils— on a dusty shelf mounted next to the door. Jason didn't move.

I wish he wouldn't stand so close, she thought, leaning over to pick up a sealed jar of lard. Why does he just stand there? It's clear he has a hangover. His eyes are puffy and he seems to be frowning and squinting at everything—except me. His voice sounds tired and defeated. Mei-Yin felt a sudden heaviness in her chest. *Defeated*. Is that it? Is that why he got drunk last night?—because he thinks he will lose at trial tomorrow? Does he believe Hok-Ling will be found guilty and executed? She stopped midway in her work, and only with great effort was she able to continue. Oh *Tianshen*, great spirits, that's it, isn't it? The attorney's miserable because he knows Hok-Ling can't be saved. But if only people knew what really happened. If only the judge and jury could hear the truth.

Here these two men are, trying to protect me, but it is Hok-Ling who needs protecting. Why are they putting me here, when it is Hok-Ling's life that is in danger? This doesn't make sense.

She heard Jason draw a long, self-conscious breath and noticed that he stepped out to look over the tangle of thorny vines in the direction of the wagon. His next movement so startled Mei-Yin that she gasped and recoiled, and in the next instant she found herself looking directly into his eyes. He had taken hold of her shoulders.

"Fan-Fei . . . " Although his voice was soft and questioning, his stare was piercing. His eyes seemed no longer sluggish or squinting.

Her heart froze then began to thrash wildly in her chest. What's he doing? She twisted to free herself. "Please! Let go of me!" she cried in Cantonese. He released her slowly, but continued to hold her in his gaze. I knew it! He's just like the others, like the men at the camp who gawk at me and desire one thing. Or the men on the ship. Jason's eyes broke free of their ice-like intensity and began to wander wistfully over her face. A wave of fear swept through Mei-Yin. She took two steps back. Is he going to rape me?

"*You* . . . Fan-Fei . . . Fan-Fei . . . "

She took another step back. The soft and thoughtful tone in his voice, the evident desire to communicate, arrested her momentarily. But then the weight of an unfathomable anxiety and expectation began to descend. The instinct to survive began to take hold.

"You are so beautiful," Jason whispered. "Do you understand? *Beautiful.*"

There is too much need in his eyes. I must get away from him.

"I have never seen a more beautiful woman in all my—"

"Aaee!" Mei-Yin turned and ran as fast as she could down the winding path through the swollen mounds of blackberries. Within a few moments, she heard Jason's footsteps behind her. Then his voice.

"Wait, Fan-Fei! Fan-Fei! What's wrong?"

She let out a scream as she reached the open field. Turning, she saw Lei Chi-Man in the distance, walking toward her with a box in one hand and a large canvas bag thrown over the other shoulder. She veered and ran straight for him. Her knees and elbows churned rapidly over the stubble field. He dropped what he was carrying and began to run toward her. When Jason appeared at the bottom of the wall of blackberry vines, Lei Chi-Man stopped abruptly. Jason, too, stopped running. Jason's hands went out to his side as if to say "What in the world . . . ?" Then both men continued to run, although at lesser speed, for they were converging on what each knew would be an unpleasantness between men.

Mei-Yin's cheeks were wet with tears. At first, she was too winded to speak. She circled around Lei Chi-Man, ensuring that he stood between her and the attorney. Jason trotted up to them and stopped. He, too, breathed heavily.

"What is it, Ja-sawn?" said Lei Chi-Man. He turned to Mei-Yin. "What is it? What happened?"

"He grabbed me!" Mei-Yin cried between gulps of air. "He was going to . . . " Something inside Mei-Yin stopped her from saying it. But if it was not rape, what was it? she thought. Was he going to kiss her, touch her breast? Whatever it was, it was awful. "He . . . he tried to touch me, to harm me!"

Lei Chi-Man turned back to Jason and squared his shoulders. His stared ominously. "What's the meaning of this?" he demanded. "What have you done?"

"Listen, Charlie," Jason cried, "she misunderstood me. I was trying to tell her—"

"She says you touched her!" Lei Chi-Man shouted. He seemed on the verge of springing for his employer's neck. "Did you touch her?"

"I was trying to—"

"Did you touch her?"

"I touched her shoulders. I was trying to tell her that I . . . that I think she's beautiful."

Lei Chi-Man hesitated. His own chest was heaving now. He blinked and in time looked away, trying to calm himself. Then he turned back to Jason. "I have tried to tell you this before, Ja-sawn. You cannot touch a Chinese woman. Do you understand? It is very offensive." Most of the anger was out of Lei Chi-Man, but it continued to darken his face. He turned to Mei-Yin. "He says he did not mean to frighten you, and that he was not trying to harm you."

She began to cry. "He put his hands on me, Lei Chi-Man. I could see in his eyes what he was planning to do."

Lei Chi-Man took a deep breath. He set his gaze somewhere between Mei-Yin and Jason. "Do you see what you've done?" he said. "She thinks you were preparing to rape her."

"Rape her?" cried Jason. He put both hands on top of his head and turned in disbelief. "Charlie, you've got to tell her," he said at last, lowering his hands and spreading them wide. "Tell her she misunderstood—that I was trying to tell her that I have feelings for her." Now Jason began to pace, and he put one hand

back on top of his head. "That I think she's beautiful. That I've fallen in love with her. You've got to tell her, Charlie. Tell her I've never felt this way about any woman before."

Lei Chi-Man stared at the ground, his lips pressed tightly together.

"Do it, Charlie. Tell her I didn't mean to scare her, or offend her in any way. That I only want what's best for her. Tell her everything!"

Lei Chi-Man began to shake his head. His hands went up. "Ja-sawn, this is not the time."

"I want her to know everything. Tell her now—please."

Mei-Yin had listened to this exchange through sobs without trying to guess its meaning. When Lei Chi-Man began to speak in Cantonese, her mouth dropped open. She covered a gasp with her hand, and her eyes darted wildly side to side. He has *what? Fallen in love with me?* "How can this be true?" she sniffed, looking up at the interpreter. She saw by Lei Chi-Man's expression that it was true. "But this is impossible."

"He was not trying to rape you. There are different rules of touching here. He was trying to explain his feelings to you, that is all."

Mei-Yin tried to comprehend this, to take Lei Chi-Man's words at face value, but it strained credulity to the breaking point. *How can this man love me? He is a devil, not a Tang person. He doesn't know me. He can't speak a word of Cantonese, and I don't speak English. No, he's making this up as a way of excusing himself! Only a brute would touch a strange woman.* Her heart beat faster. A second later she considered, *but it's true that people touch each other differently here. I've seen it.* She thought of Mrs. Stewart wrapping her arm around her, and the way Jason had helped her into Dr. Randle's office. *They do touch strangers.* She searched the ground for answers. "This is just not possible," she repeated, looking up into Lei Chi-Man's eyes.

"Mmm. I agree. But it is what he believes. I happen to know this."

"You do?"

"Yes."

Mei-Yin saw the shadow of a pained expression pass over the interpreter's face, which only confused her further. She turned her back on both men. *The attorney is in love with me?* She put her hand on her stomach. *What does this mean?* Suddenly, she felt the attorney's eyes upon her. She sensed his desire, his preoccupation with her. Hadn't she felt this when he picked her up in the wagon after she'd fled from Mrs. Stewart's house? Or when he looked up to see her in Mrs. Stewart's bedroom window? Or last night, on the porch? Wasn't it there in the way he stared at her when he first encountered her at Hope, or on subsequent visits to the camp, when he and Lei Chi-Man pressed her for information about Hok-Ling?

It's true, then, she thought. *He is infatuated with me, and it is distracting him from helping Hok-Ling. The trial starts tomorrow! Oh, how awful! How could this have happened? Did I do something to cause this?* She searched her memory but could think of nothing she had done.

Suddenly, the reality of Hok-Ling's imminent death closed in around her, robbing her of breath. She reeled and began to turn side to side as though her whole body were saying no. *It will all be because of me then! It is already so, because I came here—but now? Now I have even robbed him of an attorney who is focused and free of distraction! There is nothing left! Nothing! Only the truth can save him!* She spun around and cried out blindly, "I am not Fan-Fei! I am not Soo-Kwan's sister!" *There! She'd said it!* She took a step toward Lei Chi-Man, her face trembling. "I am Yeung Mei-Yin! Do you hear? I have been promised to Hok-Ling since I was sixteen. I came here looking for Hok-Ling. I had to! My father . . . When I got here, I was raped by the green coat. It's *his* baby. It's the green coat's baby. He raped me. He was preparing to rape me again when Hok-Ling saw him—when he saw us both below the bridge." She pointed off in the general direction of Sandpoint. "I had gone there to bathe, you see, and the green coat followed me. It was not Hok-Ling's fault! He was only protecting me. You must understand. Tell the *leuht si!* Tell him!"

Lei Chi-Man stared at Mei-Yin. He tilted his head slightly as though recounting a series of events, piecing them together. One emotion after another seemed to take hold of him.

"What is it, Charlie? What's she saying?"

Lei Chi-Man turned to Jason and extended a questioning hand, but then on the verge of speaking he turned back to Mei-Yin. "So you are Mei-Yin?"

"Yes."

"And you are the woman Hok-Ling has spoken about? The one he is promised to?"

"Yes, although I have released him from that promise, should he wish it," Mei-Yin added. She felt an anguished shudder in her heart, a foreboding of hopelessness.

"Because?"

"Because I am defiled."

Lei Chi-Man's eyebrows arched. "Oh." He pretended to be thinking of something else. "You are not Fan-Fei then."

"No."

"And how did you get here? From the Middle Kingdom, I mean?"

"Aboard a ship that sailed from Kwangchow to San Francisco and Tacoma."

"And you came alone?"

"Yes. I . . . I disguised myself as a man. I will tell you anything you want to know, Lei Chi-Man, but please! Tell the *leuht si* who I am! I beg of you!"

Lei Chi-Man stood in stunned amazement. He touched his pursed lips with the tips of his fingers. He looked down, then back up at Mei-Yin, and twice more repeated this with questions crowding behind his eyes. Finally, he turned to Jason. "She is prepared to accept your apology," he said. He seemed reluctant to go on. At last he straightened his shoulders and drew a deep breath. "There is much more, Ja-sawn. This woman is not Soo-Kwan's sister, and her name is not Fan-Fei . . . "

* * *

Hok-Ling faced the window of his cell. His forehead and cheeks, his forearms and bare chest shone with an oily perspiration. His eyes were sunken and dull in their orbits. He had not moved for over an hour. In the sheriff's office, Deputy Lambert played solitaire. Now and then he whistled softly to himself to get his mind off the game. The afternoon was sultry.

Hok-Ling swallowed. This week I die. I will leave this place. Ah, no more foul air, no more dull light. But where will I go? How will my spirit find its way back to the center of the earth? My body! I must remember to ask Lei Chi-Man to notify Soo-Kwan and Dak-Wah of my death. They will make sure my remains are returned to the Middle Kingdom. Perhaps they have already made necessary arrangements with the Six Companies. But what then? Will my ancestors be there to welcome my spirit? If they aren't, what will happen to me? Will my ghost dwell in an eternal torment—a prison cell such as this?

I have tried to live honorably. But I am too free-thinking. It was never my wish to bring shame upon my family. Where did I go wrong? Was it Mei-Yin? Did I risk too much when I allowed myself to love her? To think I came here for her! Oh, Father, had you been well I know you would have stopped me. But you were delirious with fever and said nothing.

But Father, you didn't tell me that loving a woman was playing with fire! Why are you smiling? Yes, she is very beautiful, isn't she? No, I have never seen such a pearl either. You're right, it's no excuse. There is no excuse.

How terrible to find her that way—naked, defiled, helpless. He deserved to die. But why me? Why did I have to be the one to kill him? I am just Wong Hok-Ling, the son of a fishmonger. I would never have imagined killing another man. I felt the life go out of him—felt and heard it. I feel it and hear it still. I rode him like an animal. Until I was sure. Who could have imagined this?

I am rotting away here in this white devil's prison. But it won't be long now.

What will it be like to hang? I have seen two Indians hanging in the trees, but they were long dead. The neck of that one! Oh, how could I forget it, stretched so grotesquely? His eyes were not closed, although I did not see pain in them. Perhaps it is not a painful thing to hang. His eyes were still looking.

I will close my eyes.

* * *

"Yes? Who is it?" The voice behind the door crackled with sleepiness.

"It's me. Jason."

"Good heavens! What time is it? What do you want?"

"I've come to talk to you."

"It's after midnight. I'm not dressed."

"I'm sorry. I . . . I shouldn't have come. I'll . . . "

"Is there something wrong?"

"No. Not really."

"Are you sure?"

"Yeah."

"What time is it?"

"I don't know, Esther. I'm sorry. I'll talk to you tomorrow . . . or sometime."

"Are you sure? You're not sick or anything?"

"No. I'm not sick." He stepped away from the door. "Sorry, Esther. Go back to sleep." The door squeaked open when he reached the top step. He turned and saw a sliver of her face. "I'm sorry, Esther, really."

"Nonsense. Come in. I'll get my robe."

"No. It's late."

"Come on. It's cold out there. Let me stoke the fire and make some cocoa."

He nodded. "All right."

She closed the door behind him, and when next she spoke she was neatly beyond him, mounting the stairs. "I'll be right down," she yawned.

"Thanks," Jason said. "Should I stoke the fire?"

"No. I'll be right there." With each ascending step Esther ascended out of sleep. Her bare feet slid over the landing at the top of the stairs, then faded to soft thuds and creaks over the ceiling of the parlor. Jason waited in darkness at the bottom of the stairs.

She tied the sash of her robe then sat quietly at the edge of her bed. She reached through the darkness for her hairbrush. *Now what am I to do? Of course, I must tell him.* With her heart racing, she began to brush very hard, pulling her head back with each stroke.

I can't explain it, Joe. She imagined a long-faced Joe Patterson sitting opposite her in the drawing room of his father's mansion, his legs crossed, his hands curled over the arms of the leather wingback chair. The marble and ormolu clock would be ticking loudly on the mantle. *I thought it was over, Joe. I swear I did. I thought he was out of my system completely, that I would never see him again.*

I feel so terrible! You've been so good to me, Joe. So true and kind, and—oh, I don't deserve you. I really don't! All those wonderful things you said to me the other day, why, those were the most beautiful words—

He came back, Joe. He came back in the middle of the night and apologized to me. I didn't know he would. I had no idea! He said he never meant to hurt me. That he wanted more than anything to have me back. He wanted a chance to explain, to try to make me understand why he did what he did, why he felt he had to represent the Chinaman. He said he wanted me to know all about the law, and why lawyers do the things they do.

Don't you see, Joe? I'm in a terrible pickle. Yes, I know, but I love him, Joe. I love him dearly. Can you ever forgive me? Can you? She stretched to replace her hairbrush on the nightstand.

Jason followed her down the hallway into the kitchen. He sat at the table. The pretty line of Esther's figure wrapped in a thin summer robe passed before the window. He heard a cupboard door snap open, then the sound of her fingers probing a box of matches. "I'm a perfect bastard for coming here," he moaned at last.

"I was dreaming I heard someone knocking," she said throatily, ignoring his self-reproach. "That's why I didn't come for so long. I might have gone on sleeping if you hadn't been so persistent."

"Was I persistent?"

She struck a match. The flame hissed and its light sprang up on her wry smile and dark eyes, and it threw a strange, elephantine image up behind her, against a white wall and cupboard. "I should say so," she replied. "But I'm glad you were. I've wanted to see you. I've wanted to tell you I *don't* hate you. I don't, you know. I've had a lot of time to think about this. I was just so upset when—the last time I saw you." There, she thought, that will ease the way for him to speak, to apologize and explain. The flame subsided behind her cupped hand as she moved toward the table, intent on the oil lamp. He lifted the chimney. The flame nosed across the wick, rose up with sharp sides and two severe points. The light wandered over a checkered oilskin tablecloth, over his face, revealing eyes that were round with introspection.

She carried the dying match to the stove. A few minutes later, the fire in the stove sputtered around new kindling and the first traces of heat eddied through the room. She set a pan of milk on the stovetop and returned to the table.

"Would you like something to eat?"

"No. Thank you." He looked up to find her staring at him. His own silence was unbearable to him. "How . . . have you been?"

Esther leaned over the table and the humorous, middle-of-the-night smile on her face as much as said, "I know you've got something on your mind, Jason McQuade, and you're finding it difficult to tell me. You might as well come out with it. I'm not going to bite you." But the words she spoke were, "I'm fine. How have you been?"

"Fine, fine. How's Joe? And . . . and Sarah, and everybody. Gosh, I've been so busy I hardly know what's happening anymore."

There was enough light to see some color come into Esther's face. "He's fine, Jason."

"Oh . . . that's good."

The clock in the hall struck one sonorous tone. "Good heavens!" Esther cried. "One o'clock. Have you been to bed at all?"

"No."

"Well, this must be very important." She sat up and spread her hands over the table. She smiled again but her eyes grew insistent. "I mean, it's wonderful to see you—really—but I've never had anyone call on me at one in the morning. If Daddy were alive, he'd . . . "

Jason's hands sprang out, smothering hers against the tablecloth. "Listen to me, Esther. The trial is tomorrow. You know that, right?"

Esther nodded self-consciously. If it's going to be said, it is *you* who must say it, dear. I've already told you I don't hate you. I've tried to make it easier for you, but all the same, you must say it. I long to hear it. Oh, how I long to hear it! I've missed you terribly.

He released her hands in a way that startled her, and sprang to his feet. He walked toward the window. In it were reflections of the lantern's flame, the brightly colored tablecloth, Esther's face, uplifted, bludgeoned by shadow. "You don't know the particulars," he blurted. "I've come to tell you what I've learned, to prepare you for what's going to happen."

"What?"

He turned toward her. "I came here to tell you . . . to tell you what I've discovered about your father's death. But it's horrible,

Esther—unspeakably horrible. I fear you . . . you won't believe me. And now, as I stand here, well, I'm afraid that it's simply too horrible to be believed—even though I may believe it myself." The last he mumbled to himself as he stared into the dark corner of the kitchen.

Esther stiffened. Behind a confused smile her thoughts raced. *He . . . he's not here . . . Wait a minute! Did he say . . ? Am I dreaming? Think, Esther! What's happening? Why is he here?* Oh God, what a fool I am! How could I have been such an idiot? Her eyes settled back on Jason, and her sadness and sleepiness were evident in them, and mostly there was sadness. "You came to tell me something about Daddy? Then you must tell me—at once . . . *Especially* if you believe it."

He moved toward her, and as he did, the lantern's light caught on him, sparkling in the silver buckle at his waist, lighting the buttons of his shirt, flashing in his glossy eyes. When the flames flickered, it seemed his whole frame shuddered as in a monstrous fever. He stopped within a few feet of her. Esther covered her face. But in the next minute their eyes were fastened upon each other again— his unmoving, hers tracking impatiently and angrily between his. He continued to stare and made no move to touch her.

"You *will* tell me eventually, won't you?"

He turned his head and stared helplessly into the space between Esther's face and the glowing lantern. His eyes were suddenly distant. "I . . . I will tell you this," he began slowly, as though speaking out of a dream. "I am altogether unworthy of your friendship, of your love. It is quite impossible for a man of honor and principle to blunder as I have down a path paved with such black and melancholy insinuations aimed at a man as worthy and respected as your father was. It is truly shocking . . . even to me . . . and I've spent the whole of this afternoon and tonight in the grip of an awful depression . . . a terrible depression." He turned again to Esther. "Seeing you tonight . . . now . . . I'm suddenly more depressed than ever. I'm more confused than I ever thought possible."

Esther frowned. "That makes two of us, Jason. Why are you doing this to me? Tell me. Tell me what it is." She wanted to cry, wanted nothing more than to cry at this moment.

He continued to speak as though not hearing her. "I'm very tired, Esther. It's gone too far, this whole thing, you see." His eyes grew wide and fearful. But he was looking inward. "I would quit if I could. On my word I would. But what then? Who would defend him?" Jason raised his head and stared at the wall. "He'll hang anyway. You should have heard Emory! You should have heard him, Esther!" His brow arched above a tortured expression. "He says they'll hang him for sure, Esther—regardless."

"Jason, *please!* Do not for one minute pretend that I care as you do about the man who killed my father. I can't believe . . . " Her voice cracked, and she stopped.

"They offered a deal, Esther," he said, as if just remembering it himself. "Did I tell you? Maybe I shouldn't tell you this, but—oh, no matter. I can plead Hok-Ling to second degree murder. They'll send him to prison for the rest of his life. They won't hang him. What do you think of that?"

"What am I supposed to think?" she cried. "You came to tell me *this?*"

He looked at her and recollected himself, and his eyes were active again and weighted with kindness. "You're right," he said. "I should not have come. I cannot for one minute justify myself."

"Why are you doing this to me?"

"What? I'm sorry, Esther. Truly I am." He turned as though trying to flee the lamplight. She watched him lean against the sink, shaking his head. "Can you forgive me, Esther?"

"*What?* Forgive? What are you talking about?" She examined him with increasing intensity and trepidation.

"It's true, Esther. I'm sorry."

"You're hiding something from me!"

Jason continued, still with his back to her. "No. I'm over my head, that's all. I'm not a *lawyer*—not a good one, anyway. What do I know about your father . . . or these Chinese people . . . or a murder trial? *A murder trial!* Good God, I've never tried a case in my life. Who am I to get in the middle of this? Emory said as much himself. This will be the end of me."

Esther leaned back in her chair and folded her arms stiffly beneath her bosom. "You did not wake me up to rave about these apprehensions of yours. You know damn well that I am the last person on earth who will sympathize with you! You came to tell me something about Daddy's death. Something horrible. Something that, you say, you nevertheless believe." She closed her eyes to let a painful shudder pass. When she opened them again, she said, "Tell me what it is . . . or get out."

He turned and looked at her desperately. "For the love of God, Esther." His hands started out. *"I can't."*

"Get out!"

26

J udge Essex Simmons pointed to two ladder-back chairs facing his desk. "Have a seat, fellas." He closed the door, cutting off the noise from the courtroom. His robe billowed behind him as he moved around the desk. "Looks like a full house already. Reporters from all over—far away as Helena." He smiled, then winked at Jason. "Word gets around. You boys ready?"

Jason and Emory nodded from the chairs. Tyler Forbes, the third attorney in town, who'd teamed up with Emory to prosecute Hok-Ling, leaned against the window sill and crossed his arms. "We're ready, Your Honor," he said.

"That's fine. That's fine. Let's see here. A couple of preliminary matters." Simmons picked up a piece of paper. He extended it out and adjusted his glasses in order to read it. "No, we'll do that later. That, too," he mumbled to himself, evidently reading from a list.

Jason looked down at three pages of handwritten notes that he held in his left hand over his lap. "Opening Statement" was scribbled in large letters across the top of the first page. He pushed the papers down against his leg to stop them from shaking. God! This is really happening, he thought. He tried to swallow but couldn't. The atmosphere around him seemed to thicken, making it hard to breathe. That a man's life was at stake—that what *he*, Jason McQuade, did or said in the next two to three days could spell the difference between a man living out the rest of his life or having his neck snapped at the end of a rope within a week—imbued him with a terror unlike anything he had ever experienced before. Why is this starting now? he wondered. But he knew the answer as soon as he asked the question. Before this, he had held it all at bay. It was an investigation. Mind work. Legwork. Yes, the sheriff was dead, but he had never really known the sheriff. Or liked him, for that matter. Only a few words had passed between them, pleasantries of one kind or another, although none particularly pleasant. Jason regarded him as someone potentially standing astride the line connecting him to Esther, but more often as some vague personage in the background. Everyone else was alive. It was an investigation. Oh, there was Esther's grief. That was concrete enough. But any daughter would grieve the loss of her father— or most would. No, it had all been academic until now, this case, like the hundreds of cases he'd read and re-read in Emory's law library. A murder here, a robbery there. A defendant facing a death sentence here, a defendant facing a prison sentence there.

But this was not academic. Not even close.

"We'll seat a jury this morning," continued the judge, still concentrating on the list, "and have opening statements out of the way by noon. Now we might even get a witness or two in."

Jason saw that the papers in his hand were still shaking. He cleared his throat and made a show of crossing his legs and folding his arms—sending the papers out of sight. A quick glance to his left satisfied him that neither Emory nor Forbes had noticed his shaking.

"How long do you figure for your opening statement, Emory?" Simmons asked.

Forbes interjected, "I'll be doing the opening, Judge. No more than fifteen minutes."

The judge looked at Jason. "And you?"

Suddenly, Jason recalled a defense trial strategy he'd learned from Emory, reserving the opening statement. "You have the option," Emory had explained rocking back in his office chair late one night. "You can give your opening statement to the jury immediately following the prosecution's opening, or you can reserve it until the prosecution has called all its witnesses and rested its case. There are advantages either way. By giving it early you're reminding the jury that, even as they hear the prosecution witnesses, there's another side to the story coming. You're planting the seed of that alternate story in their heads. On the other hand, the advantage of reserving your opening is that you can give it after you've heard the prosecution's case, and you can tailor the opening accordingly. It's a particularly helpful strategy if you don't know what the other side's got." Jason looked at the judge and said, "The defense will reserve, Your Honor."

"Very well. Now, it turns out the court has other business tomorrow. I apologize for the late notice. We'll get done what we can today, then reconvene on Wednesday morning." Judge Simmons put the paper back on his desk. He pulled a handkerchief from his pocket and began to use it to clean his silver wire-rim glasses. "What do you anticipate in terms of timing, Emory?"

"I would guess we'll rest sometime Wednesday morning," Emory replied. "Don't know how much Mr. McQuade has, but we should finish—what do you think, Jason?—Thursday? Wednesday afternoon?"

"I, uh . . . " He wasn't prepared for the question and didn't want to box himself in by answering it incorrectly. How am I supposed to know that? Jason wondered, his face reddening. I have no idea. It'll take as long as it takes.

The judge smiled thinly and picked up the piece of paper again. "We'll see how it goes. I'd like the jury to get the case Thursday morning, if possible."

That seemed possible to Jason, and he was relieved that that issue was out of the way. He looked up at an amateurish but brightly colored landscape painting that hung high on the wall behind Judge Simmons. They want to know how long the defense case will go. I don't even know what the defense case *is*!

He began to consider his case anew. I can't call Mei-Yin, even though that's what she wants more than anything. She's Chinese. They won't believe her. Even if they did, she'll be implicating herself in a murder. They'll scream for blood. Why hang one Chinese when you can hang two? At a minimum, she'd be charged as an accessory and imprisoned. No, I've got to keep her out of this. Emory hasn't discovered her. I don't think he has. I've got to keep her out of sight.

And saving Mei-Yin isn't the only reason I can't have her testify. If it came out that Roger Langston raped Mei-Yin, and was killed for that reason, it would destroy Esther—utterly. Her life here would never be the same. She's suffered so much already. I couldn't stand the thought of doing that to her.

I can't call Soo-Kwan or Dak-Wah either. They have turned and twisted themselves into knots trying to remember the false stories supplied by Hok-Ling and Mei-Yin, and what they actually know would fit in a matchbox. I could call them as character witnesses, but beyond that . . . two Chinese character witnesses for a Chinese defendant—ha! Now there's a strategy!

Judge Simmons mumbled something to himself as he crossed out something on his list and scribbled a note in the margin. Emory, in the meantime, signaled Tyler Forbes to come closer. He whispered something into his ear.

Jason bit his lip. I certainly can't call Hok-Ling. He's ready to admit to everything. He'd put the noose around his own neck if they'd let him. So what do I really have? I thought we had an alibi when Mei-Yin was Fan-Fei, or when I thought she was Fan-Fei. But that's long gone. Long, long gone.

Maybe I'm looking at this all wrong. My duty is to my client. I'm supposed represent him "zealously"—that's the way Emory always put it. So what if I wasn't in love with Mei-Yin? What if this was a different woman altogether? Would I let her testify— let her risk going to prison or even being executed herself in hopes that the jury would believe her and exonerate my client? Yes, of course I would! It's the truth, after all, that she speaks, and the truth could save him. I know it would hurt Esther, but . . .

What am I doing denying Hok-Ling this chance? Of course Mei-Yin has to testify. Jason felt a throbbing in the base of his neck. He pictured Mei-Yin dressed in Mrs. Stewart's nightgown gazing down at him from the bedroom window, and then that image faded and was replaced by the image of Mei-Yin in her rolled-up work clothes standing in the water at Hope, shielding her eyes. But I can't, he said to himself. I can't and won't! I won't risk the life of the woman I love to try to save him. This way, she's safe and Esther's safe. And it's the only way.

Jason looked down to find Judge Simmons staring at him over his glasses. A fatherly smile was spread over his face. "Are you all right, son?"

"Yes, of course. Thank you."

"Don't try too hard on this one, son. It might have been unfair of me to stick you in the lions' den so early in your legal career. This fellow *is* going to be convicted. There are no two ways about it." He looked at Emory. "I'm assuming you've had this discussion?"

"We have, Your Honor."

"All right," the judge continued, glancing quickly at Jason, "we'll just . . . uh . . . keep things in perspective here. Well, let's see. What else do we have?"

What do you mean he *is* going to be convicted? You mean it's *fait accompli*? What kind of rulings can I expect from a judge who's already decided the case? But of course Jason remembered the conversation he'd had with Emory, the one about inevitable "slippage" in the legal system. The people of this town want blood. They have a dead sheriff on their hands. The accused had a motive and opportunity, and he's Chinese. What else is there?

"Jason and I had a brief discussion about a possible plea bargain," Emory interjected calmly, "but I haven't heard back. This morning was the deadline."

But Jason's thoughts had circled back to the question of calling Mei-Yin as a witness, and his duty to zealously represent Hok-Ling. Does it matter to *me* if Hok-Ling's Chinese? he asked himself. That I can't talk to him? That we're from different races? What if my client were white and American? What if I were representing Bernie Page? I'd do everything in my power for Bernie. I'd spare no effort, and that's exactly my duty to Hok-Ling. Of course she has to testify! But a second later he pictured Mei-Yin walking up to the witness stand under the stares of the twelve jurors. No, never! I could never expose her to that. This back and forth, this distraction came at the cost of hearing what Emory had said. Once again, he found the judge's eyes leveled expectantly on him. "I'm sorry," Jason said, turning to Emory. "I was thinking of something. What'd you say?"

"I was just mentioning that we had discussed a possible plea bargain, but I hadn't heard back."

"Oh. Right." The plea bargain. The one way out of a sure death sentence for Hok-Ling, but so far he'd refused to even consider it. Jason replied, "I'd like you to keep that offer open, if you don't mind, until tomorrow."

"Is there some chance your client will accept it?" Emory asked.

"I don't know, to be honest. I want to talk to him again about it. Since we don't have court tomorrow, I can spend some time with him and go over some of the things we talked about."

The judge turned to Emory. "Is that acceptable to you, Counsel?"

Emory scratched the back of his neck with one finger. "Yes, that's all right."

"Okay. You guys can worry about that. I think that's it, then. Gentlemen, do you have anything else?"

"No" was the answer all round.

"Let's not leave them waiting any longer."

* * *

Of course Mei-Yin has to testify. That's his only chance. God, I should have told Esther last night. I *should* have. Jason looked over his shoulder into the crowd. He didn't see her. I can tell her tomorrow. Lord, this will ruin her though—if they believe Mei-Yin. What if they *don't?* What if they think I planted this story to save my client? Jason's blood began to tingle. Then Hok-Ling and Mei-Yin will both hang. He pulled on his lip. The sibilant edge of a laugh escaped through his nose. So Mei-Yin is dead along with Hok-Ling, Esther hates me, and my career comes to a glorious end after one case. That's hilarious! It's like Emory said.

Suddenly, the chair next to Jason slid back and he looked up, startled.

"Good morning." Lei Chi-Man sat down. He blinked with surprise. "You are not well?"

Jason coughed and chuckled simultaneously, in spite of himself. He put a hand over the interpreter's shoulder. "No, I'm fine. A little nervous is all. I'm glad you're here though."

The interpreter said, "You told me to come at nine thirty."

"I know, I know," Jason whispered, leaning over. "I guess I'm just feeling lonely all of a sudden. You know it's you and me against all these people, don't you, Charlie? Every one of them's against us."

Lei Chi-Man glanced back into the gallery then answered, "No. I just translate."

"Ha! You're right! Okay, but I still feel better. How is she this morning, Charlie?"

"She's fine. Said she managed to sleep a little."

"Did she get enough to eat?"

"Yes. And I rode in and got her some fruit juice from the hotel this morning." He leaned close. "Good for the baby."

"You should have taken milk."

Lei Chi-Man made a face. "Oh no, not for Chinese, Ja-sawn. Very few drink it in China."

"Really?" said Jason. "I had no idea."

"All rise!" The bailiff stood at attention, holding a gavel. The door to the judge's chamber swung open and Judge Simmons appeared. With a practiced air of dispassionate neutrality, he quickly mounted the platform and sat down at his desk. He glanced quickly up at the overflowing crowd and nodded, then returned to matters closer at hand. "Come to order!" the bailiff shouted. "This court is now in session, the Honorable Essex Simmons, presiding." He struck his gavel once. "Be seated."

The silence in the room was incomplete. Simmons took up his own gavel and lightly pounded the block of wood at the corner of his desk. "Quiet down, folks," he said amiably, taking only a few seconds to look up from the papers in front of him. "Thank you. Today, ladies and gentlemen, we have the matter of the People of the Territory of Idaho versus one Wong Hok-Ling, a Chinese national. Is the prosecution ready to proceed?"

Emory and Tyler Forbes were still on their feet. Emory was bent over the counsel table, sorting papers. He straightened. "Yes, we're ready, Your Honor."

The judge was sorting papers of his own. Then he picked them up as a bunch and tapped them on the desk to straighten them. He winked at Jason as he did this. "Is the defense ready?"

"Yes, Your Honor."

"Very well, then. Bring in the defendant, Mr. Lambert."

The deputy nodded and rose importantly from his chair beside the makeshift jury box. He stepped partway into a small anteroom beside the clerk's station and soon was backing out again, letting the door ride against his heels. Jason watched and was heartsick, re-experiencing the unfamiliar depths of his fear for Hok-Ling, and his anxiety over his role in what was about to happen. An aching began to tear away at his stomach.

There was a sharp clanking—the sound of chains. The courtroom began once again to buzz with anticipation. Suddenly, Hok-Ling appeared in the doorway, bound hand and foot. The clanking of his fetters competed with the gasps and murmured exclamations of the crowd and the pounding of the judge's gavel. He shuffled uncertainly over the floor, as though intoxicated. His eyes were drooped and stuporous.

"Oh my God!" whispered Jason, rising slowly to his feet. Lei Chi-Man rose as well. The prisoner was dressed in the tattered dungarees and oil-stained work shirt he had been wearing on the day of his arrest. They had not been cleaned. His matted hair was laden with filth, and one long lock hung rigidly over his left eye. His feet were bare and nearly black with dirt.

Lei Chi-Man stepped back to make room for the prisoner. Jason positioned a chair behind him. The deputy guided him down.

"You bloody bastard!" Jason seethed under his breath as he and the deputy were bending over the catatonic prisoner. "Where are the clothes I gave you? And why didn't you give him fresh water as I asked?"

"Godammit, Jason, I asked Simmons and he said 'No'— said to bring him as he is. I swear! I'd have done what you asked if it'd been up to me." He removed the handcuffs and the two men straightened. The deputy blushed deeply. "I swear that's the truth, McQuade."

"Are we ready, gentlemen?" Simmons inquired unctuously.

Jason could feel a fresh, barely controlled anger and disappointment mold itself into words. "The defense is *not* ready," he cried, stepping to the side of the counsel table. He felt a surge of emotion against his face as his voice took command of the room. So here we go, he thought. It begins. "My client stands innocent before this court until proven guilty, yet he has been brought in in chains, and unbathed. I myself bought him decent clothes to wear and asked that he be given fresh water. But Deputy Lambert here tells me that the court denied him these decencies, that you ordered him to stand trial in *this* condition. Why?"

A groundswell of sibilant utterances was beaten down, this time by the bailiff. "Order, please."

"Mr. McQuade," Simmons replied without hesitation, "this court is not interested in the *toilette* of murderers—or accused murderers. Also, it may interest you to know that the sheriff's office has been shorthanded of late. There is hardly time and manpower for attending to such matters as your client's wardrobe and personal comfort, and, indeed, I would have presumed, by the looks of things, that this man would be the last man on earth to be concerned with such—can I say trivial?—matters." No effort was made to quell the ripple of laughter and murmuring that sounded in support of the judge's explanation, although, at one point, the bailiff did pick up his gavel and could be seen turning it in his hands. This seemed to have some effect.

Jason countered in a booming voice. "Would it not be the concern of every man to stand before his accusers free of the deprecation of prison filth? Is a man's dignity really as *trivial* as you make it out?"

Simmons blushed. "This court is not a forum for a college debate, young man, nor is it a platform for rhetorical flourishes. We don't coddle prisoners here. You will remember that. Now, do you have a motion you wish to bring at this time?"

Jason glanced uneasily at Emory. The older attorney sat back in his chair, pulling at the hairs of his mustache. "I do, Your Honor. I move for a one-hour recess to allow my client an opportunity to bathe and properly dress for his trial. I think it is only f—"

"Do you wish to respond, Mr. Morse?" the judge interrupted.

Emory stood up slowly. "We have no objec—"

"Motion *denied*. Anything further, Mr. McQuade?"

Jason stepped toward the bench, completely at a nonplus. "I'm sorry, you said . . . ?"

"Motion denied. Is there anything *else* you wish to bring to the court's attention at this time?"

Their eyes locked for five seconds. "No, sir. Not at this time."

"Very well, then. Mr. Sours, call up twelve jurors and swear them for voir dire, will you? Mr. McQuade, you may sit down." The judge looked into the gallery. "Now, fellas, when your name is called for jury duty . . . "

Tyler Forbes delivered the prosecution's opening statement. There were no surprises in it. The people would prove that the defendant had a motive to kill the sheriff. That the defendant demonstrated disrespect, insolence, and malice toward the decedent on at least two occasions prior to his crime. Witnesses would be called who would place the defendant in town as well as on the Sand Creek Bridge on the night in question. And testimony concerning his flight following the murder would establish that he arrived back in Hope on the last possible boat, just before eleven o'clock, with no mail and with his clothing wet and rumpled.

This thorough foreshadowing of the people's case was met with whispered affirmations and a good deal of head shaking in the gallery. When it was quelled, Jason announced to the court that he would reserve his opening statement until the close of the prosecution's case.

"Very well," replied the judge. "Call your first witness, Mr. Morse."

Emory stood up. "The people call Mr. William Keating, Your Honor."

William Keating rose from his place on the aisle and moved with an ambassador's calm toward the gate. He was dressed impeccably in a blue-gray, three-piece suit and starched collar, and carried a silver-handled cane. His sunburned face bore an expression of smug imperturbability. He did not return the glances of either Emory or Jason as he passed the counsel tables, but instead pointed his cane carelessly in the direction of the bailiff and stepped quickly to meet him. He was sworn and waved to the stand. Before the first question was put to him, he found reason to simper red-faced toward the judge and jury, displaying what all took to be a kind of corporate homage to the territorial judicial system. He set his hat on the rail, then after quick reconsideration removed it to the floor between his legs.

Emory had followed him to the witness stand. If the rise of color in Keating's face was any indication, the attorney was standing rather closer than the witness had anticipated. "Give us your name, if you would, and spell your last name for the reporter."

Keating cleared his throat. "William Keating. K-e-a-t-i-n-g."

"Where do you work, Mr. Keating?"

"I'm the head of operations, Lake Pend d'Oreille Division, Northern Pacific Railroad."

"I see. And you're the fella in charge out there at Hope, isn't that right?"

"That's right."

"Do you know the defendant, Mr. Keating?" Emory pointed toward Hok-Ling.

"I know two of the three men seated there. Mr. McQuade, I have met once, and I recognize the defendant, yes. The other—the Chinese there in the suit—I don't know."

"When did you first meet the defendant?"

"Well, it would have been in July. I asked one of our crew bosses to select a man to go into town to get the mail. This was the man he selected."

"And was the defendant, in fact, sent to Sandpoint for that purpose?"

"Yes."

"What day was that, Mr. Keating?

"I . . . I'm not sure of the date exactly."

"It was the day of the murder, was it not? The 16th of July?"

Jason looked up from his note taking. "Objection, Your Honor. Counsel is leading the witness."

Emory turned as if to look at Jason, but stopped partway. He turned back and fixed his eyes on the witness. "By way of background, Judge."

Judge Simmons, who was also writing, did not look up. "Objection overruled. You may answer, Mr. Keating."

"Yes, that sounds right. July 16."

"What time of day would he have gone to Sandpoint?"

"Oh, I don't know. The nine o'clock boat, I imagine."

"And would that have been the *Henry Villard* or the *Mary Moody?*"

"The *Villard*. I believe the *Mary Moody* was engaged with the bridge builders on the Clark's Fork around that time."

"I see. And when did you next see the defendant?" Emory turned his back to the witness and began to walk slowly away from him.

"I . . . I'm not sure. It may be today."

"You didn't see him when he returned to Hope that afternoon or that night?"

Jason rose to his feet. "Objection. Your Honor, Mr. Morse's question assumes facts not in evidence."

"Over—"

"I'll rephrase the question, Your Honor," said Emory, with his hand in the air. "Mr. Keating, let me ask you this way. Did the defendant return to Hope on the afternoon or evening of the 16th?"

"Uh. Well, yes. Yes he did."

"And how do you know that?"

"His crew boss, Ying-Chiao—he's one of our English-speaking Chinese out there—he brought me the mail satchel and the defendant's pigtail. It was after eleven, I think."

Emory spun around. "His pigtail, did you say?"

"Yes, that's right . . . or queue, whatever you want to call it."

"Did the defendant have a queue when he went into town on the morning of July 16th?"

"Oh yes—most of them out there have queues."

"And how is it, sir, that you ended up holding this man's queue sometime after eleven o'clock that night?"

Jason stood up. "Objection, Your Honor. There's been no foundation—"

"Actually," Keating chimed in, "I *didn't* hold it. I wouldn't touch the damn thing. I told the crew boss to put it in the fire." Laughter broke out in the gallery. Jason sat down.

"And did he do so?"

"Yes, that's right."

"Why was this thing brought to you then? Do you know?"

Keating breathed deeply and crossed his arms over his chest. "Apparently, it's some kind of a sign of dishonor with the Chinese."

"Objection!" cried Jason.

"Sustained," said the judge. He turned toward the witness. "Just tell us what you know of your own personal knowledge, Mr. Keating."

"Yes, of course. I . . . uh, the crew boss brought me the pigtail and apologized for the failure of this man. That's all I know."

"By failure, do you mean his failure to get the railroad's mail?"

"Yes. I'm sorry. I thought I said that. The mail satchel was returned empty."

"And did the crew boss offer any explanation as to why the defendant didn't bring back any mail?"

"No, he didn't."

"Did you ask him for an explanation?"

The witness stopped to think. He shifted in his chair. "You know, I don't think I did. These Chinamen foul up all the time, you have to understand. I probably figured, what the hell, at least I got the satchel back, so I'm ahead of the game, right? So much for that experiment." He chuckled lamely, drawing sporadic laughter from the crowd.

Emory walked stiffly over to the counsel table and stared down at his papers. "Did you send somebody else to town the next day?"

"Yes, although I think it was a couple days later. I sent my assistant—Johnson's his name. Turns out the Overland had broken down outside of Priest River anyway. There was no mail that week."

Emory straightened and turned, and by his expression he showed that he regretted having asked the question. He thought for a moment. "It was the 16th that you sent this man in, though, the first time? The defendant, I mean."

"Yes. Right. The 16th."

"Fine. That's all I have, Mr. Keating."

Judge Simmons nodded at Jason. "Mr. McQuade?"

Jason stood up. "Thank you, Your Honor. Now Mr. Keating, you testified that this fellow Ying-Chiao—the crew boss, as you call him—brought you my client's pigtail after eleven o'clock on the night of the 16th, is that right?"

"Yes, uh-huh."

"Tell the jury, if you would, how you were able to determine that the pigtail that was presented to you was, in fact, *my client*'s pigtail?"

Keating blushed to the roots of his reddish-blond hair. "Well, I , uh . . . this is what I was told."

"That's what you were told. But you don't know of your own knowledge whose pigtail it was, do you?"

"No."

"The truth is it could have been from any one of a hundred other men, or more, couldn't it?"

"Yes, I suppose so. Although, like I say, most of them—"

"Exactly how many of your coolies out there wear pigtails, Mr. Keating?"

"Oh, I couldn't tell you that."

"More than half of them?"

"Oh, yes, I would say so. Most of them do."

Jason walked slowly toward the jury. "I see. Now you said that Hok-Ling was sent into town that morning to fetch the mail."

"Yes."

"Did he go?"

"What do you mean?"

"Did my client actually go to Sandpoint that day to get the mail?"

The witness glanced up at the judge for help. "Yes, I thought that's what I said. I'm not sure what you're driving at, McQuade."

"Did you see him get on the boat, Mr. Keating?"

"Well, no."

"Did you see him get off the boat at Sandpoint?"

"No."

"Were you in Sandpoint yourself that day?"

"No. If I—"

"Then how do you know this man—Hok-Ling—went to Sandpoint?" Jason saw that the witness had no answer. "The point is, you *don't* know, do you? *That's* what I'm driving at, Mr. Keating. You simply don't know."

Keating shielded himself with a wry grin. The gold around his teeth sparkled. "All right, Mr. McQuade. I don't know. Is that what you want?"

"Yes, exactly. That's exactly what I want. Now maybe we can get at what you do know, Mr. Keating. Shall we try to do that?"

Emory's eyes shot up to the bench. "Objection. Argumentative."

The judge said, "Sustained. Kindly keep your editorial comments to yourself, young man."

"Yes, Your Honor. My apologies." Jason turned his back on the judge and the witness stand both. He gazed out over the heads of the people who packed the gallery. "Mr. Keating, tell me something: Do you recognize any of these people out here?"

"How's that?"

He glanced back at the witness, but pointed into the gallery. "Do you recognize anybody out there? Or how about our jury members over here? Do you recognize any of these men?"

Keating hesitated. He shifted in his seat again. "Well, no, I can't say as I do."

"You don't?" Jason straightened as though shocked by the answer. "I'm surprised. Need I remind you that you met with many of these people about a month before you brought the Chinese crews up here? I believe it was on the afternoon of April 4th."

"Oh, yes! Of course. I'd forgotten about that. I'm sorry. I didn't get a chance to get to . . . well, really get to know these people that day."

"No, but you did come up here from Spokane Falls to discuss the building of the railroad, didn't you? And to discuss these people's concerns about the Chinese work crews in particular. Isn't that right?"

"Yes. That's right."

"And do you recall that you spoke to the people of this town that day for about an hour, hour and a half?"

"Yes."

"As an official representative of the railroad?"

"Yes. Uh-huh."

Jason had made his way back to his place at the counsel table. He stood in front of his chair. "Fine. Now just one more thing, Mr. Keating. Did you or did you not give your solemn promise to the people of this town that no Chinese would be allowed to enter this town unsupervised?"

Emory jumped to his feet. "Objection! What's the relevance of this?

Jason fixed the witness with his stare. "Answer the question, Mr. Keating!"

"Objection sustained. Mr. McQuade, you will wait until I rule on objections."

With the gallery abuzz behind him, Jason glanced over at Emory and bobbed his eyebrows. *What was it you taught me, Emory? You can't unring a bell.* The old attorney made a face which as much as said, "All right. I'll give you that one." Jason squeezed back a self-satisfied smile and addressed the court. "Of course, Your Honor. Allow me to withdraw the question."

27

From the outset, Hok-Ling refused to listen to Lei Chi-Man's translations. He looked down at his hands. I am here, inside myself, but there is nothing else. No one else. I feel every cell of my body—and nothing beyond it.

Beyond the cocoon of Lei Chi-Man's whispering was the rise and fall of voices. It was late afternoon. Long shafts of sunlight reached in over the heads of the jurors, illuminating the varnished wood at the base of the judge's desk. The air circulating through the open windows was filled with dust from the wagons and horses in the street. Hok-Ling raised his head now and then to look around, but it was not to see his surroundings. Rather, it was as a bear might awaken accidentally from his hibernation, to see that he is out of time, blink once, and sleep again.

Perhaps it was to see that this was real. That there was no avenue of escape. It didn't concern him that his lawyer—his *leuht si*—was standing in the open space between the counsel tables, or by the witness stand, extending his arms, his body bouncing gently with speaking. And it was of no moment to him that the witnesses seated next to the judge, and the men in the jury near the witness stand, were listening intently, with eyes fixed on the attorney. These were as objects to him.

He turned once to his left to observe the rest of the room. His narrow, dark eyes stopped momentarily on Emory Morse, the old lawyer seated at the counsel table opposite him. Emory must have seen him from the corner of his eye, as he looked up from his writing. For a short time, the two men faced one another, but Hok-Ling did not regard Emory as a man, and therefore he turned away unmoved by his decency, his humility, or his compassion.

Most of the people behind the makeshift balustrade sat in rapt attention. Their blank faces were pointed up toward the questioning attorney and answering witness, as though they were stage actors. A few women in high-collar dresses fanned themselves, but there was little movement besides. A white curtain billowed gently in front of a window at the back of the courtroom, but it fell back again and was still. Three people in the front row, two women and a man, noticed Hok-Ling staring over his shoulder and so turned to look at him, to meet his gaze as Emory had done. Although their movements attracted Hok-Ling subconsciously, his dull gaze brushed past each set of eyes unseeing. He turned back slowly and leaned back in his chair. Whatever his reason for looking, he was done.

* * *

The second witness for the prosecution was Andrew Epps, proprietor of the paint store. He recalled with nervous excitement the first confrontation between the defendant and Sheriff Langston.

Emory put his foot up and leaned over the rail of the jury box. He was the picture of tranquility, the opposite of Epps. "Why do you suppose Sheriff Langston took a whip to this other fella, Andy?"

"Oh, I know the answer to that, Emory. This heathen—not this one here," Epps sputtered, pointing at Hok-Ling, "but the other one. A taller fella. He spat at one of the ladies in the street. Mrs. Crowder, I think it was—up from Bayview to visit her sister. I saw him do it."

"Actually spit?"

"Yes, sir. And Roger . . . Sheriff Langston, he saw it too, and took out after him."

"But that wasn't this fella?" asked Emory, nodding toward the defense table.

"No, sure wasn't."

"Okay. What, if anything, did you see this fella do that day, Andy?"

"Well, course most of you's saw it for yourselves," the witness rejoiced, flushing. "This here Chinaman," he nodded at Hok-Ling, "snuck up in the crowd and tore the whip right out of the sheriff's hand, just as he was trying to steady his horse and bring things to order. Came up and just tore it away, like that! Then he threw the damn thing up on the roof of the hotel." Epps put a challenge to the jury. "You all remember that, don't you?"

"Just answer my questions, Andy. Don't you be asking questions. What'd the sheriff do next?"

The witness's spirit was wounded by Emory's rebuff. He covered half his mouth with a soiled hand and stared off like an old soldier recalling defeat. It was half a minute before he looked back and said softly, "You know, I don't know that I know for sure, Emory. I know he didn't arrest the fella. I guess maybe this one just took off an' ran into the crowd an' got away. There was a whole shit-load of Chinamen around here that day."

The gallery erupted with a chorus of laughter. The witness looked around, confused. The judge's gavel was thunderous.

"Quiet in the court!" he shouted. Andrew Epps looked up at the judge like a dog vaguely aware of some wrongdoing. His lips were blue. "Don't use that kind of talk in here, Mr. Epps."

"Well, I . . . "

"Now, you could have said, 'there were lots of Chinamen' or 'plenty of Chinamen,' see? You didn't need to say it that way."

The witness hung his head stupidly. "Sorry, Judge Simmons."

Emory smiled up at the judge. "That's all I have, Your Honor."

"Any cross-examination, Mr. McQuade?"

Jason hesitated. "No. Not at this time, Your Honor."

"Very well, then." The judge fumbled beneath his robe and pulled out a gold pocket watch. "I see it's almost four o'clock. I think we'll adjourn for the day. This court will be in recess until nine o'clock Wednesday morning."

The clerk banged his gavel and stood up. "All rise!"

Hok-Ling was startled out of his dreaming by Lei Chi-Man, who grasped his arm and lifted him to his feet. The prisoner eyed the interpreter suspiciously. "You must rise when the others rise," Lei Chi-Man whispered. "It is a sign of respect."

Hok-Ling jerked his arm free. "And do you think that I respect them, Lei Chi-Man?"

"It would behoove you to pretend as much. But I do not blame you in any case."

The judge disappeared into his chambers, shutting the door behind him. Deputy Lambert advanced toward the defense table, working a tangle out of his handcuffs, while Jason, who had taken his seat again, was bent over the table, writing furiously. Hok-Ling looked down over Jason's head. "Tell me, friend," he said to Lei Chi-Man haltingly, "does this man believe that I should live?"

Lei Chi-Man did not answer for a time. "He believes in finding the truth," he said at last. Hok-Ling placed his hands behind his back automatically when the deputy stepped around him. "Whether that means you should live? I don't know. That is a different question."

The prisoner's gaze grew intense and the start of a smile played at the corners of his lips. He looked up at the interpreter. "There's one place where the ocean may be crossed with a single step—"

"And its name is the same on either shore," Lei Chi-Man interrupted, retrieving the verse from a childhood memory. They finished the verse in unison. "It is known here and there as Truth." Lei Chi-Man's brow arched appreciatively. "Hmmm," he smiled. "I'd almost forgotten it."

Hok-Ling nodded weakly at the interpreter, then turned of his own accord and was led away.

* * *

"He said he likes tea but prefers coffee."

Mei-Yin smiled as she brought the refilled kettle back to the fire and balanced it on three well-placed stones. She knelt and sat back on her heels. The light of the fire began to glint in the eyes of the interpreter and the attorney. She looked up to see the first star shining through the veil of night. When she reached for her tea, Jason and Lei Chi-Man reached for theirs, as well—a pattern all three had grown used to. "Please tell him that I am a poor hostess. I have only tea at the moment."

The translation was made but there was no response. Mei-Yin glanced at the attorney as he set his teacup back on the ground. He seems preoccupied. I wonder what's going through his mind. She looked at the interpreter, who also seemed lost in the flames. According to Lei Chi-Man, the trial did not go badly today, she thought. In fact, the attorney was impressive, he said. So why are they distracted? She did not have long to wait for the answer.

"Tell her, Charlie, that I am very sorry for touching her yesterday and for scaring her." Lei Chi-Man looked up at Jason as if he were a quarter mile away. "Do it," Jason insisted.

Lei Chi-Man began to speak in a soft, reticent tone. Mei-Yin was shocked that this subject would be raised. She stared at the ground and nodded. Her heart began to accelerate in anticipation of what was to come.

"Tell her it is very, very difficult for me not to be able to talk to her directly."

Lei Chi-Man shook his head as if to warn Jason, but the attorney would not be deterred. "He says he wishes he could speak to you directly."

Jason went on. "But because I can't, I need to tell her things through you. I am from Boston. Do you know where that is?"

Mei-Yin shook her head. Jason took a stick from the fire and drew the shape of North America in the dirt. "We are here, now," he said, jabbing the stick in the earth, "and Boston is here. Oh, and China is way over here." Lei Chi-Man translated for Mei-Yin, pointing to the drawing. "I have one brother, Andrew. He's older than me. Do you have any brothers or sisters?"

Mei-Yin whispered to Lei Chi-Man. "I have two older sisters. Lei Chi-Man, why is he doing this?"

"Because he has affection for you and is haunted by it. I know it is wrong, but I am paid to translate. What are your sisters' names please?" A moment later, Lei Chi-Man turned to Jason. "Two older sisters, Lei-Jong and Shi-Jiao."

"My father owns a large textile company called McQuade Textiles. His company has many offices on the East Coast. Here, here, here, and here. My mother keeps a peaceful home and is kind to the help. Her name is Margaret. My father's name is Robert McQuade. Tell me about your parents." And so it went for the better part of twenty minutes. However, Mei-Yin answered each question as though it were being asked by the interpreter. That is, she did not acknowledge Jason as the source of the questions, or face him in answering. She smiled now and then, with her eyes mainly—and very quickly and subtly—for she could tell that Lei Chi-Man was relaying her answers in an unfamiliar monotone, trying to discourage the attorney.

I don't want to hurt the *leuht si*, she thought. He is confused. He doesn't know me, but now he's trying to make up for that. I must try to put an end to this. "Lei Chi-Man, please tell the attorney that, while I am happy to learn these things about his family, we are simply different. Our differences are too great. Tell him, please, what my grandfather once told me:

It is our differences that define us—that make us who we are." In the intervals provided by Mei-Yin over the next few minutes, Lei Chi-Man translated. However, he evidently found it more and more difficult to look at Jason as he translated and began to escape into the glowing embers of the fire.

Mei-Yin explained. "I am a son of Han. If all people were sons of Han, we would not have this phrase 'son of Han.' These were my grandfather's words. He said: 'It is only possible to know what a son of Han is because some people are not sons of Han.' Do you see?"

Jason nodded vaguely.

"We know what it means to be tall or short because people are of different heights. If all people were the same height, would we say of any man, 'Look. He is tall?'" Mei-Yin faced Lei Chi-Man, but she turned her head to follow this question as it was given to the attorney. When the attorney said nothing, she looked down. I am talking too much—like my grandfather did! It feels awkward, and the *leuht si* is beside himself. But I must help him understand. He must forget about me and concentrate on Hok-Ling's case. If I don't say this, he will continue to pursue me. "I am from a land far away," she said tentatively, staring at the edge of the fire. "A very ancient land. We do not share your language or beliefs. Our people do not share your customs. Many of the things that people do here are strictly forbidden in the Middle Kingdom. We even look different. Except what you have told me this evening, I know so little about you. You know little about me—almost nothing—for who can claim to understand these tidbits by themselves. We are different. And it is through our differences that we know ourselves."

"But I want to know more," Jason said. "You're right, of course, about our differences. There are many, but surely they are not too great. You are a woman and I am a man. I want to get to know you. I will learn about your customs—even your language, if I can." He looked up to find Lei Chi-Man staring coldly at him over the fire. "Tell her this!" he demanded.

Lei Chi-Man swallowed. "I will tell her. But you are making a mistake."

"Why? I don't think it's a mistake at all. It's the one chance I have to tell her how I feel."

"She knows how you feel. You've made that clear, Ja-sawn. She is trying to explain to you why she cannot return these feelings. It is not right for a white man to speak this way to a Chinese woman. And there is the matter of Hok-Ling."

"What?"

Mei-Yin saw that the two were at the point of arguing and said preemptively, "I must say more, Lei Chi-Man." Both men stopped. She stared at the barn, embarrassed, thinking, Mei-Yin, you have never spoken so boldly! In a softer tone, she said, "I have never forgotten my grandfather's words. You see, he was trying to console me. I was eleven, and a friend—a girl I thought was a friend—had spoken ill of me behind my back. She told others that I looked like a boy. After my tears dried, my grandfather said: 'It is not just that we are different—or that our minds can perceive human differences only through awareness of defining oppositions. There is a third piece. We are prone— all of us—to deep emotional responses in the face of some of these oppositions. Sometimes we are attracted by oppositions— such as beauty. Sometimes we are neutral to them. But a good deal of the time we are wounded, repulsed, or left afraid.'" Mei-Yin hesitated. "People who do not share the same race, who do not share the same religion, history, and culture, who do not speak the same language, are strangers to each other. They are buffeted with negative feelings from these oppositions which they cannot help. Such people are not meant to be together. *We* are not meant to be together."

Mei-Yin looked expectantly at Jason as the last of her grand-father's wisdom was being translated. The fire was now bright against his face. The night had crept close. Does he understand? she wondered. I think he does. His face is drawn. At least he is thinking about what I have said. It pains me to hurt him. I'm sure he is a good man—not like the green coat. But I do not feel as he does. For me, our differences are too great. Even if I were not promised to Hok-Ling, I would never consider marrying a white devil.

For several minutes, the only sound was the snapping of the fire and the chirring of crickets in the field below.

* * *

Jason tossed the stick back to let it burn. *If only we had more time and I could speak to her alone,* he thought. *I know she would feel differently.* He thought of Josephine and Esther, of other women he had known in Boston. *I'm not unappealing to women—even beautiful, intelligent women. I'm responsible to a fault, educated, articulate. I'm a gentleman. Why doesn't* she *see this?* He looked at Mei-Yin and allowed himself to imagine her lying naked next to him, sleeping. A shudder ran the length of his body. *Nothing would be more perfect,* he thought. *Oh, if only we had more time! If only I could speak to her directly!*

Lei Chi-Man and Mei-Yin exchanged a few whispered words, then Mei-Yin got up, bowed to Jason, and disappeared into the barn. Jason turned to Lei Chi-Man. "Is she going to bed?"

"Yes. She said she would leave us alone now, and to thank you for all you're doing for Hok-Ling."

It felt like a punch to the stomach. Jason drew his next three breaths through his mouth. He picked up his tea and drank deeply from the cup to hide his disappointment. When he'd recovered sufficiently, he said to Lei Chi-Man, barely suppressing anger, "Charlie, I'm going to plead Hok-Ling. Second-degree murder. Life in prison." He drained the rest of his lukewarm tea.

"*What?*"

"It's his best chance. He's going to hang otherwise."

"How do you know?"

A shudder brought goose bumps to Jason's arms. He rubbed them out. What am I doing? he asked himself. Doing my duty to Hok-Ling or simply trying to arrange it so that I will have time with Mei-Yin? He looked up. "What did you say?"

"I said, how do you know?"

"I just do." With enough time, he knew he could convince her—show her who he really was, wear her down with kindness, if nothing else. He avoided Lei Chi-Man's eyes. Against the threat of a rising tide of guilt, he heard Emory's voice within, "You're right. You can't win this case—and Hok-Ling *is* going to hang. The judge has convicted him already, and if *he* has, the jury most certainly will. *Slippage*—remember? There's nothing anyone can do." Jason leaned over his knees and locked his fingers together. Working his lips and looking up at last, he met Lei Chi-Man's skeptical gaze. The interpreter's face was orange and scarlet in the firelight. "There's only one way to save this man's life, Charlie, and that's to plead him. I've asked Emory to keep the offer open until tomorrow."

"But Mei-Yin hasn't testified. The truth hasn't come out."

"She doesn't need to testify. The offer's there. All we have to do is take it."

"What about Hok-Ling? He's already rejected the offer."

Jason picked up a small pebble and tossed it into the fire. "We're going to talk him into it. You and I—tomorrow morning. We're going to sit on him until he says yes."

Lei Chi-Man sat very still. Only his eyes were active. "Think carefully, Ja-sawn. Do you really think this will save him?"

"It's for his own good," Jason added with emphasis, not having heard Lei Chi-Man. How could anyone with knowledge of the facts argue otherwise? he asked himself. But he had an ulterior motive, and he knew it. There came to him an image of Mei-Yin sitting beside him again on Mrs. Stewart's steps. This time it was midday and Mrs. Stewart wasn't there. He was reading *Blackstone's Commentaries*, and she—with a relaxed expression—was replacing a button on one of his shirts.

"What about the truth?" Lei Chi-Man protested. "Mei-Yin was raped. He was about to rape her again. This was not murder."

"You and I know that, but the jury won't believe it. It's her word against . . . well, their thirst for retribution. And she's . . . " He checked himself.

"She's Chinese," said Lei Chi-Man.

"Yes. It would only endanger her to put her on the stand. Oh, I know she wants to testify. But the minute she acknowledges that she was there, they're just as apt to demand her head, as well. I won't take that chance."

A noise from inside the barn drew their attention. Mei-Yin emerged from the shadows carrying a glass toward the water jug. Lei Chi-Man called to her. She stood in the doorway. "Yes, Lei Chi-Man."

The interpreter turned to Jason. "I must tell her of your decision. She expects to testify on Hok-Ling's behalf, and deserves to know what you've told me." Jason watched as the information was conveyed. Mei-Yin placed a hand on her stomach, and leaned back, nearly falling over. Once she had steadied herself, she stepped forward into the firelight. The pained expression on her face made her look like a different person. She and Lei Chi-Man exchanged rapid-fire sentences. Mei-Yin's words were spoken in ever higher pitches, and her free hand gesticulated wildly.

The interpreter turned to Jason. Mei-Yin approached and squatted over the ground where she had rested and taken tea before. She leaned toward Lei Chi-Man and demanded something, the meaning of which Jason guessed: "Tell him!"

"She insists that she be allowed to testify. She will not take no for an answer."

Jason saw the woman stare at him now in a way she had never looked at him before. The muscles of her jaw pulsed as she blinked back tears. He could not hold her gaze and averted his eyes. "Tell her . . . " he began, but his words were drowned out by another rapid-fire appeal from Mei-Yin.

"She insists. The truth must be told. She must be allowed to explain what happened." Mei-Yin continued to talk, her voice rising until it seemed it could go no higher. "She says this is the only way to save Hok-Ling. Only the truth can save his life. She begs you a thousand times—a thousand times a thousand. Do not let Hok-Ling die. Do not send him to prison, for he will be killed in the white man's prison." The tears in her eyes flashed as she turned to watch Jason jump to his feet and walk away from the fire. He stood with his back to them, one hand at the back of his neck.

Mei-Yin sprang to her feet, as well, but did not move. "Please!" she said in her native Cantonese. She turned to Lei Chi-Man. "Please! Tell him I'll do anything—*anything!* I must be allowed to testify! They must know what happened!"

Lei Chi-Man was unable to prevent a scowl from forming. He drew a weary breath. "She says if you care about her, you will let the truth be told. You will not accept this so-called bargain."

Jason threw his hands up and spun around. "She said that?"

"Yes."

Jason took a step toward Mei-Yin. "Do you understand what this means?" He remembered himself. "Charlie, tell her that, if she testifies, there's a good chance the jury won't believe her. The Chinese are hated here. They will think she helped Hok-Ling murder the sheriff. How else could such a small man kill such a large one, and an armed one at that? Then she will be charged and convicted of the murder herself, and both of them will hang."

After the translation, Mei-Yin said through the interpreter, "Then I shall die. My duty is to Hok-Ling, and to the truth."

Jason's heart stopped. He stood with his hands at his sides, staring at Mei-Yin, unable to speak. He saw stark determination etched in her face.

Lei Chi-Man rose to his feet and moved in the opposite direction around the fire. When he stopped, he looked momentarily at Mei-Yin, then turned and gazed out over the invisible landscape of tangled blackberry mounds and neglected hay fields, all encased in darkness. "What about this man Eddie?" he asked. "Can you have him testify that Mei-Yin arrived in town that night? That he and his friend brought her in their wagon?"

Jason moved closer to Lei Chi-Man. Now the three of them formed a triangle. "Yes. But what does that prove?"

"It would corroborate Mei-Yin's testimony, would it not?"

"It would place her in town on the night the sheriff was killed, yes."

"And Dr. Randle . . . couldn't he confirm Mei-Yin's pregnancy and the date of conception? Doesn't that fit with her testimony that she was raped?"

"It fits, but it doesn't prove that the sheriff fathered the child. It could have been anybody. She might have gotten pregnant—" Jason hesitated, "another way." He looked at Mei-Yin and was glad this part of the conversation was not being translated. "Look, Charlie," he continued. "We know the sheriff was killed with Mei-Yin's knife. Do you think that wouldn't come out in cross-examination? How does that look? It's her knife—she killed the sheriff. Mei-Yin hangs. Pretty straightforward." Lei Chi-Man started to speak in Cantonese, but Jason interrupted him. "It's all very plausible. The rule in town is 'no Chinese without a white chaperone,' right? Here comes this Chinese woman walking into town at night, alone. She's looking for the boat to Hope when the sheriff sees her. He catches up to her on the Sand Creek Bridge. It's pitch-black out. When he tries to arrest her, she surprises him with a knife and kills him. He's standing next to the railing and falls over it, into the grass below. There. We have a sheriff just trying to do his job, and a Chinese woman who kills him on the spot."

Lei Chi-Man spoke at length to Mei-Yin. She shook her head and her reply came at once. "She says that is nonsense. But it doesn't matter to her. All that matters is that the truth be told before Hok-Ling is judged."

"Look!" Jason shouted. "This is my case, and I must handle it as best I know how."

Mei-Yin had no trouble seeing through him. "She says it will be wrong if you hide the truth. She tells me, if you care about her, you must allow her to testify, period. I believe she means it."

"Aaaaaargh!" Jason shouted. He put both hands on top of his head, turned around, and stared forlornly up at the canopy of stars overhead. I can't do it! I've got to listen to Emory. There's slippage everywhere, especially where the Chinese are concerned. They will hang Mei-Yin or at least imprison her for life. I'm sure of it. Mei-Yin and Hok-Ling are both dead within a week. And Esther's happiness is shattered. There's *got* to be another way. Jason leaned back and closed his eyes. There's *got* to be another way! He began to move his hands back and forth across his scalp. Think! A few seconds later, he was pacing, the tips of his fingers arched inches from his lips. Suddenly he stopped. "Wait a minute." He turned toward Lei Chi-Man. "Wait a minute." His eyes widened to take in some new, unexpressed possibility. "Charlie!" he cried, running toward the interpreter. "Didn't you say they were concerned about a labor strike because of the way Hok-Ling had been treated?"

"Yes, that's what the crew boss, Ho Ying-Chiao, told me."

"And he said his job was at stake, right? He was worried that he'd lose his job if the crews went out on strike."

"Yes, that's right."

Jason's eyes darted left and right, only settling on Lei Chi-Man's face when he said, "Wouldn't he have sent somebody else in?"

"What?"

"Ho Ying-Chiao. Wouldn't he have sent another coolie into town to look for Hok-Ling?"

"How do you know that—?"

"That's it! He had to send another man in. There were two coolies in town when the sheriff was killed!" Jason grabbed Lei Chi-Man's shoulders and smiled excitedly. "I'll bet you anything, Charlie!"

"So you mean . . ?"

"Listen! Hok-Ling takes an early morning boat to Sandpoint. He's due back by noon—maybe earlier. He doesn't show up. Ho Ying-Chiao remembers the trouble Hok-Ling had with the sheriff when the crews marched through town. He starts to think, 'What if something's happened to Hok-Ling? The crews will blame the railroad and go out on strike. I'll lose my job.' What does he do? He sends somebody into town to look for him, that's what!"

"So you think there were two coolies in town when the sheriff was killed?"

"Exactly. I'll bet if we go out there tomorrow and talk to Ho Ying-Chiao, we'll find out that's exactly what happened. Two coolies and one body makes for a reasonable doubt, Charlie. All the coolies out there had a motive to kill the sheriff after what he did to Soo-Kwan."

Mei-Yin stepped toward them. "What is it, Lei Chi-Man? What's he saying?"

"He thinks Ho Ying-Chiao may have sent a second man into town on the day of the murder, someone to look for Hok-Ling. If there was a second man, a reasonable doubt arises as to which coolie may have killed the sheriff."

"But there was a second man," Mei-Yin exclaimed.

"*What?*"

"Yes. I saw him. I was below the bridge. I had just arrived. A boat whistle sounded, and a few minutes later I saw a coolie running across the bridge in the direction of the boat. I saw him clearly."

Lei Chi-Man turned to Jason. A rare smile crossed his lips. "Well, Ja-sawn. I have some good news."

28

J ason lay awake in his dark room, staring up at the ceiling. He'd thought of getting up and making coffee, but it was too early to make noise. Roosters were beginning to crow at a half-dozen different points on the compass, including Mrs. Stewart's own Mr. Lucky, a Rhode Island Red, of whom she'd once warned "when he gets his steam up you can hear him all the way to Laclede." The chill morning air was tinged with the sweet smell of fresh-cut alfalfa. Mrs. Stewart would be up soon, and the knocking of the stove top would be his signal to rise.

In the meantime, there was Mei-Yin to think of, and the trial, and the second man. Who would it be? What additional information would he learn today that might solidify or call into question his defense? No, it would not call it into question. He was there. Mei-Yin saw him—and this was minutes before she was raped. It's just a matter of confirming who he was and which boat the man took back to Hope.

Suddenly, Jason pictured the second man—gave him a face. He was struck at once with a terrible thought. This man's innocent! I'm going to implicate him in a murder he didn't commit to try to save the man *who I know did kill the sheriff!* He lifted himself up on his elbows and stared into the gloom. Oh my God! Why didn't I think of this before? Can I do this? Is it ethical? I'm supposed to represent Hok-Ling zealously. Pointing out that a second coolie was in town at the time of the killing can't be a bad thing—can it? But this other man's innocent, and I'm exposing him to a possible murder charge! This man could be executed for something he didn't do. Jason fell back against his pillow. Dash! Why didn't I think of this before? He closed his eyes. Think! What would Emory say? God, I wish I could talk to him about this. He'd know the answer.

I'm not accusing the second man. I'm just saying he was there, right? He *was* in town. I'm creating a reasonable doubt. It's the old dilemma, the one Emory described last year. Three men walk into a hotel room, two walk out, the one inside is dead. Neither man talks. Who's the murderer?

Jason was up on his elbows again. But what about the fact that these are Chinese, and the sheriff was white? What about *slippage?*

* * *

Jason and Lei Chi-Man's last interview with Ho Ying-Chiao took place in a morning thunderstorm and downpour. The cacophonous racket caused each of the three men, more than once, to stop and look out past the open door of the wall tent. Visible beyond the dripping canvas doorway were dozens of coolies in conical hats and rain-soaked blue coats and trousers digging with pickaxes and shovels, or pushing wheelbarrows piled high with dirt and stones. No sooner had the interview ended than Ho Ying-Chiao put on his own hat and ducked out into the rain. Within seconds he was barking orders and tromping through the mud like an army field commander. When one of his crew slipped, upsetting his wheelbarrow, he stopped to help the man up. The sibilant rain and an irregular clanking was all that could be heard inside the tent as Jason and Lei Chi-Man watched Ho Ying-Chiao and the man replace the stones in the barrow, one by one.

Jason buttoned his coat and looked over at two drenched horses tied to the trunk of a fir tree fifty yards away. It was an hour-and-a-half-ride to Hope. "Are you ready, Charlie?" he asked.

"Ready."

Jason winked and smiled at the interpreter, and the two dashed out of the tent together.

They were almost dry by the time the *Henry Villard* was off Bottle Bay with the mist-shrouded Sandpoint dock and the *Mary Moody* in sight. Jason and Lei Chi-Man sat alone in the passenger cabin on opposite sides of a small potbellied stove. Lei Chi-Man was lost in a paperback that he'd produced from an inside pocket of his frock coat fifteen minutes earlier in response to Jason's protracted silence. The latter held a handful of papers and a pencil. The top page was covered with scribbled details and still bore the imprint of his carefully written note to Emory that morning thanking him for—but rejecting once and for all—the proffered plea bargain. Jason stared off through the silvery, rain-spotted window. He'd let the rumble of the engine, the pelting of the rain on the roof, and the flat, gray water passing by lull him into a reverie.

So where are we? We have our second man. But is that enough? It should be. Both were in town. Both had a motive. There were no witnesses to the killing—none that the jury will know about. Can the jury find beyond a reasonable doubt that Hok-Ling killed the sheriff? That it might have been Hok-Ling—certainly. But proven beyond a reasonable doubt? He pulled a folded sheet from his shirt pocket and unfolded it. Printed in his best hand was the jury instruction on "reasonable doubt" he intended to ask Judge Simmons to read to the jury at the close of the case. He read it over carefully.

The burden is on the Territory to prove beyond a reasonable doubt that the defendant, Hok-Ling, is guilty of the charge made against him. Proof beyond a reasonable doubt does not mean proof beyond all possible doubt, for everything in the lives of human beings is open to some possible or imaginary doubt.

A charge is proved beyond a reasonable doubt if, after you have compared and considered all of the evidence, you have in your minds an abiding conviction, to a moral certainty, that the charge is true. Every person is presumed to be innocent until he is proved guilty, and the burden of proof is on the prosecutor. If you evaluate all the evidence and you still have a reasonable doubt remaining, the defendant is entitled to the benefit of that doubt and must be acquitted.

It is not enough for the Territory to establish a probability, even a strong probability, that the defendant is more likely to be guilty than not guilty. That is not enough. Instead, the evidence must convince you of the defendant's guilt to a reasonable and moral certainty; a certainty that convinces your understanding and satisfies your reason and judgment as jurors who are sworn to act conscientiously on the evidence.

He refolded the sheet, nervously blowing out a large volume of air.

What was this fellow's name? Jason looked at his fistful of papers again and flipped through the pages. Yee Chun-Wah.

Next to the name were the words "dead—tunnel collapse two weeks ago."

Ho Ying-Chiao can testify that he sent Yee Chun-Wah into town, and what time he got back. That's not a problem.

Dead in a tunnel collapse. What irony, he thought, remembering the question that roiled him and drove him out of bed at five thirty that morning. Was he exposing an innocent man to a possible death sentence? Yee Chun-Wah was dead—killed with twelve other coolies in a tunnel accident east of Heron. Jason looked out at the gray, still surface pocked with raindrops. He wouldn't have to worry about it now.

He set his head back against the hard bench. There won't be a time for us, will there, Mei-Yin? No time. Differences. That's what you said, and of course you're right. Differences. What was I thinking? I don't know you at all, do I? But you are so beautiful.

I want you to be happy and safe, Mei-Yin. I want you to live to an old age surrounded by people you love, who love you. He thought of Esther. I feel the same about you. And you, Josephine, you, too. And then he thought of himself. And you, too.

A few minutes later, he found himself staring down at his notes again. An unsettled feeling began to creep over him. With Yee Chun-Wah dead they'll feel cheated, he thought. You can't hang a dead man. Jason sat bolt upright. They can't slake their collective thirst for justice. That means they'll find Hok-Ling guilty, no matter what. They'll convict him just to have someone to hang! What good will the court's instruction do?

Do I dare call Mei-Yin to the stand? *No!*

When the vessel landed, the two men walked silently along the path, through the narrow finger of woods to the Sand Creek Bridge. Crossing the bridge, they stopped at the corner of Bridge Street and Main. Jason turned his collar up. He could feel the approach of fall in the rain. Explaining that he had more work to do, he instructed Lei Chi-Man to return to the barn and report to court no later than 8:30 the next morning. Lei Chi-Man nodded. The two shook hands, and departed in opposite directions.

Jason passed three people in the first block, and he squinted at them through the rain, preparing to offer a greeting. None would make eye contact, and two frowned and made a show of their disdain. Will this end when the trial is over? he wondered. He turned on Lake Street. As he sidestepped the puddles and scuttled under the dripping boughs of giant maples, bound for Mrs. Stewart's house, he couldn't help but compare the reactions of so many of the townspeople to his father's rejection. They were of a piece, he thought. To them his acceptability as a person—his worth—was ever in doubt, contingent, fleeting. He slowed his pace. And what it meant was that if something about him were different, if he had done something differently somewhere along the line, something better, if he were exceptional—that's what his father had in mind—the sun of acceptance would never set and the lingering wound in his soul would heal. But, alas, he was mortal, and they were free to reject him, just as Mei-Yin had. The freedom to reject, to hate, to disdain, he mused. It's everywhere. He stopped in the street. Freedom and differences, he said to himself. Differences and freedom. His gaze was now set on the open gate of a garden fence beside an unpainted two-story house, but he didn't have the gate in mind, as such. The freedom to hate. The dark side of freedom. The unmentionable side of freedom. Differences. He turned and began to walk slowly back toward Main Street. "A bottle of Old Crow, please," he murmured to the rain-sodden road.

* * *

Jason looked up as Mrs. Stewart entered the kitchen. Her movements stirred the air and brought the smell of wood smoke over the table. "May I buy you a drink, madam?" Jason asked, pointing toward the half-empty bottle. "It'll cure what ails you."

Mrs. Stewart held her sewing against her bosom with one hand and poured herself some coffee. A needle and thread were in her mouth. "Why, yes," she mumbled, extending her cup toward Jason. The white thread at the end of the needle bounced as she spoke. "Just a drop, mind you. As my husband used to say, 'I'll take that drink so others don't have to.'" Jason laughed, which made him clank the bottle against the rim of Mrs. Stewart's coffee cup. "That's good!" she said. She stood tall and looked over the papers scattered on the table. "How's it coming in here? You've been at it quite awhile."

"It's coming along," Jason answered. He splashed more whiskey into his own glass. "Slow but sure."

"Well, good. Better light the lamp. With these low clouds it'll get dark early."

"Thanks. I'll do that."

"We'll eat about five thirty or so," she said, making her way back to the parlor.

He picked up his dip pen and looked down at the page in front of him. So far, he'd written under 'Ideas for Closing Argument':

> Freedom—includes the freedom to hate— human differences: tall/short, German/Dutch/ American, man/woman. All hum. differences are part of a duality—each has a "defining opposition"—the human mind can't comprehend one side without awareness of other. White/ nonwhite, CHINESE/non-Chinese . . . "If all people had the same skin color, the freedom to hate wouldn't attach to skin color." Skin color wouldn't be a human difference, like nationality, religion, language, culture.

> Being Chinese—if all of us across the planet were Chinese, the freedom to hate wouldn't attach to being Chinese. The freedom to hate attaches to human differences.

Jason tipped his glass and drank the whiskey in two gulps. He sat back and shook his head in response to the fire erupting in his throat. Differences, he said to himself. The freedom to hate. He threw the pen down. Defining oppositions. How am I doing, Mei-Yin? I guess it's your grandfather I'm really talking to, isn't it? Hello, sir. I don't know your name, but allow me to tell you that I love your granddaughter. You laugh? You think that's funny. Well, I guess it is. You see, she doesn't feel the same about me. He poured more whiskey and held it up as though preparing to toast the ghost of Mei-Yin's grandfather. "You, sir, have bested me," he said aloud. But a frown tugged at his lips. He put the glass back on the table. There are more than differences, old man. What about samenesses? What about loving children, or the desire for health? What about the need for sleep and getting old? Do any of those happen in China?

Jason put his elbow on the table and rested his forehead against his fist. He stared at the paper in front of him. "There are no defining oppositions for human samenesses. Do you get that?" he said aloud. He lifted his head. So there are two spheres, he said to himself. Two spheres of experience, human differences and human samenesses. Yes, there's the freedom to hate, but it attaches only to the sphere of human differences. If you want to hate someone for being a foreign devil, or being tall, or speaking English—you want to hate someone for being Chinese—go ahead. But make sure you see them completely. He picked up his pen and dipped the nib.

> All men are created equal.
>
> All men are entitled to the presumption of innocence. Is it because of our differences, or what we have in common?

Does the presumption of innocence belong only to men, to white men, to fair-skinned people—who speak English? To the wealthy?

Beyond a reasonable doubt—the standard for all people. Don't apply it ~~without seeing the defendant completely~~ until you've seen the def. completely.

Jason sat back and exhaled slowly. See his differences, but also see his humanity—that's where the burden of proof attaches to him. He stared into the corner of the kitchen, and his eyes drifted down slowly. On the floor near a box of kindling was the dumbbell Mrs. Stewart used as a doorstop. He went from not seeing it—that is, paying it no attention, for it was always there—to examining it closely. An idea began to form in his mind. He got up from his chair, too quickly, and staggered. He steadied himself against the edge of the table, then walked across the room and picked up the dumbbell. He put his free hand out toward the wall to keep from falling, but then decided he didn't need that. He held the ten-pound pewter-colored weight in front of him and began to turn it one way and another. He lifted it to eye level, closed one eye, and turned it one direction until only one of its two spheres was visible to him—the further sphere having been eclipsed by the nearer. Then he turned it back until the two spheres changed places. "Huh," he mumbled. He repeated the maneuver. "Human differences," he mumbled, focusing on the first sphere, and turning the object again to see the second sphere only, he said, "human samenesses." Turning the dumbbell partway back so that both spheres were visible, he opened both eyes and smiled to himself. "The whole man." Ten seconds later he was in the parlor, holding the dumbbell out for Mrs. Stewart to see. He wobbled in a circle where he stood. "Can I borrow this?" he said.

Mrs. Stewart looked up over round, silver spectacles. "Son," she began. She lowered her sewing as though preparing to speak freely, but then she checked herself. "Of course you can."

29

"**N**ow, George, why don't you start by telling us where you were on the night of July 16, a Wednesday?" asked Emory on the second day of trial. He addressed George Reynolds, a shift supervisor for the Patterson Lumber Company. Reynolds was a tall, slight man of thirty-two. His gaunt, clean-shaven face was punctuated by dark, surprised eyes that peaked out beneath sharp brows. Like most of the male witnesses, and all the jurors, he wore his Sunday suit to court.

"I was at the Copper Penny. My brother Tom and I and Paul Dobbins and Roy Beals and a couple of other fellas was playing cards."

"What time was this?"

"Oh, I don't know. We were there till about, oh, eleven, I guess. Maybe eleven thirty. Tom was losing and wouldn't let nobody go home there for a while."

The first ripples of laughter from the gallery brought a smile to Emory's face. "What time did you arrive at the Copper Penny?"

"About eight o'clock. I had supper at home."

Emory turned to face the jury. He sunk his hands into the pockets of his trousers. "Did you have occasion to step out on the back porch of the saloon that night?"

"Yeah, I sure did. About nine or so, I went out there for some air and . . . Well, for some air."

"Did you see anyone . . . anybody . . . while you were out there? Anybody on the Sand Creek Bridge, for example?"

"Yeah. I saw this fella here," the witness replied, pointing to Hok-Ling. The prisoner sat slumped in the same chair as before, staring down at his lap, but today he wore a suit of new clothes, his hair and body were clean, and there were boots on his feet. "He was running along, kind of crouched over, seems to me."

"Crouched over? What do you mean?"

"Well, like he didn't want to be seen."

Jason set his hands on the edge of the counsel table. "Objection, Your Honor."

"Sustained."

Jason touched his aching head. Did I shout that? he wondered. He blinked at the leaden dumbbell resting at the corner of the defense counsel table. I've got to get over this headache. He took a deep breath. With any luck, that second cup of coffee will kick in any minute.

He'd produced the dumbbell, wrapped in burlap, upon arriving in court at 8:45. Without speaking to Lei Chi-Man, Hok-Ling, or anyone else, he'd slowly unwrapped it, folded the burlap into a suitable base, and placed the object on top. Since then, he'd succeeded in ignoring it. But others seemed incapable of doing so, especially the jury members—a propitious sign, Jason thought.

Emory followed their glances, looked over his shoulder at Jason, and then down at the dumbbell. A shadow of irritation crossed his face as he turned back to face the witness. "Just tell us what you saw, George."

"Like I said, it was this fella here, crouched down, running."

"And you're sure it was the defendant?"

"Sure I'm sure."

"And again this was about nine or so?"

"That's right."

Emory turned and walked toward the prosecution's table. "Your witness, counsel."

Jason stood up but didn't move from the defense table. He looked down at his notes for a few moments and the hint of smile played at the corners of his mouth. He remembered a trial strategy Emory had taught him. "In a capital murder case, if you're defending the accused, you want to get the jury laughing at something—anything—during trial. Jurors who've spent time laughing at your jokes don't like to go into jury rooms and start talking about hanging your client." Jason stepped away from the counsel table. "Now Mr. Reynolds, you said your brother Tom was losing that night and wouldn't let anybody go home."

The witness smiled and blushed. "Not for a while, no."

"Is Tom here today?" Jason grinned and turned toward the gallery. "Tom, are you out there?"

"He's there, all right," George Reynolds laughed. "He's hiding behind Sally Montgomery."

"Oh yeah, I see him. We see you, Tom." Jason turned back and winked at one of the jurors. All twelve men were smiling now. "When I was kid, we used to make up nicknames for people just to see if we could get them to stick." He turned to the witness. "Does your brother have a nickname, George?"

"No. Tommy, I guess."

"Well, Tommy, yeah. But that's different. I mean a real nickname—and I've got one for Tom Reynolds over here. I propose we call him 'Late Night Reynolds.' 'Late Night' for short. What do you think?" The audience erupted in laughter and so did the jury.

"I don't think his wife's going to like it," someone called out from the gallery, and the laughter shook the room.

Jason turned back to the witness, smiling. With an effort, he resisted making eye contact with Judge Simmons. "Well, back to business here, Mr. Reynolds. So you're playing cards, and you step out on the back porch for a break, is that it?"

"That's right."

"And then you saw a Chinese man scampering across the bridge."

"Right."

"I don't know if you mentioned which way he was going, but I take it he was heading in the direction of the docks—is that right?"

"Yes."

"So leaving town and heading for one of the boats, probably."

"I would imagine so."

Jason turned and walked back to the far corner of the jury box. Another trick Emory had taught him. When the attorney asks his questions from there, the witness has no choice but to face the jury while testifying. "This man who was running along there, you recognized him as one of the coolies from the clothes he was wearing, right?"

"Certainly."

"I mean, you don't know any of those Chinese fellows out there at Hope personally, do you?"

"No."

"It would've been getting on toward dark at that hour, I suppose?"

"Yes, as I recall, it was dark. There was some light from some of the buildings—that's how I saw him."

"So when this fellow got to the other end of the bridge, I'm guessing you lost sight of him." Jason began to pace in front of the counsel tables, his head down.

"Well, that's right."

"You didn't see him get down off that bridge and go down by the water or anything?"

"No."

"And you didn't see anybody else over there at the time?"

"No."

"So, to be clear, what you saw was one of these coolies running across the bridge in the direction of the boat dock around nine o'clock or so?"

"That's right."

Jason spun around and faced the witness. "Were you in court on Monday when William Keating, the supervisor out there at Hope, testified that my client was sent into town that day to fetch the mail?"

"Yes."

"Do you know my client, Mr. Reynolds?"

"No."

"As you sit here today, do you recognize him as someone you've met or seen before?"

"No, can't say as I do."

"So when you testified a few moments ago that you saw my client running across the bridge that night, isn't it safe to say you were *assuming* it was him because you knew Mr. Keating had sent him into town that day? You did the logical thing and put two and two together—like anyone would—isn't that right?

"Yes, I guess I did. I mean—"

"You didn't see the man's face that night. You just saw a coolie running away from you."

"That's right."

Next, Buster James was called. He was followed by Jake Prescott, Edda Farlan, and David Jackson, the pilot of the *Henry Villard*.

Buster James was questioned by Tyler Forbes, who stood planted like a quince in the middle of the courtroom. "I'm not sure I understand you, Buster. You're sure it was this man who looked cross-eyed at your wife?"

"Yep."

"But I thought you said you and Bertha were down in front of the print shop watching the Chinese come through town. The scuffle with Sheriff Langston started back in front of the Carson Hotel."

"So?"

"So how could the defendant . . ? I mean, look, Buster, everybody knows it was this fella who got mixed up with the sheriff. Took his whip and all. Now how could he have been back there if he'd already passed the print shop up the street, like you say."

"What'd I say?"

"You said he'd already come up as far as the print shop."

"If I said that, then that's right."

"Well, if he was up there already, how come he showed up all of a sudden when the sheriff took the whip after that other one?"

Buster James rubbed his chin, and you could hear the rasp of his whiskers across the room. "Could you repeat the question?"

* * *

"Edda, when I spoke to you a couple of weeks ago you mentioned that you and Sue Ann Conrad had been to the market at about 10 a.m., and you were on your way home when you saw the defendant. Is that right?"

"That's right, Mr. Morse. We'd just been over to Carpenter's General Store to pick up sugar, yeast, food coloring, and other sundries for the church social. I'd promised Reverend Buck that if he'd make a point of remembering my little great-grand-daughter Betsy Asbury in his prayers, why, I'd make a nice—"

"That's fine, Edda. You don't need to go into that. The point is, though, you and Sue Ann saw this man on the morning of the 16th. Isn't that right?"

"Right."

"What time of day did you actually see him? Do you remember?"

"Oh, it must of been around 10:30 or 10:40. It wasn't very much after 10:00." Edda McFarland shifted in the chair and made a minute adjustment to the lay of her dress over her lap. She was growing comfortable in the witness stand. She smiled inwardly. The incessant twitching of her thin, gray lips was an annoyance to everyone but herself. "Let's call it 10:30."

"Ten thirty. And where was the defendant at ten thirty that morning, when you saw him?"

"He was right there in front of Anthony's."

"Anthony's Lockers?"

"Yes. Right there in the street."

"Do you remember what he was wearing, Edda?"

"No. Pants, I guess, and a shirt. He didn't have shoes. I remember that."

"Did he have anything else with him—a mailbag, for instance?"

"He may have. I don't remember. I don't remember him having anything except a very mean disposition."

"Objection, Your Honor!" Jason raised himself out of his chair, but not all the way. "The witness is editorializing."

Judge Simmons raised his hand, then looked over at the witness and smiled good-naturedly. "Miss Edda, in court here you can only talk about what you saw and what you heard. You're not entitled to tell the jury what you think someone's disposition was. That's for them to decide. That's all right, though. You didn't know that. Go ahead, Mr. Morse."

"Thank you, Your Honor. Edda, why don't you tell the jury what you saw that morning?"

"Well, like I said, Sue Ann and I were on our way home when we came across this heathen out there in the street. And there were some boys there, too, and the sheriff. We— "

"You say the sheriff was there?"

"Oh yes. And it took all these boys and the sheriff just to surround this Chinaman. That's how mean he was."

"Objection!"

"Sustained."

The old woman placed a frail hand over her chest. She looked up at the judge, surprised. "Oh, I'm sorry, Essex. I'm not supposed to say how mean he was, am I?"

The gallery rang out with laughter. At first neither the judge nor the clerk moved against the disruption, but then it was the clerk who spanked the wooden block on his desk two times. The judge, smiling, red-faced, leaned over toward the witness at last. "No, Edda, you're not," he chuckled. "But that's okay. Don't mind us. You're doing fine."

Jason was on his feet. His glower caught the judge by surprise. "Your Honor," he called out over the rippling laughter in the courtroom, "the defense requests that the court instruct the jury to disregard Miss McFarland's comments entirely."

Judge Simmons's smile wilted and he turned a darker shade of red. He waved his hand as if to pat the defense attorney back down into his chair. "Sit down, counsel—and shut up. I've known Miss Edda here for over thirty years. There's not a more honest person on the face of the earth. This court fairly bristles at the impertinence of your suggestion."

The Territory's last two witnesses were Dr. Randle and Ho Ying-Chiao. Dr. Randle testified to the cause of death—seventeen stab wounds with a five-and-a-half-inch, non-serrated knife of unknown manufacture. The fatal blow partially severed the aorta two and a quarter inches above the left atrium of the sheriff's heart.

Ho Ying-Chiao's testimony began shortly after 11:00 a.m.

"Your name is Ho Ying-Chiao?"

"*Hai.* Yes."

"You are a crew boss?"

"Yes, crew boss."

Emory stood at the far end of the jury box, but the Chinese persisted in answering with his head down and his eyes pointed toward the black silk skullcap that he held with both hands on his lap.

"You must look up and answer aloud," Emory cautioned.

"Oh. Yes. Sorry."

"Look up, Mr. Ho!"

"Yes, yes. Okay." Ho Ying-Chiao's thin face twitched nervously, as he sought by every means possible to avoid looking at the jury.

"You have sworn to tell the truth—*sworn*—do you understand what that means?"

"Sworn?"

"Yes."

"Tell truth."

"Yes, that's right." Emory smiled. "And you promise to do this?" Ho Ying-Chiao grimaced and tilted his head. He laughed self-consciously through crooked yellow teeth. "Do you understand, Mr. Ho?"

"Mmm, no."

"You will not tell the truth?"

"Oh, yes-yes. Tell true. Yes. Mmm."

Jason stood up. "Your Honor, if counsel would find it helpful, we have a court-certified interpreter here." He nodded toward Lei Chi-Man. "Mr. Lee is more than capable of translating, and I intended to use him on cross-examination of this witness in any event. I suspect the witness might be more comfortable testifying in his native language."

The judge looked at Emory. "It might make things clearer for the jury. What do you think, Emory?"

Emory hesitated a moment, then said, "Yes, let's do that. Thank you, Jason."

Lei Chi-Man was called forward by the judge, interrogated briefly about his experiences translating in the California courts, and then sworn in. A chair was brought in and placed beside the witness stand.

"Very well. Mr. Ho, do you know the defendant—this man?" Emory asked, stepping over toward Hok-Ling and pointing.

"Yes, of course."

"And how long have you known him?"

"More than three years." Ho Ying-Chiao looked closely at Hok-Ling.

"You were his crew boss."

"Yes."

"Did you see Hok-Ling on July 16, the day of the murder?"

"Did I see him?"

"Yes. Did you see the defendant, Hok-Ling?"

"Yes."

"When?"

There was a short discussion between the witness and Lei Chi-Man, then the interpreter turned to face Emory. "I saw him early in the morning, and again late that night."

"When did you see him in the morning? What time?"

"I'm not sure of the exact time. It was before seven thirty, I know that."

"Hok-Ling came here—to Sandpoint—to get the railroad mail. Isn't that right?

Ho Ying-Chiao nodded as the question was interpreted. Lei Chi-Man answered, "Yes."

"When he returned to Hope, did he have the mail with him?"

Ho Ying-Chiao stared at his skullcap again. He didn't wait for the interpreter. "No. Bag was empty."

"I want you to wait for the interpreter, Mr. Ho. Do you understand?"

Lei Chi-Man interpreted this. "Yes."

"Why didn't he have the mail?"

The witness looked up as Lei Chi-Man relayed his answer in English. "I have no idea. He could have smoked opium that day for all I know. I'm not even sure he got on the boat."

"Did you speak to him that night?"

"Yes."

"What did he say?"

Ho Ying-Chiao looked long at Emory. Lei Chi-Man answered, "I don't remember."

"You don't remember? Did you ask him where the mail was, Mr. Ho?"

"I might have. I don't remember"

"What did he look like? What did his clothes look like?"

"I don't remember."

"Do you know what jail is, Mr. Ho?"

"Jail? Yes."

"Then with the court's permission I will tell this witness that he is going to jail if doesn't tell the truth! Do you understand that? You will go to jail for lying."

"No!" Ho Ying-Chiao blurted, again without waiting for the translation. "No lie!" Lei Chi-Man put his hand on the witness's arm while he translated. Ho Ying-Chiao's eyes darted from the lawyer to the judge, then to the bailiff. "I remember now. Hok-Ling said some boys beat him up—they wouldn't let him go—the mailbag was empty—his trousers and shirt were crumpled and wet. This is all true."

"That's better, Mr. Ho. Now tell the jury about his queue—his long pigtail. What happened to his pigtail that night?"

* * *

The cross-examination of Ho Ying-Chiao began just after eleven o'clock. The judge had ordered a fifteen-minute break at 10:50, and the jury and public had just returned to their seats. During the recess, Jason had been busy working on his closing argument, oblivious to the man shackled to the counsel table next to him.

"Are you ready to proceed, Mr. McQuade?"

"I am, Your Honor." Jason rose from the counsel table. Before approaching the witness stand he glanced back into the gallery. He scanned the receding lines of faces ten rows deep, and those of the people standing along the back wall. Finally, he saw Esther Langston. Their eyes met and he offered the hint of a smile. It was not returned. Esther was dressed in a navy blue dress with standing collar. Her blond hair was pulled back and tied in a chignon at the crown of her head. She wore short, curly bangs. Sitting next to her was Joe Patterson, dressed in a black ditto suit with gray and black striped tie. I'm glad he's there for her, he thought. This must be torture for her. He turned and looked at the two Chinese men waiting for him to approach. "Mr. Ho," Jason began, "You testified that after sending my client into town on the 16th, you did not see him again until late that night. Do I have that right?"

"Yes."

"How many hours passed between the time you sent him—strike that. What time did you send him into town that day?"

"He took the 8:10 boat."

"That's 8:10 in the morning?"

"Yes."

"Did he have orders to do anything else in town besides get the mail and bring it back?"

"No."

"So tell the jury, if you would, what time you expected him back in camp."

"I don't know. Shortly before noon, I guess."

"Did it concern you when he didn't show up before noon?"

"Yes, I was aware that he was late."

"So I imagine you were very concerned when he didn't return on any of the early afternoon boats."

"Yes, I was concerned."

"What did you think had happened to him?

"I didn't know. I had no way of knowing."

Jason turned his back on the witness and Lei Chi-Man and began to walk away with his hands behind his back. He compensated by raising his voice. "Now, Mr. Ho, is it not true that your job depended on the success of Hok-Ling's errand?"

"I'm not sure I understand you."

"Were you aware that the coolies at Hope were threatening to go out on strike because of how Hok-Ling had been treated?"

"Objection," said Emory. "Lack of foundation. Assumes facts not in evidence."

"Sustained," said Judge Simmons.

Jason turned to the judge. "I'll rephrase the question, Your Honor." He stepped toward the witness stand again. "Tell the jury what, if any, labor problems, or potential labor problems, you were aware of on the day you sent my client, Hok-Ling, into town for the mail?"

"The men believed that Hok-Ling had been cheated by the railroad. They denied him his voucher after three years' work and made him come to Idaho. They believed the railroad stole his money, or arranged for it to be stolen, so that he could not run. They are convinced of this and there has been talk of a slowdown or strike."

"This talk had already started before July 16th?

"Oh yes."

"Your boss is Mr. Keating, right?"

"Yes."

"Tell the jury what, if any, warnings you had received from Mr. Keating concerning what would happen if the men went out on strike."

"Objection," said Emory, rising to his feet. "Hearsay."

"Sus—"

"Your Honor, this is not hearsay. It's not offered to prove the truth of any warnings, but rather to show Mr. Ho's state of mind on July 16th."

Judge Simmons glanced over at the witness, then at Emory. "I'll allow it for that purpose."

"Do you understand the question, Mr. Ho?"

"Yes. It is essential to finish the track to the Cabinet Gorge by winter. He . . . Mr. Keating . . . told me that if the men strike or slow down, he would fire me."

"Did you take this threat seriously?"

"Yes."

"You've testified that the men were concerned about Hok-Ling's treatment. Did this have a bearing on how you reacted when Hok-Ling didn't return to Hope in a timely fashion on July 16?

"Yes."

"Tell the court what you did."

"I sent a man in after him—to look for him."

"You sent a man in. What do you mean?"

"I sent one of my men into Sandpoint to look for Hok-Ling."

"Was this on the 16th?"

"Yes."

"Who was this man?"

"His name was Yee Chun-Wah."

"So you sent another coolie into Sandpoint. What time was this?"

"He left on the 1:40 boat."

A stirring began in the gallery. Jason glanced over his shoulder just as Tyler Forbes and Emory were leaning together, whispering. The latter was shaking his head vigorously.

"What time did he come back, Mr. Ho?"

"He returned on the next-to-last boat. That boat arrives at 10:20.

Individual voices could be heard punctuating an uncomfortable murmuring emanating from the gallery. The judge tapped his gavel once. "Quiet in the court, please."

"So this Yee Chun-Wah was in town all that time?"

"Yes."

"And he returned about an hour before the last boat that night."

"That's right."

"I take it he did not find Hok-Ling?"

"No. He said he couldn't find him. He said he looked everywhere. When it got dark, he said the boat's warning whistle blew, and he ran to catch the *Mary Moody*."

"This would have been sometime after nine o'clock then?

"Yes."

"And to get to the boat, he would have had to cross the Sand Creek Bridge, is that right?"

"Yes, of course."

"Where is this man now, Mr. Ho?"

"He's dead."

Someone in the gallery said, *"What!"* But it was only one voice in a sudden upwelling of indistinct vocalizations. Several members of the jury shifted in their seats. The judge struck his gavel twice more. "Quiet!" he shouted.

Jason took his position at the far end of the jury box. "What do you mean 'he's dead,' Mr. Ho?"

"He was killed with twelve other men in the tunnel collapse two weeks ago up at Cabinet Gorge."

The crowd's reaction was barely restrained. Jason nodded as he walked back to the counsel table and leaned over the notes he'd left beside the dumbbell. He let several seconds pass, then stood up again facing the witness.

"Unfortunate—not only for him, but for us, as well. Tell me, Mr. Ho, did you witness the sheriff's whipping of Soo-Kwan, the event we've heard so much about in this trial?"

"Yes, I was there. I came upon it as it was happening."

"Did you see this man Yee Chun-Wah at that time?"

"Yes."

"What was he doing?"

"He was knocked over by the sheriff's horse."

"What do you mean? Explain that."

"The sheriff was whipping Soo-Kwan, and his horse was turning in circles in the street. Before Hok-Ling stepped forward and grabbed the whip out of the sheriff's hand, I saw Yee Chun-Wah run forward to try to save Soo-Kwan. Unfortunately, this was just as the sheriff's horse was spinning in the road, and its rump and hind leg struck Yee Chun-Wah, knocking him over. A few seconds later Hok-Ling stepped forward."

"So when Hok-Ling . . ?"

"Yee Chun-Wah was knocked to the ground. He lost face . . . at the hands of another."

"What is the significance of this, Mr. Ho? Of losing face at the hands of another?"

"In Chinese culture, when a person loses face at the hands of another, it is common to seek revenge."

"That's all I have, Mr. Ho. Thank you."

30

J udge Simmons read aloud a series of instructions to the jury. Each appeared on a separate sheet of paper that he picked up— after wetting his thumb and the tips of two fingers—from a stack on the extreme left side of his desk. After each instruction was read, he carefully turned the page over and set it down again in front of him, keeping them in order. Jason's instruction on reasonable doubt was given. When the judge picked up the last sheet, he swiveled in his chair toward the jury box. He abandoned the monotone of the last quarter hour, which lent weight to the view that Hok-Ling's fate would soon be in the hands of the twelve jurors. "I have outlined for you the rules of law applicable to this case," he began. "You have heard the evidence, and both sides have rested. In a few minutes, you will hear the closing arguments of counsel. Closing arguments, while often helpful to the jury, are not evidence and should not be considered as such. It is your duty to give careful attention to the arguments of counsel. If you remember the facts differently from the way the attorneys have stated them, you should base your decision on what you remember. You are the ones to determine what evidence was given in this case, as well as what conclusions of fact should be drawn therefrom. After the attorneys have given their closing arguments, you will retire to the jury room. As jurors you have a duty to consult with one another and to deliberate before making your individual decisions. Once you have reached a verdict, the jury foreman will complete and sign the verdict form, and advise the bailiff that you are ready."

Judge Simmons turned back and faced the counsel tables. "Is the Territory ready for closing argument?"

Emory stood up. "We are, Your Honor."

Jason watched Emory lean over to get last-minute input from Tyler Forbes. Jason pulled out his pocket watch. It was 1:43. Emory will probably go twenty minutes, he thought, and I'll go twenty or thirty. The jury will have the case this afternoon. While replacing the watch, he looked down at the iron chain that drooped over the leg of the man seated next to him—his client. He sat back, looked out the window. Don't think about it, he told himself. He remembered a Harvard assistant coach who habitually uttered the same words—"Don't think about it"— before every crew race. What a fool, he thought, then and now.

A handful of brightly lit cumulous clouds were casting dark shadows over the sunlit flank of Black Rock Mountain. Jason tried to distract himself by locating the granite outcrop above which, in a grass clearing, he and Esther had lain together. But in the next instant his mind traveled northeast to the barn where Mei-Yin was ensconced. What is she doing right now? he wondered. He tried to picture her sitting in the sun, sewing, but with the first words of Emory's closing argument filling the courtroom, he knew the answer. Worrying.

Emory hammered home each point of the prosecution's case and made no apology for the fact that the Territory was relying on circumstantial evidence. Indeed, he had no reason to apologize. "How many murders happen in front of witnesses?" he asked rhetorically. "What percentage? Certainly some do. But we all know that a great many crimes—dare we say most?—are committed in the shadows, around corners, behind doors—out of view. Don't be dissuaded, gentlemen, by the fact that Hok-Ling chose to kill in the shadows. As Judge Simmons has instructed you, circumstantial evidence is just as valid as direct, eyewitness testimony. Allow me to read it to you again." With this, Emory strode to the judge's desk and asked for instruction number five. The judge fingered through the pile and handed him the instruction. "Thank you." He turned to the jury. "Here it is, instruction number five. 'There is no reason to be prejudiced against evidence simply because it is circumstantial evidence. You make decisions on the basis of circumstantial evidence in the everyday affairs of life. There is no reason why decisions based on circumstantial evidence should not be made in the courtroom. In fact, proof by circumstantial evidence may be as conclusive as would be the testimony of witnesses speaking on the basis of their own observation. Circumstantial evidence, therefore, is offered to prove a certain fact from which you are asked to infer the existence of another fact or set of facts. Before you decide that a fact has been proved by circumstantial evidence, you must consider all of the evidence in light of reason, experience, and common sense.'" Emory returned the instruction to the judge, who nodded. "So you see, gentlemen," Emory continued, walking back to the jury, "you may reach a verdict of guilty beyond a reasonable doubt on the basis of circumstantial evidence, and that's exactly what you should do in this case. There were no eyewitnesses to this crime, but don't worry about that. Sheriff Langston was killed on the evening of July 16, 1882, and based on the evidence presented to you in this case, you know who did it and why. Justice requires that you return a verdict of guilty." Emory pulled his frock coat back and plunged his hands into the pockets of his trousers. With his eyes cast down, he began to pace. "Let's review the facts . . . "

At 2:10, Judge Simmons put down a crescendo of whispers and low talk from the gallery, then looked over his spectacles at Jason. "We will now hear the defense closing argument. Mr. McQuade?"

Jason felt a lump at the base of his throat. He nodded toward the bench. This is it, he told himself. His heart began to flail in his chest like a pheasant startled from a thicket. More than ever, he wished he could communicate with Hok-Ling. He would lean over and say to him if he could: "I've done my best, Hok-Ling. I want you to know that." The gulf between the two men had never seemed painful to Jason before, but it did now.

Emory had argued his case well and convincingly. Plus, Jason thought, he's a fixture here. Everyone knows and respects Emory. And here I am. People hardly know me at all. What chance does Hok-Ling have? Jason put his hands on the edge of the counsel table and rose slowly. "Thank you, Your Honor." He glanced at Emory. The old attorney was sitting back, leaning over an elbow. His face was pale, and his slumping posture betrayed the fact that for him the case was over. He had done all he could. Emory looked over at his protégé and gave him a weary, almost imperceptible nod.

Jason drew a deep breath and pushed back from the table. "May it please the court." He looked down at the dumbbell as he walked past the corner of the counsel table and took a position in the middle of the room, facing the jury box. "Gentlemen of the jury, you have now heard the prosecution's case—all of it. You know as much about this killing as Mr. Morse and Mr. Forbes are able to tell you—as much as they ever knew— as much as Judge Simmons knows, or Deputy Lambert, or William Keating, or George Reynolds or any of the other witnesses for the prosecution. So the question to ask yourselves is this: What is it *you* know? What facts have been established beyond a reasonable doubt?"

"That the sheriff is dead—yes, unfortunately." He turned away from the jury and his eyes settled on William Keating, sitting with his legs crossed and his hands folded on his lap in the front row of the gallery. He seemed genuinely concerned about the fate of his employee. To Keating's left was Ho Ying-Chiao, wearing a black silk skullcap and a gold and black coat embossed with white brocade. Jason stepped along the balustrade, trying to avoid looking at Esther. But at the same time he was tempted to, and he gave way to the temptation. The moment their eyes met he spun away. "But who killed him? Isn't that the question, gentlemen? Where's the murder weapon? Where's a single witness to the crime?"

"I'll tell you who killed Sheriff Langston," Jason continued, his voice becoming fuller. He took off his frock coat and draped it over the back of his chair. "It was Charlie Hackett." Jason turned to the sound of multiple murmurings in the audience. "Do you remember him? He was that cattle rustler that stole fourteen head of cattle—from *you,* Fred Polson." Jason pointed toward a heavy-set man standing along the wall at the back of the courtroom. "*You* remember him, don't you, Fred? Of course you do. And some of you other folks remember him, too. And do you know why Hackett killed Sheriff Langston? Because four years ago the sheriff caught up with him outside of Priest River—over by the Thompson place—do you remember? And he brought him in, and he was tried right here in this room. I wasn't around here then, but many of you were. Hackett swore he'd have his revenge before they sent him to prison. Two years ago he escaped."

"Or was it Robert Tippett? Everyone here knows who Robert Tippett is. He's probably the slickest bank robber this side of St. Louis. Tippett's younger brother, Hardy, wasn't so slick though, was he?" Jason's eyes glinted. He raised a finger into the air. "I'm told his career started and ended right here in our little town seven years ago, at the age of sixteen. He's buried right up there off the Cougar Mountain Road—isn't he, Bart?—I see Mrs. White shaking her head over here. That's right, isn't it, Mrs. White?"

A fair, rosy-cheeked woman dressed in a black pongee traveling dress, with a head of unruly red curly hair, leaned toward her husband and grimaced at the attention her nodding had brought her. From another part of the courtroom, a man called out, "That's right, McQuade. He's buried up off the Pine Hill Loop."

"With a bullet in his head from Sheriff Langston's rifle!" Jason said. "Am I right?"

"Right," several male voices responded.

Jason aimed an insinuating smirk at the jury. "So there you have it. His brother Robert paid our little town a visit on the night of July 16th. Took care of some business. It's possible, isn't it? For all that's been proven here in this trial, that theory's as good as any other."

There was whispering, followed by a low, restive grumbling in the gallery, but it died out when Jason pivoted away from the jury box. He glanced icily over the balustrade, then turned and lowered his eyes to the ground. "It's possible," he repeated. Then he looked up as though remembering something. He spun back toward the jury. "Can any of you tell me it *wasn't* Charlie Hackett, or Robert Tippett? Or how about Tex Sasser, the fella they've been looking for down at Rathdrum? They say he killed two men. Or Shoshone Jack? Isn't he the renegade they say led a band of Indians against the Talbot family up there at Bonners Ferry? Why not *him*?"

Jason measured off a long pause. When he started in again, his voice was almost a whisper. "None of you can tell me that it *wasn't* because, you see, none of you know who did it. And that's the simple fact of the matter. That's where we are." Full-voiced again, he continued. "Mr. Morse here, and Mr. Forbes, they think it must have been *this* man," he said, pointing to Hok-Ling, "because he had a motive and was seen on the bridge on the night of the killing. But *was* he seen?" Jason moved close to the jury and leaned over the railing. "Was it Hok-Ling that George Reynolds saw on the night of July 16? Or was it Yee

Chun-Wah? You see, there was a second man in town, a second coolie. And like Charlie Hackett, like Robert Tippett—yes, even like my client—Yee Chun-Wah had reason to seek revenge from the sheriff."

"I don't doubt that my client crossed the Sand Creek Bridge sometime that afternoon or night. We know he got back to Hope. But there's been no evidence presented by the Territory telling us which boat Hok-Ling was on, whereas Ho Ying-Chiao testified that Yee Chun-Wah arrived on the 10:20 boat. That would have put Yee Chun-Wah on the Sand Creek Bridge just after nine o'clock, the exact hour described by George Reynolds. And when was the sheriff last seen alive? A quarter to nine."

"What we have here, gentlemen, is reasonable doubt. In fact, you could not have a clearer example of it. A moment ago, Mr. Morse read from the instruction on circumstantial evidence. That was appropriate, for, you see, all the instructions are equally valid and binding. They provide the legal framework for your deliberations. You are not free to ignore them or depart from them." Jason moved to the bench. "Your Honor, may I have instruction number eight?"

When the sheet was handed to him, Jason paused for a few seconds to read from it, then he took a position midway along the length of the jury box. "I'm reading from the second paragraph. 'A charge is proved beyond a reasonable doubt if, after you have compared and considered all of the evidence, you have in your minds an abiding conviction, to a moral certainty, that the charge is true. Every person is presumed to be innocent until he is proven guilty, and the burden of proof is on the prosecutor. If you evaluate all the evidence and you still have a reasonable doubt remaining, the defendant is entitled to the benefit of that doubt and must be acquitted.'" He held the sheet up and looked into the eyes of each juror in turn. Their impassive stares sent a shudder down his spine. It doesn't matter to them, he thought. Not one of these men is disposed to acquit Hok-Ling. He felt the presence of Emory behind him, and remembered

Emory's low, confidential warning encased in the laughter and hubbub of the Copper Penny Saloon. "There's slippage in the system. This one has slippage built into it. I can see it coming. These people have a dead sheriff on their hands, and your man's Chinese. This town's going to hang that Chinaman of yours."

God, how'd I get myself involved in this? Jason thought as he walked back to the bench and handed the instruction to the judge. He stood for a moment, staring out the window, with his back to the jury. It doesn't matter what I say. It doesn't matter what the instructions say. It's all subjective, isn't it? Reasonable doubt. Moral certainty. Whose reason? Whose moral certainty? He's not even a man to them, he's a Johnny, a Chinaman. An ironic smile lifted one corner of his mouth. And who are we to them? Foreign devils. Uncouth, uncivilized, pale-skinned brutes. This is a fine state of affairs.

Jason felt a sudden, unexpected lightness in his being, a tectonic shift, a strange psychological cleansing that he could not account for—unless, he thought as he turned to stare into the empty space above the heads of the gallery—unless the two hatreds cancel each other out. Or abide in the same freedom. Yes, that's it, he thought. The freedom to hate human differences—or love them, it doesn't matter. It belongs to us all. He turned around and gazed at the jury members. It belongs to them.

A wide smile crossed Jason's face. Several of the men shifted positions. One took a sudden interest in the point of his boot. "Forgive me," Jason said, approaching the jury box. His blue eyes held his smile and sparkled with fresh intensity. "I was thinking just now about freedom. Yours, mine, theirs," he said, waving toward the gallery. "All of ours. Even my client's— although he sits here in chains. It's not physical freedom I'm talking about, but the freedom to hate. That's a jarring word— hate—and some of you," he continued, turning quickly toward the gallery, "some of you are telling yourselves this very instant that you do not hate any man—that that's not the Christian way—am I right? And how dare this attorney suggest otherwise. But, you see, I don't accuse any of you of hating." Jason turned back to the jury. "I accuse you . . . no, that's not the right word. I *celebrate* with you your freedom. And if freedom means what we all know it means, then it includes the freedom to hate. Just as we are free to love, we are free to hate. And let us not shy away from freedom. Let us not deny here in this court of law who and what we are." Jason turned and stared at Judge Simmons without seeing him. "I mentioned Charlie Hackett a minute ago. We all know what we feel about cattle rustlers." He turned back to the jury. "Now I want to do an experiment— bear with me. I want you to imagine that we live in a world where cattle are everywhere, as thick as fleas. You can't turn around without bumping into one, and if you left your gate open for the night, you wouldn't lose cattle, you'd double your herd without thinking about it. In this imaginary world, every man feels free to take cattle out of another man's field anytime he wants to—in fact, it's almost considered a courtesy. Now, tell me, in that world, would we have cattle rustlers?"

Jason stepped to the end of the jury box and spoke directly to juror number twelve. "Mr. Strickland, how tall are you?"

"Six foot three," the juror replied.

Jason smiled and nodded. "That's why I asked. I knew you were tall—one of the taller people in town I don't wonder. But gentlemen," he continued, addressing the entire panel, "what if all human beings, all men and women, grew to exactly six foot three like John Strickland here. Would we look at John and say, 'Now there's a tall fellow'? Of course not. In fact, we wouldn't even have the word 'tall' to describe each other, would we?"

"Being tall is a human difference, and I want to underline that phrase, because, you see, human differences can't be understood by themselves. I can't understand what it means to be tall unless—at the same time—I know that some people are not tall. Speaking English is a human difference. Not everyone does it. But now imagine that they did. Imagine there were no

other languages besides English. Would we say of our neigh-
bor, "Oh, that's Harvey. He speaks English"? No, of course not.
We wouldn't have that word to describe human beings. And
the only reason we do is that some people *don't* speak English.
Do you see this? If everyone took cattle from everyone else's
fields whenever they wanted, if that was just something we all
did willy-nilly, we wouldn't have the phrase 'cattle rustler.' We
wouldn't say, 'Oh, that's Charlie Hackett. He's a cattle rustler.'"

Jason paused and considered whether to introduce the phrase
'defining oppositions.' He decided against it. "I'm talking about
human differences, you see, because that's where the freedom
to hate attaches. That's a whole sphere of experience that we all
have that's separate from another sphere, our shared humanity."

"The sphere of human samenesses contains things that all
human beings experience, no matter who they are, or what
their differences: the love of children, the desire for health and
knowledge, concern for the safety of loved ones. The sphere of
human samenesses contains the need for food and water, and
the processes of birth, aging, and death. The desire to be understood when we speak. The desire to be treated fairly by others.
You will find these things in every person—of every nationality,
of every skin color. They are part of what makes us what we are.
They are not the only part—don't forget, we have that whole
other sphere of differences—but they are an integral part.

"Mr. Strickland, your love for your children is a big part
of who you are. No one could ever doubt that. And you, Mr.
Smith," Jason continued, pointing to juror number four, "you're
exactly like me in that you require food and rest, you use sounds
and symbols to communicate, and—sorry to say—you and I are
getting older each day, leading to that time when we won't be
alive anymore." Smith nodded. Jason stepped toward the counsel table and picked up the dumbbell. "No doubt you gentlemen have noticed this. I brought it in this morning.

"I've talked about two spheres of experience, a sphere of
human differences and sphere of human samenesses. Speaking

broadly, this dumbbell is a fair representation of each one of us." He turned and looked at Hok-Ling, then at Ho Ying-Chiao. "*Each* one of us. Every human being," he went on, turning back to the jury, "has a sphere of human differences." Jason pointed to the left-hand ball. "Just a minute," he said. He fished in the pocket of his waistcoat and produced a small piece of chalk. "Let's mark this ball with a D for differences." The resulting 'D' was skewed by the object's shape and rough surface, but was legible. "In this sphere," he continued, "are the languages we speak, the color of our skin, our nationality, whether we are male or female, our particular intellect, our sense of humor, our family history. Anything and everything that is not shared by people everywhere. And in this ball," he continued, writing an S on the other sphere, "we find all those characteristics, experiences, concerns, and desires that are shared by people everywhere." He held the dumbbell up, and turned it once in each direction so that the gallery and judge could see the markings.

"This is a fair representation of each of us," he told the jury. "But, is it the way we see each other? When you see me, do you see my differences as well as all that I have in common with people everywhere? When you look at my client,' he continued, "do you see both spheres of his experience?" He let the question hang in the air for a few moments. "I'm going to answer the question for all of us, gentlemen, for when we see another person, we don't see both spheres of his or her experience. We see their differences." Jason turned the dumbbell so that only the ball marked 'D' was visible, and swept it in an arc to make his point to all twelve jurors. "We are drawn to each other's differences—mesmerized by them, in fact. *This* is how we see each other. We take account of each other's differences—and for good reason. But we don't turn the dumbbell in our dealings with others. We don't get around to that. And that's a problem.

"You see, human beings are not just different—they're different *and* the same. And just as the freedom to hate attaches to the sphere of differences, which we always have in view, the presumption of innocence and the requirement of proof beyond a reasonable doubt attach to the sphere of human samenesses, the one we oftentimes don't see at all. You see, the presumption of innocence and the requirement of proof beyond a reasonable doubt have nothing to do with the color of your skin, your nationality, what language you speak, or what you believe. It is rooted in one thing, all that human beings have in common. It is rooted *here,* in the sphere of our common humanity.

"Gentlemen of the jury, you are free men, free to hate or love what you see in the world around you. My client is Chinese. He is a coolie laborer. Do you hate him for his hair, for his skin color, for the shape of his eyes? Do you hate him because he has taken a job that could be filled by a white man? Fine. There he is. You're free to hate him. You are in good company. I ask only one thing. I don't ask you to leave your hatred at the door when you enter the jury room. No, take it in with you. If you have it, you have it. What I ask is what any man should ask. I ask you to see my client completely. Turn the dumbbell. See his humanity. Then decide. Has the prosecution proven beyond a reasonable doubt that *this man*, Wong Hok-Ling, of Canton, China, killed Sheriff Roger Langston on July 16? If the answer is no, or you're not sure, you must acquit him. You must. Turn the dumbbell . . . then decide."

* * *

They walked in the blue light of dusk. Each man buttoned his frock coat. Lei Chi-Man buried his hands in his pockets. A smiling dog trotted out of the open door of the livery to greet them. Jason stopped, leaned over, and patted the turning, twisting animal. Rocky was as close to a "town dog" as there was. Jason brushed the dog hair from his pants and stood up. "Do I have you for a couple more days, Charlie?"

"Yes, I leave Tuesday morning. I didn't know how long the trial would take, so I added a few days to be on the safe side. I sent a cable to my parents yesterday."

"And you're going by train?"

"Yes, there's a Chinese car scheduled for the 3:50 out of Rathdrum."

They started walking again. Jason took a deep breath. "I'll need your bill, so I can submit it to the court."

"Sure."

"What are your plans when you get back to San Francisco?"

Lei Chi-Man smiled inwardly. "Back to normal. Help my father in the store. Visit nieces and nephews. Visit old friends. Wait for the next case. Who knows? I might even clean my apartment."

Jason laughed. "Don't hurt yourself. Don't they have companies that will come in and do that for you?"

Lei Chi-Man chuckled. "That's a good idea. I may look into that."

A long period of silence ensued that did not separate the two men, but joined them. They turned on Third Avenue and walked toward a cluster of houses in the distance, in front of which a large group of children were playing in the road, kicking up a great cloud of dust. Both men listened for the church bell that would signal a verdict had been reached.

"And what about you?" Lei Chi-Man said at last.

"I'm not sure, Charlie. I don't imagine there's much I can do around here. You've seen how the people hate me."

Lei Chi-Man stopped. "Hate you? Oh no, I don't think so, Ja-sawn. They're angry and upset, but when it's all said and done, you'll see they're not angry at you. It only looks that way."

"You think so?"

They started walking again. Lei Chi-Man's "I do" ushered in another long spell of silence. Jason remembered the piece of chalk in his waistcoat pocket. He brought it out, tossed it in the air once, then threw it sidearm into the bushes. "I hope I did the right thing," he said. "I think I did. I mean, it was a gamble—wasn't it?—but it was the right thing to do. By not calling Mei-Yin we saved her life, at least potentially—or if not her life, we saved her from a long prison term. And we saved

Esther from a lifetime of anguish if it came out that her father was a rapist. If we'd gone with the truth, that Hok-Ling killed the sheriff, even if it was to protect Mei-Yin, they'd hang him. Now, at least, there's a chance. They're taking their time." Both men reached for their pocket watches.

"It's been almost three hours," Lei Chi-Man said.

"They're thinking about it. Our best shot was to argue reasonable doubt." Jason looked into Lei Chi-Man's eyes. "You don't seem convinced."

Lei Chi-Man replaced his watch. "I'm just the interpreter."

Jason shoved him good-naturedly. "Oh, that's right. You don't think." Both men laughed. Suddenly, the pealing of a church bell filled the air. Jason and Lei Chi-Man stopped and looked at each other. "They have a verdict," Jason said. They turned together and nearly tripped over Rocky, who'd been walking two steps behind.

* * *

The jurors stared at Hok-Ling as they marched in under the glow of the burning store lamps and sat down, each in his appointed place. "Has the jury reached a verdict?" came Judge Simmons's weary voice.

"We have, Your Honor," the foreman replied.

"Hand it to the bailiff, then, will you please." A small, folded piece of paper was tucked into the bailiff's palm. The bailiff opened it and handed it to the judge.

A chorus of whispering rose up from the gallery.

Bang, bang. "Quiet in the court!" *Bang, bang.* "Quiet! Mr. Strickland, is this the true verdict of the jury?"

"Yes, Your Honor. That's it."

"Very well, then." Judge Simmons handed the verdict back to the bailiff. "Mr. McQuade, would you ask the defendant to rise please." Hok-Ling stood under his own power, his chin held high. "All right. Mr. Sours will read the verdict."

The bailiff turned and faced the gallery. "We, the jury in the matter of the Territory of Idaho versus Wong Hok-Ling, being duly impaneled, having heard the evidence, find the defendant *not guilty* of the charge of first-degree murder."

Gasps and outcries from the gallery were tamped down immediately by the judge, and a temporary silence descended like a pall over the courtroom. It was broken a few moments later by the squeaking of the door at the back of the gallery. Jason turned to see Esther and Joe Patterson disappear out the door into the deepening blue twilight. With the banging of the door, a chorus of excited whispers and side talk erupted again in the gallery. One man rose to his feet and swatted the air. "What did he say? Did he say not guilty?" The women sitting on either side of him held their hands to their mouths. Jason felt a trembling commence from deep within him. He looked down at his hands. Did this really happen? he wondered. Did I hear that correctly? He turned to see Lei Chi-Man whisper into Hok-Ling's ear, and the prisoner's eyes grew wide with disbelief. His chains rattled as he staggered backwards and went limp, his body sagging down toward his chair. Lei Chi-Man and Jason tried to lift him, but the judge said, "It's all right. Let him sit." When Jason looked up again, the judge was removing his glasses. "Deputy Lambert, unchain the defendant. He's free to go. Counsel, I want to thank you all for a well-tried case. Mr. McQuade, not bad. Not bad at all. You're to be commended, as is Mr. Morse for his fine mentorship."

Jason found enough breath to whisper, "Thank you, sir."

The judge stood up and struck his gavel one last time. "This case is dismissed." He stepped down from the bench and disappeared into his makeshift chambers.

Jason saw Emory approach him as if through a fog. The old man stepped past him then stopped. He felt Emory's hand on his shoulder. "I'm proud of you, son. Very much so. Let's talk tomorrow." In the next instant, Jason found himself shaking hands with Tyler Forbes, and then William Keating, whose smile under the oil lights revealed moist teeth framed in gold. "Congratulations, McQuade. That was impressive. I'm sure the Northern Pacific will have plenty of legal work for you if you want it."

The gallery had filed out to a chorus of restive whispers and the jury box was empty. Only Mr. Sours, the bailiff, remained at his desk, writing. Jason warmly received the outstretched hand of Lei Chi-Man. "You did it," said the interpreter. "I knew you could."

"Thanks, Charlie. I couldn't have done it without you."

Hok-Ling also extended his hand. "Thank you," he said in English, his face still pale with shock.

"You're most welcome, Hok-Ling." Lei Chi-Man translated, and a smile crossed Hok-Ling's face as he rubbed his wrists where his shackles had been.

A thought occurred to Jason. "Charlie, we should . . . would you be willing to accompany Hok-Ling back to Hope tonight? I want someone with him. The jury may have acquitted him, but there are others out there who—"

Keating, who was within earshot, interrupted. "Ying-Chiao and I can do that, Mr. McQuade. We're heading back there right now."

Jason looked at Lei Chi-Man and nodded, prompting him to translate. Hok-Ling shook his head and said in Cantonese, "Yes, that's fine. I will go with Master Keating and Ho Ying-Chiao."

"Charlie, you better go out to the barn then," said Jason, "and bring Mei-Yin into town in the morning, will you? Nine o'clock—at the office."

"Sure." Lei Chi-Man gave a quick bow in the direction of Ho Ying-Chiao and Hok-Ling and departed. Ho Ying-Chiao then spoke to Hok-Ling, and the two men walked off together, followed by Keating, who was lighting a cigar. A spirited conversation in Cantonese was cut off by the closing door.

Jason sat down at the counsel table again. He stared up at the judge's desk, and his mind went blank. Finally, the sound of the bailiff locking his desk drawers and rising to leave brought him back. "Good night, counsel," the bailiff said. "You can leave the lamps on. The judge will get them on his way out."

"All right. Good night." Twenty minutes passed, and Jason still had no inclination to get up, to be done with this room. He looked over at the twelve empty chairs in the jury box. Finally, he leaned over and picked up the dumbbell. For the first time, he used it as it was intended, to exercise his biceps. But he wasn't thinking about the dumbbell or the two spheres that rose and fell in his field of vision. "I . . . I did the right thing."

31

Mrs. Stewart insisted on a pancake, bacon, and egg breakfast with fresh-cut flowers on the table. She poured Jason's third cup of coffee into a cup that he tried to cover with his hand. "Now, you stop that," she scolded, tipping the pot.

"Really, Mrs. Stewart, I've got to get going."

"Me, too," said Eddie with his mouth full. "I gotta get to that fence."

"You just sit tight, both of you. Humor an old woman." She put the pot back on the stove and took the third and last seat at the kitchen table. "If there's one thing I've learned, it's that we have to celebrate the little victories along the way." She produced a bottle of whiskey from the pocket of her apron, opened it, and poured three or four drops into each of the three coffees. Jason and Eddie laughed.

"All right!" said Eddie. He slid thick fingers over his disheveled hair. "Not a minute too soon."

"Oh my," Jason said, picking up his cup and looking into it.

"And in that vein," Mrs. Stewart declared, lifting her cup, "let's have a morning toast to the hard work and perseverance of Jason McQuade, Esquire. To you, son."

"Thank you," Jason blushed.

"To you," Eddie nodded.

"Thanks, Eddie. Thank you both."

* * *

The note on the office door said, "Back at 8:45. Emory." Jason tried the handle. It was unlocked. He stepped inside and was met by familiar smells—pungent kerosene, the time-heavy odor of wood ash and book mold, the welcoming scent of leather. He looked at his desk. It was piled high with scattered pieces of paper, scribbled notes, open law books stacked three and four deep. The debris of trial preparation. But there was something else, an envelope placed on top of the tier of drawers behind the writing surface—positioned just so, it seemed—with his name rendered in a bold, unfamiliar script. As he stepped closer he saw that the envelope had a return address printed in a blue typeface. 'Northern Pacific RR, Pend d'Oreille Division, Hope, I.T.' He opened the envelope and pulled out a folded piece of paper. He unfolded it and read, 'Voucher for Travel' across the top. It was a printed form acknowledging payment of all 'debts, liabilities, and obligations.' He looked down quickly to see the name Wong Hok-Ling written in a neat hand. It was signed by William T. Keating. A smile crossed Jason's face. "I'll be damned," he said. He folded the voucher and put it back in the envelope.

The door opened behind him. "Good morning."

Jason turned. "Good morning." His heart stopped for a moment as he watched Emory set his briefcase on his desk, then take off his hat and coat and hang them on the coat tree. How am I supposed to act? he wondered. What should I say?

Emory returned to his desk and started removing legal files and handfuls of loose papers from his briefcase. He smiled up at Jason. "So, how are you feeling this morning?"

Jason hesitated. "I'm all right. You?"

"On top of the world," Emory winked. He finished emptying the briefcase, snapped it shut, and set it on the floor beside his desk—its normal resting place. "Do you have a minute?"

"Of course."

"Have a seat." Each man sat at his desk. Jason swiveled his chair around to face Emory, as he had done hundreds of times over the last three years. Emory leaned back and put his feet up on his desk. "I meant what I said yesterday. I'm proud of you." He picked up a pencil from his desk. "I don't think there's ten attorneys in the whole damn country who could have done what you did—or would have, for that matter."

Jason blushed. "Oh, I don't know about that. I was lucky. I . . . "

Emory chuckled. "Lucky, huh?"

Jason watched Emory idly tapping the end of the pencil on a case file. "I had no idea it would turn out that way," Jason said. "It was a shot in the dark."

The older attorney looked out the window. "Looks like another nice day, doesn't it? What are you fixing to do today?"

"Lei Chi-Man is meeting me here at nine. I'm sending him out to Hope to deliver Hok-Ling's money and *this*." He picked up the envelope. He knew he'd omitted Mei-Yin's name. *I'm not telling him anything about her*, he thought. *He'll no doubt see her, but he can jolly well guess at who she is. I'm not saying a word.*

"Oh, yeah. A fellow brought that by for you this morning. What is it, if I can ask?"

"It's a travel voucher for Hok-Ling. It's proof that he's paid his debts and allows him to board a ship for China, if that's what he wants."

Emory nodded. "And you've got that jar of money of his in the safe, right?"

"Right. That'll go back today, too."

Emory dropped the pencil and put both hands on top of his head. "And you? What are you doing today?

Jason felt a hot surge against his face. He wants me out, he thought. He wants my stuff out, now. Without thinking about it, he'd allowed himself to lean back comfortably, and now he straightened and began to look around the office. His eyes settled on the top of his desk. "I guess I'll get started with this mess."

"Can I give you a piece of advice?"

Jason looked at Emory, startled. "Sure."

"Forget the mess. Take a couple of days off. It'll do you good—you've earned it."

"But—"

"Come back on Monday. I need you to pick up where you left off on the Ballinger and Henry cases, and I've got a new case that came in on Tuesday that looks like it might be interesting. I'd like you to take the lead on it." Emory swung his feet down and leaned over his desk to pick up a small stack of papers. "I've got some notes right here. Take a look at them when you come back, and let's talk about it." Emory got up from his chair. He walked over and grabbed his hat. "I'd invite you to coffee, but I know you're meeting Mr. Lee here in a few minutes. I'll leave you to it."

Jason was thunderstruck. Emory moved toward the door and opened it. He turned back. "I saw an article in the *Spokane Times* last night. Villard and his entourage are going to be in Spokane Falls next weekend for another reception. Why don't you go in and play your duet again—get your mind off your troubles." Emory waited for an answer.

"I'll think about it," Jason replied.

Jason was busy at his desk when he heard a knock on the door. Turning, he saw Lei Chi-Man and Mei-Yin. She stood behind the interpreter. Only her left arm and shoulder and a windswept wedge of her black hair were visible through the glass. He could see that she was clad in a shimmering red silk coat. A pang of longing swept through him, but he let it pass.

I'm not going to be tortured over this, he told himself. He waved them in.

"Good morning, Ja-sawn."

Jason stood. Mei-Yin entered and stood beside Lei Chi-Man. She smiled warmly at the attorney, her face fresh and relaxed. He had never seen her more beautiful, more youthful looking. "Good mo-ning, Ja-sawn," she whispered. She pressed her hands together and bowed deeply. He set his jaw and commanded his heart not to break. She stood up and placed her hands over her heart. "Thank you . . . so very . . . much," she added. She looked at Lei Chi-Man for confirmation. He nodded. She mouthed the words 'so very much' again, smiling and wiping away a tear, averting her eyes.

Jason bowed his head. "You are very welcome, Mei-Yin.' He was glad to be able to turn away as Lei Chi-Man translated. He walked toward the safe at the back of the office, aware of a growing sense of strength and self-possession with each step. "There are a couple of things I need you to take to Hok-Ling, Charlie."

"Yes, of course." Lei Chi-Man's tone betrayed surprise and relief at Jason's sudden shift to business matters.

"Here it is." Jason extracted the jar of money from the safe and walked back to his desk to pick up the voucher. He handed the envelope to Mei-Yin and the jar to Lei Chi-Man. "Please take these to Hok-Ling," he said to Lei Chi-Man evenly. "Explain to Mei-Yin that the money has always been Hok-Ling's, and that I don't want any of it. And tell her that this is his voucher from the railroad. He's free to leave the railroad now, and return to China whenever he wants." Jason waited for the translation. He extended his hand to Lei Chi-Man, and the two men shook hands. "Thanks, Charlie." He turned and smiled at Mei-Yin and bowed his head again slightly. "Thank you, Mei-Yin." She bowed in reply. He stepped around them and opened the door.

Mei-Yin and Lei Chi-Man walked out onto the sidewalk. Lei Chi-Man stopped. Turning back, he said, "I don't know what's going to happen—between *them*, I mean."

Jason rested his forearm on the door. "Me neither, Charlie."

* * *

Hok-Ling was squatting at her fire, feeding it, when Mei-Yin and Lei Chi-Man arrived at the edge of the forest. They stopped, unnoticed. Lei Chi-Man turned to Mei-Yin. He extended the jar of money to her. "I will say good-bye now."

Mei-Yin took the money and bowed. "You have been so kind. How can I ever repay you?"

"You needn't repay me. I have merely done my job."

A gentle, knowing smile crossed her lips. "May heaven double your wages then, Lei Chi-Man."

When Lei Chi-Man was gone, she waited several minutes more to gather herself. Good! He brought a bucket of water, she said to herself. It's nearly noon. He will want rice and dried fish. I hope the animals haven't gotten into my food. If I have nothing to offer, he will scold me and tell me what a poor hostess I am. These things she said to herself, but falsely; for in truth, at the back of her mind, something else loomed—something dire and unspeakable. She drew her shoulders back and began to walk as steadily as she could toward him. A wedge of hair slipped down over her right eye, but she cleared it with a practiced sweep of her fingers just as Hok-Ling turned.

She bowed, then placed the jar of money and envelope beside Hok-Ling. Hok-Ling did not speak, or rise, although, unlike Mei-Yin, his eyes were fastened to her eyes.

Her heart throbbed painfully at the base of her throat. "You await your tea, and the water is as cold as ice," she said, kneeling. She lifted the bucket with trembling hands and began to fill the tin pot that stood nearby. The sound of water splashing in the bottom of the pot framed Hok-Ling's silence, and when that sound rose up and died, it was the low wheezing of the fire. Mei-Yin placed the pot beside the flame. With a single motion she stood up. "Are you hungry?"

"No."

"I have carrots and dried fish and hard tack."

"No."

"I will prepare rice for you."

"No. I am not hungry, Mei-Yin. I have eaten."

A bottomless dread yawned open in Mei-Yin's chest. This showed on her face as a look of sudden surprise. She tried to impose calm on herself by clapping her hands soundlessly beneath her chin and forcing a smile onto her lips.

"I must go inside for bowls and tea leaves," she said, and inside her tent she tarried. Why does he look at me this way? She made sure of noises so that she would have as much time as she needed to think. You mustn't assume the worst, she told herself. You mustn't.

At last, she felt her hope returning—its tide slowly rising. Perhaps he has come to rebuke me and nothing else. To tell me that I was wrong to come to Gold Mountain without his permission. That I should never do such a thing again. Yes, of course! He will say that I acted in a way most unwomanly! And he will demand my assurance it will not happen again. She smiled and placed a hand over her mouth, imagining her response. "You of course have my word, dear one."

When she emerged from the tent, Mei-Yin was no longer beside herself. She cocked her head slightly and bowed to Hok-Ling a second time before kneeling.

The contents of the envelope lay open beside him. Hok-Ling's eyes were fixed on the fire. "I have my voucher. I am free to return to Kwangchow." He seemed to wait for Mei-Yin to speak. She didn't speak, but stared into the fire, as well. And after awhile when she saw in the corner of her eye that Hok-Ling was scrutinizing her, she looked up into his eyes, but only for the briefest moment. She picked up one of the small, blue and white porcelain bowls and rinsed it with water from the bucket.

"It was a great opportunity," he said. "I have been irresponsible. I have begun to act like a demon these last months—asserting my will, refusing to comply with the inevitable—all to the dissatisfaction of heaven. My death would have rectified this. The ancient and venerable ancestor has made this clear—that I was to die here. It is the will of the gods. I have had many premonitions. My death would have restored honor to my family, and I would have been welcomed into the house of my ancestors."

Mei-Yin took up the second bowl. "You have mentioned this before, Hok-Ling, about the will of the gods. I must tell you this surprises me, for it seems the gods have been busy arranging something else." She produced a clean cloth from her sleeve and began to dry the bowls. "Do you not give them credit for removing you from the danger of the blast that killed the boy on the cliff? Have you not thought that perhaps it was *he* who was being summoned into heaven? What about the theft of your money? Could that have been the gods telling you, 'Although your three years are up, do not return to Kwangchow, for Mei-Yin is coming in search of you'?" She placed both bowls between them, turning them just so. She bowed over them slightly. "And what about the livery man, Hok-Ling, who prevented the green coat from shooting you?—and now the *leuht si*, who has saved you with his impassioned words? Could it be that the will of the gods is not to see you dead, but to see us together, as we were promised to be?"

"I have sought to be worthy of the ancestors." Hok-Ling tried to cover his confusion at what he had just heard. It was clear from the darting of his eyes that he had not thought of any of this, not in this way. "I have been certain of death," he said.

"Yes." She leaned over and placed her hand on the pot to gauge its warmth. She dropped fragments of green tea into the water. After a few moments, she wrapped her hand with a cloth and lifted the steaming pot with some difficulty. As she began to pour, she freed one hand to encircle each cup. In this way she shielded Hok-Ling from spray.

They drank the tea slowly, in a ponderous, grinding silence. This reminded Mei-Yin of the silence that sat easily with

Lai-Ping and Jong Suk-Wah, and once again she found it insuf-
ferable. I have spoken too boldly, she scolded herself. I must
let him speak. He is the man. But three minutes on, she heard
herself say, "What are you thinking?" She steeled herself for the
answer.

"What? Oh, of Kwangchow, of how it was with us."

"Yes."

"Of the sons we planned, for example."

"Mmm. Yes."

He mumbled something that she could not hear, then added
in a round, serious, manly tone, "It is a son's privilege to bring
honor to his family."

She took up a stick and prodded the fire unnecessarily. Her
heart thrashed violently in her chest. "Of course. And his *duty*
in all events is to avoid bringing dishonor."

Hok-Ling looked up at her quizzically. "Yes."

Mei-Yin nodded.

After a while, he said, "I, too, am a son, Mei-Yin."

"Yes. You also."

"I need to speak with you, Mei-Yin," said Hok-Ling, staring into his tea bowl.

She could not bear it any longer. "I know." Tears began to
spill and run unchecked down her cheeks. "You have already
said it. I am defiled. I carry the child of a demon, and therefore
I am unworthy of you. You would bring only dishonor to your
family by marrying me." She sprang to her feet and made a half-
turn toward her tent. But then, just as quickly, she stopped.
The edge of a scream escaped her lips, but she fought back the
rest, bouncing and bending a little to hold it in. With both
hands she covered her mouth. She closed her eyes so tightly that
new tears that might not have fallen spilled freely over her pale
cheeks. Hok-Ling jumped to his feet and took a step toward her.

"Why did it happen this way? *Why did you come?*"

Mei-Yin was silent. She stood with her head bowed, her
eyes closed. When at last she looked up, she found something in

Hok-Ling's expression that was unbearable. She quickly turned away.

"Listen to me, Mei-Yin," he pleaded. "Please. You must try to understand. I have great caring, but you must realize that I have lost face now."

Mei-Yin nodded.

"You have brought dishonor upon me. You did not mean to, but now . . . what is there to do? As long as I am with you, I will not have a place at the table of my father. I will have no peace in the house of my ancestors. You carry a white devil's seed. Your child will be half-demon. I have pity for you, Mei-Yin. It is most unfortunate." She opened her mouth as if to scream and closed her eyes against a searing pain that began in her chest and neck and spread down her arms and legs to the tips of her fingers and toes. When it was at its fullest she opened her eyes slowly, still facing the veiled obscurity of the woods.

"You know my family would not welcome the birth of such a child," he continued. "If it's a boy-child, will my mother and sisters rush to purchase eggs and dye them and present them to our friends and neighbors? Could my father welcome a demon grandson? I couldn't ask such a thing of him! Such things are impossible!"

She folded her arms stiffly, as though the pain in her chest might explode, tearing her apart. "But there is more," cried Hok-Ling.

He was not done, and she shuddered and stared at the blackened trees all around her.

"You have disobeyed your father, and now you have disobeyed me. Perhaps I am alive because of your disobedience, Mei-Yin. I don't know. But the word of man is law. I told you *not* to talk to them, to tell them you were Soo-Kwan's sister and nothing else. Tell me, how am I to save face after this? Your defiance has robbed me of respect, just as you robbed your father of respect!"

Now Mei-Yin's head slumped forward and came to rest against the fingertips of her right hand. She made no answer.

"I'm sorry, Mei-Yin. You are kind and generous of spirit. You are beautiful. But it was never to be like this." Hok-Ling stared at the ground. "It cannot be like this."

Mei-Yin answered in her own time. She spoke in a slowly rising voice, and with emphasis. "I understand what you are telling me, Hok-Ling. I disobeyed you, and I am sorry for the loss of face you evidently feel you have suffered because of me. But tell me, please, why do you bring so much of the Middle Kingdom to this place? Did I come so far only to find you again on the streets of Kwangchow, where we grew up?" She turned on him, and her gaze was at once fixed and penetrating. "This is not Kwangchow! Look at us! Look where we are!" She extended her arms out to her sides. "This is not the Middle Kingdom. Where are all the people? Where are the markets? The pagodas? The teahouses? Where is White Cloud Mountain, Hok-Ling? Can you smell the Pearl River? Or spices? Do you smell spices? No! Breathe, Hok-Ling! Breathe!" Mei-Yin inhaled mightily. "This is not Kwangchow. It is a different world, a different place altogether." Her eyes grew intense, her nostrils flared. "I am *not* sorry for the dishonor I have brought to the house of my father! Why should I be? I am nothing to him, less than nothing, a *girl*-child. Do you think he is sorry that he lost me in a wager? Or that he wagered me at all in a drunken game of mahjong? Do you? What about his promise to you? Does that mean anything? *No!* He stole your money, Hok-Ling—all of it. Do you know that? When my mother complained, he would beat her. And I would lie in my bed and listen to him tell her once again how he had always planned to sell me on the street for ten *tael* anyway, or that he was negotiating with Zhe Zhou-Zhu, the matchmaker, to find me a poor husband in the country."

"He is not sorry, for, unlike you, he is incapable of caring about anything. He is a spoiled man. He hates women. But now you say that *you* have lost face because I have dishonored him?"

Hok-Ling said nothing.

"For you, it is the same, because you are both sons of fathers, and I am a woman, a lowly woman. That is the way of the Han, it is true, but we are not in the Middle Kingdom now. If only you could see this! It is different here. I knew it was different, Hok-Ling. I knew from the stories told by Lai-Ping, from the foreigners in the trading houses along the quay, and from stories brought back to Kwangchow by the men who came here years ago, in search of gold. I would not have come otherwise."

She walked away from him and folded her arms. "The land of the occidentals is not a paradise for women, but it is not the Middle Kingdom, either. Here, a woman may speak in public. Here, she may not be sold or wagered away. Here, she may defend her life, as well as she is able, and whatever else is rightfully hers she may likewise defend. Don't you see?" she said, turning back to him. "It is the law. The law defends women as well as men. You, among of all the Tang people, should appreciate this. You, who are gentle and kind. That is why you are alive, not because I told them who I am."

She stopped, intent on every movement and glimmer in Hok-Ling's eyes, every flutter of his hair, every twitch in the muscles that flanked his jaw. A mirthless smile came and went from her lips as she struggled to catch her breath. Slowly her hand rose up and she touched the side of her face. "We are in a different world here, Hok-Ling. But we are together. At last we are together."

A single tear had fallen over Hok-Ling's cheek. "To what end are we together?" he demanded. He stepped closer, and his eyes began to dart between hers. "I am a sojourner. I came here to work, to earn the high wages paid by the American railroad, and then to return. I am not like Wu Cheong or Chin Tai, who came here to escape their nagging wives, or Lei Hong, who is a thief and cannot expect to enjoy a single day's breath if he returns. There is nothing for me here—*nothing!* And besides, my family awaits. You were supposed to wait."

"As the wife of a water carrier?"

Hok-Ling was stunned for a moment. He inhaled angrily. "Do you think I want to stay here, in this uncivilized place? We are hated here! Do you know what we are, Mei-Yin . . . you and I . . . and Soo-Kwan . . . and Dak-Wah? We are the 'yellow peril!'"

"For *some*, Hok-Ling, this is true. But there are good and kind people here, too. You have seen them yourself. The attorney, the old woman who cared for me and gave me her bed, the livery man, the doctor, the man who rode in the caskets. The jury, Hok-Ling! Think of them! They are just men and did not hate you enough to kill you. But in the Middle Kingdom, do you think you would have been spared for killing a green coat?"

"For every *leuht si*, there are fifty like the green coat!" Hok-Ling snapped.

"Then we can return *together*," exclaimed Mei-Yin impulsively, desperately.

"*No!*" Hok-Ling cried. His face blackened. "Don't you see? That's exactly what we can*not* do." He stepped away from her angrily, and his effort to be angry was theatrical. He turned, throwing his hands up in the air. After looking around, he padded past the fire toward an object lying on the other side of the tent. He pulled it up with a jerk. It was his rucksack. He cradled it awkwardly and tore at its straps. He ran to the money jar and voucher, dropped to his knees, and stuffed the articles inside.

"This is something you have no right to ask of me!" He stopped suddenly, as though sapped of every ounce of strength. At last, with a great effort, he got up and stumbled then ran toward the woods. Mei-Yin stepped after him, but a second later he had disappeared into the darkness.

"I am Han!" he cried out helplessly, thrashing through the brittle tamarack.

* * *

"You're still here," Emory said.

"I'm just getting ready to leave." Jason didn't look up. He was studying the volume numbers on the spines of four thick books that he balanced in his left arm, putting each one in its proper place in Emory's bookcase. When he finished, he closed the glass doors of the bookcase and strode to his desk. He picked up a jumble of papers and tamped them into a neat pile. "I'm going to take you up on your offer of a few days off," he said, opening his desk drawer and putting his dip pen and bottle of ink inside. "At first, I couldn't think of what I'd do, but then I remembered that Eddie's been busy replacing Mrs. Stewart's fence. I think I'll give him a hand for a couple of days."

"Splendid idea," said Emory, tossing his hat on his desk and dropping into his chair. He carried a bundle of mail in his left hand. He put his feet up and started going through it.

Jason walked to the coat tree and lifted his frock coat from the hook. He began to put it on then looked out at the sunny street. I'm going to carry it instead, he said to himself. "All right, Emory. I'll see you Monday."

Without looking up, Emory said, "See if you can get Antonea to make some of those oatmeal cookies again, will you?" Jason laughed. He walked past Emory's desk, opened the door, and felt the first caress of fresh mountain air against his face. "Hold on there," Emory said. "This one's for you." The old attorney held out an envelope and Jason took it, slowly stepping back into the office to examine it. Within a few seconds, he was aware of every beat of his heart, and his breaths, though shallow and not troubled, were audible to him. His eyes fastened on a style of handwriting that he had committed to memory since the age of eight and would know anywhere. He looked at the return address to confirm what needed no confirmation: it was a letter from his father. Jason turned the envelope over and felt its thickness. He walked back to his desk then he held it out in front of him again. A letter addressed to Jason R. McQuade, Esq., Sandpoint, Idaho Territory, from Robert McQuade, 96 Beacon Street, Boston, Mass. Three and a half years and one letter, he scoffed. I've been out here three and a half years, and now you're dropping me a line? He smiled inwardly and shook his head. He carelessly tossed the envelope on his desk and headed back for the door.

"See you Monday, Emory. Eight o'clock."

* * *

Mei-Yin emerged from the narrow curtain of woods above the camp and began to make her way down the path toward the lakeshore. Hunched over, her eyes puffy from crying, she carried her belongings in a blue blanket tossed over her shoulder and a bulging pillowcase that she held close to her stomach. As she approached one coolie and another, the men stepped off the path to give way, but made no attempt to assist. To a man, they stood in their tracks long after she passed to gaze after her. Navigating the first switchback, with her eyes fixed on the steep dirt and rock path in front of her, she was suddenly aware of the weight of the blanket and its contents being lifted from her back. She gasped and turned to find herself looking into the eyes of Lei Chi-Man.

"Let me help you with that," he said. He swung the bundle over his shoulder easily. "And that, too," he added, pointing to the pillowcase. Unable to believe what was happening, she handed him the pillowcase slowly, as though relinquishing it to a specter.

"I . . . I thought you had gone two hours ago," she said at last. Her voice was hoarse. "Why are you still here?"

Lei Chi-Man glanced over his shoulder at the lake, then turned and gazed at Mei-Yin. "I wanted to make sure you were all right." She studied his face closely. An appreciative smile began to take shape. Although quickly extinguished by the pain in her heart, it unveiled the fierceness of her beauty. Lei Chi-Man swallowed. "I thought I would make sure," he added self-consciously. "Here," he continued, "I've found a comfortable spot on this outcrop. We can wait here until the boat gets closer. It's at least forty-five minutes out."

Mei-Yin followed him and they sat together looking out over the silver-blue expanse of Lake Pend d'Oreille.

Lei Chi-Man turned to Mei-Yin. "What is your plan, if I may I ask?"

"I will try to get back to Tacoma," Mei-Yin answered. "Wu Tai-Hing—the ship's cook—told me of a Chinese community there."

"And what will you do?"

Mei-Yin pulled a strand of hair away from her mouth. "I don't know. Perhaps find work as a seamstress."

Lei Chi-Man brushed grass seeds off his knees. "My aunt is a seamstress in San Francisco. In Chinatown. She needs help."

"She . . . ?"

"Yes. I . . . please consider this. I would like you to consider this."

A westerly breeze stirred the brown grasses in front of them and lifted some of the heat—and dust—from Miner's Mountain. It was a mild nuisance. Twice, while waiting for the *Henry Villard,* they turned away together and closed their eyes to a spinning dust cloud rising up from the camp.

About the Author

Scott Wyatt was born in Portland, Oregon on March 3, 1951. He grew up in Sandpoint, Idaho, attended Stanford University and the University of Washington School of Law, and entered the practice of law in 1976. In 1999, he founded the Companion Flag Project to elevate and sustain public awareness of all that human beings have in common, their differences notwithstanding. The underpinnings of that  campaign are reflected in the closing arguments of attorney Jason McQuade in *Beyond the Sand Creek Bridge.* Scott has four children and five grandchildren. He continues to write and work from a hilltop home located sixteen miles east of Seattle—a home he shares with his wife Rochelle.